Call Me Irresistible

ALSO BY SUSAN ELIZABETH PHILLIPS

What I Did for Love
Glitter Baby
Natural Born Charmer
Match Me If You Can
Ain't She Sweet
Breathing Room
This Heart of Mine
Just Imagine
First Lady
Lady Be Good
Dream a Little Dream
Nobody's Baby But Mine
Kiss an Angel
Heaven, Texas
It Had to Be You

Call Me Irresistible

SUSAN ELIZABETH PHILLIPS

WILLIAM MORROW
An Imprint of HarperCollins*Publishers*

CALL ME IRRESISTIBLE. Copyright © 2011 by Susan Elizabeth Phillips. All rights reserved. Printed in the United States of America. No part of this book may be used or reproduced in any manner whatsoever without written permission except in the case of brief quotations embodied in critical articles and reviews. For information address HarperCollins Publishers, 10 East 53rd Street, New York, NY 10022.

HarperCollins books may be purchased for educational, business, or sales promotional use. For information please write: Special Markets Department, HarperCollins Publishers, 10 East 53rd Street, New York, NY 10022.

Designed by Jamie Lynn Kerner

Library of Congress Cataloging-in-Publication Data has been applied for.

ISBN 978-0-06-135152-5 (hardcover)
ISBN 978-0-06-206421-9 (international edition)

11 12 13 14 15 ov/rrd 10 9 8 7 6 5 4 3 2

To Iris, Miss Irresistible

Before Teddy knew it, his mom was hugging him and Dallie was hugging her, and the three of them were standing right there in the middle of the Statue of Liberty security office hugging each other and crying like a dumb old bunch of babies.

—FROM *FANCY PANTS*

Call Me Irresistible

chapter one

M ORE THAN A FEW RESIDENTS of Wynette, Texas, thought Ted
Beaudine was marrying beneath himself. It wasn't as if the
bride's mother was *still* the president of the United States. Cornelia
Jorik had been out of office for over a year. And Ted Beaudine was,
after all, Ted Beaudine.

The younger residents wanted him to marry a multiplatinum rock
star, but he'd already had that chance and turned her down. Ditto a
reigning actress-fashionista. Most, however, thought he should have
chosen someone from the world of women's professional sports, specifically the LPGA. As it was, Lucy Jorik didn't even play golf.

That didn't stop the local merchants from stamping Lucy's and
Ted's faces on some special-edition golf balls. But the dimpling made
them look a little cross-eyed, so most of the tourists who crowded the
town to catch a glimpse of the weekend festivities favored the more
flattering golf towels. Other bestsellers included the commemorative

plates and mugs mass-produced by the town's Golden Agers, with the proceeds going to repairing the fire-damaged Wynette Public Library.

As the hometown of two of the greatest players in professional golf, Wynette, Texas, was used to seeing celebrities walking its streets, although not a former president of the United States. Every hotel and motel within a fifty-mile radius was filled with politicians, athletes, movie stars, and heads of state. Secret Service agents had popped up all over, and way too many journalists were taking up valuable bar space at the Roustabout. But with only one industry to support the local economy, the town had fallen on tough times, and Wynette's citizens welcomed the business. The Kiwanis had gotten particularly inventive by selling bleacher seats across the street from Wynette Presbyterian for twenty dollars each.

The general public had been shocked when the bride had chosen the small Texas town for the ceremony instead of having a Beltway wedding, but Ted was a Hill Country boy through and through, and the locals had never imagined he'd marry anyplace else. He'd grown into a man under their watchful eyes, and they knew him as well as they knew their own families. Not a soul in town could muster up a single bad thing to say about him. Even his ex-girlfriends couldn't do more than muster sighs of regret. That's the kind of man Ted Beaudine was.

Meg Koranda might be the daughter of Hollywood royalty, but she was also broke, homeless, and desperate, which didn't exactly put her in the mood to be a bridesmaid at her best friend's wedding. Especially when she suspected her best friend just might be making the mistake of a lifetime by marrying the favorite son of Wynette, Texas.

Lucy Jorik, the bride-to-be, paced the carpet of her suite at the Wynette Country Inn, which her illustrious family had taken over for the festivities. "They won't say it to my face, Meg, but everybody in this town believes Ted is marrying *down*!"

Lucy looked so upset that Meg wanted to hug her, or maybe she wanted that comfort for herself. She vowed not to add her own misery to her friend's distress. "An interesting conclusion for these hayseeds to make, considering you're only the oldest daughter of the former president of the United States. Not exactly a nobody."

"Adopted daughter. I'm serious, Meg. The people in Wynette *interrogate* me. Every time I go out."

This wasn't entirely new information, since Meg talked to Lucy on the phone several times a week, but their phone calls hadn't revealed the tense lines that seemed to have taken up permanent residence above the bridge of Lucy's small nose. Meg tugged on one of her silver earrings, which might or might not be Sung dynasty, depending on whether she believed the Shanghai rickshaw driver who'd sold them to her. "I'm guessing you're more than a match for the good citizens of Wynette."

"It's just so unnerving," Lucy said. "They try to be cagey about it, but I can't walk down the street without somebody stopping to ask if I happen to know what year Ted won the U.S. Amateur Golf Championship or how much time passed between his bachelor's and master's degrees—a trick question because he earned them together."

Meg had dropped out of college before she earned even one degree, so the idea of earning two together struck her as more than a little demented. Still, Lucy could be a tad obsessive herself. "It's a new experience, that's all. Not having everybody suck up to you."

"Believe me, no danger of that." Lucy pushed a lock of light brown hair behind her ear. "At a party last week, somebody asked me very casually, as if everybody has this conversation over a cheese ball, if I happened to know Ted's IQ, which I didn't, but I figured she didn't know, either, so I said one thirty-eight. But, oh no . . . As it turns out, I made a *huge* mistake. Apparently Ted scored one hundred and *fifty-one* the last time he was tested. And according to the bartender, Ted had the flu or he'd have done better."

Meg wanted to ask Lucy if she'd really thought this marriage thing through, but, unlike Meg, Lucy didn't do anything impulsively.

They'd met in college when Meg had been a rebellious freshman and Lucy a savvy, but lonely, sophomore. Since Meg had also grown up with famous parents, she understood Lucy's suspicion of new friendships, but gradually the two of them had bonded despite their very different personalities, and it hadn't taken Meg long to see something others missed. Beneath Lucy Jorik's fierce determination to avoid embarrassing her family beat the heart of a natural-born hell-raiser. Not that anyone would know that from her appearance.

Lucy's elfin features and thick, little-girl eyelashes made her look younger than her thirty-one years. She'd grown out her shiny brown hair since her college days and sometimes held it back from her face with an assortment of velvet headbands that Meg wouldn't be caught dead wearing, just as she'd never have chosen Lucy's ladylike aqua sheath with its tidy black grosgrain belt. Instead, Meg had wrapped her long, gangly body in several lengths of jewel-toned silk that she'd twisted and tied at one shoulder. Vintage black gladiator sandals— size eleven—laced up her calves, and an ornate silver pendant she'd made from an antique betel-nut container she'd purchased at an open-air market in central Sumatra rested between her breasts. She'd complemented her probably fake Sung dynasty earrings with a stack of bangles she'd bought for six dollars at T.J. Maxx and embellished with African trade beads. Fashion ran in her blood.

And travels a crooked path, her famous New York couturier uncle had said.

Lucy twisted the strand of demure pearls at her neck. "Ted is . . . He's the closest the universe has come to creating the perfect man. Look at my wedding present? What kind of man gives his bride a church?"

"Impressive, I have to admit." Earlier that afternoon, Lucy had taken Meg to see the abandoned wooden church nestled at the end of a narrow lane on the outskirts of town. Ted had bought it to save it from demolition, then lived in it for a few months while his current house was being built. Although it was now unfurnished, it was a charming old building, and Meg didn't have any trouble understanding why Lucy loved it.

"He said that every married woman needs a place of her own to keep her sane. Can you imagine anything more thoughtful?"

Meg had a more cynical interpretation. What better strategy for a wealthy married man to employ if he intended to set up a private space for himself?

"Pretty incredible" was all she said. "I can't wait to meet him." She cursed the series of personal and financial crises that had kept her from hopping a plane months ago to meet Lucy's fiancé. As it was, she'd missed Lucy's showers and been forced to drive to the wedding from L.A. in a junker she'd bought from her parents' gardener.

With a sigh, Lucy settled on the couch next to Meg. "As long as Ted and I live in Wynette, I'll always come up short."

Meg could no longer resist hugging her friend. "You've never come up short in your life. You single-handedly saved yourself and your sister from a childhood in foster homes. You adapted to the White House like a champion. As for brains . . . you have a master's degree."

Lucy leaped up. "Which I didn't earn until *after* I'd gotten my bachelor's."

Meg ignored that piece of craziness. "Your work advocating for kids has changed lives, and in my opinion, that counts for more than an astronomical IQ."

Lucy sighed. "I love him, but sometimes . . ."

"What?"

Lucy waved a freshly manicured hand displaying fingernails polished the palest blush instead of the emerald green Meg currently preferred. "It's stupid. Last-minute jitters. Never mind."

Meg's concern grew. "Lucy, we've been best friends for twelve years. We know each other's darkest secrets. If there's something wrong . . ."

"Nothing's exactly wrong. I'm just nervous about the wedding and all the attention it's getting. The press is everywhere." She settled on the edge of the bed and pulled a pillow to her chest, just as she used to do in college when something upset her. "But . . . What if he's too good for me? I'm smart, but he's smarter. I'm pretty, but he's gorgeous. I try to be a decent person, but he's practically a saint."

Meg tamped down a mounting sense of anger. "You're brainwashed."

"The three of us grew up with famous parents. You, me, and Ted . . . But Ted made his own fortune."

"Not a fair comparison. You've been working in nonprofit, not exactly a launching pad for multimillionaires." But Lucy still had the ability to support herself, something Meg had never managed. She'd been too busy traveling to remote locations on the pretext of studying local environmental issues and researching indigenous crafts, but really just enjoying herself. She loved her parents, but she didn't love the way they'd cut her off. And why now? Maybe if they'd done it when she was twenty-one instead of thirty she wouldn't feel like such a loser.

Lucy propped her small chin on the edge of the pillow so that it bunched around her cheeks. "My parents worship him, and you know how they are about the guys I've dated."

"Not nearly as openly hostile as my parents are about the ones I date."

"That's because you date world-class losers."

Meg couldn't argue the point. Those losers had most recently included a schizoid surfer she'd met in Indonesia and an Australian rafting guide with serious anger-management issues. Some women learned from their mistakes. She obviously wasn't one of them.

Lucy tossed the pillow aside. "Ted made his fortune when he was twenty-six inventing some kind of genius software system that helps communities stop from wasting power. A big step toward creating a national smart grid. Now he picks and chooses the consulting jobs he wants. When he's home, he drives an old Ford truck with a hydrogen fuel cell he built himself, along with this solar-powered air-conditioning system and all kinds of other stuff I don't understand. Do you have any idea how many patents Ted holds? No? Well, I don't, either, although I'm sure every grocery store clerk in town does. Worst of all, nothing makes him mad. Nothing!"

"He sounds like Jesus. Except rich and sexy."

"Watch it, Meg. In this town joking about Jesus could get you shot. You've never seen so many of the faithful who're armed." Lucy's worried expression indicated she might be concerned about getting shot herself.

They had to leave for the rehearsal soon, and Meg was running out of time for subtlety. "What about your sex life? You've been annoyingly stingy with details, other than the stupid, three-month sexual moratorium you insisted on."

"I want our wedding night to be special." She tugged at her bottom lip with her teeth. "He's the most incredible lover I've ever had."

"Not the longest list in the world."

"He's legendary. And don't ask how I found that out. He's every woman's dream lover. Totally unselfish. Romantic. It's like he knows what a woman wants before she does." She gave a long sigh. "And he's mine. For life."

Lucy didn't sound nearly as happy about that as she should. Meg pulled her knees under her. "There has to be one bad thing about him."

"Nothing."

"Backward baseball cap. Morning breath. A secret passion for Kid Rock. There has to be something."

"Well . . ." A look of helplessness flashed over Lucy's face. "He's perfect. That's what's wrong."

Right then, Meg understood. Lucy couldn't risk disappointing the people she loved, and now her future husband had become one more person she needed to live up to.

Lucy's mother, the former president of the United States, chose that moment to stick her head in the bedroom. "Time to go, you two."

Meg shot up from the couch. Even though she'd been raised around celebrities, she'd never quite lost her sense of awe in the presence of President Cornelia Case Jorik.

Nealy Jorik's serene patrician features, highlighted honey brown hair, and trademark designer suits were familiar from thousands of photographs, but few of them showed the real person behind the American flag lapel pin, the complicated woman who'd once fled the White House for a cross-country adventure that had led her to Lucy and her sister Tracy, as well as Nealy's beloved husband, journalist Mat Jorik.

Nealy gazed at them. "Seeing the two of you together . . . It seems like yesterday you were both college students." A sentimental wash of tears softened the steely blue eyes of the former leader of the free world. "Meg, you've been a good friend to Lucy."

"Somebody had to be."

The president smiled. "I'm sorry your parents couldn't be here."

Meg wasn't. "They can't stand being separated for long, and this was the only time Mom could get away from work to join Dad while he's filming in China."

"I'm looking forward to his new movie. He's never predictable."

"I know they wish they could see Lucy get married," Meg replied. "Mom, especially. You know how she feels about her."

"The same way I feel about you," the president said, too kindly, because in comparison to Lucy, Meg had turned out to be a major disappointment. Now, however, wasn't the time to dwell on her past failures and dismal future. She needed to mull over her growing conviction that her best friend was about to make the mistake of a lifetime.

Lucy had elected to have only four attendants, her three sisters and Meg. They congregated at the altar while they waited for the arrival of the groom and his parents. Holly and Charlotte, Mat and Nealy's biological daughters, clustered near their parents, along with Lucy's half sister Tracy, who was eighteen, and their adopted seventeen-year-old African American brother, Andre. In his widely read newspaper column, Mat had stated, "If families have pedigrees, ours is American mutt." Meg's throat tightened. As much as her brothers made her feel inferior, she missed them right now.

Out of nowhere, the church doors blew open. And there he stood, silhouetted against the setting sun. Theodore Day Beaudine.

Trumpets began to sound. Honest-to-God trumpets blowing a chorus of hallelujahs.

"Jesus," she whispered.

"I know," Lucy whispered back. "Stuff like this happens to him all the time. He says it's accidental."

Despite everything Lucy had told her, Meg still wasn't prepared for her first sight of Ted Beaudine. He had perfectly bladed cheekbones, a flawlessly straight nose, and a square, movie-star jaw. He could have stepped down off a Times Square billboard, except he didn't have the artifice of a male model.

He strode down the center aisle with a long, easy gait, his dark brown hair kissed with copper. Jeweled light from the stained-glass windows flung precious gems in his path, as if a simple red carpet weren't good enough for such a man to walk upon. Meg barely noticed his famous parents following a few steps behind. She couldn't look away from her best friend's bridegroom.

He greeted his bride's family in a low-pitched, pleasant voice. The trumpets practicing in the choir loft reached a crescendo, he turned, and Meg got sucker punched.

Those eyes . . . Golden amber touched with honey and rimmed with flint. Eyes that blazed with intelligence and perception. Eyes that cut to the quick. As she stood before him, she felt Ted Beaudine gazing inside her and taking note of everything she worked so hard to hide—her aimlessness, her inadequacy, her absolute failure to claim a worthy place in the world.

We both know you're a screwup, his eyes said, *but I'm sure you'll grow out of it someday. If not . . . Well . . . How much can anyone expect from an overindulged child of Hollywood?*

Lucy was introducing them. " . . . so glad the two of you can finally meet. My best friend and my future husband."

Meg prided herself on her tough veneer, but she barely managed a perfunctory nod.

"If I could have your attention . . ." the minister said.

Ted squeezed Lucy's hand and smiled into his bride's upturned face, a fond, satisfied smile that never once disturbed the detachment in those tiger quartz eyes. Meg's alarm grew. Whatever emotions he felt for Lucy, none of them included the fierce passion her best friend deserved.

THE GROOM'S PARENTS WERE HOSTING the rehearsal dinner, a lavish barbecue for one hundred, at the local country club, a place that represented everything Meg detested—overindulged rich white people too fixated on their own pleasure to spare a thought for the damage their chemically poisoned, water-guzzling golf course was inflicting on the planet. Even Lucy's explanation that it was only a semiprivate club and anyone could play didn't change her opinion. Secret Service kept the international press corps hovering by the gates, along with a crowd of curious onlookers hoping to glimpse a famous face.

And famous faces were everywhere, not just in the bridal party. The groom's mother and father were world renowned. Dallas Beaudine was a legend in professional golf, and Ted's mother, Francesca, was one of the first and best of television's celebrity interviewers. The rich and prominent spilled from the back veranda of the antebellum-style clubhouse as far as the first tee—politicians, movie stars, the elite athletes of the professional golfing world, and a contingent of locals of various ages and ethnicities: schoolteachers and shopkeepers, mechanics and plumbers, the town barber, and a very scary-looking biker.

Meg watched Ted move through the crowd. He was low-key and self-effacing, yet an invisible klieg light seemed to follow him everywhere. Lucy stayed at his side, practically vibrating with tension as one person after another stopped them to chat. Through it all, Ted remained unruffled, and even though the room hummed with happy chatter, Meg found it increasingly difficult to keep a smile on her face.

He struck her more as a man executing a carefully calculated mission than a loving bridegroom on the eve of his wedding.

She'd just finished a predictable conversation with a former television newscaster about how she didn't look anything like her incredibly beautiful mother when Ted and Lucy appeared at her side. "What did I tell you?" Lucy grabbed her third glass of champagne from a passing waiter. "Isn't he great?"

Without acknowledging the compliment, Ted studied Meg through those eyes that had seen it all, even though he couldn't have traveled to half the places Meg had visited.

You call yourself a citizen of the world, his eyes whispered, *but that only means you don't belong anywhere.*

She needed to focus on Lucy's plight, not her own, and she had to do something quickly. So what if she came across as rude? Lucy was used to Meg's bluntness, and Ted Beaudine's good opinion meant nothing to her. She touched the fabric knot at her shoulder. "Lucy neglected to mention that you're also the mayor of Wynette . . . in addition to being its patron saint."

He didn't seem either offended, flattered, or taken aback by Meg's crack. "Lucy exaggerates."

"I do not," Lucy said. "I swear that woman standing by the trophy case genuflected when you walked by."

Ted grinned, and Meg caught her breath. That slow grin gave him a dangerous boyish look that Meg didn't buy for a moment. She plunged in. "Lucy is my dearest friend—the sister I always wanted—but do you have any idea how many annoying habits she has?"

Lucy frowned, but she didn't try to derail the conversation, which spoke volumes.

"Her flaws are small compared to mine." His eyebrows were darker than his hair, but his lashes were pale, tipped with gold, as if they'd been dipped in stars.

Meg edged closer. "Exactly what would those flaws be?"

Lucy seemed as interested in his answer as Meg herself.

"I can be a little naive," he said. "For example, I let myself be roped into the mayor's job even though I didn't want it."

"So you're a people pleaser." Meg didn't try to make it sound like anything other than an accusation. Maybe she could rattle him.

"I'm not exactly a people pleaser," he said mildly. "I was just taken by surprise when my name showed up on the ballot. I should have anticipated."

"You're sort of a people pleaser," Lucy said hesitantly. "I can't think of a single person you don't please."

He kissed her on the nose. Like she was his pet. "As long as I please you."

Meg left the border of polite conversation behind. "So you're a naive people pleaser. What else?"

Ted didn't blink. "I try not to be boring, but sometimes I get carried away with topics that aren't always of general interest."

"Nerd," Meg concluded.

"Exactly," he said.

Lucy remained loyal. "I don't mind. You're a very interesting person."

"I'm glad you think so."

He took a sip of his beer, still giving Meg's rudeness serious consideration. "I'm a terrible cook."

"That's true!" Lucy looked as though she'd stumbled on a gold mine.

Her delight amused him, and once again that slow grin claimed his face. "I'm not taking cooking lessons, either, so you'll have to live with it."

Lucy got a little starry-eyed, and Meg realized Ted's self-inventory of flaws was only making him more winning, so she redirected her attack. "Lucy needs a man who'll let her be herself."

"I don't think Lucy needs a man to let her be anything," he countered quietly. "She's her own person."

Which showed how little he understood this woman he was planning to marry. "Lucy hasn't been her own person since she was fourteen years old and met up with her future parents," Meg retorted. "She's a rebel. She was born to cause trouble, but she won't stir the pot because she doesn't want to embarrass the people she cares about. Are you prepared to deal with that?"

He cut right to the chase. "You seem to have some doubts about Lucy and me."

Lucy confirmed every one of Meg's misgivings by toying with her lame-ass pearls instead of jumping in to defend her decision to marry. Meg dug in. "You're obviously a terrific guy." She couldn't make it sound like a compliment. "What if you're too terrific?"

"I'm afraid I'm not following you."

Which must be a new experience for someone so crazy smart. "What if . . ." Meg said, " . . . you're a little too good for her?"

Instead of protesting, Lucy set her mouth in her White House smile and fingered her pearls like they were prayer beads.

Ted laughed. "If you knew me better, you'd understand just how ludicrous that is. Now if you'll excuse us, I want Lucy to meet my old Boy Scout leader." He slipped his arm around Lucy's shoulders and drew her away.

Meg needed to regroup, and she made a dash for the ladies' room only to get ambushed by a short, fireplug of a woman with razor-cut vermilion hair and lots of carefully applied makeup. "I'm Birdie Kittle," she said, taking Meg in with a sweep of her heavily mascaraed eyelashes. "You must be Lucy's friend. You don't look anything like your mother."

Birdie was probably in her mid to late thirties, which would have made her a child during the heyday of Fleur Savagar Koranda's modeling career, but her observation didn't surprise Meg. Everyone who knew anything about celebrities had heard of her mother. Fleur Koranda had put modeling behind her years ago to establish one of the most powerful talent agencies in the country, but to the general public, she'd always be the Glitter Baby.

Meg plastered on Lucy's White House smile. "That's because my mother is one of the most beautiful women in the world, and I'm not." Which was true, even though Meg and her mother shared more than a few physical characteristics, mainly the bad ones. Meg had inherited the Glitter Baby's marking-pen eyebrows, as well as her big hands, paddleboat feet, and all but two inches of her mother's nearly six feet of height. But the olive skin, brown hair, and more irregular features she'd inherited from her father kept her from staking any claim to her mother's extravagant beauty, although her eyes were an interesting combination of green and blue that changed color depending on the light. Unfortunately, she hadn't inherited either the talent or ambition both of her parents possessed in abundance.

"You're attractive in your own way, I guess." Birdie ran a manicured thumbnail over the jeweled clasp on her black evening bag. "Kind of exotic. These days they throw that supermodel word at anybody who stands in front of a camera. But the Glitter Baby was the real thing. And look at the way she turned herself into such a successful businesswoman. As a businesswoman myself, I admire that."

"Yes, she's remarkable." Meg loved her mother, but that didn't keep her from wishing Fleur Savagar Koranda would sometimes stumble—lose a top client, blow an important negotiation, get a zit. But all her mother's bad luck had come early in her life, before Meg was born, leaving her daughter with the title of family screwup.

"I guess you look more like your daddy," Birdie went on. "I swear I've seen every one of his pictures. Except the depressing ones."

"Like the film that earned him his Oscar?"

"Oh, I saw that one."

Meg's father was a triple threat. World-famous actor, Pulitzer Prize–winning playwright, and best-selling book author. With such mega-successful parents, who could blame her for being seriously messed up? No child could live up to that kind of legacy.

Except her two younger brothers . . .

Birdie adjusted the straps on her heart-necked black sheath, which fit a bit too snugly around her waist. "Your friend Lucy is a pretty little thang." It didn't sound like an accolade. "I hope she appreciates what she has in Teddy."

Meg worked at keeping her composure. "I'm sure she appreciates him just as much as he does her. Lucy is a very special person."

Birdie jumped at the opportunity to take offense. "Not as special as Ted, but then you'd have to live around here to understand."

Meg wasn't getting into a spitting contest with this woman, no matter how much she wanted to, so she kept her smile firmly in place. "I live in L.A. I understand a lot."

"All I'm saying is that just because she's the president's daughter doesn't mean she's got anything on Ted or that everybody's going to give her special treatment. He's the finest young man in this state. She'll have to earn our respect."

Meg struggled to hold on to her temper. "Lucy doesn't have to earn anyone's respect. She's a kind, intelligent, sophisticated woman. Ted's the lucky one."

"Are you saying he's not sophisticated?"

"No. I'm merely pointing out—"

"Wynette, Texas, may not look like much to you, but it happens to be a very sophisticated town, and we don't appreciate having outsiders come in and pass judgment on us just because we're not big Washington hotshots." She snapped her purse shut. "Or Hollywood celebrities."

"Lucy is not—"

"People have to make their own mark here. Nobody's going to kiss anybody's bee-hind just because of who her parents are."

Meg didn't know whether Birdie was talking about Meg herself or about Lucy, and she no longer cared. "I've visited small towns all over the world, and the ones with nothing to prove always seem to welcome strangers. It's the down-and-out places—the burgs that have lost their luster—that see every new face as a threat."

Birdie's penciled-in russet eyebrows shot to her hairline. "There is not one thing down-and-out about Wynette. Is that what *she* thinks?"

"No, it's what *I* think."

Birdie's face pinched. "Well, that tells me a lot, now doesn't it."

The door flew open, and an older teen with long, light brown hair stuck her head in. "Mom! Lady Emma and the others want you for pictures."

Darting Meg a last hostile glance, Birdie shot out of the room, primed to repeat their conversation to all who would listen.

Meg grimaced. In her attempt to defend Lucy, she'd done more harm than good. This weekend couldn't be over soon enough. She retied her dress at the shoulder, ran her fingers through her short, crazy haircut, and forced herself back to the party.

As the crowd raved about the barbecue and laughter spilled over the veranda, Meg seemed to be the only one who wasn't having fun. When she found herself alone with Lucy's mother, she knew she had to say something, but even though she chose her words carefully, the conversation didn't go well.

"Are you really suggesting that Lucy shouldn't marry Ted?" Nealy Jorik said in the voice she reserved for the opposition party.

"Not exactly. Just that—"

"Meg, I know you're going through a difficult time, and I'm truly sorry about that, but don't let your emotional state cast a shadow over Lucy's happiness. She couldn't have chosen better than Ted Beaudine. I promise, your doubts are groundless. And I want your promise that you'll keep them to yourself."

"What doubts?" said a voice with a faint British accent.

Meg spun around and saw Ted's mother standing at her elbow. Francesca Beaudine looked like a modern-day Vivien Leigh with a heart-shaped face, cloud of mahogany hair, and moss green wrap dress hugging her still-trim figure. For the three decades that *Francesca Today* had been on the air, she'd challenged Barbara Walters as queen of the prime-time celebrity interviewers. While Walters was the superior journalist, Francesca was more fun to watch.

Nealy quickly smoothed the waters. "Bridesmaid jitters . . . Francesca, this is the loveliest evening. I can't tell you how much Mat and I are enjoying ourselves."

Francesca Beaudine was no fool. She gave Meg a cool, assessing look, then led Nealy away toward a group that included the red-haired fireplug from the ladies' room and Emma Traveler, the wife of Ted's best man, Kenny Traveler, another of professional golf's superstars.

After that, Meg sought out the most unsuitable guest she could find, a biker who professed to be one of Ted's friends, but even the distraction of a great set of pecs couldn't cheer her up. Instead, the biker made her think about how overjoyed her parents would have been if she'd ever brought home anyone remotely resembling Ted Beaudine.

Lucy was right. He was perfect. And he couldn't be more wrong for her friend.

No matter how Lucy adjusted the pillows, she couldn't get comfortable. Her sister Tracy slept soundlessly at her side after insisting she share Lucy's bed tonight. *Our last night to be just sisters . . .* Still, Tracy wasn't sad about the wedding. She adored Ted just like everyone else.

Lucy and Ted had their mothers to thank for fixing them up. *"He's incredible, Luce,"* Nealy had said. *"Wait till you meet him."*

And he was incredible . . . Meg shouldn't have planted all those doubts in her head. Except the doubts had been there for months, even as Lucy kept reasoning them away. What woman in her right mind wouldn't fall in love with Ted Beaudine? He dazzled her.

Lucy kicked the sheet free. This was all Meg's fault. That was the problem with Meg. She turned everything upside down. Being Meg's best friend didn't make Lucy blind to her faults. Meg was spoiled, reckless, and irresponsible, looking for purpose over the next mountaintop instead of inside herself. She was also decent, caring, loyal, and the best friend Lucy had ever had. Each of them had found her own way to live in the shadow of famous parents—Lucy by conforming, Meg by racing around the world, trying to outrun her parents' legacies.

Meg didn't know her own strengths—the considerable intelligence she'd inherited from her parents but never figured out how to use to her advantage; the gangly, unconventional appearance that made her far more arresting than more predictably beautiful women. Meg was good at so many things that she'd concluded she wasn't good at anything. Instead, she'd resigned herself to being inadequate, and no one—not her parents, not Lucy—could shake her conviction.

Lucy turned her face into her pillow, trying to shut out the memory of that awful moment tonight after they'd returned to the inn when Meg had pulled Lucy into a hug. "Luce, he's wonderful," she'd whispered. "Everything you said. And you absolutely cannot marry him."

Meg's warning hadn't been nearly as frightening as Lucy's own response. "I know," she'd heard herself whisper back. "But I'm going to anyway. It's too late to back out."

Meg had given her a fierce shake. "It's not too late. I'll help you. I'll do whatever I can."

Lucy had pulled away and hurried into her room. Meg didn't understand. She was a child of Hollywood, where the outrageous was ordinary, but Lucy was Washington's child, and she understood the country's conservative heart. The public was invested in this wedding. They'd watched the Jorik kids grow up and embraced them through more than a few youthful missteps. News outlets all over the world had shown up to cover the wedding, and Lucy couldn't call things off for a reason she wasn't able to articulate. Besides, if Ted was so wrong for her, wouldn't someone else have noticed? Her parents? Tracy? Wouldn't Ted, who saw everything so clearly, have figured it out?

The reminder of Ted Beaudine's infallible judgment brought her just enough comfort to settle into a shallow, uneasy sleep. By the next afternoon, however, that comfort had vanished.

chapter two

THE NARTHEX OF THE WYNETTE Presbyterian Church smelled of old hymnals and long-forgotten potluck dinners. Outside, organized chaos reigned. The special section set aside for the press bulged with reporters, and spectators packed the bleachers, with the overflow spilling onto the side streets. As the bridal party lined up to enter the sanctuary, Meg glanced back at Lucy. The perfectly fitted lace gown flattered her small frame, but not even skillfully airbrushed makeup could mask her tension. She'd been so jittery all day that Meg hadn't had the heart to say another word about this ill-advised wedding. Not that she could have anyway with Nealy Case Jorik watching her every move.

The chamber ensemble concluded the prelude, and the trumpets rang out announcing the beginning of the bridal procession. Lucy's two youngest sisters stood at the front, with Meg next, and then eighteen-year-old Tracy, who was Lucy's maid of honor. They all wore simple gowns of champagne silk crepe de chine accented with the smoky topaz earrings that were Lucy's gift to her attendants.

Thirteen-year-old Holly started down the aisle. When she reached the midpoint, her sister Charlotte stepped off. Meg smiled over her shoulder at Lucy, who'd elected to enter the sanctuary by herself and meet both her parents halfway down as a symbol of the way they'd come into her life. Meg moved into position in front of Tracy for her own entrance, but as she got ready to take her first step, she heard a rustle and a hand shot out to grab her arm. "I have to talk to Ted right now," Lucy said in a panicky whisper.

Tracy, whose blond hair had been arranged in an intricate twist, gave a choked gasp. "Luce, what are you doing?"

Lucy ignored her sister. "Get him for me, Meg. Please."

Meg was hardly a slave to convention, but this was rash even for her. "Now? You don't think you could have done this a couple of hours ago?"

"You were right. Everything you said. You were completely right." Even through yards of tulle, Lucy's face looked pale and stricken. "Help me. Please."

Tracy spun on Meg. "I don't understand. What did you say to her?" She didn't wait for an answer but grabbed her sister's hand. "Luce, you're having a panic attack. It's going to be okay."

"No. I—I have to talk to Ted."

"Now?" Tracy said, echoing Meg. "You can't talk to him now."

But she had to. Meg understood that, even if Tracy didn't. Tightening her grip on a bouquet of miniature calla lilies, Meg plastered a smile on her face and stepped out onto the pristine white runner.

A horizontal aisle divided the front of the sanctuary from the back. The former president of the United States and her husband waited there, moist-eyed and proud, to escort their daughter on her final walk as a single woman. Ted Beaudine stood at the altar, along with his best man and three groomsmen. A shaft of sunlight fell directly on his head giving him—what else?—a halo.

Meg had been politely admonished at last night's rehearsal for walking too quickly down the aisle, but that wasn't a problem now as she reduced her customary long stride to baby steps. What had she done? The guests had turned in anticipation, waiting for the appearance of the bride. Meg reached the altar much too soon and stopped in front of Ted instead of taking her place next to Charlotte.

He regarded her quizzically. She focused on his forehead so she wouldn't have to meet those unsettling tiger quartz eyes. "Lucy would like to talk to you," she whispered.

He cocked his head while he processed that information. Any other man might have asked a few questions, but not Ted Beaudine. His puzzlement shifted to concern. With a purposeful stride, and no hint of embarrassment, he strode up the aisle.

The president and first husband gazed at each other as he passed, then immediately took off after him. A buzz rose from the guests. The groom's mother came to her feet, and then his father. Meg couldn't let Lucy face this alone, and she hurried back up the aisle. With each step her sense of dread grew stronger.

When she got to the narthex, she spotted the frothy top of Lucy's veil over Ted's shoulder as Tracy and her parents gathered around her. A pair of Secret Service agents stood at full alert by the doors. The groom's parents appeared just as Ted pulled Lucy away from the group. With a firm grip on her arm, he led her toward a small door off to the side. Lucy turned, searching for someone. She found Meg, and even through the tulle waterfall, her entreaty was clear. *Help me.*

Meg rushed toward her only to have mild-mannered Ted Beaudine pin her with a look that stopped her in her tracks, a look as dangerous as anything her father had conjured up in his Bird Dog Caliber movies. Lucy shook her head, and Meg somehow understood her friend hadn't been pleading for her to intercede with Ted. Lucy wanted her to deal with the mess out here, as if Meg had even a clue how to go about that.

As the door shut behind the bride and groom, the former first husband of the United States advanced on her. "Meg, what's going on? Tracy said you know about this."

Meg gripped her bridesmaid's bouquet. Why did Lucy have to wait so long to rediscover her rebel's heart? "Uhm . . . Lucy needed to talk to Ted."

"That's obvious. About what?"

"She's . . ." She saw Lucy's stricken face in her mind. "She's having some doubts."

"Doubts?" Francesca Beaudine, furious in fawn Chanel, shot forward. "You're responsible for this. I heard you last night. This is your doing." She charged toward the room where her son had disappeared only to be restrained at the last moment by her husband.

"Hold on, Francesca," Dallas Beaudine said, his Texas drawl in marked contrast to his wife's clipped British accent. "They have to sort this out for themselves."

The bridesmaids and groomsmen rushed into the narthex from the sanctuary. Lucy's siblings clustered together: her brother, Andre; Charlotte and Holly; Tracy, who was darting murderous looks at Meg. The minister went to the president, and the two engaged in a quick conversation. The minister nodded and returned to the sanctuary, where Meg heard him apologize for the "short delay" and ask the guests to stay where they were.

The chamber ensemble began to play. The door at the side of the narthex remained closed. Meg was starting to feel sick.

Tracy broke away from her family and charged toward Meg, her rosebud mouth puckered in outrage. "Lucy was happy till you showed up. This is your fault!"

Her father came to her side and put his hand on her shoulder as he regarded Meg coldly. "Nealy told me about your conversation last night. What do you know about this?"

The groom's parents heard his question and closed in. Meg knew Lucy was counting on her and fought the urge to back away. "Lucy . . . tries so hard not to disappoint the people she loves." She licked her dry lips. "Sometimes she can . . . forget to be true to herself."

Mat Jorik was from the No Bullshit School of Journalism. "Exactly what are you saying? Spell it out."

All eyes fastened on her. Meg tightened her grip on the calla lily bouquet. No matter how much she wanted to run she had to try to make this at least a little easier on Lucy by laying the groundwork for the difficult conversations that lay ahead. She licked her lips again. "Lucy isn't as happy as she should be. She has some doubts."

"Rubbish!" Ted's mother exclaimed. "She had no doubts. Not until you manufactured them for her."

"This is the first any of us have heard about doubts," Dallas Beaudine said.

Meg briefly considered pleading ignorance, but Lucy was the sister she'd never had, and she could at least do this much for her. "Lucy realized she might be marrying Ted for the wrong reasons. That he . . . might not be the right man for her."

"That's preposterous." Francesca's green eyes shot poisoned darts. "Do you know how many women would give anything to marry Teddy?"

"A lot, I'm sure."

His mother wasn't pacified. "I had breakfast with Lucy on

Saturday morning, and she told me she'd never been happier. But that changed after you arrived. What did you say to her?"

Meg tried to dodge the question. "She might not have been quite as happy as she seemed. Lucy's good at faking it."

"I'm something of an expert on people who are faking it," Francesca snapped. "Lucy wasn't."

"She's really good."

"Let me offer up another scenario." The groom's petite mother bore down with the authority of a prosecuting attorney. "Is it possible that you—for reasons only you know—decided to capitalize on a perfectly normal case of bridal nerves?"

"No. That's not possible." She twisted the bronze bouquet ribbon through her fingers. Her palms had begun to sweat. "Lucy knew how much all of you wanted them together, so she convinced herself it would work out. But it wasn't what she really wanted."

"I don't believe you!" Tracy's blue eyes flooded with tears. "Lucy loves Ted. You're jealous! That's why you did this."

Tracy had always worshiped Meg, and her hostility hurt. "That's not true."

"Then tell us what you said to her," Tracy demanded. "Let everybody hear."

One of the bouquet ribbons shredded in her damp fingers. "All I did was remind her she needs to be true to herself."

"She was!" Tracy cried. "You've ruined everything."

"I want Lucy to be happy just like the rest of you. And she wasn't."

"You figured all this out in one conversation yesterday afternoon?" Ted's father said, his voice dangerously low.

"I know her pretty well."

"And we don't?" Mat Jorik said coldly.

Tracy's lips trembled. "Everything was wonderful until you showed up."

"It wasn't wonderful." Meg felt a trickle of perspiration slide between her breasts. "That's only what Lucy wanted you to believe."

President Jorik subjected Meg to a long, searching gaze and finally broke her silence. "Meg," she said quietly. "What have you done?"

Her soft condemnation told Meg what she should have known from the beginning. They were going to blame her. And maybe they were right. No one else believed this marriage was such a terrible idea. Why should a confirmed loser think she knew better than all the rest of them?

She wilted under the powerful force of the president's Mayflower blue eyes. "I—I didn't mean—Lucy wasn't . . ." Seeing such disappointment reflected in the expression of a woman she admired so much was even worse than enduring her own parents' censure. At least Meg was used to that. "I'm—I'm sorry."

President Jorik shook her head. The bridegroom's mother, who'd been known to annihilate puffed-up celebrities in her television interviews, got ready to annihilate Meg until the cooler voice of her husband interceded. "We may be overreacting. They're probably patching things up right now."

But they weren't patching anything up. Meg knew it, and so did Nealy Jorik. Lucy's mother understood her daughter well enough to know Lucy would never subject her family to this kind of distress if she hadn't made up her mind.

One by one, they turned their backs on Meg. Both sets of parents. Lucy's siblings. The groomsmen and best man. It was as if she no longer existed. First her parents, and now this. Everybody she cared about—everyone she loved—had written her off.

She wasn't a crier, but tears pressed against her lids, and she knew she had to get away. No one noticed as she began to edge toward the front doors. She twisted the knob and slipped outside only to realize her mistake too late.

Strobes fired. Television cameras whirred. The sudden appearance of a bridesmaid at the exact moment when the wedding vows should have been being exchanged set off a frenzy. Some of the onlookers in the bleachers across from the church rose to see what the commotion was about. Reporters surged forward. Meg dropped her bouquet, spun around, and grabbed the heavy iron knob with both hands. It refused to turn. Of course. The doors were locked for security. She was trapped.

The reporters rushed her, pressing against the security detail at the bottom of the steps.

What's happening in there?

Has something gone wrong?

Has there been an accident?

Is President Jorik all right?

Meg's spine flattened against the door. Their questions grew louder, more demanding.

Where are the bride and groom?

Is the ceremony over?

Tell us what's happening.

"I—I'm not feeling well, that's all . . ."

Their shouts swallowed her weak response. Somebody screamed for everybody to "Shut the hell up!" She'd faced down con artists in Thailand and street thugs in Morocco, but she'd never felt so far out of her element. Once again, she turned toward the door, crushing her bouquet beneath her heel, but the lock wouldn't budge. Either no one inside realized her predicament or they'd tossed her to the wolves.

The bleacher crowd was on its feet. She looked desperately around and spotted two narrow steps leading to a walkway that ran around the side of the church. She rushed down them, nearly tripping. The onlookers who'd been shut out of the bleachers clustered on the sidewalk beyond the churchyard fence, some of them with strollers, others with drink coolers. She picked up her skirt and ran along the uneven brick path toward the parking lot at the rear. Surely someone from the security detail would let her back in the church. An awful prospect, but better than facing the press.

Just as she reached the asphalt, she spotted one of the groomsmen with his back toward her as he opened the door of a dark gray Benz. The ceremony had definitely been canceled. She couldn't imagine riding back to the inn in the same limo as the other members of the wedding party, and she rushed toward the Benz. She tugged open the passenger door just as the ignition turned over. "Could you drop me off at the inn?"

"No."

She looked up and met the cool eyes of Ted Beaudine. One glance at that stubborn jaw told her he'd never believe she wasn't responsible for what had happened, especially not after the way she'd interrogated him at the rehearsal dinner. She started to say she was sorry for the pain this was causing him, but he didn't look pained. He seemed more inconvenienced. He was an emotional robot, and Lucy had been right to dump him.

Meg pulled her skirt around her and took a faltering step backward. "Uh . . . Okay then."

He took his time leaving the parking lot. No squealing tires or roaring engine. He even shot a brief wave to a couple of people on the sidewalk. He'd just been ditched by the daughter of the former president of the United States while the whole world looked on, yet he showed no sign that something monumental had happened.

She dragged herself to the nearest security guard, who finally let her back into the church, where her reappearance received exactly the hostile reception she expected.

OUTSIDE THE CHURCH, THE PRESIDENT'S press secretary delivered a hurried statement that offered no details, only a brief announcement that the ceremony was canceled. After an obligatory request for the public to respect the couple's privacy, the press secretary hurried back inside without taking questions. Through the commotion that followed, no one noticed a small figure dressed in a royal blue choir robe and white satin pumps slip out the side door and disappear into the neighboring backyards.

chapter three

Emma Traveler had never seen Francesca Beaudine so distraught. Four days had passed since Lucy Jorik had disappeared, and they were sitting under the pergola in the shady courtyard behind the Beaudine home. A silver gazing ball nestled among the roses made Francesca seem even tinier than she was. In all the years they'd known each other, Emma had never seen her friend cry, but Francesca had a telling mascara smear under one of her emerald eyes, her chestnut hair was disheveled, and weary lines etched her heart-shaped face.

Although Francesca was fifty-four, nearly fifteen years older than Emma and far more beautiful, their deep friendship had its roots in common bonds. They were both British, both married to famous professional golfers, and both far more interested in reading a good book than venturing near a putting green. Most important, they both loved Ted Beaudine—Francesca, with a fierce maternal love, and Emma, with a steadfast loyalty that had begun the day they'd met.

"That bloody Meg Koranda did something horrible to Lucy. I know it." Francesca stared blindly at a swallowtail butterfly flitting through the lilies. "I had doubts about her even before I met her, despite all Lucy's glowing reports. If Meg was such a close friend, why didn't we meet her until the day before the wedding? What kind of friend couldn't spare the time to attend even one of Lucy's bridal showers?"

Emma had wondered the same thing. Thanks to the power of Google, unfavorable gossip about Meg Koranda's aimless lifestyle had begun to swirl as soon as the list of bridesmaids was announced. Still, Emma didn't believe in judging people without sufficient evidence, and she'd refused to take part in rumormongering. Unfortunately, this time the gossips seemed to have been right.

Emma's husband, Kenny, who was Ted's best friend, couldn't comprehend why people were so much more hostile toward Meg than to the runaway bride, but Emma understood. The locals liked Lucy, at least as much as they could like an outsider who'd landed their Ted, and they'd been prepared to accept her right up to the night of the rehearsal dinner when she'd changed before their eyes. She'd spent more time huddled with Meg Koranda than with her own fiancé. She'd been short with the guests, distracted, and she'd barely smiled during even the funniest of the toasts.

Francesca pulled a wadded tissue from the pocket of the wrinkled white cotton capris she wore with an old T-shirt, Italian sandals, and her ever-present diamonds. "I've been around too many spoiled Hollywood brats not to recognize another one. Girls like Meg Koranda have never had to work a day in their lives, and they think their famous last names give them license to do whatever they want. That's precisely why Dallie and I made sure Ted always knew he'd have to work for a living." She dabbed at her nose. "I'll tell you what

I think. I think she took one look at my Teddy and wanted him for herself."

Although it was true that women lost their good sense after meeting Ted Beaudine, Emma didn't believe even Meg Koranda could regard breaking up Ted's wedding as the best strategy toward snagging him for herself. Hers, however, was a minority opinion. Emma subscribed to the less widely held theory that Meg had spoiled Lucy's happiness because she was jealous that her friend was making a success of her life. But what Emma couldn't understand was how Meg had been able to work so quickly.

"Lucy was already like a daughter to me." Francesca twisted her fingers in her lap. "I'd lost hope that he'd ever meet anyone special enough for him. But she was perfect. Everybody who saw them together knew that."

A warm breeze ruffled the leaves that shaded the pergola. "If only he'd go after Lucy, but he won't," Francesca went on. "I understand pride. God knows, his father and I have more than enough of it. But I wish he could set that aside." Fresh tears leaked from her eyes. "You should have seen Teddy when he was little. So quiet and serious. So dear. He was an amazing child. The most amazing child ever."

Emma considered her own three children the most amazing ever, but she didn't challenge Francesca, who gave a rueful laugh. "He was completely uncoordinated. He could hardly walk across a room without tripping. Trust me when I tell you his athletic talent came late in his childhood. And thank God he outgrew his allergies." She blew her nose. "He was homely, too. It took him years to grow into his looks. And he was so smart, smarter than everybody around him—certainly smarter than me—but he never condescended to people." Her watery smile broke Emma's heart. "He's always believed everybody has something to teach him."

Emma was glad Francesca and Dallie were leaving for New York soon. Francesca thrived on hard work, and taping her next series of interviews would be a good distraction. Once they'd settled into their Manhattan town house, they could immerse themselves in the diversion of big-city life, much healthier than staying in Wynette.

Francesca rose from the bench and rubbed her cheek. "Lucy was the answer to my prayers for Teddy. I thought he'd finally met a woman who was worthy of him. Someone intelligent and decent, someone who understood what it was like to be raised with privilege but hadn't been spoiled by her upbringing. I thought she had character." Her expression hardened. "I was wrong there, now wasn't I?"

"We all were."

The tissue shredded in her fingers, and she spoke so softly Emma could barely hear her. "I so desperately want grandchildren, Emma. I—I dream about them—holding them, smelling their soft little heads. Teddy's babies . . ."

Emma knew enough about Francesca and Dallie's history to understand Francesca was expressing more than a fifty-four-year-old woman's simple yearning for a grandchild. Dallie and Francesca had been estranged for the first nine years of Ted's life, right up until the time Dallie learned that he had a son. A grandchild would help fill that empty hole in their lives.

As if reading her thoughts, Francesca said, "Dallie and I never got to watch first steps together, to hear first words." Her voice grew bitter. "Meg Koranda stole Ted's babies from us. She stole Lucy, and she stole our grandchildren."

Emma couldn't bear her sadness. She rose from the bench and hugged her. "You'll still have those grandchildren, love. There'll be another woman for Ted. A woman far better than Lucy Jorik."

Francesca didn't believe her. Emma could see that. And she

decided right then not to tell Francesca the worst of it. That Meg Koranda was still in town.

"Do you have another credit card, Ms. Koranda?" the beautiful blond desk clerk asked. "This one seems to have been rejected."

"Rejected?" Meg acted as though she didn't understand the word, but she understood it all right. With a soft *whoosh,* her last remaining credit card disappeared into the middle drawer of the front desk at the Wynette Country Inn.

The desk clerk didn't try to hide her satisfaction. Meg had become public enemy number one in Wynette, as a twisted version of her role in the wedding debacle that had subjected the town's sainted mayor to international humiliation had spread like an airborne virus through the small town where a few members of the press still lingered. A grossly exaggerated account of Meg's confrontation with Birdie Kittle the night of the rehearsal dinner had also become public fodder. If only Meg had been able to leave Wynette right away, she could have avoided this, but that had proven to be impossible.

Lucy's family had left Wynette on Sunday, twenty-four hours after Lucy had run off. Meg suspected they'd still be here, hoping Lucy would return, but the president had committed to attending the World Health Organization's global conference in Barcelona along with Lucy's father, who was hosting a gathering of international medical journalists. Meg was the only one who'd spoken to Lucy since she'd run away.

She'd gotten the phone call late Saturday night, around the time the bride and groom should have been leaving the wedding reception for their honeymoon. The signal was weak, and she barely recognized Lucy's voice, which sounded thin and unsteady.

"Meg, it's me."

"Luce? Are you all right?"

Lucy gave a choked, semihysterical laugh. "Matter of opinion. You know that wild side of me you're always talking about? I guess I found it."

"Oh, honey . . ."

"I'm—I'm a coward, Meg. I can't face my family."

"Luce, they love you. They'll understand."

"Tell them I'm sorry." Her voice broke. "Tell them I love them, and I know I've made a horrible mess of everything, and that I'll come back and clean it up, but . . . Not yet. I can't do it yet."

"All right. I'll tell them. But—"

She disconnected before Meg could say anything else.

Meg steeled herself and told Lucy's parents about the call. "She's doing this of her own free will," the president had said, perhaps remembering her own long-ago rebellious escape. "For now, we have to give her the space she needs." She made Meg promise to remain in Wynette for a few more days in case Lucy reappeared. "It's the least you can do after causing this mess." Meg was too weighed down with guilt to refuse. Unfortunately, neither the president nor her husband had thought to cover the cost of Meg's extended stay at the inn.

"That's odd," Meg said to the desk clerk. In addition to her natural beauty, the clerk's highlighted hair, perfect makeup, blindingly white teeth, and assortment of bracelets and rings tagged her as someone who spent a lot more time and money on her appearance than Meg did. "Unfortunately, I don't have another card with me. I'll write a check." Impossible, since she'd emptied out her checking account three months ago, and she'd been living on her precious last credit card ever since. She shuffled through her purse. "Oh, no. I forgot my checkbook."

"No problem. There's an ATM right around the corner."

"Excellent." Meg grabbed her suitcase. "I'll drop this in my car on the way."

The clerk shot around the counter and wrenched the suitcase away. "We'll have it waiting for you when you get back."

Meg gave the woman her most withering look and spoke words she'd never imagined would ever come out of her mouth. "Do you know who I am?" *I'm a nobody. An absolute nobody.*

"Oh, yes. *Everybody* does. But we have our policies."

"Fine." She hoisted her purse, a hand-me-down Prada hobo from her mother, and swept from the lobby. By the time she reached the parking lot, she'd broken out in a cold sweat.

Her gas-guzzling fifteen-year-old Buick Century sat like a rusty wart between a shiny new Lexus and a Cadillac CTS. Despite repeated vacuuming, the Rustmobile still smelled of cigarettes, sweat, fast food, and peat moss. She lowered the windows to let in some air. A sheen of perspiration had formed beneath the gauzy top she wore with jeans, a pair of hammered silver earrings she'd made from some buckles she'd found in Laos, and a vintage maroon felt cloche hat that her favorite L.A. resale shop advertised as having come from the estate of Ginger Rogers.

She rested her forehead against the steering wheel, but no matter how hard she thought, she couldn't see a way out. She pulled her cell from her purse and did what she'd promised never to do. She called her brother Dylan.

Even though he was three years younger, he was already a hugely successful financial whiz. Her mind tended to wander when he talked about what he did, but she knew he did it extremely well. Since he refused to give her his work number, she called his cell. "Hey, Dyl, call me right away. It's an emergency. I mean it. You have to call me back right now."

It was useless to call Clay, who was Dylan's twin. Clay was still a starving actor, barely making the rent, although that wouldn't last much longer, since he had a degree from Yale drama school, a growing list of off-Broadway credits, and the talent to back up the last name of Koranda. Unlike herself, neither of her brothers had taken anything from their parents since they'd graduated from college.

She snatched up her phone as it rang.

"The only reason I'm calling you back," Dylan said, "is curiosity. Why did Lucy bail on her wedding? My secretary told me an online gossip site is saying you're the one who talked her out of getting married. What's going on down there?"

"Nothing good. Dyl, I need a loan."

"Mom said this would happen. The answer's no."

"Dyl, I'm not kidding. I'm in a jam. They took my credit card, and—"

"Grow up, Meg. You're thirty years old. It's sink-or-swim time."

"I know. And I'm going to make some changes. But—"

"Whatever you've gotten yourself into, you can get yourself out of. You're a lot smarter than you think. I have faith in you, even if you don't."

"I appreciate that, but I need help now. Really. You have to help me."

"Jesus, Meg. Don't you have any pride?"

"That's a shitty thing to say."

"Then don't make me say it. You're capable of handling your own life. Get a job. You know what that is, right?"

"Dyl—"

"You're my sister, and I love you, and because I love you, I'm hanging up now."

She stared at the dead phone, angry but not surprised at this evidence of a family conspiracy. Her parents were in China, and they'd made it blazingly clear they wouldn't rescue her again. Her creepy grandmother Belinda didn't give out freebies. She'd force Meg to enroll in acting classes or something equally insidious. As for her uncle Michel . . . The last time they'd visited, he'd delivered a biting lecture on personal responsibility. With Lucy on the run, that left Meg's three other close friends, all of whom were rich and any one of whom would lend her money.

Or would they? That was the thing about them. Georgie, April, and Sasha were all independent, unpredictable women who'd been telling Meg for years that she needed to stop screwing around and commit to something. Still, if she explained how desperate she was . . .

Don't you have any pride?

Did she really want to give her accomplished friends more evidence of her worthlessness? On the other hand, what were her options? She had barely a hundred dollars in her wallet, no credit cards, an empty checking account, less than half a tank of gas, and a car that could break down at any moment. Dylan was right. However much she might hate it, she needed to get a job . . . and fast.

She thought it over. As the town bad guy, she could never get a job here, but both San Antonio and Austin were less than two hours away, just about reachable on half a tank of gas. Surely she could find work in one of those places. It would mean skipping out on her bill, something she'd never done in her life, but she'd run out of options.

Her palms were sweaty on the steering wheel as she pulled slowly out of the parking lot. The roar of the bad muffler made her long for the hybrid Nissan Ultima she'd had to give up when her father stopped making the payments. She had only the clothes on her back and the contents of her purse. Leaving her suitcase behind made her crazy, but since she owed the Wynette Country Inn for three nights, well over four hundred dollars, there wasn't much she could do about it. She'd pay them back with interest as soon as she found a job. What that job would be, she had no idea. Something temporary and, hopefully, well paying, until she figured out what to do next.

A woman pushing a stroller stopped to stare at the brown Buick as it belched a cloud of oily smoke. That, combined with her bellowing muffler, hardly made the Rustmobile an ideal getaway car, and she tried to sink lower in the seat. She passed the limestone courthouse and the fenced-off public library as she edged toward the town's outskirts. Finally, she spotted the city limits sign.

YOU ARE LEAVING
WYNETTE, TEXAS
Theodore Beaudine, Mayor

She hadn't seen Ted since their awful encounter in the church parking lot, and now she wouldn't have to. She'd bet anything that women all over the country had already lined up to take Lucy's place.

A siren shrieked behind her. Her eyes shot to the rearview mirror, and she saw the flashing red light of a police cruiser. Her fingers clenched the steering wheel. She pulled to the shoulder of the road, praying her noisy muffler was to blame and cursing herself for not having had it fixed before she left L.A.

Dread pooled in her stomach as she waited for the two officers to check out her plates. Finally, the officer behind the wheel emerged and ambled toward her, his beer belly hanging over his belt. He had ruddy skin, a big nose, and steel wool hair sprouting from beneath his hat.

She rolled down her window and plastered on a smile. "Hello, Officer." *Please, God, let this be about my bad muffler and not skipping out on my bill.* She handed over her license and registration before he asked for it. "Is there a problem?"

He studied her license, then took in her felt cloche. She thought about telling him Ginger Rogers had once worn it, but he didn't look like much of an old film buff. "Ma'am, we have a report that you left the inn without paying your bill."

Her stomach dipped. "Me? That's ridiculous." Out of the corner of her eye, she saw movement in the outside mirror as his backup decided to join the party. Except his backup wore jeans and a black T-shirt instead of a uniform. And his backup—

She stared more closely into the mirror. *No!*

Shoes crunched in the gravel. A shadow fell over the side of the car. She lifted her gaze and found herself staring into the impassive amber eyes of Ted Beaudine.

"Hello, Meg."

chapter four

Ted!" She tried to act as though he was the person she most wanted to see instead of her worst nightmare. "Have you joined the police force?"

"Doing a ride-along." He propped his elbow on the roof of her car. As he took in her appearance, she got the impression that he didn't like her cloche either—or anything else about her. "My schedule for the next two weeks suddenly opened up."

"Ah."

"So I hear you skipped out on your bill at the inn."

"Me? No. A mistake. I didn't—I was just taking a ride. Beautiful day. Skip out? No. They have my suitcase. How could I skip out?"

"I guess by getting in your car and driving off," Ted said, as if he were the cop. "Where are you headed?"

"Nowhere. Exploring. I like to do that when I visit new places."

"Best to pay your bill before you go off exploring."

"You're absolutely right. I wasn't thinking. I'll take care of it right away." Except she couldn't do that.

A truck roared by, heading into town, and another trickle of perspiration slipped between her breasts. She needed to throw herself on someone's mercy, and it didn't take long to make her choice. "Officer, could I talk to you privately?"

Ted shrugged and moved to the rear of the car. The officer scratched his chest. Meg caught her bottom lip between her teeth and lowered her voice. "See, the thing is . . . I made this stupid mistake. With all my traveling, my mail didn't catch up with me, and that's caused a small difficulty with my credit card. I'll have to ask the inn to bill me. I don't think it will be a problem." She flushed with shame, and her throat closed so tight she could barely get out the words. "I'm sure you know who my parents are."

"Yes, ma'am, I do." The cop reared back his head, which sat on a short, squat neck. "Ted, looks like we've got a vagrant here."

A *vagrant*! She threw herself out of the car. "Now wait just a minute! I'm not a—"

"Stay right where you are, ma'am." The cop's hand went to his holster. Ted propped his foot on her rear bumper and watched with interest.

Meg spun on him. "Asking the inn to send me a bill doesn't make me a vagrant!"

"Did you hear what I said, ma'am?" the cop barked out. "Back in the car."

Before she had time to move, Ted approached again. "She's not cooperating, Sheldon. I guess you'll have to arrest her."

"Arrest me?"

Ted looked vaguely sad about that, leading her to conclude that he had a sadistic streak. She jumped back into her car. Ted stepped away.

"Sheldon, what do you say we follow Miz Koranda back to the inn so she can take care of her unfinished business?"

"Sure thing." Officer Surly pointed down the road a few feet. "Turn around in that drive, ma'am. We'll be right behind you."

Ten minutes later, she was once again approaching the front desk of the Wynette Country Inn, but this time Ted Beaudine walked at her side while Officer Surly stopped by the door and spoke into the mike on his lapel.

The beautiful blond desk clerk sprang to attention as soon as she spotted Ted. Her lips curled in a wide smile. Even her hair seemed to perk up. At the same time she furrowed her brow with concern. "Hey there, Ted. How are you doing?"

"Just fine, Kayla. Yourself?" He had a way of lowering his chin when he smiled. Meg had watched him do it to Lucy at the rehearsal dinner. He didn't drop it far, maybe only an inch, just enough to turn his smile into a curriculum vitae of clean living and honorable intentions. Now he was offering the identical smile he'd bestowed on Lucy to the desk clerk at the Wynette Inn. So much for his broken heart.

"No complaints," Kayla said. "We've all been prayin' for you."

He didn't look remotely like a man in need of prayer, but he nodded. "I appreciate it."

Kayla tilted her head so that her sweep of shiny blond hair fell over one shoulder. "Why don't you join Daddy and me for dinner at the club this weekend? You know what a good time you and Daddy always have."

"Just might do that."

They chatted for a few minutes about Daddy, the weather, and Ted's mayoral responsibilities. Kayla pulled out all the stops, tossing her hair, batting her lashes, doing the Tyra Banks eye-thing, basically giving it everything she had. "We've all been talkin' about that phone call you got yesterday. Everybody thought for sure Spencer Skipjack had forgotten about us. We can hardly believe Wynette's back in the running. But I said all along you'd pull this off."

"I appreciate the vote of confidence, but it's a long way from a done deal. Remember that up until last Friday, Spence was set on San Antone."

"If anybody can convince him to change his mind and build in Wynette, it's you. We sure do need the jobs."

"Don't I know it."

Meg's hopes that they'd continue their conversation were short-lived as Ted turned his attention back to her. "I understand Miz Koranda here owes you money. She seems to think she can work it out."

"Oh, I hope so."

The clerk didn't look as though she hoped any such thing, and a panicky flush crept from Meg's face to her chest. She licked her dry lips. "Maybe I could . . . speak to the manager."

Ted seemed dubious. "I don't think that's a good idea."

"She'll have to," Kayla said. "I'm only helping out today. This is way beyond the realm of my responsibilities."

He smiled. "Oh, what the heck. We could all use a little day-brightener. Go on and get her."

Officer Surly piped up from the door. "Ted, there's been an accident out on Cemetery Road. Can you handle things here?"

"Sure thing, Sheldon. Anybody hurt?"

"Don't think so." He nodded toward Meg. "Walk her over to the station when you're done."

"Will do."

Walk her over to the station? They really were going to arrest her?

The cop left, and Ted leaned against the desk, comfortable in the world that had crowned him king. She tightened her grip on her purse. "What did you mean when you said talking to the manager wasn't a good idea?"

Ted gazed around the small, homey lobby and seemed satisfied with what he saw. "Just that she's not exactly a member of your fan club."

"But I've never met her."

"Oh, you met her, all right. And from what I hear, it didn't go well. Word is, she doesn't appreciate your attitude toward Wynette . . . or toward me."

The door behind the desk swung open, and a woman with woodpecker red hair and a turquoise knit suit emerged.

It was Birdie Kittle.

"Afternoon, Birdie," Ted said as the inn's owner came toward them, her short, fiery hair blazing against the neutral backdrop of the beige walls. "You're lookin' fine today."

"Oh, Ted . . ." She appeared ready to cry. "I'm so sorry about the wedding. I don't even know what to say."

Most men would be mortified by all that pity flowing at them, but he didn't seem even mildly embarrassed. "Things happen. I appreciate your concern." He nodded toward Meg. "Sheldon stopped Miz Koranda here on the highway—fleeing the scene of the crime, so to speak. But there's been an accident out on Cemetery Road, so he asked me to handle it. He doesn't think anybody's hurt."

"We have too many accidents out there. Remember Jinny Morris's daughter? We need to bulldoze that curve."

"It sure would be nice, but you know as well as anybody what the budget's like."

"Things'll be a lot better once you get us that golf resort. I'm so excited I can hardly stand it. The inn'll pick up business from all the guests who want to play the golf course but don't want to pay the resort's room prices. Plus, I'll finally be able to open up the tearoom and bookstore next door like I've always wanted. I'm thinkin' of calling it the Sip 'N' Browse."

"Sounds good. But the resort is far from being sewed up."

"It will be, Ted. You'll make sure of it. We need those jobs so bad."

Ted nodded, as if he had every confidence in the world he'd be able to deliver them.

Birdie finally turned her sparrow eyes on Meg. Her lids bore the lightest dusting of frosted copper shadow, and she looked even more unfriendly than during their confrontation in the ladies' room. "I hear you didn't get around to settling up your account before you took off." She came around from behind the desk. "Maybe hotels in L.A. let their guests stay for free, but we're not as *sophisticated* here in Wynette."

"There was a mistake," Meg said. "Silly, really. I thought the, uhm, Joriks were taking care of it. I mean, I assumed . . . I . . ." She was only making herself sound more incompetent.

Birdie crossed her arms over her breasts. "How do you intend to pay your bill, Miz Koranda?"

Meg reminded herself that she'd never have to see Ted Beaudine after today. "I—I can't help but notice that you're a very well dressed person. I have an incredible pair of earrings from the Sung dynasty in my suitcase. One of a kind. I bought them in Shanghai. They're worth a lot more than four hundred dollars." At least they were if she chose to believe the rickshaw driver. Which she did. "Would you be interested in barter?"

"I'm not into wearing other people's castoffs. I guess that's more an L.A. thing."

Ruling out Ginger Rogers's cloche.

Meg tried again. "The earrings really aren't castoffs. They're valuable pieces of antiquity."

"Can you pay your bill or not, Miz Koranda?"

Meg tried to come up with a response but couldn't.

"I guess that answers the question." Ted gestured toward the desk phone. "Is there somebody you can call? I sure would hate to have to take you across the street."

She didn't believe him for a moment. He'd love nothing more than to book her himself. He'd probably even volunteer to do the strip search.

Bend over, Miz Koranda.

She shivered, and Ted offered up that slow smile, as if he'd read her mind.

Birdie displayed her first show of enthusiasm. "I have an idea. I'd be more than happy to talk to your father for you. Explain the situation."

I'll just bet you would. "Unfortunately, my father is out of reach right now."

"Maybe Miz Koranda could work it off," Ted said. "Didn't I hear you were short a maid?"

"A maid?" Birdie said. "Oh, she's way too *sophisticated* to clean hotel rooms."

Meg swallowed hard. "I'd be . . . happy to help you out here."

"You'd better think this through," Ted said. "What are you paying, Birdie? Seven—seven-fifty an hour? Once Uncle Sam gets his share—and assuming she works a full shift—that's a couple weeks' work. I doubt Miz Koranda could handle cleaning bathrooms for that long."

"You have no idea what Miz Koranda can handle," Meg said,

trying to look much tougher than she felt. "I've been on a cattle drive in Australia and hiked the Annapurna circuit in Nepal." Only ten miles of it, but still . . .

Birdie lifted her penciled eyebrows and exchanged a look with Ted that they both seemed to understand. "Well . . . I do need a maid," Birdie said. "But if you think you can work off your bill by loafing around, you're in for an unhappy surprise."

"I don't think that at all."

"All right, then. Do your job, and I won't press charges. But if you try to skip out, you'll find yourself in the Wynette City Jail."

"Fair enough," Ted said. "I only wish all disputes could be solved so peacefully. It'd be a better world, now wouldn't it?"

"It sure would," Birdie said. She turned her attention back to Meg and pointed toward the door behind the desk. "I'll take you to meet Arlis Hoover, our head housekeeper. You'll be working for her."

"Arlis Hoover?" Ted said. "Damn, I forgot about that."

"She was here when I took over the place," Birdie said. "How could you forget?"

"I don't know." Ted dug a set of car keys from the pocket of his jeans. "I guess she's just one of those people I try to put out of my mind."

"Tell me about it," Birdie muttered.

And with those ominous words, she led Meg from the lobby into the bowels of the hospitality industry.

chapter five

Emma Traveler loved the creamy limestone ranch house she and Kenny shared with their three children. In the pasture beyond the live oaks, the horses grazed in contentment, and a mockingbird called from its perch on the newly whitewashed fence. Before long, the first peaches in their orchard would be ready for picking.

All but one member of the Wynette Public Library Rebuilding Committee had gathered around the pool for their Saturday afternoon meeting. Kenny had taken the children into town so the committee could conduct business without any interruptions, although Emma knew from long experience that no business could ever be conducted until each member, whose ages ranged from thirty-two to her own ancient forty, had finished discussing whatever happened to be on her mind.

"I've been saving for years to afford college for Haley, and now she doesn't want to go." Birdie Kittle tugged on her new Tommy Bahama suit, with its diagonal ruching to help camouflage her middle. Her daughter had graduated from Wynette High a few weeks earlier with straight As. Birdie couldn't accept Haley's insistence on attending the county community college in the fall instead of the University of Texas, just as she couldn't accept her looming fortieth birthday. "I was hopin' you could talk some sense into her, Lady Emma."

As the only child of the long-deceased fifth Earl of Woodbourne, Emma was entitled to the honorific "Lady" but never used it. That, however, hadn't stopped the entire population of Wynette—minus Emma's children and Francesca—from addressing her as "Lady" no matter how many times she'd pleaded with them not to. Even her own husband did it. Unless, of course, they were in bed, in which case . . .

Emma struggled not to drift into an X-rated reverie. She was a former teacher, a longtime member of the board of education, the town's cultural director, and president of the Friends of the Wynette Public Library, so she was accustomed to questions about other people's children. "Haley is quite bright, Birdie. You'll have to trust her."

"I don't know where she got her brains because it sure wasn't from her ex-father or me." Birdie polished off one of the lemon bars that Patrick, the Travelers' longtime housekeeper, had put out for the group.

Shelby Traveler, who was both Emma's friend and, at thirty-seven, her very young mother-in-law, slipped a floppy sun hat over her ex-sorority girl's blond bob. "Look on the bright side. She wants to keep living at home. I couldn't wait to get away from my mother."

"It doesn't have anything to do with me." Birdie swiped at the crumbs on her bathing suit. "If Kyle Bascom was going to U.T. instead of County Community, Haley'd be packing her suitcases for Austin right now. And he doesn't even know she's alive. I can't stand the idea of one more Kittle woman throwing away her future for a man. I tried to get Ted to talk to her—you know how much she respects him—but he said she's old enough to make her own decisions, which she's not."

They looked up as Kayla Garvin hurried around the corner of the house, the top of her two-piece swimsuit generously displaying the implants her father had bought her several years ago in hopes she could lure Ted into joining the Garvin family. "Sorry I'm late. New arrivals at the shop." She wrinkled her nose, showing her distaste for the clothing resale shop she ran part-time to keep herself busy, but her expression brightened when she saw that Torie hadn't shown up. Even though Torie was a close friend, Kayla didn't like being around anyone whose body was as good as her own, not when she was wearing a swimsuit.

Today, Kayla had piled her blond hair into a fashionably unkempt knot on top of her head and wrapped a white lace sarong low on her hips. As usual, she wore full makeup and her new pavé diamond star necklace. She settled on the chaise next to Emma. "I swear, if one more woman tries to pawn off another old lady Christmas sweater on me, I'm going to lock up that resale shop and go to work for you, Birdie."

"Thanks again for helping me out last week. That's the second time this month Mary Alice has called in sick." Birdie moved her freckled legs out of the sun. "Even though I need the business, I'm glad the press has finally left town. They were like a bunch of crows, poking around in our business and making fun of the town. They dogged Ted everywhere."

Kayla reached for her favorite MAC lip gloss. "I should be thankin' you for letting me help out that day. I wish y'all had been there when Miss Hollywood started scrambling to pay her bill. 'Do you know who I am?' she says, like I'm supposed to start bowing." Kayla slicked the wand over her lips.

"She's got more attitude than anybody I've ever met." Zoey

Daniels wore a conservative one-piece nut brown bathing suit a few shades darker than her skin. Believing that African American women needed to be just as vigilant against sun damage as their pale sisters, she'd chosen to sit under one of the striped umbrellas.

At thirty-two, Zoey and Kayla were the youngest members of the group. Despite their differences—one was a fashion-obsessed blond beauty queen; the other the studious young principal of Sybil Chandler Elementary School—they'd been best friends since childhood. Barely five feet tall and slender, Zoey had short, natural hair, large golden-brown eyes, and an air of worry that had become more pronounced as class sizes had grown and budgets had been cut.

She tugged on a brightly colored stretchy bracelet strung with what seemed to be lumps of dried Play-Doh. "Just the sight of that girl depresses me. I can't wait for her to leave town. Poor Ted."

Shelby Traveler rubbed sunblock on the tops of her feet. "He's being so brave about what happened. It just about breaks my heart."

Ted was special to each of them. Birdie adored him, and he'd been in and out of Shelby's house ever since she'd married Kenny's father, Warren. Kayla and Zoey had both been in love with him, a serious test of their friendship. All Kayla would say about it these days was that those were the best six months of her life. Zoey just sighed and got depressed, so they'd stopped talking about it.

"Maybe it was jealousy that made her do it." Zoey retrieved a copy of *Social Studies in Elementary School* that had fallen out of her book bag and stuffed it back in. "Either she didn't want Lucy to have him, or she took one look at him and wanted him for herself."

"We all know women who've gotten more than a little obsessive about Ted." Shelby didn't look at either Zoey or Kayla, but she didn't have to. "I sure would like to know what she said to Lucy to convince her to call off the wedding."

Kayla fiddled with her star necklace. "Y'all know how Ted is. Sweet to everybody. But not to Miss I've-Got-Famous-Parents." Kayla shivered. "Who knew Ted Beaudine had a dark side."

"It only makes him hotter." Zoey gave another of her poignant sighs.

Birdie smirked. "Jake Koranda's daughter is scrubbin' my toilets . . ."

Emma pulled on her sun hat, a perky straw number. "It's difficult for me to understand why her parents aren't helping her."

"They've cut her off," Kayla said firmly. "And it's not hard to figure out why. Meg Koranda is on drugs."

"We don't know that for sure," Zoey said.

"You always want to think the best of everybody," Kayla retorted. "But it's clear as anything. I'll bet her family finally decided they'd had enough."

This was exactly the kind of gossip Emma most disliked. "Best not to start rumors we can't prove," she said, even though she knew she was wasting her breath.

Kayla readjusted her bikini top. "Make sure your cash drawer is locked up tight, Birdie. Drug addicts will steal you blind."

"I'm not worried," Birdie said smugly. "Arlis Hoover's keeping an eye on her."

Shelby made the sign of the cross, and they all laughed.

"Perhaps you'll get lucky and Arlis will take a job at the new golf resort."

Emma had meant to be funny, but a silence fell over the group as each of them pondered how the proposed golf resort and condo complex could change her life for the better. Birdie would have her tearoom and bookstore, Kayla would be able to open the upscale fashion boutique she dreamed of, and the school system would get the extra revenue Zoey yearned for.

Emma exchanged a look with Shelby. Her young mother-in-law would no longer have to watch her husband deal with the stress of being the only large employer in a town where too many were jobless. As for Emma herself . . . She and Kenny had enough money to live comfortably, regardless of what happened with the golf resort, but so many of the people they cared about didn't, and the well-being of their hometown meant everything to them.

Emma, however, didn't believe in moping. "Golf resort or not," she said briskly, "we need to discuss how we're going to find the money to get our library repaired and back in operation. Even with the insurance check, we're still miserably short of what we need."

Kayla refastened her blond topknot. "I can't stand having another stupid bake sale. Zoey and I did enough of that in junior high."

"Or a silent auction," Shelby said.

"Or a car wash or a raffle." Zoey swatted at a fly.

"We need something big," Birdie said. "Something that will attract everybody's attention."

They talked for another hour, but no one could come up with a single idea about what that might be.

ARLIS HOOVER POINTED A STUBBY finger toward the bathtub Meg had just scrubbed for the second time. "You call that clean, Miss Movie Star? I don't call that clean."

Meg no longer bothered pointing out she wasn't a movie star. Arlis knew that very well. Exactly why she kept repeating it.

Arlis had dyed black hair and a body like gnawed gristle. She fed off a permanent sense of injustice, certain that only bad luck separated her from wealth, beauty, and opportunity. She listened to wacko radio shows as she worked, shows that proved Hillary Clinton had once eaten the flesh of a newborn child and that PBS was entirely funded by left-wing movie stars bent on giving homosexuals control of the world. Like they'd really want it.

Arlis was so mean that Meg suspected even Birdie was a little afraid of her, although Arlis did her best to curb her more psychotic impulses when she was around her employer. But she saved Birdie money by getting the most out of a tiny housekeeping staff, so Birdie left her alone.

"Dominga, come over here and look at this bathtub. Is that what you folks in Mexico call clean?"

Dominga was an illegal, in no position to disagree with Arlis, and she shook her head. "No. *Muy sucia.*"

Meg hated Arlis Hoover more than she'd ever hated anyone, with the possible exception of Ted Beaudine.

What are you paying your housekeepers, Birdie? Seven, seven-fifty an hour?

No. Birdie paid them ten-fifty an hour, as Ted surely knew. All of them except Meg.

Her back ached, her knees throbbed, she'd cut her thumb on a broken mirror, and she was hungry. For the past week, she'd been existing on pillow mints and the inn's leftover breakfast muffins, smuggled to her by Carlos, the maintenance man. But those economies couldn't make up for her mistake that first night when she'd taken a room in a cheap motel, only to wake up the next morning realizing that even cheap motels cost money, and that the one hundred dollars in her wallet had shrunk to fifty dollars overnight. She'd been sleeping in her car out by the gravel quarry ever since and waiting until Arlis left for the day before sneaking into an unoccupied room to shower.

It was a miserable existence, but she hadn't yet picked up the phone. She hadn't tried to reach Dylan again, or called Clay. She hadn't phoned Georgie, Sasha, or April. Most important, she hadn't mentioned her situation to her parents when they'd called. She hugged that knowledge to herself every time she unclogged another fetid toilet or dug one more scummy hair plug from a bathtub drain. In a week or so, she'd be out of here. Then what? She had no idea.

With a large family reunion scheduled to arrive soon, Arlis could only spare a few minutes to torture Meg. "Turn that mattress before you change the sheets, Miss Movie Star, and I want all the sliding doors on this floor washed. Don't let me find one fingerprint."

"Afraid the FBI will discover it belongs to you?" Meg said sweetly. "What do they want you for anyway?"

Arlis nearly went catatonic whenever Meg talked back to her, and an angry rash exploded on her veiny cheeks. "All I have to do is say one word to Birdie, and you'll be locked behind bars."

Maybe, but with the inn filling up for the weekend and a shortage of housekeepers, Arlis couldn't afford to lose her right now. Still, best not to press it.

When Meg was finally alone, she gazed longingly at the sparkling bathtub. Last night, Arlis had stayed late to check inventory, so Meg hadn't been able to sneak in a shower, and with the inn booked up, the prospects didn't look much better for tonight. She reminded herself that she'd spent days on muddy trails without giving a thought to indoor plumbing. But those excursions had been recreational, not her real life, although now that she looked back, it seemed as though recreation had been her real life.

She was struggling to flip the mattress when she sensed someone behind her. She prepared herself for another confrontation with Arlis only to see Ted Beaudine in the doorway.

He leaned against the doorjamb with one shoulder, his ankles crossed, perfectly at home in the kingdom over which he ruled. Sweat glued her mint green polyester maid's dress to her skin, and she dabbed her forehead against her arm. "My lucky day. A visit from the Chosen One. Cured any lepers lately?"

"Too busy with the loaves and fishes thing."

He didn't even smile. Bastard. A couple of times this week as she'd adjusted drapes or wiped off a windowsill with one of the toxic products the inn insisted on using, she'd spotted him outside. City Hall, it turned out, occupied the same building as the police station. This morning, she'd stood in a second-floor window and watched him honest-to-God stop fricking traffic to help an old lady across the street. She'd also noticed a lot of young women entering the building through the side door that led directly to the municipal offices. Maybe on city business. More likely monkey business.

He nodded toward the mattress. "Looks like you could use some help with that?"

She was exhausted, the mattress was heavy, and she swallowed her pride. "Thanks."

He looked behind him into the hallway. "Nope. Don't see anybody."

Letting herself get suckered in gave her the willpower to wedge her shoulder under the bottom corner of the mattress and hoist it. "What do you want?" she grunted.

"Checking up on you. One of my duties as mayor is to make sure our vagrant population isn't accosting innocent citizens."

She jammed her shoulder farther under the mattress and retaliated with the rottenest thing she could think of. "Lucy's been texting me. So far, she hasn't mentioned you." Or much of anything, just a sentence or two saying she was all right and she didn't want to talk. Meg heaved the mattress higher.

"Give her my best," he said, as casually as if he were referring to a distant cousin.

"You don't even care where she is, do you?" Meg lifted the mattress another few inches. "Whether she's all right or not? She could have been kidnapped by terrorists." Fascinating how easily a basically nice person like herself could turn nasty.

"I'm sure someone would have mentioned it."

She struggled to catch her breath. "It seems to have escaped your supposedly gigantic brain that I'm not responsible for Lucy ditching you, so why make me your personal punching bag?"

"I have to take out my boundless fury on somebody." He recrossed his ankles.

"You're pathetic." But she'd barely gotten the words out of her mouth when she lost her balance and tumbled over the box spring. The mattress slammed on top of her.

Cool air slithered over the backs of her bare thighs. The skirt of her uniform bunched above her hips, giving him an unrestricted view of her bright yellow panties and possibly the dragon inked on her hip. God had punished her for being rude to his Perfect Creation by turning her into a big Posturepedic sandwich.

She heard his muffled voice. "You all right in there?"

The mattress didn't move.

She squirmed, trying to work herself free and getting no help. Her skirt crept to her waist. Putting the image of yellow panties and a dragon tattoo out of her head, she vowed not to let him see her defeated by a mattress. Struggling for air, she curled her toes into the carpet and, with one final contortion, pushed the bulky weight onto the floor.

Ted gave a low whistle. "Damn, that is one heavy son of a bitch."

She stood up and shoved her skirt down. "How would you know?"

He let his gaze drift over her legs and smiled. "Educated guess."

She lunged for the corner of the mattress and somehow managed to gather enough traction to turn the awful thing and pull it back onto the box spring.

"Well done," he said.

She pushed a spike of hair out of her eyes. "You're a vindictive, cold-blooded psycho."

"Harsh."

"Am I the only person in the world who sees through your St. Ted routine?"

"Just about."

"Look at you. Not even two weeks ago, Lucy was the love of your life. Now you barely seem to remember her name." She kicked the mattress forward a few inches.

"Time heals."

"Eleven days?"

He shrugged and wandered across the room to investigate the Internet connection. She stomped after him. "Stop taking what happened out on me. It wasn't my fault that Lucy ran off." Not entirely true, but close enough.

He squatted down to inspect the cable connection. "Things were fine before you got here."

"You only think they were."

He reset the jack and rose to his feet. "Here's the way I see it. For reasons only you know—although I have a fair idea what they are— you brainwashed a wonderful woman into making a mistake she'll have to live with for the rest of her life."

"It wasn't a mistake. Lucy deserves more than you were prepared to give her."

"You have no idea what I was prepared to give her," he said as he headed for the door.

"Not your unbridled passion, that's for sure."

"Stop pretending you know what you're talking about."

She charged after him. "If you'd loved Lucy the way she deserved to be loved, you'd be doing everything in your power to find her and convince her to take you back. And I didn't have any hidden agenda. All I care about is Lucy's happiness."

His steps slowed, and he turned. "We both know that's not quite true."

The way he studied her made her feel as though he understood something about her that she didn't. Her hands fisted at her sides. "You think I was jealous? Is that what you're saying? That I set out to somehow sabotage her? I have a lot of faults, but I don't screw over my friends. Ever."

"Then why did you screw over Lucy?"

His lethal, unfair attack sent an angry rush through her. "Get out."

He was already leaving, but not before he sent a final dart her way. "Nice dragon."

BY THE TIME HER SHIFT was over, all the inn's rooms were occupied, making it impossible for her to sneak in a shower. Carlos had smuggled her a muffin, her lone meal of the day. Besides Carlos, the only other person who didn't seem to hate her was Birdie Kittle's eighteen-year-old daughter, Haley, which was something of a surprise, since she identified herself as Ted's personal assistant. But Meg soon figured out that meant she merely ran occasional errands for him.

Haley had a summer job at the country club, so Meg didn't see her much, but she sometimes stopped in a room Meg was cleaning. "I know Lucy's your friend," she said one afternoon as she helped Meg tuck in a clean sheet. "And she was super nice to everybody. But she didn't seem like she'd be happy in Wynette."

Haley bore little resemblance to her mother. A few inches taller, with a long face and straight, light brown hair, she wore her clothes too small and applied more makeup than her delicate features warranted. Meg gathered from an exchange she'd overheard between Birdie and her daughter that the eighteen-year-old's entry into skankdom was fairly recent.

"Lucy is pretty adaptable," Meg said as she slipped on a fresh pillowcase.

"Still, she seemed more like a big-city person to me, and even though Ted travels all over when he does consulting, this is where he lives."

Meg appreciated knowing someone else in this town had shared her doubts, but it didn't help shake off her growing despondence. When she left the inn that evening, she was dirty and hungry. She lived in a rusty Buick she parked each night in a deserted patch of scrub by the town gravel quarry where she prayed no one would discover her. Her body felt heavy despite her empty stomach, and as she approached the car that had become her home, her steps slowed. Something didn't seem right. She looked more closely.

The rear of the car on the driver's side sagged almost imperceptibly. She had a flat tire.

She stood there without moving, trying to absorb this latest disaster. Her car was all she had left. In the past when she'd had a flat, she'd simply called someone and paid to have it changed, but she had barely twenty dollars left. And even if she could figure out how to change it herself, she didn't know whether the spare had air. If there was a spare.

With a catch in her throat, she opened the trunk and pulled up the mangy carpet, filthy with oil, dirt, and who knew what else? She found the spare tire, but it was flat. She'd have to drive on the bad tire to the town's nearest service station and pray she didn't damage the rim on the way.

The owner knew who she was, just like everybody else in town. He delivered a cutting remark about this only being a hick small-town garage, then launched into a rambling story extolling the way saintly Ted Beaudine had single-handedly saved the county food pantry from closing. When he wound down, he demanded twenty dollars in advance to replace the original tire with the balding spare.

"I've got nineteen."

"Hand it over."

She emptied her wallet and stomped inside the service station while he changed the tire. The coins that had collected in the bottom of her purse were all she had left. As she stared at the snack dispensers filled with goodies she could no longer afford, Ted Beaudine's old powder blue Ford pickup pulled to a pump. She'd seen him drive the truck through town, and she remembered Lucy mentioning that he'd modified it with some of his inventions, but it still looked like an old beater to her.

A woman with long brunette hair sat in the passenger seat. As Ted got out, she lifted her arm and pushed her hair away from her face with a gesture as graceful as a ballerina's. Meg recalled seeing her at the rehearsal dinner, but there had been so many people, and they hadn't been introduced.

Ted slipped back inside the car as the tank filled. The woman curled her hand around his neck. He tilted his face toward her, and they kissed. Meg watched with disgust. So much for Lucy's guilt over breaking Ted's heart.

The truck didn't seem to take much gas—maybe the hydrogen

fuel cell Lucy had mentioned. Ordinarily Meg would have been interested in something like that, but now all she cared about was counting the change in the bottom of her purse. One dollar and six cents.

As she drove away from the service station, she finally accepted the fact she least wanted to face. She'd hit bottom. She was famished, filthy, and the only home she had was nearly out of gas. Of all her friends, Georgie York Shepard was the softest touch. Indefatigable Georgie, who'd been supporting herself since she was a child.

Georgie, it's me. I'm aimless and undisciplined, and I need you to take care of me because I can't take care of myself.

An RV chugged past, heading into town. She couldn't face driving back to the gravel pit and spending another night trying to convince herself this was simply a new travel adventure. Sure, she'd slept in dark, scary places before, but only for a few days and always with a friendly guide nearby and a four-star hotel waiting at the end of the trip. This, on the other hand, was homelessness. One step away from pushing a shopping cart down the street.

She wanted her father. She wanted him to hug her close and tell her everything would be all right. She wanted her mother to stroke her hair and promise that no monsters lurked in the closet. She wanted to curl up in her old bedroom in the house where she'd always felt so restless.

But as much as her parents loved her, they'd never respected her. Neither had Dylan, Clay, or her uncle Michel. And once she hit Georgie up for money, her friend would join the list.

She started to cry. Big, drippy tears of self-disgust for hungry, homeless Meg Koranda, who'd been born with every advantage and still couldn't make anything of herself. She pulled off the road onto the crumbling parking lot of a shuttered roadhouse. She needed to call Georgie now, before her father remembered he was still paying her phone bill and he cut that off, too.

She ran her thumb over the buttons and tried to figure out how Lucy was managing. Lucy hadn't gone home, either. What was she doing to get by that Meg hadn't figured out how to do for herself?

A church bell tolled six o'clock, reminding her of the church Ted had given Lucy as a wedding present. A pickup rattled by with a dog in the back, and the phone slipped from Meg's fingers. *Lucy's church!* Sitting empty.

She remembered passing the country club when they'd driven there because Lucy had pointed it out. She recalled lots of twists and turns, but Wynette had so many back roads. Which ones had Lucy taken?

Two hours later, just as Meg was about to give up, she found what she was looking for.

chapter six

THE OLD WOODEN CHURCH SAT on a rise at the end of a gravel lane. Meg's headlights picked out the squat white steeple just above the central doors. In the dark, she couldn't see the overgrown graveyard off to the right, but she remembered it was there. She also remembered Lucy retrieving a hidden key from somewhere near the base of the steps. She shone her headlights on the front of the building and began fumbling around among the stones and shrubbery. The gravel ground into her knees, and she scraped her knuckles, but she couldn't find any evidence of a key. Breaking a window seemed sacrilegious, but she had to get in.

The glare of the headlights sent her shadow shooting grotesquely up the simple wooden facade. As she turned back to her car, she spotted a roughly carved stone frog perched underneath a shrub. She picked it up and found the key beneath. Tucking it deep in her pocket for safekeeping, she parked the Rustmobile, retrieved her suitcase, and climbed the five wooden steps.

According to Lucy, the Lutherans had abandoned the tiny country church sometime in the 1960s. A pair of arched windows bracketed the double front doors. The key turned easily in the lock. The inside was musty, the air hot from the day. When she'd last visited, the interior had been washed in sunlight, but now the darkness reminded her of every horror movie she'd ever seen. She fumbled for a switch, hoping the electricity was turned on. Magically, two white wall globes sprang to life. She couldn't leave them on long for fear someone would see—just long enough to explore. She dropped her suitcase and locked the door behind her.

The pews were gone, leaving an empty, echoing space. The founding fathers hadn't believed in ornamentation. No stained-glass windows, soaring vaults, or stone columns for these stern Lutherans. The room was narrow, not even thirty feet wide, with scrubbed pine floors and a pair of ceiling fans hanging from a simple stamped-metal ceiling. Five long transom windows lined each wall. An austere staircase led to a small wooden choir loft at the rear, the church's only extravagance.

Lucy had said that Ted had lived in the church for a few months while his house was being built, but whatever furniture he'd brought here was gone. Only an ugly easy chair with stuffing showing through a corner of its brown upholstery remained, along with a black metal futon she discovered in the choir loft. Lucy had planned to furnish the space with cozy seating areas, painted tables, and folk art. All Meg cared about right now was the possibility of running water.

Her sneakers squeaked on the old pine floor as she made her way toward the small door positioned to the right of what had once been the altar. Beyond it lay a room barely ten feet deep that served as both kitchen and storage space. An ancient, silent refrigerator, the kind with rounded corners, rested next to a small side window. The kitchen also held an old-fashioned four-burner enameled stove, a metal cupboard, and a porcelain sink. Perpendicular to the back door another door led to a bathroom more modern than the rest of the church with a toilet, white pedestal sink, and shower stall. She gazed at the X-shaped porcelain faucets and slowly, hopefully, twisted one handle.

Fresh water gushed from the spout. So basic. So luxurious.

She didn't care that there was no hot water. Within minutes, she'd retrieved her suitcase, peeled off her clothes, grabbed the shampoo and soap she'd pilfered from the inn, and stepped inside. She gasped as the cold splashed over her. Never again would she take this luxury for granted.

After she dried off, she tied the silk wrap she'd worn to the rehearsal dinner under her arms. She'd just located an unopened box of saltines and six cans of tomato soup in the metal cupboard when her phone rang. She picked it up and heard a familiar voice.

"Meg?"

She set the soup can aside. "Luce? Honey, are you all right?" It had been almost two weeks since the night Lucy had run away, and that was the last time they'd spoken.

"I'm fine," Lucy said.

"Why are you whispering?"

"Because . . ." A pause. "Would I be . . . like . . . a total skank if I slept with another guy now? Like in about ten minutes?"

Meg stood straighter. "I don't know. Maybe."

"That's what I thought."

"Do you like him?"

"Kind of. He's no Ted Beaudine, but . . ."

"Then you should *definitely* sleep with him." Meg spoke more forcefully than she'd intended, but Lucy didn't pick up on it.

"I want to, but . . ."

"Be a skank, Luce. It'll be good for you."

"I guess if I'd seriously wanted to be talked out of this, I'd have called somebody else."

"That tells you a lot, then."

"You're right." Meg heard the sound of water being shut off in the background. "I have to go," Lucy said in a rush. "I'll call when I can. Love you." She hung up.

Lucy sounded frazzled, but excited, too. Meg thought about the call as she finished a bowl of soup. Maybe this would all turn out okay in the end. At least for Lucy.

With a sigh, she washed the saucepan, then laundered her dirty clothes with some dishwashing detergent she found under the sink amid a scatter of mouse turds. Every morning, she'd have to wipe out the signs that she'd been here, pack her possessions, and stow them in her car in case Ted stopped by. But for now, she had food, shelter, and running water. She'd bought herself a little more time.

THE NEXT FEW WEEKS WERE the worst of her life. As Arlis made her days increasingly miserable, Meg dreamed of returning to L.A., but even if she could have gotten back, she had nowhere to stay. Not with her parents, whose tough-love speech was seared into her brain. Not with her friends, all of whom had families, which was fine for an overnight stay, but not for an extended visit. When Birdie grudgingly informed her that she'd finally worked off her debt, Meg felt nothing but despair. She couldn't quit the inn until she had another source of income, and she couldn't move as long as Lucy's church was her only shelter. She needed to find another job, one in Wynette. Preferably a job that provided immediate tip money.

She applied to wait tables at the Roustabout, the honky-tonk that served as the town's gathering place. "You screwed up Ted's wedding," the owner said, "and you tried to stiff Birdie. Why would I hire you?"

So much for the Roustabout.

Over the next several days, she stopped at every bar and restaurant in town, but none was hiring. Or at least they weren't hiring her. Her food supply was nonexistent, she was purchasing gas three gallons at a time, and she had to buy Tampax soon. She needed cash, and she needed it fast.

As she removed still another revolting hair plug from still another crusty bathtub, she thought about how many times she'd forgotten to tip the housekeepers who cleaned the hotel rooms after her. So far, all she'd picked up in tips was a measly twenty-eight bucks. It would have been more, but Arlis had an uncanny ability to spot the guests most likely to be generous and make sure she checked their rooms first. The upcoming weekend might be lucrative if Meg could figure out how to outsmart her.

Ted's former best man, Kenny Traveler, was hosting a golf outing for his friends who were flying in from all over the country and staying at the inn. Meg might regard the sport with contempt for the way it gobbled up natural resources, but money was to be made from its disciples, and all day Thursday, she thought about how she could profit from the weekend. By evening, she had a plan. It involved an expenditure she could ill afford, but she made herself stop at the grocery after work and turn over twenty dollars from her meager paycheck as an investment in her immediate future.

The next day she waited until the golfers began trickling in from their Friday afternoon rounds. When Arlis wasn't looking, she grabbed some towels and started knocking on doors. "Good afternoon, Mr. Samuels." She plastered on a big smile for the gray-haired man who answered. "I thought you might like some extra towels. Sure is hot out there." She set one of the precious candy bars she'd bought the night before on top. "I hope you had a good round, but here's a little sugar in case you didn't. My compliments."

"Thanks, honey. That's real thoughtful." Mr. Samuels pulled out his money clip and peeled off a five-dollar bill.

By the time she left the inn that night, she'd made forty dollars. She was as proud of herself as if she'd made her first million. But if she intended to repeat her scheme on Saturday afternoon, she needed a new twist, and that was going to involve another small expenditure.

"Damn. I haven't had one of those in years," Mr. Samuels said when he answered the door on Saturday afternoon.

"Homemade." She gave him her biggest, most winning smile and handed over the fresh towels, along with one of the individually wrapped Rice Krispies treats she'd stayed up until well past midnight last night making. Cookies would have been better, but her culinary skills were limited. "I only wish it were a cold beer," she said. "We sure appreciate you gentlemen staying here."

This time he gave her a ten.

Arlis, already suspicious over their dwindling towel inventory, nearly caught her twice, but Meg managed to dodge her, and as she approached the third-floor suite, registered to a Dexter O'Connor, her uniform pocket held a comfortable weight. Mr. O'Connor had been out yesterday when she'd stopped, but today a tall, strikingly beautiful woman wrapped in one of the inn's white terry robes answered the door. Even just out of the shower, with her face scrubbed free of makeup and strands of inky hair clinging to her neck, she was flawless—tall and thin with bold green eyes and iceberg-size diamond studs in her ears. She didn't look like a Dexter. And neither did the man Meg glimpsed over her shoulder.

Ted Beaudine sat in the room's easy chair, his shoes kicked off, a beer in hand. Something clicked, and Meg recognized the brunette as the woman Ted had kissed at the gas station a few weeks ago.

"Oh, good. Extra towels." Her splashy diamond wedding ring sparkled as she grabbed the package on top. "And a homemade Rice Krispies treat! Look, Teddy! How long has it been since you've had a Rice Krispies treat?"

"Can't say as I recall," *Teddy* replied.

The woman tucked the towels under her arm and pulled at the plastic wrap. "I love these things. Give her a ten, will you?"

He didn't move. "I'm fresh out of tens. Or any other currency."

"Hold on." The woman turned, presumably to get her purse, only to whip back around. "Holy Jesus!" She dropped the towels. "You're the wedding wrecker! I didn't recognize you in your uniform."

Ted unwound from the chair and approached the door. "Selling baked goods without a license, Meg? That's a direct violation of city code."

"These are gifts, Mr. Mayor."

"Do Birdie and Arlis know about your gifts?"

The brunette pushed in front of him. "Never mind that." Her green eyes glittered with excitement. "The wedding wrecker. I can't believe it. Come on in. I have some questions for you." She shoved the door fully open and tugged on Meg's arm. "I want to hear exactly why you thought What's-Her-Name was so wrong for Teddy."

Meg had finally met someone other than Haley Kittle who didn't hate her for what she'd done. It wasn't exactly shocking that this person would be Ted's apparently married lover.

Ted stepped in front of the woman and disconnected her hand from Meg's arm. "Best for you to get back to work, Meg. I'll be sure to let Birdie know how diligent you are."

Meg gritted her teeth, but Ted wasn't quite done. "The next time you talk to Lucy, be sure to tell her how much I miss her?" With a flick of his finger, he tugged open the loose knot on the front of the woman's robe, pulled her against him, and kissed her hard.

Moments later, the door slammed in Meg's face.

MEG HATED HYPOCRISY, AND KNOWING everybody in town regarded Ted as a model of decency when he was banging a married woman made her crazy. She'd bet anything the affair had been going on while he and Lucy were engaged.

She pulled up to the church that evening and began the laborious process of dragging all her possessions back inside—her suitcase, towels, food, the bed linens she'd borrowed from the inn and intended to return as soon as she could. She refused to spend another second thinking about Ted Beaudine. Better to concentrate on the positive. Thanks to the golfers, she had money for gas, Tampax, and some groceries. Not a huge accomplishment, but enough so she could postpone making any humiliating phone calls to her friends.

But her relief was short-lived. On Sunday, the very next evening, as she was about to leave work, she discovered that one of the golfers—and it didn't take any great detective skills to figure out which one—had complained to Birdie about a maid trolling for tips. Birdie called Meg to her office and, with a great deal of satisfaction, fired her on the spot.

THE LIBRARY REBUILDING COMMITTEE SAT in Birdie's living room enjoying a pitcher of her famous pineapple mojitos. "Haley's mad at me again." Their hostess leaned back into the streamlined midcentury armchair she'd just had reupholstered in vanilla linen, a fabric that wouldn't have lasted a day at Emma's house. "Because I fired Meg

Koranda, of all things. She says Meg won't be able to find another job. I pay my maids more than a fair wage, and Miss Hollywood shouldn't have been deliberately soliciting tips."

The women exchanged glances. They all knew Birdie had paid Meg three dollars less an hour than she was paying everybody else, something that had never sat quite right with Emma, even though Ted had come up with the idea.

Zoey toyed with a glittery pink pasta shell that had dropped off the pin she'd stuck to the collar of her sleeveless white blouse. "Haley's always had a soft heart. I'll bet Meg took advantage of it."

"A soft head is more like it," Birdie said. "I know y'all have noticed the way she's been dressing lately, and I appreciate that none of you have mentioned it. She thinks lettin' her boobs hang out will make Kyle Bascom notice her."

"I had him when I taught sixth grade," Zoey said. "And let me just say that Haley is way too smart for that boy."

"Try telling her that." Birdie drummed her fingers on the chair arm.

Kayla put down her lip gloss and picked up her mojito. "Haley's right about one thing. Nobody in this town is going to hire Meg Koranda, not if they want to look Ted Beaudine in the face."

Emma had never liked bullying, and the town's vindictiveness toward Meg was starting to make her uncomfortable. At the same time, she couldn't forgive Meg for the part she'd played in hurting one of her favorite people.

"I've been thinking a lot about Ted lately." Shelby hooked one side of her blond bob behind her ear and gazed down at her new peep-toe ballerinas.

"Haven't we all." Kayla frowned and touched her pavé diamond star necklace.

"Way too much." Zoey started to chew on her bottom lip.

Ted's newly single status had once again raised their hopes. Emma wished they'd both accept the fact that he would never commit to either of them. Kayla was too high maintenance, and Zoey inspired his admiration but not his love.

It was time to draw the conversation back to the subject they'd been avoiding, how they were going to raise the rest of the money to repair the library. The town's normal sources of big money, which included Emma and husband Kenny, still hadn't recovered from the hits their portfolios had taken in the last economic downturn, and they'd already been tapped out by half a dozen other vital local charities in need of rescue. "Anyone have any new fund-raising idea?" Emma asked.

Shelby clicked her index finger against her front tooth. "I might."

Birdie groaned. "No more bake sales. Last time, four people got food poisoning from Mollie Dodge's coconut custard pie."

"The quilt raffle was a dreadful embarrassment," Emma couldn't help but add, even though she didn't like contributing to the general negativity.

"Who wants a dead squirrel staring back at them every time they go into their bedroom?" Kayla said.

"It was a kitten, not a dead squirrel," Zoey declared.

"It sure looked like a dead squirrel to me," Kayla retorted.

"Not a bake sale and not a quilt raffle." Shelby had a faraway look in her eyes. "Something else. Something . . . bigger. More interesting."

They all regarded her inquisitively, but Shelby shook her head. "I need to think about it first."

No matter how hard they tried, they couldn't get any more out of her.

NOBODY WOULD HIRE MEG. Not even at the ten-unit motel on the edge of town. "You got any idea how many permits it takes to keep this place open?" the ruddy-faced manager told her. "I ain't doin' nothin' to piss off Ted Beaudine, not as long as he's mayor. Hell, even if he wasn't mayor . . ."

So Meg drove from one business to the next, her car guzzling gas like a construction worker gulping water on a summer afternoon. Three days passed, then four. By the fifth day, as she gazed across the desk at the newly hired assistant manager of Windmill Creek Country Club, her desperation had developed a bitter center. As soon as this interview fell through, she'd have to swallow her final shard of pride and call Georgie.

The assistant manager was an officious preppy type, thin, with glasses and a neatly trimmed beard he tugged on as he explained that, despite the club's lowly status, being only semiprivate and not nearly as prestigious as his former place of employment, Windmill Creek was still the home of Dallas Beaudine and Kenny Traveler, two of the biggest legends in professional golf. As if she didn't know.

Windmill Creek was also the home club of Ted Beaudine and his cronies, and she'd never have wasted gas coming here if she hadn't seen the item in the *Wynette Weekly* announcing that the club's newly hired assistant manager had last worked at a golf club in Waco, which made him a stranger in town. On the chance that he didn't yet know she was the Voldemort of Wynette, she'd immediately picked up the phone and, to her shock, snagged this afternoon's interview.

"The job's eight to five," he said, "with Mondays off."

She'd gotten so used to rejection that she'd let her mind wander. She had no idea what job he was talking about, or if he'd actually offered it to her. "That's—that's perfect," she said. "Eight to five is perfect."

"The pay's not much, but if you do your job right, the tips should be good, especially on weekends."

Tips! "I'll take it!"

He eyed her fictionalized résumé, then took in the outfit she'd pulled together from her desperately limited wardrobe—a gauzy petal skirt, white tank, studded black belt, gladiator sandals, and her Sung dynasty earrings. "Are you sure?" he said doubtfully. "Driving a drink cart isn't much of a job."

She bit back the urge to tell him she wasn't much of an employee. "It's perfect for me." Desperation made it alarmingly easy to set aside her beliefs about golf courses destroying the environment.

As he led her outside to the snack shop to meet her supervisor, she could barely comprehend that she finally had a job. "Exclusive courses don't have drink carts," he sniffed. "But the members here can't seem to wait for the turn to grab their next beer."

Meg had grown up around horses, and she had no idea what "the turn" was. She didn't care. She had a job.

When she got home later that afternoon, she parked behind an old storage shed she'd discovered in the undergrowth beyond the stone fence that surrounded the graveyard. It had long ago lost its roof, and vines, prickly pear, and dried grasses grew around its collapsing walls. She blew her curls off her sweaty forehead as she hauled her suitcase out of the trunk. At least she'd been able to hide her small stash of groceries behind some abandoned kitchen appliances, but even so, the constant packing and unpacking were wearing on her. As she lugged her possessions through the graveyard, she dreamed of air-conditioning and a place to stay where she wouldn't have to erase her presence every morning.

It was nearly July, and the church felt hotter than ever. Dust motes flew as she turned on the overhead fans. They did nothing more than stir the air, but she couldn't risk opening the windows, just as she tried to avoid turning the lights on after dark. It left her with nothing to do other than go to bed around the same time she used to head out for the evening.

She peeled down to her tank and underpants, slipped into her flip-flops, and let herself out the back door. As she wove through the graveyard, she glanced at the names on the tombstones. DIETZEL. MEUSEBACH. ERNST. The hardships she faced were nothing compared with what those good Germans must have endured when they left the familiar behind to make a home in this hostile country.

A thicket of trees lay beyond the graveyard. On the other side, a wide creek fed by the Pedernales River formed a secluded swimming hole she'd discovered not long after she'd moved into the church. The clear water was deep at the center, and she'd started coming here every afternoon to cool off. As she dove in, she wrestled with the unhappy knowledge that Ted Beaudine's fan club would try to get her fired as soon as they spotted her. She had to make sure she didn't give them a reason beyond basic hatred. What did it say about her life that her highest aspiration was not to screw up driving a drink cart?

THAT NIGHT THE CHOIR LOFT was especially hot, and she tossed on the lumpy futon. She had to be at the country club early, and she tried to will herself to fall asleep, but just as she finally drifted off, a noise jarred her awake. It took a few seconds to identify the sound of the doors below opening.

She shot up in bed as the lights came on. Her travel alarm read midnight, and her heart pounded. She'd been prepared for Ted to show up at the church during the day while she was gone, but she'd never expected a nighttime visit. She tried to remember if she'd left anything out in the main room. She eased off the bed and sneaked a peek over the choir loft railing.

A man who was not Ted Beaudine stood in the middle of the old sanctuary. Although they were about the same height, his hair was darker, almost blue-black, and he was a few pounds heavier. It was Kenny Traveler, golf legend and Ted Beaudine's best man. She'd met him and his British wife, Emma, at the rehearsal dinner.

Her heart kicked up another notch as she heard the crunch of a second set of tires. She lifted her head a little higher but couldn't see any signs of abandoned clothes or shoes. "Somebody left the door un-locked," Kenny said a few moments later as the person entered.

"Lucy must have forgotten to close up the last time she was here," an unpleasantly familiar male voice replied. Barely a month had passed since his aborted wedding ceremony, but he uttered Lucy's name im-personally.

She inched up her head again. Ted had wandered into the center of the sanctuary and stood before the place where the altar had once been. He wore jeans and a T-shirt instead of a robe and sandals, but she still half expected him to raise his arms and start addressing the Almighty.

Kenny was in his early forties, tall, well built, as exceptionally good-looking in his way as Ted. Wynette definitely had more than its fair share of male stunners. Kenny took one of the beers Ted handed him and carried it over to the far side of the room, where he sat against the wall between the second and third windows. "What does it say about this town that we have to sneak away to have a private conversa-tion?" he said as he popped the top.

"It says more about your nosy wife than about the town." Ted sat next to him with his own beer.

"Lady Emma does like to know what's going on." The way Kenny caressed his wife's name spoke volumes about his feelings for her. "She's been on my ass ever since the wedding to spend more *quality* time with you. Thinks you need the solace of male friends and all that bullshit."

"That's Lady Emma for you." Ted sipped his beer. "Did you ask her what she meant by quality time?"

"Afraid to hear her answer."

"No question she's real big on book clubs these days."

"You should never have appointed her the town's cultural director. You know how seriously she takes things like that."

"You need to get her pregnant again. She doesn't have as much energy when she's pregnant."

"Three kids is enough. Especially our kids." Once again, his pride shone through his words.

The men drank in silence for a while. Meg allowed herself a flicker of hope. As long as they didn't wander into the back where her clothes were scattered, this could still turn out all right for her.

"You think he'll buy the land this time?" Kenny said.

"Hard to tell. Spencer Skipjack's unpredictable. Six weeks ago he told us he'd decided on San Antone for sure, but now here he is again."

Meg had overheard enough conversations to know Spencer Skipjack was the owner of Viceroy Industries, the giant plumbing company, and the man they were all counting on to build some kind of local upscale golf resort and condo complex that would attract both tourists and retirees and rescue the town from its economic doldrums. Apparently Wynette's only decent-size industry was an electronics company partially owned by Kenny's father, Warren Traveler. But one company wasn't enough to sustain the local economy, and the town was in bad need of jobs along with a fresh source of revenue.

"We have to show Spence the time of his life tomorrow," Ted said. "Let him see what his future'll be like if he chooses Wynette. I'll wait until dinner to get down to business—lay out the tax incentives, remind him of the bargain he'll be getting on that land. You know the drill."

"If only we had enough acreage at Windmill Creek to bulldoze the place and put the resort there." The way Kenny said it suggested this was something they'd frequently discussed.

"It would be a lot cheaper to build, that's for sure." Ted set his beer can aside with a thud. "Torie wanted to play with us tomorrow, so I told her if I saw her anywhere near the club, I'd have her arrested."

"That won't stop her," Kenny said, "and having my sister show up is the last thing we need. Spence knows he can't outplay us, but he'd hate getting beat by a woman, and Torie's short game is practically as good as mine."

"Dex is going to tell Shelby she has to keep Torie away."

Meg wondered if Dex was short for Dexter, the name that Ted's love nest at the inn had been registered under.

Ted leaned against the wall. "As soon as I got wind of Torie's plan to fill out our foursome, I made Dad fly back from New York."

"That'll definitely pump up Spence's ego. Playing with the great Dallas Beaudine." Meg detected a trace of petulance in Kenny's tone, and apparently Ted did, too.

"Stop acting like a girl. You're almost as famous as Dad." Ted's smile faded, and he dropped his hands between his bent knees. "If we don't pull this off, the town's going to suffer in more ways than I want to think about."

"It's time you let people know exactly how serious the situation is."

"They already do. But for now, I don't want anybody saying it out loud."

Another silence fell as the men finished their beers. Finally, Kenny stood to leave. "This isn't your fault, Ted. Things were already in the crapper before you let yourself get elected mayor."

"I know that."

"You're not a miracle worker. All you can do is give it your best effort."

"You've been married to Lady Emma too long," Ted grumbled. "You sound just like her. Next thing, you'll be inviting me to join your damn book club."

The men kept on like that, jabbing at each other as they made their way outside. Their voices faded. A car engine roared to life. Meg sagged back on her heels and let herself breathe.

And then she realized the lights were still on.

The door opened again, and a single set of footsteps echoed on the pine floors. She peered down. Ted stood in the middle of the room, his thumbs tucked in the back pockets of his jeans. He gazed toward the place where the altar had been, but this time his shoulders sagged ever so slightly, offering her a rare glimpse of the unguarded man beneath the self-possessed exterior.

The moment passed quickly. He moved toward the door that led to the kitchen. Her stomach tightened with dread. A moment later, she heard a very loud, very angry curse.

She ducked her head and buried her face in her hands. The angry thud of feet echoed through the church. Maybe, if she stayed very quiet . . .

"Meg!"

chapter seven

M EG DASHED TOWARD THE FUTON. "I'm trying to sleep up here," she shouted, girding herself for battle. "Do you mind?"

Ted thundered up the steps to the loft, the floor trembling under his feet. "What the *hell* do you think you're doing?"

She sat on the edge of the futon and tried to look as though she'd just awakened. "Obviously, not sleeping. What's up with you, anyway? Barging in here in the middle of the night . . . And you shouldn't curse in church."

"How long have you been staying here?"

She stretched and yawned, trying to pull off her cool act. It would have been easier to do if she were wearing something more impressive than pirate-skull panties and the HAPPY PRINTING COMPANY T-shirt left behind by one of the guests. "Do you have to yell so loud?" she said. "You're disturbing the neighbors. And they're dead."

"How long?"

"I'm not sure. Some of those headstones date all the way back to the 1840s."

"I'm talking about *you*."

"Oh. I've been here for a while. Where did you think I'd been staying?"

"I didn't think about it at all. And you know why? Because I didn't give a damn. I want you out of here."

"I believe you, but this is Lucy's church, and she told me I could stay as long as I want." At least she would have if Meg had ever asked her.

"Wrong. This is my church, and you're leaving here first thing tomorrow and not coming back."

"Hold on. You gave this church to Lucy."

"A wedding present. No wedding. No present."

"I don't think that will hold up in a court of law."

"There wasn't a legal contract!"

"You're either a person who stands by his word or you're not. Frankly, I'm beginning to think not."

His eyebrows slammed together. "It's my church, and you're trespassing."

"You see it your way. I see it mine. This is America. We're entitled to our opinions."

"Wrong. This is Texas. And my opinion is the only one that counts."

A lot truer than she cared to acknowledge. "Lucy wants me to stay here, so I'm staying." She absolutely would want Meg to stay here if she knew about it.

He planted a hand on the loft railing. "At first it was fun torturing you, but the game's gotten old." He dipped into his pocket and withdrew a money clip. "I want you out of town tomorrow. This is going to speed you on your way."

He removed the bills, stuck the empty clip back in his pocket, and fanned the money in his fingers so she could count it. Five one-hundred-dollar bills. She swallowed hard. "You shouldn't carry so much cash."

"Normally I don't, but a local property owner dropped by City Hall after the bank closed and paid the balance on an old tax bill. Aren't you glad I couldn't leave all that money lying around?" He dropped the bills on the futon. "Once you get back in Daddy's good graces, have him write me a check." He turned toward the stairs.

She couldn't let him have the last word. "That was an interesting scene I walked in on Saturday at the inn. Were you screwing around on Lucy through all of your engagement or only part of it?"

He turned back and let his eyes slip over her, deliberately lingering on the HAPPY PRINTING COMPANY logo across her breasts. "I've always screwed around on Lucy. But don't worry. She never suspected a thing."

He disappeared down the stairs. A few moments later, the church went dark and the front door snapped closed behind him.

SHE DROVE BLEARY-EYED TO HER job the next morning, the money burning a radioactive hole in the pocket of her revolting new khaki Bermuda shorts. With Ted's five hundred dollars, she could finally get back to L.A. where she could hole up in a cheap motel while she landed a job. Once her parents saw that she was capable of working hard at something, surely they'd relent and help her get a genuine fresh start.

But no. Instead of making a run for the city limits with Ted's money, she was sticking around to begin a dead-end job as a country-club drink-cart girl.

At least the uniform wasn't as bad as her polyester maid's dress, although it ran a close second. At the end of her interview, the assistant manager had handed over a preppy yellow polo shirt bearing the country-club logo in hunter green. She'd been forced to use her precious tip money to buy her own regulation-length khaki shorts as well as a pair of cheap white sneakers and some odious pom-pom sneaker socks she couldn't bear looking at.

As she turned into the club's service drive, she was furious with herself for being too stubborn to grab Ted's money and run. If the cash had come from anyone else, she might have, but she couldn't tolerate taking a penny from him. Her decision was all the more lamebrained because she knew he'd do his best to get her fired as soon as he discovered she was working at the club. She could no longer pretend, even to herself, that she knew what she was doing.

The employee parking lot was emptier than she'd expected at eight o'clock. As she headed into the club through the service entrance, she reminded herself she had to keep Ted and his cronies from spotting her. She made her way to the assistant manager's office, but it was locked and the club's main floor deserted. She went back outside. A few golfers were on the course, but the only employee in sight was a worker watering the roses. When she asked where everyone was, he replied in Spanish, something about people being sick. He pointed her toward a door on the club's lower level.

The pro shop was decorated like an old English pub with dark wood, brass fixtures, and a low-pile navy-and-green-plaid carpet. Pyramids of golf clubs stood guard between racks of neatly organized golf clothes, shoes, and visors bearing the club logo. The shop was empty except for a clean-cut guy behind the counter who was frantically punching at his cell. As she came closer, she read his name tag. MARK. He wasn't quite her height, in his mid- to late twenties, with a slight build, neatly cut light brown hair, and good teeth—a former frat boy who, unlike her, was at home in a polo shirt emblazoned with a country-club logo.

As she introduced herself, he looked up from his cell. "You picked a heck of a day to start work here," he said. "Tell me you've caddied before, or at least play the game."

"No. I'm the new *cart* girl."

"Yeah, I understand. But you've caddied, right?"

"I've seen *Caddy Shack*. Does that count?"

He didn't possess a great sense of humor. "Look, I don't have time to screw around. A very important foursome is going to be here any minute." After last night's conversation, she didn't need to think hard to identify the members of that important foursome. "I've just found out that all but one of our caddies is laid up with food poisoning, along with most of the staff. The kitchen put out some bad coleslaw yesterday for the employee lunch, and believe me, somebody's going to lose a job over that."

She didn't like the direction of this conversation. Didn't like it at all.

"I'm going to caddy for our VIP guest," he said, coming out from behind the counter. "Lenny—he's one of our regular loopers—hates coleslaw, and he's on his way in now. Skeet's caddying for Dallie, as usual, so that's a big break. But I'm still short one caddy, and there's no time left to find anybody."

She swallowed. "That nice man watering the roses by the flagpole . . ."

"Doesn't speak English." He began steering her toward a door in the rear of the pro shop.

"Surely there's somebody else on the staff who didn't eat the coleslaw."

"Yeah, our bartender, who has a broken ankle, and Jenny in billing, who's eighty years old." As he opened the door and gestured her through it, she felt him assessing her. "You don't look like you'll have any trouble carrying a bag for eighteen holes."

"But I've never played golf, and I don't know anything about it. I don't even respect the game. All those trees chopped down and pesticides giving people cancer. It'll be a disaster." More than he could imagine. Only minutes earlier, she'd been contemplating how she'd stay out of Ted Beaudine's sight. And now this.

"I'll talk you through it. You do well, and you'll earn a lot more than you can driving the drink cart. The fee for a beginning caddy is twenty-five dollars, but all these men are big tippers. You'll get at least forty more." He held the door open for her. "This is the caddy room."

The cluttered space held a sagging couch and some metal folding chairs. A bulletin board displaying a NO GAMBLING sign hung above a folding table scattered with a deck of cards and some poker chips. He turned on the small television and pulled a DVD from the shelf. "This is the training video we show the kids in the junior caddy program. Watch it till I come back to get you. Remember to stick close to your player, but not close enough to distract him. Keep your eye on the ball, his clubs clean. Carry a towel at all times. Fix his divots on the fairway, his ball marks on the green—watch me. And don't talk. Not unless one of the players talks to you."

"I'm not good at not talking."

"You'd better be today, especially when it comes to your opinions about golf courses." He stopped at the door. "And never address a club member as anything other than 'sir' or 'mister.' No first names. Ever."

She slumped onto the sagging couch as he disappeared. The training video came on. No way was she calling Ted Beaudine "sir." Not for all the tip money in the world.

HALF AN HOUR LATER, SHE stood outside the pro shop with a nauseating hip-length green caddy bib tied over her polo shirt, doing her best to make herself invisible by hiding behind Mark. Since she had him by at least two inches, it wasn't going well. Fortunately, the approaching foursome was too engrossed in a conversation about the breakfast they'd just finished and the dinner they planned to consume that night to notice her.

With the exception of a man she assumed to be Spencer Skipjack, she recognized them all: Ted; his father, Dallie; and Kenny Traveler. And with the exception of Spencer Skipjack, she couldn't remember ever seeing so much male perfection grouped together, not even on a red carpet. None of these three gods of golf showed signs of hair transplants, shoe lifts, or subtle dabs of bronzer. These were Texas men—tall, lean, steely-eyed, and rugged—manly men who'd never heard of male mois-turizers, chest waxes, or paying more than twenty dollars for a haircut. They were the genuine article—the archetypal American hero civiliz-ing the West with a set of golf clubs instead of a Winchester.

Other than possessing the same height and build, Ted and his father didn't look much alike. Ted had amber eyes, while Dallie's were a brilliant blue, undimmed by the passing years. Where Ted had angles, Dallie's edges had been smoothed. His mouth was fuller than his son's, almost feminine, and his profile softer, but they were both stunners, and with their easy strides and confident bearing, no one could mistake them for anything other than father and son.

A grizzled man with a graying ponytail, small eyes, and a pressed-over nose came out of what she'd learned was the bag room. This could only be Skeet Cooper, the man Mark had told her was Dallie Beaudine's best friend and lifelong caddy. As Mark strode over to the group, she dipped her head, dropped to one knee, and pretended to tie her shoe. "Good morning, gentlemen," she heard Mark say. "Mr. Skipjack, I'll be caddying for you today, sir. I've heard you have quite a game, and I'm looking forward to watching you play."

Until this precise moment she hadn't thought far enough ahead to ponder exactly which player Mark would assign her to.

Lenny, the coleslaw-hating caddy, wandered out. He was short, weather-beaten, and tooth challenged. He picked up one of the enormous golf bags resting against the bag rack, slung it over his shoulder as if it were a summer jacket, and headed straight for Kenny Traveler.

That left . . . But of course she'd end up caddying for Ted. With her life in free fall, what else could she expect?

He still hadn't spotted her, and she began retying her other sneaker. "Mr. Beaudine," Mark said, "you're breaking in a new caddy today . . ."

She set her jaw, conjured up her father in his most menacing screen role as Bird Dog Caliber, and stood.

"I know Meg will do a good job for you," Mark said.

Ted went absolutely still. Kenny regarded her with interest, Dallie with open hostility. She lifted her chin, squared her shoulders, and made Bird Dog meet the frozen amber eyes of Ted Beaudine.

A muscle ticked in the corner of his jaw. "Meg."

As long as Spencer Skipjack was within earshot, she realized Ted couldn't say what he wanted to. She nodded, smiled, but didn't offer even a simple "hello," nothing that would force her to call him "sir." Instead, she headed for the rack and hoisted the remaining bag.

It was exactly as heavy as it looked, and she staggered ever so slightly. As she heaved the wide strap across her shoulder, she tried to figure out how she was going to lug this thing over five miles of a hilly golf course in the blazing Texas sun. She'd go back to college. Finish her bachelor's and then get a law degree. Or a degree in accounting. But she didn't want to be a lawyer or an accountant. She wanted to be a rich woman with an unlimited checking account that allowed her to travel all over the world, meet interesting people, take in the local crafts, and find a lover who wasn't either crazy or a jerk.

The group began moving toward the practice range to warm up.

Ted tried to lag behind so he could rip her a new one, but he couldn't get away from his honored guest. She trotted after them, already breathing hard from the weight of the bag.

Mark sidled up next to her and spoke softly. "Ted's going to want his sand wedge when he gets to the range. Then his nine-iron, seven-iron, probably his three, and finally his driver. Remember to clean them off when he's done. And don't lose his new head covers."

All these instructions were starting to jumble together. Skeet Cooper, Dallie's caddy, glanced over at her and studied her with his beady eyes. Beneath his ball cap, his grizzled ponytail fell well below his shoulders, and his skin reminded her of sun-dried leather.

As they reached the practice range, she set down Ted's clubs and pulled out an iron marked with an *S*. He nearly tore off her hand wrenching it away from her. The men began to warm up at the practice tees, and she finally had a chance to study Spencer Skipjack, the plumbing giant. In his fifties, he had a rawboned, Johnny Cash sort of face, and a waistline that had begun to thicken but hadn't yet developed a paunch. Although he was clean-shaven, his jaw bore the shadow of a heavy beard. A straw Panama hat decked out with a snakeskin band sat on thick dark hair shot with gray. The black stone in his silver pinky ring glinted on his little finger, and an expensive chronometer encircled a hairy wrist. He had a big, booming voice and a demeanor that reflected both a powerful ego and the expectation of everyone's attention.

"I played Pebble last week with a couple of the boys from the tour," he announced as he pulled on a golf glove. "Picked up all the green fees. Played damn good, too."

"Afraid we can't compete with Pebble," Ted said. "But we'll do our best to keep you entertained."

The men began to hit their practice shots. Skipjack looked like an expert player to her, but she suspected he was out of his league competing against two golf pros and Ted, who'd won the U.S. Amateur, as she'd heard repeatedly. She sat on one of the wooden benches to watch.

"Get up," Mark hissed at her. "Caddies don't ever sit."

Of course not. That would make too much sense.

When they finally left the range, the caddies lagged behind the golfers, who were discussing their upcoming match. She pieced together enough to understand they were playing a team game called "best ball," in which Ted and Dallie would be matched up against Kenny and Spencer Skipjack. At the end of each hole, whichever player had the lowest score for that hole would win a point for his team. The team with the most points at the end won the match.

"How about a twenty-dollar Nassau to keep the game interesting?" Kenny said.

"Shit, boys," Skipjack countered, "me and my buddies play a thousand-dollar Nassau every Saturday."

"Against our religion," Dallie drawled. "We're Baptists."

Doubtful, since Ted's wedding had been at the Presbyterian church and Kenny Traveler was a Catholic.

When they reached the first tee, Ted came toward her, his hand out, his eyes venomous. "Driver."

"Since I was sixteen," she replied. "You?"

He reached past her, snatched off one of the head covers, and pulled out the longest club.

Skipjack teed up first. Mark whispered that the other players would have to give him a total of seven strokes overall to make the game fair. His shot looked impressive, but nobody said anything, so it must not have been. Kenny went next, then Ted. Even she could see the power and grace in his practice swing, but when it came time for the real thing, something went wrong. Just as he neared the point of impact, he lost his balance and sent the ball careening off to the left.

They all turned to look at her. Ted offered up his public Jesus smile, but the fires of hell burned in his eyes. "Meg, if you wouldn't mind . . ."

"What did I do?"

Mark quickly pulled her aside and explained that letting a couple of golf clubs rattle together during a player's swing was this big, whoppin' crime against humanity. Like polluting streambeds and screwing up wetlands didn't count.

After that Ted did his best to get her alone, but she managed to avoid him until the third hole when a crappy drive put him in a fairway sand trap—a bunker, they called it. The whole subservient routine of lugging his bag and being instructed to call him "sir"—which she'd so far managed to avoid—made it imperative that she strike first.

"None of this would have happened if you hadn't gotten me fired from the inn."

He had the audacity to look outraged. "I didn't get you fired. It was Larry Stellman. You woke him up from his nap two days in a row."

"That five hundred dollars you offered me is in the top pocket of your bag. I'll expect some of it back as a very generous tip."

He clenched his jaw. "Do you have any idea how important today is?"

"I was eavesdropping on your conversation last night, remember? So I know exactly what's at stake and how much you want to impress your hotshot guest today."

"And yet here you are."

"Yes, well, this is one disaster you can't blame on me. Although I can see you're going to."

"I don't know how you managed to talk your way into caddying, but if you think for one minute—"

"Listen up, Theodore." She slapped one hand on the edge of his bag. "I was coerced into this. I hate golf, and I don't have a clue what I'm doing. None whatsoever, got it? So I suggest you try really hard not to make me any more nervous than I already am." She stepped back. "Now stop talking and hit the damned ball. And this time I'd appreciate it if you hit it straight so I don't have to keep walking all over the place after you."

He gave her a murderous look totally out of place with his saintly reputation and yanked a club from his bag, proving he was perfectly capable of dealing with his own equipment. "As soon as this is over, you and I are going to have our final reckoning." He struck the ball with a massive, rage-fueled swing that sent sand flying. The shot bounced ten yards in front of the green, rolled up the slope to the pin, hung on the lip of the cup, and dropped in.

"Impressive," she said. "I didn't know I was such a good golf coach."

He threw the club at her feet and stalked away as the other players called out their congratulations from across the fairway.

"How 'bout you toss some of that luck my way?" Skipjack's Texas drawl couldn't be genuine, since he was from Indiana, but he was clearly a man who liked to be one of the boys.

On the next green, she was the caddy closest to the flag. As Ted lined up his putt, Mark sent her a subtle nod. She'd already learned her lesson about not making sudden moves, so even though everybody started to yell, she waited until Ted's ball hit the flag and dropped in before she pulled the pin from the cup.

Dallie groaned. Kenny grinned. Ted lowered his head, and Spencer Skipjack crowed. "Looks like your caddy just took you out of this hole, Ted."

Meg forgot she was supposed to be mute—along with efficient, cheerful, and subservient. "What did I do?"

Mark had gone pale from his forehead to his polo shirt logo. "I'm really sorry about that, Mr. Beaudine." He addressed her with grim patience. "Meg, you can't let the ball hit the pin. It's a penalty."

"The player gets penalized for a caddy's mistake?" she said. "That's stupid. The ball would have gone in anyway."

"Don't feel bad, honey," Skipjack said cheerfully. "It could have happened to anybody."

Because of his handicap, Skipjack got an extra stroke, and he didn't try to hold back his glee after they'd all putted out. "Looks like my net birdie just won us the hole, partner." He slapped Kenny on the back. "Reminds me of the time I played with Bill Murray and Ray Romano at Cypress Point. Talk about characters . . ."

Ted and Dallie were now one hole down, but Ted put a good public face on it—no surprise. "We'll make it up on the next hole." The private glare he shot her sent a message she had no trouble interpreting.

"This is a ridiculous game," she muttered a little over twenty minutes later after she once again took Ted out of competition by violating another ridiculous rule. Trying to be a good caddy, she'd picked up Ted's ball to clean off some muck only to discover she wasn't allowed to do that until it was on the green and marked. Like that made any sense.

"Good thing you birdied one and two, son," Dallie said. "You sure do have some bad luck going for us."

She saw no sense in ignoring the obvious. "I'm the bad luck."

Mark shot her a warning glare for violating the no-talking rule and not calling Dallie "sir," but Spencer Skipjack chuckled. "At least she's honest. More than I can say for most women."

It was Ted's turn to send her a warning glare, this one forbidding her to comment on the idiocy of a man stereotyping an entire gender. She didn't like the way Ted was reading her mind. And she really didn't like Spencer Skipjack, who was a blowhard and a name-dropper.

"Last time I was in Vegas, I ran into Michael Jordan in one of the private rooms . . ."

She managed to survive the seventh hole without breaking any more rules, but her shoulders ached, her new sneakers were rubbing a blister on her little toe, the heat was getting to her, and she had eleven miserable holes to go. Being forced to lug around a thirty-five-pound bag of golf clubs for a six-foot-two athletic champion, who was perfectly capable of doing the job himself, seemed increasingly ludicrous. If these healthy, strong-bodied men were too lazy to carry their own clubs, why didn't they take golf carts? The whole caddying thing made no sense. Except . . .

"Fine shot, Mr. Skipjack. You really nailed that one," Mark said with an admiring nod.

"Way to play the wind, Mr. Traveler," Lenny said.

"You spun that like a top," Skeet Cooper offered up to Ted's father.

As she listened to the caddies praise the players, she concluded this was all about ego. About having your personal cheering squad. She decided to test her theory. "Wow!" she exclaimed on the next tee after Ted hit. "Cool drive. You really hit that far. Very far. All the way . . . down there."

The men turned to stare at her. There was a long pause. Finally, Kenny spoke. "I sure wish I could hit a ball like that." Another long pause. "Far."

She vowed not to say another word, and she might have been able to stick to that vow if Spencer Skipjack hadn't liked to talk so much. "Pay attention, Miz Meg. I'm gonna use a little tip I picked up from Phil Mickelson to set this one right next to the pin."

Ted tensed up just as he'd been doing whenever Skipjack addressed her. He expected her to sabotage him, and she definitely would have if only his happiness and well-being were at stake. But something else hung in the balance.

She was facing an impossible dilemma. The last thing the planet needed was another golf course sucking up its natural resources, but it was obvious even to her how much the town was suffering. Each issue of the local paper reported another small business closing or one more hard-pressed charity unable to keep up with an increased demand for its services. And how could she be judgmental of others when she was living a life that was anything but green, starting with her gas-guzzling car? No matter what she did now, she'd be a hypocrite, so she followed her instincts, abandoned a few more of her principles, and played the good soldier for the town that hated her. "Watching you hit a golf ball is pure pleasure, Mr. Skipjack."

"Naw. I'm only a hacker compared to these boys."

"But they get to play golf full-time," she said. "You have a *real* job."

She thought she heard Kenny Traveler snort.

Skipjack laughed and told her he wished she was his caddy, even though she didn't know a damn thing about golf and he'd need more than seven strokes to make up for her mistakes.

When they stopped at the clubhouse between the ninth and tenth holes, the match was even—four holes for Ted and Dallie, four for Kenny and Spencer, one hole tied. She got a short break—not the nap she dreamed of, but enough time to splash cold water on her face and tape up her blisters. Mark pulled her aside and dressed her down for getting too familiar with the members, making too much noise on the course, not sticking close enough to her player, and shooting Ted dirty looks. "Ted Beaudine is the nicest guy in the club. I don't know what's wrong with you. He treats everybody on the staff with respect, and he gives big tips."

Somehow she suspected that might not apply to her.

As Mark walked off to suck up to Kenny, she approached Ted's big navy bag with loathing. The gold head covers matched the bag's stitching. Only two head covers. Apparently she'd already lost one. Ted came up behind her, frowned at the missing head cover, then at her. "You're getting way too cozy with Skipjack. Back off."

So much for playing the good soldier. She kept her voice low. "I grew up in Hollywood, so I understand ego-driven men like him better than you ever will."

"That's what you think." He jammed the ball cap he was carrying on her head. "Wear a damn cap. We've got real sun here, not that watered-down California crap you're used to."

On the back nine, she knocked Ted and his father out of another hole because she yanked up a couple of weeds to give Ted a better shot. Yet even with the three holes she'd cost them—and Ted's occasional errant shot when he tried too hard to conceal how pissed off he was at her—he was still highly competitive. "You're playin' a strange game today, son," Dallie said. "Glimpses of brilliance paired with some mind-bogglin' lunacy. I haven't seen you play this good—or this bad—in years."

"Heartbreak'll do that to a man." Kenny putted from the edge of the green. "Makes 'em go a little crazy." His ball stopped a few inches short of the cup.

"Plus the humiliation of everybody in town still feeling sorry for him behind his back." Skeet, the only caddy allowed to be on familiar terms with the players, brushed away some debris that had fallen on the green.

Dallie stepped up to his putt. "I tried to show him by example how to hold on to a woman. Kid didn't pay attention."

The men seemed to delight in poking fun at one another's vulnerabilities. Even Ted's own father. A test of manhood or something. If her girlfriends had gone after one another the way these guys did, somebody would have ended up in tears. But Ted merely delivered his leisurely smile, waited his turn, and sank his putt from ten feet away.

As the men walked off the green, Kenny Traveler, for a reason she couldn't fathom, decided to tell Spencer Skipjack who her parents were. Skipjack's eyes lit up. "Jake Koranda's your father? Now that is really something. Here I thought you were caddying for money." He shot a look between her and Ted. "You two a couple now?"

"No!" she said.

"Afraid not," Ted said easily. "As you might guess, I'm still trying to recover from my broken engagement."

"I don't think they call it a broken engagement when you get dumped at the altar," Kenny pointed out. "That's more commonly known as a catastrophe."

How could Ted be so worried about her embarrassing him today when his own friends were doing the job so well? But Skipjack seemed to be having the time of his life, and she realized their insider chatter made him feel as if he were one of them. Kenny and Dallie, for all their dumb-ass, good ol' boy ways, had his number.

After the revelation of her famous parents, Skipjack wouldn't leave her alone. "So what was it like growing up with Jake Koranda as a father?"

She'd heard that question a thousand times and still found it offensive that people didn't also acknowledge her mother, who was just as accomplished as her father. She delivered her pat answer. "Both of my parents are just Mom and Dad to me."

Ted finally realized she might have some value to him. "Meg's mother is famous, too. She runs a big talent agency, but before that she was a famous model and actress."

Her mother had appeared in exactly one film, *Sunday Morning Eclipse,* where she'd met Meg's father.

"Wait a minute!" Spencer exclaimed. "Son of a— I had this poster of your mother on the back of my bedroom door when I was a kid."

Another statement she'd heard a few zillion times too many. "Imagine that." Ted slanted her another of his looks.

Skipjack didn't stop talking about her famous parents until they approached the seventeenth hole. Thanks to some bad putting, Kenny and Skipjack were down one hole, and Skipjack wasn't happy. He grew even unhappier when Kenny took a phone call from his wife before he teed off and learned that she'd cut her hand while she was gardening and had driven herself to the doctor to get a couple of stitches. It was apparent from Kenny's end of the conversation that the injury was minor and his wife wouldn't hear of him dropping out of the match, but from then on he was distracted.

Meg could see how much Skipjack wanted to win, just as she could see that it didn't occur to either Ted or Dallie to back off, not even for the future of the town. Dallie had played consistently well, and Ted's erratic play was now a thing of the past. She was getting the weird feeling that he might even be enjoying the challenge of making up the three holes she'd cost them.

Skipjack snapped at Mark for taking too long to hand over a club. He could feel his win slipping away and, along with it, the chance to brag that he and Kenny Traveler had beaten Dallie and Ted Beaudine on their home course. He even stopped pestering Meg.

All Team Beaudine had to do was miss a few putts, and they'd put

Spencer Skipjack in a magnanimous mood for future negotiations, but they didn't seem to get that. She couldn't understand it. They should be catering to their guest's enormous ego instead of playing as though only the outcome of the match mattered. Apparently they thought tossing jokes at one another and letting Skipjack feel like an insider was enough. But Skipjack was a sulker. If Ted wanted him to be receptive, he and his father needed to lose this match. Instead, they were pressing even harder to maintain their one-hole advantage.

Fortunately, Kenny came to life on the seventeenth green and sank a twenty-five-foot putt that tied up the teams.

Meg didn't like the determined glint in Ted's eye as he teed off on the final hole. He lined up his drive, adjusted his stance, and launched his swing . . . at the exact moment she accidentally on purpose dropped his bag of golf clubs . . .

chapter eight

THE CLUBS LANDED WITH A CRASH. All seven men standing on the tee spun around to stare at her. She tried to look abashed. "Oops. Dang. Big mistake."

Ted had pulled his drive into the far left rough, and Skipjack grinned. "Miz Meg, I sure am glad you're not caddying for me."

She stubbed her sneaker into the ground. "I'm really sorry." *Not.*

And what did Ted do in response to her blunder? Did he thank her for reminding him of what was most important today? Conversely, did he stalk over and wrap one of his clubs around her neck as she knew he wanted to? Oh, no. Mr. Perfect was way too cool for any of that. Instead, he gave them his choirboy smile, wandered back to her with his easy lope, and righted the bag himself. "Now don't you stress, Meg. You've just made the match more interesting."

He was the best bullshit artist she'd ever known, but even if the others couldn't see it, she knew he was furious.

They all set off down the fairway. Skipjack's face was flushed, his golf shirt sticking to his barrel chest. She understood the game well enough by now to know what needed to happen. Because of his handicap, Skipjack got an extra stroke on this hole, so if everybody parred it, Skipjack would win the hole for his team. But if either Dallie or Ted birdied the hole, Skipjack would need a birdie himself to win the hole, something that seemed highly unlikely. Otherwise, the match would end in an unsatisfying tie.

Thanks to her interference, Ted was farthest from the pin, so he was up first for his second shot. Since no one was close enough to overhear, she could tell him exactly what she thought. "Let him win, you idiot! Can't you see how much this means to him?"

Instead of listening to her, he drilled a four-iron down the fairway, putting him in what even she could see was perfect position. "Butthead," she muttered. "If you birdie, you've just about guaranteed your guest can't win. Do you really think that's the best way to put him in a good mood for your odious negotiations?"

He tossed his club at her. "I know how the game is played, Meg, and so does Skipjack. He's not a kid." He stalked away.

Dallie, Kenny, and a glowering Skipjack put their third shots on the green, but Ted was only lying two. He'd abandoned common sense. Apparently losing a game was a mortal sin for those who worshipped in the holy cathedral of golf.

Meg reached Ted's ball first. It perched on top of a big tuft of chemically nurtured grass in perfect position to set up an easy birdie shot. She lowered his bag, contemplated her principles once again, then brought her sneaker down as hard as she could on the ball.

As she heard Ted come up behind her, she shook her head sadly. "Too bad. It looks like you landed in a hole."

"A hole?" He pushed her aside to see his ball mashed deeply into the grass.

As she stepped back, she spotted Skeet Cooper standing on the fringe of the green watching her with his small, sun-wrinkled eyes. Ted gazed down at the ball. "What in the—?"

"Some kind of rodent." Skeet said it in a way that let her know he'd witnessed exactly what she'd done.

"Rodent? There aren't any—" Ted spun on her. "Don't tell me . . ."

"You can thank me later," she said.

"Problem over there?" Skipjack called from the opposite fringe.

"Ted's in trouble," Skeet called back.

Ted used up two strokes getting out of the hole she'd dug him into. He still made par, but par wasn't good enough. Kenny and Skipjack won the match.

Kenny seemed more concerned about getting home to his wife than relishing the victory, but Spencer chortled all the way into the clubhouse. "Now that was a golf game. Too bad you lost it there at the end, Ted. Bad luck." As he spoke, he was peeling away at a wad of bills to tip Mark. "Good job today. You can caddy for me anytime."

"Thank you, sir. It was my pleasure."

Kenny passed some twenties over to Lenny, shook hands with his partner, and took off for home. Ted dug into his own pocket, pressed a tip into her palm, then closed her fingers around it. "No hard feelings, Meg. You did your best."

"Thanks." She'd forgotten she was dealing with a saint.

Spencer Skipjack came up behind her, settled his hand into the small of her back, and rubbed. Way too creepy. "Miz Meg, Ted and his friends are taking me to dinner tonight. I'd be honored if you'd be my date."

"Gosh, I'd like to, but—"

"She'd love to," Ted said. "Wouldn't you, Meg?"

"Ordinarily yes, but—"

"Don't be shy. We'll pick you up at seven. Meg's current home is hard to find, so I'll drive." He gazed at her, and the flint in his eyes sent a clear message that told her she'd be looking for a new home if she didn't cooperate. She swallowed. "Casual dress?"

"Real casual," he said.

As the men walked away, she contemplated the evils of being forced on a date with an egotistic blowhard who was practically as old as her father. Bad enough by itself, but even more depressing with Ted watching her every move.

She rubbed her aching shoulder, then uncurled her fingers to check out the tip she'd received for spending four and a half hours hauling thirty-five pounds of golf clubs uphill and down in the hot Texas sun.

A one-dollar bill looked back at her.

NEON BEER SIGNS, ANTLERS, and sports memorabilia decked out the square wooden bar that sat in the center of the Roustabout. Booths lined two of the honky-tonk's walls, pool tables and video games another. On weekends, a country band played, but for now, Toby Keith blasted from the jukebox near a small, scarred dance floor.

Meg was the only woman at the table, which left her feeling a little like a working girl at a gentleman's club, although she was glad neither Dallie's nor Kenny's wife was present, since both women hated her. She sat between Spencer and Kenny, with Ted directly across the table along with his father and Dallie's faithful caddy, Skeet Cooper.

"The Roustabout's an institution around here," Ted said as Skipjack finished polishing off a platter of ribs. "It's seen a lot of history. Good, bad, and ugly."

"I sure do remember the ugly," Skeet said. "Like the time Dallie and Francie had an altercation in the parking lot. Happened more'n thirty years ago, long before they were married, but people still talk about it today."

"That's true," Ted said. "I can't tell you how often I've heard that story. My mother forgot she's half my father's size and tried to take him down."

"Damn near succeeded. She was a wildcat that night, I can tell you," Skeet said. "Me and Dallie's ex-wife couldn't hardly break up that fight."

"It's not exactly the way they're making it sound," Dallie said.

"It's exactly the way it sounded." Kenny pocketed his cell after checking on his wife.

"How would you know?" Dallie grumbled. "You were a kid then, and you weren't even there. Besides, you've got your own history with the Roustabout parking lot. Like the night Lady Emma got upset with you and stole your car. You had to run down the highway after her."

"It didn't take too long to catch up," Kenny said. "My wife wasn't much of a driver."

"Still isn't," Ted said. "Slowest driver in the county. Just last week she caused a big backup out on Stone Quarry Road. Three people called me to complain."

Kenny shrugged. "No matter how hard we all try, we can't convince her that our posted speed limits are only polite recommendations."

It had been going on like that all evening, the five of them entertaining Skipjack with their good ol' boy patter, while Spence, as she'd been instructed to call him, soaked it in with a combination of amusement and the faintest hint of arrogance. He loved being courted by these famous men—loved knowing he had something they wanted, something he had it within his power to withhold. He dragged his napkin over his mouth to wipe off some barbecue sauce. "You've got strange ways in this town."

Ted leaned back in his chair, as relaxed as ever. "We're not hampered by a lot of bureaucracy, that's for sure. People around here don't see the sense in all kinds of red tape. If we want to make something happen, we go ahead and do it."

Spence smiled at Meg. "I think I'm about to hear a paid political announcement."

It was long past time. She was bone tired and wanted nothing more than to curl up in her choir loft and go to sleep. After her disastrous caddying round, she'd spent the rest of the day on the drink cart. Unfortunately, her immediate boss was a stoner kid with minimal communication skills and no idea how her predecessor had set up the beverages. How was she to know that the club's female golfers were addicted to diet Arizona iced tea and got huffy if it wasn't waiting for them by the fourteenth tee? Still, that hadn't been as bad as running out of Bud Light. In a curious case of mass self-delusion, the club's overweight male golfers seemed to have concluded the word *light* meant they could drink twice as much. Their bellies should have pointed out their faulty reasoning, but apparently not.

The most surprising part of today, however, was how much she hadn't hated it. She should have detested working at a country club, but she loved being outside, even if she wasn't allowed to drive all over the course the way she wanted and had to stay parked at either the fifth or fourteenth tee. Not getting fired was a bonus.

Spence tried to sneak a surreptitious look down the top she'd fashioned from one length of the rehearsal-dinner silk wrap she now wore with jeans. All evening, he'd been touching her, tracing a bone on her wrist, caressing her shoulder, the small of her back, feigning curiosity over her earrings as an excuse to rub her lobe. Ted had taken in every touch and, for the first time since they'd met, seemed happy she was around. Spence leaned in too close. "Here's my dilemma, Miz Meg."

She edged nearer Kenny, something she'd been doing all evening until she was practically in his lap. He seemed oblivious, apparently so used to women hitting on him that it no longer registered. But Ted was registering, and he wanted her to stay put, right where Skipjack could paw her. Since his easy smile never changed, she didn't know how she knew this, but she did, and the next time she got him alone, she intended to tell him to add "pimp" to his big, impressive résumé.

Spence toyed with her fingers. "I'm looking at two sweet pieces of property—one on the outskirts of San Antone, a city that's a hotbed of commercial activity. The other in the middle of nowhere."

Ted hated cat-and-mouse games. She knew because he leaned farther back in his chair, as unruffled as a man could be. "The most beautiful part of nowhere anybody's ever seen," he said.

And one they wanted to destroy with a hotel, condos, manicured fairways, and pristine greens.

"Don't forget there's a landing strip not twenty miles out of town." Kenny fingered his cell.

"But not much else to speak of," Spence said. "No upscale boutiques for the ladies. No nightclubs or fine dining."

Skeet scratched his jaw, his nails rasping over the graying stubble. "I don't see that's much of a disadvantage. All it means is people'll spend more money at your resort."

"When they're not coming into Wynette to get their fix of small-town Americana," Ted said. "The Roustabout, for example. This is the real thing—no phonied-up national franchise with mass-produced steer horns hanging on the wall. We all know how much rich people appreciate authenticity."

An interesting observation coming from a multimillionaire. It occurred to her that everybody at this table was filthy rich except her. Even Skeet Cooper must have a couple of million tucked away from all the prize money he'd earned caddying for Dallie.

Spence curled his hand over Meg's wrist. "Let's dance, Miz Meg. I need to work off my dinner."

She didn't want to dance with him, and she extracted her hand with the excuse of reaching for her napkin. "I don't understand exactly why you're so eager to build a resort. You're already the head of a big company. Why make your life more complicated?"

"Some things a man's destined to do." It sounded like a line from one of her father's worst movies. "You ever heard of a guy named Herb Kohler?"

"I don't think so."

"Kohler Company. Plumbing. My biggest rival."

She didn't pay much attention to bathroom fixtures, but even she'd heard of Kohler, and she nodded.

"Herb owns the American Club in Kohler, Wisconsin, along with four of the Midwest's best golf courses. Each room at the American Club is outfitted with the latest plumbing fixtures. There's even a plumbing museum. Every year the place is top ranked."

"Herb Kohler's an important man," Ted said with such a lack of guile that she nearly rolled her eyes. Was she the only person who saw through him? "He sure has made himself a legend in the golfing world."

And Spencer Skipjack wanted to outdo his rival. That's why building this resort was so important to him.

"It's too bad Herb didn't build his place somewhere people could play year-round," Dallie said. "Wisconsin's a damn cold state."

"The reason I was smart enough to choose Texas," Skipjack said. "I came down here a lot from Indiana when I was a kid to visit my mother's family. I've always felt at home in the Lone Star State. More Texan than Hoosier." He turned his attention back to Meg. "Wherever I build, you be sure and tell your father he's invited to play anytime as my guest."

"I'll do that." Her athletic father still loved basketball, and thanks to her mother, now rode horseback for pleasure, but she couldn't imagine him swinging a golf club.

She'd had separate phone conversations with both of her parents today, but instead of begging them to send money, she'd told them that she'd gotten a great job in hospitality at an important Texas country club. Although she didn't say she was the activities coordinator, neither did she correct her mother when she came to that conclusion and said how wonderful it was Meg had finally found a useful outlet for her natural creativity. Her dad was just happy she had a job.

She couldn't keep quiet about this any longer. "Have any of you thought about leaving that land alone? I mean, does the world really need another golf course eating up more of our natural resources?"

Ted's frown was almost imperceptible. "Recreational green spaces keep people healthy."

"Damn right they do," Spence said before Meg could bring up the golfers and their Bud Light. "Ted and I have talked a lot about that." He pushed back his chair. "Come on, Miz Meg. I like this song."

Spence might have her arm, but Meg could have sworn she felt Ted's invisible hand shoving her to the dance floor.

Spence was a decent dancer, and the song was up tempo, so things started out all right. But when a ballad came on, he pulled her so close his belt buckle pressed against her, not to mention something more objectionable. "I don't know what happened to make you fall on hard times." Spence nuzzled her ear. "But it looks like you could use somebody to watch out for you until you're back on your feet."

She hoped he didn't mean what she thought he meant, but the evidence below his belt buckle seemed to indicate he did.

"Now I'm not talking about anything that would make you uncomfortable," he said. "Just the two of us spending some time together."

She deliberately tripped over his foot. "Oops. I need to sit down. I picked up a couple of blisters today."

Spence didn't have any choice but to follow her back to the table. "She can't keep up with me," he grumbled.

"Not many people can, I'll bet," Mayor Suck-up said.

Spence pulled his chair closer and draped his arm around her shoulders. "I got a great idea, Miss Meg. Let's fly to Vegas tonight. You, too, Ted. Ring up a girlfriend and come with us. I'll call my pilot."

He was so certain of their compliance that he reached for his cell, and since not one of the men at the table did anything to dissuade him, she realized she was on her own. "Sorry, Spence. I have to work tomorrow."

He winked at Ted. "That's not much of a country club you work for, and I'll bet Ted could talk your boss into giving you a couple of days off. What do you think, Ted?"

"If he can't, I can," Dallie said, tossing her to the wolves.

Kenny piled on. "Let me do it. I'll be happy to make a call."

Ted gazed at her over the top of his longneck, saying nothing. She stared right back, so angry her skin burned. She'd put up with a lot lately, but she wouldn't put up with this. "The thing is . . ." She bit off the syllables. "I'm not exactly free. Emotionally."

"How's that?" Spence asked.

"It's . . . complicated." She was starting to feel nauseated. Why couldn't life come with a pause button? More than anything, that's what she needed right now, because without a chance to think this through, she was going to say the first thing that sprang into her mind, the stupidest thing, but again, no pause button. "Ted and me."

Ted's beer bottle clinked against his teeth. Kenny perked up. Spence looked confused. "This morning you said the two of you weren't a couple."

She pinched her mouth into a smile. "We're not," she said. "Yet.

But I have hopes." The word caught in her throat like a bone. She had just validated everything people believed about her motivation for stopping the wedding.

But Kenny kicked back in his chair, more amused than accusatory. "Ted does this to women all the time. None of us can figure out how."

"I sure can't." Ted's father slanted her a peculiar look. "Homeliest kid you ever saw."

Ted ground his words around the edges of a lazy smile. "It's not going to happen, Meg."

"Time will tell." Now that she saw how much she'd aggravated him, she warmed to the topic, despite its larger implications. "I have a bad history of falling for the *worst* men." She let that settle in for a moment. "Not that Ted isn't perfect. A little too perfect, obviously, but . . . attraction isn't always logical."

Spence's heavy dark brows met in the middle. "Wasn't it last month he was all ready to marry the president's daughter?"

"The end of May," she said. "And Lucy is my best friend. It was a total debacle, as I'm sure you know from all the press." Ted watched her, his easy smile fixed in place, a microscopic nerve jumping at the corner of his eye. She began to enjoy herself. "But Lucy was never the right woman for him. Thanks to me, he knows that now, and frankly, his gratitude would be embarrassing if I weren't so head over heels."

"Gratitude?" Ted's voice was tempered steel.

To hell with it. She waved an airy hand and began to embellish with all the skill of her actor-playwright father. "I could play coy and pretend I haven't fallen totally—and I mean *totally*—in love with him, but I've never been the kind of woman to play games. I throw my cards right on the table. It's better in the long run."

"Honesty's an admirable quality," Kenny said, openly enjoying himself.

"I know what you're all thinking. That I couldn't possibly have fallen for him so quickly because, no matter what anybody says, I did *not* break up that wedding. But . . ." She shot Ted an adoring look. "This time it's different for me. So different." She couldn't resist fanning the flames. "And . . . Judging from Ted's late-night visit yesterday . . ."

"You two had a late-night visit?" his father said.

"Pretty romantic, right?" She manufactured a dreamy smile. "At midnight. In the choir—"

Ted shot to his feet. "Let's dance."

With a tilt of her head, she transformed herself into the mother of all sorrows. "Blister."

"Slow dance," he said silkily. "You can stand on my feet."

Before she could come up with a way out, Ted had her arm and was dragging her toward the crowded dance floor. He tucked her against him—one step from a chokehold. At least he wasn't wearing a belt, so she didn't have to put up with a buckle . . . or any other object pressing into her flesh. The only thing hard about Ted Beaudine was the expression in his eyes. "Every time I think you can't cause more trouble, you manage to surprise me."

"What was I supposed to do?" she retorted. "Fly off to Vegas with him? And when did 'pimp' become part of your job description?"

"It wouldn't have gone that far. All you had to do was be nice."

"Why should I? I hate this town, remember? And I don't care if your stupid golf resort gets built. I don't *want* it to get built."

"Then why have you gone along with this so far?"

"Because I've sold out. To put food in my stomach."

"Is that the only reason?"

"I don't know . . . It seemed like the right thing to do. God knows why. Contrary to popular opinion, I'm not the evil bitch everybody's made me out to be. But that doesn't mean that I'm willing to turn hooker for the good of *y'all*."

"I never said you were evil." He actually had the nerve to look wounded.

"You know he's only interested in me because of my father," she hissed. "He's a little man with a big ego. Being around famous people, even an auxiliary person like me, makes him feel important. If it weren't for my parents, he wouldn't look at me twice."

"I wouldn't be so sure about that."

"Come on, Ted. I'm not exactly the type to be a rich man's bimbo."

"That's true." A world of compassion softened his voice. "Bimbos are generally good-hearted women who are pleasant to be around."

"Spoken from experience, I'm sure. By the way, you may be God Almighty on the golf course, but you're a lousy dancer. Let me lead."

He lost a step, then looked at her oddly, as if she'd finally taken him by surprise, although she couldn't imagine why, and she relaunched her attack. "Here's an idea. Why don't you and your lover fly to Vegas with Spence? I'm sure the two of you could show him a great time."

"That really galls you, doesn't it?"

"The fact that you screwed around on Lucy? Oh, yes. Right now she's eaten up with guilt. And don't think for a second that I won't fill her in on all the sordid details of your extracurricular activities as soon as we get the chance for a long chat."

"Doubt she'll believe you."

"I don't get why you proposed to her in the first place."

"Not being married was starting to hold me back," he said. "I was ready to move on to the next stage of my life, and I needed a wife for that. Someone spectacular. The daughter of the president fit the bill perfectly."

"Did you ever love her? Even a little?"

"Are you crazy? It was a sham right from the beginning."

Something told her he was throwing up a smoke screen, but the mind-reading thing she'd been doing all evening failed her. "It must be hard being you," she said. "Mr. Perfect on the outside. Dr. Evil on the inside."

"It's not that hard. The rest of the world isn't as insightful as you."

His easy smile slid over her, and a tiny zap—almost imperceptible—so small it was hardly worth noting—but still *there*— hit her nerve endings. Not all of them. Just a couple. The ones located somewhere south of her belly button.

"Crap!" he exclaimed, voicing her feelings perfectly.

She turned her head and saw what had caught his attention. His beautiful brunette lover making a beeline for Spence.

Ted abandoned Meg and ambled back to the table, his amble so full of purpose Meg was surprised he didn't leave tread marks on the floor. He hit the brakes just as his lover held out her hand to their visitor.

"Hi, there. Torie Traveler O'Connor."

chapter nine

TORIE TRAVELER O'CONNOR? MEG REMEMBERED the conversation she'd overheard the night before between Ted and Kenny. Ted's married lover was Kenny's sister?

Torie's Texas drawl was liquid decadence. "I heard you tore up the back nine today, Spence. You don't mind if I call you Spence, do you? I had to meet the man who took these ol' boys to the cleaners."

Spence looked temporarily awestruck. It was easy to see how Torie could do that with her flawless features, swirl of inky hair, and long legs hugged by ultraexpensive jeans. A trio of small silver charms dangled at the open neck of her scooped top, an enormous diamond winked on her left hand, and two others, nearly as large, played at her earlobes.

Kenny frowned at her. Seen together, their over-the-top good looks made it obvious they were siblings. "Why aren't you home minding my nieces?"

"Because they're finally asleep. It took a couple of Xanax cleverly concealed inside some Twinkies, but oh well . . . Monsters."

"They miss their father," Kenny said. "The only stabilizing influence in their lives."

Torie grinned. "He'll be back tomorrow." She poked her brother. "I just talked to Lady Emma. She told me her hand is fine, and if you call her one more time, she won't put out tonight." She kissed Ted's cheek. "Hey, there, Mr. Mayor. Word is you played real ugly today."

"Except for a hole-out eagle and a few birdies," her brother said. "Damnedest game I ever saw."

She looked around for a place to sit, and not spotting an open chair, perched on Ted's right thigh. "Weird. You're usually so consistent."

"Spence intimidated me," Ted said with all kinds of sincerity. "He's as good a seven handicap as I've ever played with."

Kenny tilted back in his chair. "Lots of interesting events happening around here today, Torie. Meg was just filling Spence in on her unrequited love for Ted. Who knew, right?"

Torie's eyes widened with surprise, followed almost immediately by anticipation. Right then Meg understood. Even with Torie balanced like a sleek, man-eating panther on Ted's thigh and one arm draped over his shoulders, Meg knew they weren't lovers. She didn't understand exactly what their relationship was, or why they'd been together in the suite at the inn with Torie wrapped only in a towel, or why Torie had kissed him that night in his car. Despite all the evidence to the contrary—and despite Ted's own words—she knew with absolute certainty these two were not intimate.

Torie took a sip from Ted's beer and turned her attention to Meg. "I never get tired of hearing women's stories, especially ones involving men. I swear, I'd read a romance novel every day if I didn't have to chase after my kids. Did you just blurt it right out—tell Ted how you feel?"

Meg tried to look sincere. "I believe in honesty."

"She's pretty sure he'll come around," Kenny said.

Torie handed Ted's beer back without taking her eyes off Meg. "I admire your self-confidence."

Meg extended her hands, palms out. "Why wouldn't he come around? Look at me."

She expected snickers, but it didn't happen. "Interesting," Torie said.

"Not interesting." Ted slid his beer out of Torie's reach.

Torie took in Meg's Sung dynasty earrings. "Probably best you haven't heard about my stepmother's new plan to raise money for the library repairs."

"Shelby hasn't talked to me about any plan," Ted said.

Torie waved him off. "I'm sure someone will mention it to you sooner or later. The committee hasn't finished ironing out the details."

Ted eyed Kenny. "Lady Emma say anything about this to you?"

"Not a word."

Torie was a woman on a mission, and she wouldn't let herself be distracted for long. "Your honesty is refreshing, Meg. Exactly when did you realize you were in love with Ted? Before or after Lucy ditched him?"

"Lay off," Ted said pleasantly.

Torie stuck her perfectly shaped nose in the air. "I wasn't talking to you. When it comes to women, you always leave out the interesting parts."

"*After* she left," Meg said, and then, more carefully, "there's really nothing more to tell at this point. I'm still hoping to . . . work through Ted's issues."

"Remind me what those issues are," Torie said. "Ted being so perfect." A tiny gasp slipped through her glossy lips. "Oh, God, Teddy . . . Not *that* issue! You told us the Viagra helped." She leaned toward Spence, and in a fake whisper said, "Ted's been fighting a courageous battle against erectile dysfunction."

Skeet choked on his beer. Kenny laughed. Dallie winced, and Spence frowned. He wasn't exactly certain whether or not Torie was joking, and he didn't like feeling excluded. Meg experienced her first flash of sympathy, not for Spence, but for Ted, who looked as serene as ever, even though he definitely wasn't. "Torie's kidding, Spence." Meg gave a superexaggerated eye roll. "She's really, *really* kidding." And then, with fake guilt, "At least from what I've heard."

"Okay, that's enough." Ted nearly dumped Torie as he came up out of his chair and caught her wrist. "Let's dance."

"If I wanted to dance, I'd ask my brother," Torie retorted. "Somebody who doesn't have two left feet."

"I'm not that bad," Ted said.

"Bad enough."

Kenny addressed Spence. "My sister is the only woman in Wynette—probably the entire universe—who's ever told Ted the truth about his lack of ballroom skills. The rest of them bat their eyes and pretend he's Justin Timberlake. Funnier'n hell."

Ted's eyes grazed Meg's, just for an instant, before he turned away and pulled Torie toward the jukebox.

Spence watched them. "Your sister's an unusual woman."

"Tell me about it."

"Her and Ted seem real close."

"Torie's been Ted's best female friend since he was a kid," Kenny said. "I swear, she's the only woman under sixty who's never been in love with him."

"Her husband doesn't mind their friendship?"

"Dex?" Kenny smiled. "No. Dex is pretty self-confident."

Ted seemed to be doing more lecturing than dancing, and when he and Torie returned to the table, he made a point of grabbing an empty chair and seating her as far away from Spence as he could manage. That didn't stop Torie from touting the advantages of Wynette as the perfect location for a golf resort, trying to figure out how much Spence was worth, inviting him to her stepmother's Fourth of July party on Monday, and coercing him into a Saturday afternoon golf match.

Ted looked pained and quickly announced that he and Kenny would join them. Torie glanced at Meg, and the mischievous glimmer in her eyes explained why Ted wanted to keep her far away from Skipjack. "Meg's going to caddy for Ted again, right?"

Ted and Meg both spoke up. "No!"

But Kenny, for some unfathomable reason, decided that was a great idea, and with Spence saying the match wouldn't be half as much fun without Meg, the handwriting was blood-spattered all over the wall.

When Spence disappeared to the men's room, the conversation grew more sober. "Here's what I can't figure out," Torie said to Ted. "Spence's people made it clear last spring that he'd eliminated Wynette and decided on San Antone. Then a month ago, without any warning, he pops up again and says Wynette's back in the running. I'd like to know what happened to change his mind."

"The folks in San Antone are as surprised as we are," Ted said. "They thought they had it sewn up."

"Too bad for them." Torie waved at someone across the room. "We need this more than they do."

When it was time to leave, Dallie insisted on dropping Spence off at the inn, which was how Meg ended up alone in Ted's Benz. She waited until they reached the highway before she broke the silence. "You're not having an affair with Kenny's sister."

"I'd better tell her that."

"And you never screwed around on Luce."

"Whatever you say."

"And"—she studied the easy way his hands curled over the steering wheel and wondered if anything ever came hard to this charmed creature—"if you want my continued cooperation with Spence—which I assure you that you do—we need to come to an understanding."

"Who says I need your cooperation?"

"Oh, you need it, all right." She slipped her fingers into her hair. "It's fascinating, isn't it, how impressed Spence is with my father and, by extension, with me? Insulting to my mother, of course, considering how powerful she is in the industry, not to mention being one of the most beautiful women in the world. Still, Spence did mention that he had her poster on his bedroom wall, and he's definitely smitten with me, for whatever twisted reason. That means I've gone from a liability to an asset, and you, my friend, need to work a little harder to please me, starting with those cheapskate tips. Spence gave Mark a hundred dollars today."

"Mark didn't cost Spence three holes and I don't know how many bad shots. But fine. Tomorrow I'll tip you a hundred. Minus fifty dollars for every hole you cost me."

"Minus ten dollars for every hole I cost you, and it's a deal. By the way, I'm not big on diamonds and roses, but an open account at the grocery wouldn't go unappreciated."

He slanted her one of his saintly looks. "I thought you were too proud to take my money."

"Take it, yes. Earn it? Definitely not."

"Spence didn't get where he is by being stupid. I doubt he bought that cockamamie story of your unrequited passion for me."

"He'd better have bought it because I won't let that man paw me again, not for all the golf resorts in the world, and irresistible you is my excuse."

He lifted an eyebrow at her, then turned into the dark, narrow lane that led to her temporary home. "Maybe you should reconsider. He's a decent-looking guy, and he's rich. Frankly, he could be the answer to your prayers."

"If I were going to put a price tag on my lady parts, I'd find a more appetizing buyer."

Ted liked that, and he was still grinning when they pulled up to the church. She opened the passenger door to get out. He slipped his arm over the back of her seat and gave her a look she couldn't quite fathom. "I assume I'm invited in," he said. "Considering the intensity of your feelings for me?"

He had her in his high beams, those amber eyes delivering his personal elixir of rapt attention, perfect understanding, deep appreciation, and forgiveness for all her sins.

He was totally messing with her.

She pulled a tragic sigh. "I need to get past your otherworldly perfection before I can begin to think about exposing you to my lusty side."

"How lusty?"

"Off the charts." She slid out of the car. "Good night, Theodore. Sweet dreams."

She climbed the stairs to the church doors with the glare from his headlights lighting her way. When she reached the top, she slipped the key in the lock and let herself inside. The church enfolded her. Dark, empty, lonely.

SHE SPENT THE NEXT DAY on the drink cart without getting fired, something she regarded as a major accomplishment, since she hadn't been able to resist reminding a few of the golfers to dump their freaking beverage cans in the recycling containers instead of the trash bins. Bruce Garvin, the father of Birdie's friend Kayla, was particularly hostile, and Meg suspected she had Spencer Skipjack's interest in her to thank for her continued employment. She was also deeply grateful that news of her fake declaration of love for Ted didn't seem to have spread. Apparently last night's witnesses had decided to keep quiet, a miracle in a small town.

She greeted Birdie's daughter, Haley, when she went into the snack shop to get fresh ice and replenish the beverages in the cart. Haley had either taken in the seams on her employee's polo shirt or traded with someone smaller because the outline of her breasts was on full display. "Mr. Collins is playing today," she said, "and he's big on Gatorade, so make sure you have plenty."

"Thanks for the tip." Meg pointed toward the candy bar display. "Mind if I take some of these? I'll toss them on top of the ice and see if they sell."

"Good idea. And if you run into Ted, would you tell him I need to talk to him?"

Meg sincerely hoped she didn't run into him.

"He's turned off his cell," Haley said, "and I'm supposed to do his grocery shopping today."

"You do his grocery shopping?"

"I run errands for him. Mail packages. Do things he doesn't have time for himself." She lifted some hot dogs out of the steamer. "I think I told you I'm his personal assistant."

"That's right. You did." Meg concealed her amusement. She'd grown up around personal assistants, and they did a lot more than run errands.

When she got home that evening, she opened the windows, glad the need for secrecy was gone, then took a quick swim in the creek. Afterward, she sat cross-legged on the floor and examined some unclaimed costume jewelry she'd gotten permission to take from the club's lost-and-found box. She liked working with jewelry, and the glimmer of an idea had been poking at her for the last few days. She retrieved a pair of ancient long-nosed pliers she'd found in a kitchen drawer and began taking apart an inexpensive charm bracelet.

A car pulled up outside, and a few moments later, Ted wandered in looking sloppy and gorgeous in navy slacks and a wrinkled gray sport shirt.

"Ever hear of knocking?" she said.

"Ever hear of trespassing?"

His open shirt collar revealed the suntanned hollow at the base of his throat. She stared at it for a moment too long, then jabbed at the jump ring attached to the bracelet's clasp. "I got a text message from Lucy today."

"I don't care." He moved deeper into the room, bringing with him the nauseating scent of undiluted goodness.

"She still won't tell me what she's doing or exactly where she is." The pliers slipped. She winced as she pinched her finger. "All she'll say is that no terrorists have captured her and I shouldn't worry."

"Repeat. Don't care."

She sucked her finger. "Yes, you do, although not in the way most abandoned bridegrooms would care. Your pride's injured, but your heart doesn't even seem bruised, let alone broken."

"You don't know anything about my heart."

The need to be disagreeable wouldn't let go, and as she once again dragged her eyes away from that odious open shirt collar, she recalled a tidbit she'd picked up from Haley. "Don't you think it's a little embarrassing for a man your age to still live with his parents?"

"I don't live with my parents."

"Close enough. You have a house on the same property."

"It's a big property, and they like having me nearby."

Unlike her own parents, who'd booted her out the door. "How sweet," she said. "Does Yummy Mummy tuck you in at night?"

"Not unless I ask her to. And you're not exactly in a position to make Yummy Mummy cracks."

"True. But I don't live with mine." She didn't like him looming over her, so she uncoiled from the floor and wandered toward her only piece of living room furniture, the ugly brown upholstered chair Ted had left behind. "What do you want?"

"Nothing. Just relaxing." He meandered over to a window and ran his thumb along one side of the frame.

She perched on the chair arm. "You have a tough life for sure. Do you actually work? I mean aside from your so-called mayor's job."

Her question seemed to amuse him. "Sure I work. I have a desk and a pencil sharpener and everything."

"Where?"

"Secret location."

"All the better to keep the women away?"

"To keep everybody away."

She thought that over. "I know you invented some kind of whiz-bang software system that made you a gazillion dollars, but I haven't heard much talk about it. What kind of job do you have?"

"A lucrative job." He gave a quick, apologetic tilt of his head. "Sorry. Foreign word you wouldn't understand."

"That's just mean."

He smiled and gazed up at the ceiling fan. "I can't believe how hot it is in here, and it's only the first of July. Hard to imagine how much worse it'll get." He shook his head, his expression as guileless as a saint's. "I was going to put in air-conditioning for Lucy, but I'm glad now that I didn't. Adding all those fluorocarbons to the atmosphere would have kept you awake at night. Do you have any beer?"

She glowered at him. "I can barely afford milk for cereal."

"You're living here rent free," he pointed out. "The least you could do is keep beer in the refrigerator for company."

"You're not company. You're an infestation. What do you want?"

"This is my place, remember? I don't have to want anything." He pointed the toe of a scuffed, but very expensive, loafer toward the jewelry laid out on the floor. "What's all this?"

"Some costume jewelry." She knelt down and began to gather it up.

"I hope you didn't pay real money for it. Eye of the beholder, I guess."

She gazed up at him. "Does this place have a postal address?"

"Sure it has an address. Why do you want to know?"

"I want to know where I live, that's all." She also needed some things sent to her that were packed away in her closet back home. She found a scrap of paper and wrote down the address he gave her. She nodded toward the front of the church. "As long as you're here, will you turn on the hot water? I'm getting tired of cold showers."

"Tell me about it."

She smiled. "You can't still be suffering from the effects of Lucy's three-month sexual moratorium?"

"Damn, but you women sure do like to talk."

"I told her it was stupid." She wished she were evil enough to pass on the news that Lucy had already taken a lover.

"We finally agree on something," he said.

"Still . . ." She returned to putting the jewelry away. "Everybody knows you can have any brainless woman in Wynette. I don't exactly see what your problem is finding sexual companionship."

He looked at her as though she'd just joined the Idiots Club.

"Right," she said. "This is Wynette, and you're Ted Beaudine. If you do one of them, you'd have to do them all."

He grinned.

She'd intended to annoy, not to amuse, and she took another swipe. "Too bad I was wrong about you and Torie. A clandestine affair with a married woman would answer your problem. Almost as good as being married to Lucy."

"What do you mean by that?"

She extended her legs and leaned back on her hands. "No messy emotional crap. You know. Like real love and genuine passion."

He stared at her a moment, those tiger eyes inscrutable. "You think Lucy and I didn't have passion?"

"Not to be insulting—okay, maybe a little insulting—but I sincerely doubt you have a passionate bone in your body."

An ordinary mortal would have been offended, but not St. Theodore. He merely looked thoughtful. "Let me get this straight. A screwup like you is analyzing me?"

"Fresh viewpoint."

He nodded. Contemplated. And then he did a very un–Ted Beaudine–like thing. He dropped his lids and gave her a wicked eye-rake. Starting at the top of her head and sliding down her body, lingering here and there along the way. Her mouth. Her breasts. The apex of her thighs. Leaving hot little eddies of desire behind.

The absolute horror of not being immune to him hurled her into action, and she jumped up from the floor. "Waste of effort, Mr. B. Unless, of course, you're paying."

"Paying?"

"You know. A big wad of twenties on the dresser afterward. Oops . . . I don't have a dresser. Oh, well, there goes that idea."

She'd finally managed to annoy him. He stalked into the back room to either turn on the hot water or blow the place up. She sincerely hoped it was the former. Not long after, she heard the back door close, and a few moments later, his car pulling away. She was strangely disappointed.

THE FOURSOME TEED OFF the next day. Ted and Torie playing Kenny and Spence.

"I had to go to Austin yesterday," Spence told Meg, "and every time I saw a beautiful woman, I thought about you."

"Jeez, why?"

Ted gave her a surreptitious poke. Spence threw back his head and laughed. "You're something, Miz Meg. You know who you remind me of?"

"I'm hoping a young Julia Roberts."

"You remind me of me, that's who." He resettled his straw Panama on his head. "I had a lot of challenges in my life, but I always faced them down."

Ted whapped her on the back. "That's our Meg, all right."

By the time they reached the third green, she was wilting from the heat but still happy to be outside. She forced herself to concentrate on being the perfect caddy, along with shooting Ted adoring glances every time Spence got too cozy.

"Would you stop that!" Ted said, when they were out of earshot.

"What do you care?"

"It's unnerving, that's all," he complained. "Like being trapped in an alternate reality."

"You should be used to adoring glances."

"Not from *you*."

It was soon evident, even to Meg, that Torie was a highly competitive athlete, but on the back nine, she suddenly began missing putts. Ted never lost his easy charm, not until he was alone with Meg when he confirmed her suspicions that Torie was doing it deliberately. "That was barely a three-foot putt," he groused, "and Torie lips the cup. Spence could be around for weeks. Anybody who thinks I'm going to let him win every match is crazy."

"Which is obviously why Torie missed that putt." At least someone other than herself understood Spence's ego. She glanced around for the most recent head cover she seemed to have misplaced. "Concentrate on the big picture, Mr. Mayor. If you're determined to destroy the local environment with this project, you need to be more like Torie and work harder to make Spence happy."

He ignored her jab. "Look who's talking about making Spence happy. It wouldn't hurt you to be nicer to him. I swear I'm going to stage a public fight with you so he knows exactly how unrequited your passion for me is."

He put a long wedge shot on the green, tossed the club at her, and stalked off.

Thanks to Torie, Spence and Kenny pulled off a one-hole victory. Afterward, Meg headed for the ladies' locker room, which, technically, employees weren't supposed to use, but since it was equipped with a vast array of personal-care products sadly missing from her own collection, she used it anyway. As she splashed her heat-flushed face with cold water, Torie joined her at the sink. Unlike Meg, the heat didn't seem to have affected Torie, who merely pulled off her visor to refasten her ponytail, then looked around to make sure the locker room was empty. "So what's really between you and Ted?"

"What do you mean? Haven't you heard the rumors about how I drove Lucy away so I could have him for myself?"

"I'm a lot brighter than I look. And you're not a woman who'd fall for a guy who basically hates your guts."

"I don't think he hates me as much as he did. Now it's more your run-of-the-mill loathing."

"Interesting." Torie shook out her long hair, then gathered it together again.

Meg grabbed a washcloth from the pile by the sink and ran it under the cold water. "You don't seem to hate me, either. Why is that? Everybody else in town does."

"I have my reasons." She snapped the elastic back into place. "Which isn't to say I wouldn't scratch your eyes out if I really believed you were a threat to Ted."

"I broke up his marriage, remember?"

Torie gave a noncommittal shrug.

Meg studied her, but Torie wasn't giving anything more away. Meg rubbed the cold washcloth over the back of her neck. "Since we're having this heart-to-heart, I'm curious how your husband would feel if he knew you were practically naked in a hotel room with Ted?"

"Oh, Dex didn't mind the naked part—I'd just come out of the shower—but he wasn't happy about Ted kissing me like that, even after I pointed out that I was an innocent bystander." She disappeared into the nearest stall, still talking. "Dex got all huffy and informed Ted that he drew the line at kissing. I told Dex I wished he'd draw it someplace else because, even though I doubted that kiss was Ted's best effort, it was still kind of fun. Then Dex said he'd show me all the fun I could handle, which, if you knew my husband, would make you laugh, but Dex was feeling crabby because, a couple of weeks ago, I'd tricked him into staying with the girls while I went with Ted to test the new GPS he made for his truck. Dex wanted to do the test run himself."

That must have been the night Meg had seen them together. She was getting more than a little curious about Dexter O'Connor. "So your husband knew you were alone in a room at the inn with Ted?" She grabbed the sunblock. "You must have a very understanding husband."

The toilet flushed. "What do you mean alone? Dex was in the shower. It was our room. Ted just stopped by."

"Your room? I thought you lived in Wynette."

Torie came out of the stall and regarded her with faint pity. "We have kids, Meg. *K-i-d-s.* Two fabulous little girls I love with all my heart, but they definitely take after me, which means Dex and I try to get away, just the two of us, every couple of months." She washed her hands. "Sometimes we manage a long weekend in Dallas or New Orleans. Usually, though, it's a night at the inn."

Meg had more questions, but she needed to put away Ted's clubs and collect her tip money.

She found him by the pro shop, talking to Kenny. He reached into his pocket as she approached. She held her breath. True, she'd lost his last two head covers, but she hadn't cost him a single hole, and if that cheapskate . . .

"Here you go, Meg."

The full one hundred dollars. "Wow," she whispered. "I thought I needed to buy a bedroom dresser before I could make this kind of money."

"Don't get used to it," he said. "Your days caddying for me are over."

Just then, Spence emerged from the pro shop along with a young woman dressed for business in a sleeveless black shift, pearls, and a dark green Birkin bag. She was tall and full figured, although not even close to fat. She had strong features—a long face with well-defined, dark eyebrows, an important nose, and a full, sensuous mouth. Subtle highlights brightened the dark brown hair that curved in long, straight layers around her face. Although she looked to be in her late twenties, she carried herself with the confidence of an older woman combined with the sexy assurance of a younger one used to getting her own way.

Skipjack slipped his arm around her. "Ted, you've already met Sunny, but I don't think the rest of you know my beautiful daughter."

Sunny shook hands briskly, repeating each name and locking it in her memory, starting with Kenny, then Torie—assessing Meg—and pausing when she reached Ted. "It's great to see you again, Ted." She studied him as if he were a prized piece of horseflesh, which offended Meg.

"You, too, Sunny."

Spence squeezed her arm. "Torie here invited us both to a little Fourth of July shindig. A good chance to meet more of the locals and get the lay of the land."

Sunny smiled at Ted. "Sounds great."

"Do you want us to pick you up, Meg?" Spence asked. "Torie invited you, too. Sunny and I'll be happy to stop on our way."

Meg pulled a long face. "Sorry, I have to work."

Ted thumped her on the back. Extra hard. "I wish all the club's employees were so dedicated." He slipped his thumb under her shoulder blade, finding what just might be one of those lethal pressure points only assassins knew about. "Fortunately, Shelby's party doesn't start until late afternoon. You can come over as soon as you get off work."

She managed a weak smile, then decided that a free meal, her curiosity about Sunny Skipjack, and the opportunity to irritate Ted outweighed spending another night alone. "All right. But I'll drive myself."

Sunny, in the meantime, was having a hard time tearing her eyes away from Ted. "You're quite the public servant."

"I do my best."

Her teeth were large and perfect as she smiled. "I suppose the least I can do is put in my own bid."

Ted cocked his head. "Beg pardon?"

"The auction," she said. "I'll definitely put in a bid."

"You've got me at a disadvantage, Sunny."

She snapped open her Birkin and extracted a bright red flyer. "I found this under the windshield of my rental car after I stopped in town."

Ted glanced down at the flyer. It might have been Meg's imagination, but she thought he flinched.

Kenny, Torie, and Spence moved closer to read over his shoulder. Spence shot Meg a speculative look. Kenny shook his head. "This is Shelby's big idea. I heard her talking about it to Lady E., but I never thought it would get this far."

Torie let out a hoot. "I'm definitely bidding. I don't care what Dex says."

Kenny arched a dark brow. "Lady E. sure isn't bidding."

"That's what you think," his sister retorted. She extended the flyer toward Meg. "Take a look at this. Too bad you're poor."

The flyer was simply printed in bold black letters:

WIN A WEEKEND WITH TED BEAUDINE

Join Wynette's favorite bachelor
for a romantic weekend in San Francisco.

Sightseeing, fine dining,
romantic nighttime boat cruise,
and more. Much more . . .

Ladies, place your bids.
($100.00 minimum)

Married! Single! Old! Young!
Everyone welcome.
The weekend can be as friendly (or intimate) as you like.

www.weekendwithted.com

All proceeds benefit the
Wynette Public Library
rebuilding effort.

Ted snatched the flyer from her, studied it, then crumpled it in his fist. "Of all the stupid, asinine . . . !"

Meg tapped him on the shoulder and whispered, "I'd buy a dresser, if I were you."

Torie threw back her head and laughed. "I *love* this town!"

chapter ten

O N HER WAY HOME FROM WORK that evening, Meg passed the town's resale shop. She loved good vintage stores and decided to stop. Another of the red flyers hung in the window advertising the Win a Weekend with Ted Beaudine contest. She opened the heavy, old-fashioned wooden door. The sunny yellow interior smelled faintly musty, the way most resale shops did, but the merchandise was well organized, with antique tables and chests serving both as display areas and section dividers. Meg recognized the clerk as Birdie's friend Kayla, the blonde who'd been behind the front desk at the inn the day of Meg's humiliation.

Kayla's sleeveless pink and gray camouflage-print dress definitely wasn't resale. She wore it with stilettos and a set of tasseled black enamel bangles. Even though it was nearly closing time, her makeup was still flawless—eyeliner, contoured cheekbones, glossy mocha mouth, the personification of a Texas beauty queen. She didn't pretend not to know who Meg was, and like everybody else in this stupid town, she had no regard for tact. "I hear Spencer Skipjack's got a thing for you," she said as she stepped away from the jewelry rack.

"I don't have a thing for him." A quick glance at the merchandise revealed boring preppy sportswear, pastel church suits, and grandma sweatshirts decorated with Halloween pumpkins and cartoon characters—all of it hard to reconcile with this stylish creature.

"That doesn't mean you can't be nice to him," Kayla said.

"I am nice to him."

Kayla planted a hand on her hip. "Do you have any idea how many jobs that golf resort will give people in this town? Or the new businesses that will spring up?"

Useless to mention the ecosystems it would also destroy. "Quite a few, I imagine."

Kayla retrieved a belt that had fallen off a rack. "I know people around here haven't exactly put out the welcome mat for you, but I'm sure everybody would appreciate it if you didn't use that as an excuse to screw us over with Spencer Skipjack. Some things are more important than holding on to petty grudges."

"I'll keep that in mind." Just as Meg turned to leave, a display caught her eye—a gray menswear shirt with a matching bandeau top and short shorts with a paper-bag waist. The pieces were edgy updates of 1950s summer fashion, and she walked over to examine them more closely. When she found the label, she couldn't believe what she saw. "This is Zac Posen."

"I know."

She blinked at the price tag. Forty dollars? For a three-piece Zac Posen? She didn't have forty dollars to spare at the moment, not even with Ted's tip, but still, an incredible bargain. Hanging nearby was an avant-garde dress with a beautifully constructed green and melon corset top, at least two thousand dollars new, but now priced at one hundred. The label bore her uncle's name, Michel Savagar. She examined the other clothes on the rack and found a silky chartreuse tank dress printed with the elongated head of a Modigliani female, a startling origami jacket with steel gray pencil pants, and a black-and-white Miu Miu miniskirt. She pulled a girly fuchsia cardigan with crocheted roses off the rack, imagining it with a T-shirt, jeans, and Chuck Taylors.

"Nice pieces, aren't they?" Kayla said.

"Very nice." Meg put the sweater back and fingered a Narciso Rodriguez jacket.

Kayla regarded her almost slyly. "Most women don't have the body to wear these clothes. You have to be really tall and thin."

Thank you, Mom! Meg did a quick mental calculation, and ten minutes later, she walked out of the store with the Miu Miu mini and the Modigliani tank dress.

The next day was Sunday. Most of the employees grabbed a quick lunch in the caddy room or a corner of the kitchen, but she didn't like either place. Instead, she headed toward the swimming pool with the peanut butter sandwich she'd made that morning. As she passed the dining patio, she spotted Spence, Sunny, and Ted seated at one of the umbrella-shaded tables. Sunny had her hand on Ted's arm, and Ted seemed perfectly content to leave it there. He was doing all the talking as Spence listened intently. None of them noticed her.

The pool was crowded with families enjoying the long holiday weekend. Conscious of her lowly employee status, she found a spot in the grass around the corner from the snack shop and away from the members. As she sat cross-legged on the ground Haley appeared, carrying a drink cup printed with the green country-club logo. "I brought you a Coke."

"Thanks."

Haley freed her hair from the ponytail her job required and settled next to Meg. She'd unfastened all the buttons on her yellow employees' polo, but it still pulled over her breasts. "Mr. Clements and his sons are playing at one o'clock. Dr Pepper and Bud Light."

"I saw." Meg checked tee times each morning in hopes of improving her tips by memorizing names, faces, and the members' drink preferences. She hadn't exactly received a warm welcome, but no one except Kayla's father, Bruce, had mentioned getting rid of her, something she attributed to Spencer Skipjack's interest rather than the quality of her service.

Haley gazed at the short pendant nestled inside the open collar of Meg's detestable polo. "You have the best jewelry."

"Thanks. I made it last night." She'd assembled a small, quirky necklace from bits of the rescued costume jewelry: the mother-of-pearl face of a broken Hello Kitty watch, some tiny pink glass beads she'd taken off a lone earring, and a silver fish that looked as though it might have been part of a key chain. With a little glue and wire, she'd pulled together an interesting piece, perfect for the silky black cord she'd shortened.

"You're so creative," Haley said.

"I love jewelry. Buying it, making it, wearing it. When I travel, I find local artisans and watch them work. I've learned a lot." She impulsively unclipped the cord. "Here. Enjoy."

"You're giving it to me?"

"Why not?" She fastened the pendant around Haley's neck. Its funky charm helped downplay her overly made-up face.

"That's so cool. Thanks."

The gift unlocked some of Haley's natural reticence, and while Meg ate, she talked about attending the county community college in the fall. "My mom wants me to go to U.T. instead. She's being a real rag about it, but I'm not going."

"I'm surprised you don't want to head off to the big city," Meg said.

"It's not so bad here. Zoey and Kayla are always talking about how much they'd like to move to Austin or San Antonio, but they never do anything about it." She took a sip of her Coke. "Everybody's saying Mr. Skipjack's obsessed with you."

"He's obsessed with my celebrity connections, and he's really persistent. Just between us, I've been trying to get him to back off by telling him I'm in love with Ted."

Haley's big eyes grew even larger. "You're in love with Ted?"

"God, no. I have more sense. That was the best I could come up with on short notice."

Haley pulled at a tuft of grass by her ankle. Finally, she said, "Have you ever been in love?"

"I thought I was a couple of times, but I wasn't. What about you?"

"For a while, I had this thing for this guy I graduated with. Kyle Bascom. He's going to County Community next year, too." She glanced up at the clock on the snack shop wall. "I have to get back to work. Thanks for the necklace."

Meg finished her sandwich, grabbed an empty golf cart, and drove back to the fourteenth tee. By four o'clock, the course had begun to empty, leaving her with nothing to do except obsess over her failures.

That evening when she pulled the Rustmobile up to the church, she found an unfamiliar car parked by the steps. As she got out, Sunny Skipjack came around the corner from the graveyard. She'd traded in the marigold yellow number she'd been wearing at lunch for shorts, a white top, and a pair of cherry red sunglasses. "Doesn't it bother you, living out here alone?" she asked.

Meg tilted her head toward the cemetery. "They're fairly harmless. Although a couple of those black markers give me chills."

Sunny came closer, moving with a sinuous rhythm that emphasized her round hips and full breasts. She wasn't a woman who obsessed over not being a size zero, and Meg liked that about her. What she didn't like was an aggressive attitude that signified she'd mow down anyone who had the audacity to oppose her.

"I wouldn't object to a cold beer," Sunny said. "I've spent the last two hours with my father and Ted. We've been trudging around the land Spence is considering buying."

"No beer, but I have iced tea."

Sunny wasn't someone who'd settle for less than exactly what she wanted, and she declined. Since Meg was anxious to go for a swim, she decided to speed things along. "What can I do for you?" As if she didn't know . . . Sunny was going to warn her away from Daddy.

Sunny waited a moment too long to reply. "The . . . dress code for the party tomorrow? I thought you'd know."

It was a lame excuse. Meg took a seat on the step. "It's Texas. The women tend to dress up."

Sunny barely paid attention. "How did Jake Koranda's daughter end up in a hick town like this?"

Meg had good reason to ridicule this hick town, but Sunny was merely being a snob. "I'm taking a break from L.A."

"Quite a change," Sunny said.

"Sometimes change is what we need. I guess it lets us look at our lives in a new way." And hadn't she turned into the wise philosopher?

"There's nothing I'd want to change about my life." Sunny

slipped her bright red sunglasses to the top of her head, where the stems pushed the long layers of dark brown hair away from her face and highlighted her resemblance to Spence. They had the same strong nose, full lips, and air of entitlement. "I like things just the way they are. I sit on the board of my father's company. I design products. It's a great life."

"Impressive."

"I have a bachelor's in mechanical engineering and an MBA," she added, even though Meg hadn't asked.

"Nice." Meg thought of the degree she didn't have in anything.

Sunny sat on the step above her. "You seem to have stirred up the town since you got here."

"It's a small town. Easy to stir up."

Sunny rubbed a smudge from her ankle that she must have picked up during the land survey. "My father has quite a lot to say about you. He enjoys younger women."

She'd finally gotten to the point of today's visit, and Meg couldn't have been happier.

"They obviously enjoy him, too," Sunny went on. "He's successful, outgoing, and he likes to have a good time. He keeps talking about you, so I know you've caught his interest. I'm happy for you both."

"You are?" Meg hadn't expected this. She wanted an ally, not a matchmaker. She stalled for time by untying her sneakers. "I guess I'm surprised. Don't you worry about . . . gold diggers? You might have heard that I'm broke."

Sunny shrugged. "My father's a big boy. He can take care of himself. The fact that you're a challenge makes you even more intriguing to him."

The last thing Meg wanted was to be intriguing. She slipped out of her sneakers, pulled off her socks, and said carefully, "I don't really go for older men."

"Maybe you should give one of them a try." Sunny rose from the step and came down to Meg's level. "I'm going to be straight with you. My father has been divorced from my mother for nearly ten years. He's worked hard all his life, and he deserves to enjoy himself. So don't worry about me getting in your way. I have no problem with the two of you having fun together. And who knows where it might lead? He's never been stingy with the women he dates."

"But . . ."

"I'll see you tomorrow at the party." Her business accomplished, she headed for her rental car.

As she drove off, Meg put the pieces together. Sunny had obviously heard about Meg's professed interest in Ted, and she didn't like it. She wanted to keep Meg occupied with her father so she'd have a clear field to stake out St. Sexy for herself. If she only knew the truth, she wouldn't have wasted her time.

MEG HAD NO TROUBLE FINDING the Moorish mansion where Shelby and Warren Traveler lived. According to gossip, Kenny and Torie hadn't been happy when their father had married a woman thirty years his junior who also happened to be Torie's sorority sister. Even the birth of a half brother hadn't appeased them, but eleven years had passed since then, Kenny and Torie were both married, and all seemed to be forgiven.

An impressive mosaic fountain sat in front of the house, which was built of rose-colored stucco with a crenellated tile roof straight out of the Arabian nights. One of the catering staff let her in through a set of carved wooden doors bracketed by arched windows. The English country decor was a surprise in a house with such pronounced Moorish architecture, but somehow the chintz, hunting prints, and Hepplewhite furniture Shelby Traveler had chosen sort of worked.

.   A pair of doors with mosaic inlays led to a terrace with high, stucco walls, long benches covered in jewel-toned prints, and tiled tables holding brass buckets spilling over with red, white, and blue flower arrangements augmented with small American flags. Shade trees and a mist cooling system kept the guests comfortable in the late-afternoon heat.

Meg spotted Birdie Kittle and Kayla huddled together, along with Kayla's BFF Zoey Daniels, the local elementary-school principal. Several country-club staff members were helping serve, and Meg waved at Haley, who was passing a tray of hors d'oeuvres. Kenny Traveler stood next to an attractive woman with honey brown curls and baby-doll cheeks. Meg recognized her from the rehearsal dinner as his wife, Emma.

Meg had showered in the ladies' locker room, scrunched some hair product into her rowdy curls, applied lipstick and eye makeup, then slipped into the chartreuse tank dress from the resale shop. With the elongated Modigliani woman's head printed down the front, the dress didn't require a necklace, but she hadn't been able to resist attaching a couple of quarter-size purple plastic discs to each of her Sung dynasty earrings. The dramatic juxtaposition of ancient and mod complemented the Modigliani print and pulled the whole posh-meets-kitsch look together. Her uncle Michel would have approved.

Heads began to turn at her appearance but not, she suspected, because of her great earrings. She'd expected hostility from the women, but she hadn't anticipated the amused glances some of them exchanged as they took in her tank dress. It was a perfect fit, and it looked great on her, so she didn't care.

"Can I get you something to drink?"

She turned to see a tall, thin man in his early forties with straight, slightly disheveled brown hair and wide-spaced gray eyes visible through the lenses of wire-rimmed glasses. He reminded her of a college lit professor. "Arsenic?" she asked.

"I don't think that will be necessary."

"If you say so."

"I'm Dexter O'Connor."

"No, you're not!" The words came out before she could stop them, but she couldn't believe this bookish man was the glamorous Torie Traveler O'Connor's husband. It had to be the mismatch of the century.

He smiled. "Obviously, you've met my wife."

Meg swallowed. "Uh . . . It's just that—"

"Torie is Torie, and I'm . . . not?" He raised an eyebrow.

"Well, I mean . . . I guess that could be a good thing, right? Depending on how you look at it?" She'd just unintentionally insulted his wife. He waited, a patient smile on his face. "I don't mean that Torie's not terrific . . ." She stumbled on. "Torie's practically the only nice person I've met in this town, but she's very—" Meg was only digging herself in deeper, and she finally gave up. "Crap. I'm sorry. I'm from L.A., so I have no manners. I'm Meg Koranda, as you probably know, and I like your wife."

His amusement at her discomfort seemed more appreciative than mean-spirited. "So do I."

At exactly that moment, Torie came over to join them. She was startlingly beautiful in a sleeveless, embroidered Chinese red top and royal blue mini that showed off her long, tanned legs. How could a firecracker like this be married to a man with such a quiet, scholar's manner?

Torie hooked a hand through her husband's elbow. "See, Dex. Now that you've met Meg you can see she's not the bitch everybody makes her out to be. At least I don't think so."

Dex gave his wife a tolerant smile and Meg a sympathetic one. "You'll have to forgive Torie. Whatever pops into her head comes out her mouth. She can't help it. She's spoiled beyond belief."

Torie grinned and gazed at her egghead husband with such affection that Meg felt a surprising lump form in her throat. "I don't get why you think that's a problem, Dex."

He patted her hand. "I know you don't."

Meg realized that her initial impression of Dexter O'Connor as a gullible egghead might not be accurate. He had a quiet manner, but he was no fool.

Torie dropped her husband's arm and grabbed Meg's wrist. "I'm getting bored. It's time to introduce you to some people. That'll liven things up for sure."

"I don't really think—"

But Torie was already pulling her toward Kenny Traveler's wife, who'd chosen a cheery tangerine shift with eyelet petals at the hem. The warm color enhanced her brown eyes and butterscotch curls.

"Lady Emma, I don't think you've officially met Meg Koranda," Torie said. And then, to Meg, "Just so you know . . . one of Lady Emma's closest friends is Ted's mother, Francesca. Mine, too, but I'm more broad-minded. Lady Emma pretty much hates your guts like everybody else."

Kenny's wife didn't bat an eyelash at Torie's bluntness. "You've caused Francesca a great deal of pain," she said to Meg in a quietly clipped British accent. "I don't know all the circumstances, however, so 'hates' is much too strong a word, but Torie prides herself on creating drama."

"Don't you just love the way she talks?" Torie gave the smaller woman a bright smile. "Lady Emma is a stickler for fairness."

Meg decided it was time to give these blunt-spoken females a small dose of their own medicine. "If being fair toward me is too much trouble, Lady Emma, I give you permission to set aside your principles."

She didn't even blink. "Just Emma," she said. "I have no title, merely an honorific, as everyone here very well knows."

Torie gave her a tolerant look. "Let's put it this way. If my daddy was the fifth Earl of Woodbourne like yours was, I'd sure as hell call myself Lady."

"As you've made abundantly clear." She turned her attention back to Meg. "I understand Mr. Skipjack has taken an interest in you. May I ask if you intend to use that against us?"

"Oh, so tempting," Meg said.

Ted stepped out on the patio along with Spence and Sunny. He wore a boring pair of tan shorts and an equally boring white T-shirt with a Chamber of Commerce logo over the breast. Predictably, a shaft of sunlight chose that moment to cut through the trees and spill all over him so it looked as though he'd stepped into a string of twinkle lights. He should be embarrassed.

Haley took her job as his personal assistant seriously. She abandoned the elderly man reaching for one of the buffalo wings on her tray and rushed to Ted's side to serve him.

"Oh, dear," Emma said. "Ted's here. I'd better go out to the pool and check on the children."

"Shelby's got three lifeguards on duty," Torie said. "You don't want to face him."

Emma sniffed. "The contest to spend a weekend with Ted was entirely Shelby's idea, but you know he'll blame me."

"You are president of the Friends of the Library."

"And I planned to talk to him first. Believe me, I had no idea they'd get the flyers out so quickly."

"I hear the bidding's already up to three thousand dollars," Torie said.

"Three thousand four hundred," Emma replied, a little dazed. "More than we could make in a dozen bake sales. And Kayla had trouble with the Web site last night or the bidding might have gone higher."

Torie wrinkled her nose. "Probably best not to mention the Web site to Ted. It's a sore spot."

Emma pulled a very full bottom lip between her teeth, then released it. "We all take such advantage of him."

"He doesn't mind."

"He does mind," Meg said. "I don't know why he puts up with all of you."

Torie waved her off. "You're an outsider. You have to live around here to understand." She gazed across the patio toward Sunny Skipjack, cool and sexy in white slacks and a powder blue tunic with a keyhole neckline that displayed an enticing amount of cleavage. "She sure is giving Ted the works. Look at that. She's rubbing her boob against his arm."

"He seems to be enjoying it," Emma said.

Was he? With Ted, who could tell? Only thirty-two years old, and he was carrying not only the weight of Sunny Skipjack's breast on his arm but also the burden of the entire town.

He surveyed the crowd and almost immediately found Meg. She felt her own internal twinkle lights begin to flash.

Torie lifted her long hair off her neck. "You got yourself a bit of a dilemma, Meg. Spence is champing at the bit to get his hands on you. At the same time, his daughter has your love object in her high beams. Tough situation." And then, in case Emma had missed the point, "Meg told Spence she's in love with Teddy."

"Who isn't?" Emma's smooth brow furrowed. "I'd better go talk to him."

But Ted had already turned the Skipjacks over to Shelby Traveler so he could make a beeline for Kenny's wife. First, however, he took in Meg with a slow shake of his head.

"What?" she said.

He regarded Torie and Emma. "Is anybody going to tell her?"

Torie flipped her hair. "Not me."

"Nor I," Emma said.

Ted shrugged and before Meg could ask what he was talking about, he'd pinned her with his tiger eyes. "Spence wants to see you, and you'd better cooperate. Smile at him and ask him questions about his plumbing empire. He's real big on his new Cleaner You toilet." As Meg arched an eyebrow at him, he spun on Emma. "As for you . . ."

"I know. I'm dreadfully sorry. Really. I fully intended to talk to you first about the contest."

Torie jabbed him in the shoulder with one manicured fingernail. "Don't you dare complain. The bidding's already up to thirty-four hundred dollars. Not having children yourself, you can't imagine how much the library means to the sweet little babies in our town who are crying themselves to sleep every night because they don't have any new books."

He wasn't biting. "Your expenses will eat up every penny of that thirty-four hundred. Did anybody factor that in?"

"Oh, we have the expenses all worked out," Emma said. "One of Kenny's friends has volunteered his private jet, which takes care of airfare to San Francisco. And your mother's connections will get us great hotel and restaurant discounts. Once we tell her we need them, of course."

"I wouldn't bet on her help."

"On the contrary. She'll like the idea very much . . . after I point out how brilliantly this contest has taken your mind off your recent . . ."

As Emma searched for the right word, Meg jumped in to help her out. "National humiliation? Public debasement? Looking like a weenie?"

"That's uncalled for," Torie protested. "Considering you were responsible."

"I'm not the one who dumped his sorry ass," Meg said. "Why can't you people get that through your thick heads?"

She waited for the inevitable retort. That everything had been fine until she'd come along. That she'd taken cruel advantage of Lucy's bridal nerves. That she'd been jealous and wanted Ted for herself. Instead, he waved her off and focused on Emma. "You should have known better than to go along with this harebrained contest."

"Stop looking at me like that. You know how wretched it makes me feel when you frown. Blame Shelby." Emma glanced around the patio for her mother-in-law. "Who seems to have disappeared. Coward."

Torie poked him in the ribs. "Uh-oh . . . Your newest conquest is headed this way. With her father."

Meg could swear she saw Ted frown, except all she actually saw him do was curl his mouth into one of his boringly predictable smiles. But before the Skipjacks could get to him, a shriek cut through the party noise.

"*Oh my God!*"

Everyone stopped talking and turned to locate the source of the noise. Kayla was staring at the small screen of her metallic red smartphone while Zoey stood on tiptoe to peer over her shoulder. A tendril of hair tumbled from her casually arranged updo as she lifted her head. "Somebody just raised the last bid by a thousand dollars!"

Sunny Skipjack's crimson lips curved in a satisfied smile, and Meg saw her slip her own phone into the pocket of her tunic.

"Dang," Torie grumbled. "Topping that is going to put a serious dent in my discretionary income."

"Daddy!" With a cry of distress, Kayla left Zoey behind as she dashed through the crowd to her father. Just that morning, Meg had served Bruce Garvin an orange soda and received zero tip in exchange. Kayla grabbed his arm and engaged him in a furious conversation.

Ted's lazy smile wobbled.

"Look on the bright side," Meg whispered. "The dear little babies of Wynette are that much closer to curling up with the new John Grisham."

He ignored her to address Torie. "Tell me you're not really bidding."

"Of course I'm bidding. Do you think I'd give up the chance for a weekend in San Francisco away from my kids? But Dex gets to come with us."

An overheated arm settled around Meg's waist, accompanied by the cloying scent of heavy cologne. "You don't have a drink yet, Miss Meg. Let's take care of that."

The plumbing king looked like Johnny Cash, circa 1985. The silver in his thick black hair shone, and his expensive watch glittered in a nest of wrist hair. Although most of the men wore shorts, he had on black pants and a designer polo with a small tuft of hair visible at the open neck. As he maneuvered her away from the others, he rubbed his hand across the small of her back. "You look like a movie star yourself today. That's a beautiful dress. Did you ever happen to meet Tom Cruise?"

"I never had the pleasure." It was a lie, but she wouldn't let him trap her into a discussion of every star she'd met. Out of the corner of her eye, she saw Sunny give Ted her bold smile and watched Ted smile right back. A fragment of their conversation drifted her way.

" . . . and with my software," Ted said, "communities improve their power efficiency. Dynamic load balancing."

The way Sunny licked her lips made her response sound like soft-core porn. "Optimizing their existing infrastructure. That's brilliant, Ted."

They soon formed a foursome. Sunny, Meg observed, was the whole package. Sexy, smart, accomplished. Her father obviously adored her, and he went on ad nauseum about her accomplishments, from her GRE scores to the design awards she'd won for the company. Ted introduced them to everyone, which turned out to be surprisingly entertaining, because even Birdie, Kayla, and Zoey had to be polite to Meg in front of the Skipjacks. She'd never been around so much sucking up in her life, not even in Hollywood.

"Wynette is the best-kept secret in Texas," Birdie trilled. "This is God's country for sure."

"Just walking down the street, you can run into Dallie Beaudine or Kenny Traveler," Kayla's father said. "Name another town where that could happen."

"Nobody can match our scenery," Zoey offered, "and people in Wynette know how to make strangers feel welcome."

Meg could have debated that last point, but a hand that didn't belong to Spence gave her elbow a warning pinch.

By the time the barbecue was served, Sunny was treating Ted like a long-term boyfriend. "You have to come to Indianapolis, doesn't he, Dad? You're going to love it. The most underrated city in the Midwest."

"That's what I've heard," the mayor replied with all kinds of admiration.

"Sunny's right." Spence gave his daughter a fond look. "And I guess Sunny and I already know just about everybody in town."

Kayla came over to flirt with Ted and announce that the bid had gone up another five hundred dollars. Since she seemed happy about it, Meg suspected "Daddy" was responsible. Sunny didn't seem threatened by either the higher stakes or Kayla's blond dazzle.

When Zoey joined them, Ted introduced her to the Skipjacks. Although she wasn't as obvious about it as Kayla, her gazes at Ted left no doubt how she felt about him. Meg wanted to tell both Zoey and Kayla to get a grip. It was obvious Ted liked them and just as obvious his feelings didn't stretch any further. Still, she felt more than a little sorry for both women. Ted treated all females—Meg being the lone exception—as infinitely desirable creatures, so it was no wonder they continued to hold out hope.

Sunny had grown bored. "I heard they have a beautiful pool here. Would you mind showing me, Ted?"

"Great idea," he said. "Meg's been wanting to see it, too. We'll all go."

Meg would have thanked him for making sure she wasn't left with Spence if she hadn't recognized his true motive. He didn't want to be alone with Sunny.

They all wandered out to the pool. Meg met their host, Kenny's father, Warren Traveler, who looked like an older, rougher version of his son. His wife, Shelby, came across as a bubblehead, an impression Meg knew could be deceptive in Wynette, and sure enough, she soon learned that Shelby Traveler headed the board of the British boarding school where Emma Traveler had formerly been headmistress.

"Before you start yelling at me," Shelby said to Ted, "you should know that Margo Ledbetter made an audition tape for you and sent it in to *The Bachelor.* You might want to start practicing your rose ceremony."

Ted winced, a string of firecrackers went off, and Meg leaned in close enough to whisper, "You really need to get out of this town."

The small muscle she was becoming increasingly familiar with began to tick at the corner of his jaw, but he smiled and pretended not to hear.

chapter eleven

AT THE POOL, MEG WATCHED Torie wrap two future beauty queens in beach towels. The happy kisses she planted on both noses testified that she was all bluster when it came to complaining about her kids. Kenny, in the meantime, was refereeing an argument between two young boys with hair as dark as his own, while a little girl with her mother's butterscotch curls stole the disputed rubber raft from behind their backs and ran into the pool with it.

Eventually Meg managed to excuse herself to use the bathroom only to find Spence waiting in the hallway with a fresh glass of wine as she came out. "I seem to remember you were drinking the sauvignon blanc." He hit the consonants hard, like a man with no patience for any language other than English, then poked his head into the bathroom. "Kohler toilet," he said. "But those are my faucets. Brushed nickel. Part of our Chesterfield line."

"They're . . . lovely."

"Sunny designed them. That girl is a whiz."

"She seems really accomplished." Meg tried to ease away, but he was a big man, and he blocked the hallway. His hand settled into its too-familiar spot in the middle of her back. "I have to fly back to Indy for a couple of days. After that, I need to make a quick run to London to check out a cabinet company. I know you've got a job, but"—he winked—"why don't I see if I can arrange for you to get a couple of days off and come with me?"

She was starting to feel a little queasy. "Spence, you're a great guy . . ." A great guy with a chunk of barbecued chicken wedged in his front teeth. "I'm really flattered, but . . ." She tried to look besotted. "You know I'm in love with Ted."

He gave her an indulgent smile. "Meg, honey, chasing after a guy who's not interested in you will rip the hell out of your self-respect. Better to face facts now because the longer you put it off, the harder it'll be."

She wasn't giving up that easily. "I don't actually know that Ted's not interested in me."

He moved his hand to her shoulder and squeezed. "You've seen Ted with Sunny. The way the sparks are flying between them. Even somebody half blind could tell those two are made for each other."

He was wrong. The only genuine sparks had come from Sunny. The rest had come from the Beaudine voodoo machine. She couldn't pinpoint exactly what kind of woman Ted needed, but it wasn't Spence's daughter any more than it had been Lucy. Still, what did she know? Maybe Sunny, with her advanced degree and engineering mind, was right for him.

"Now, I know he's just coming off an engagement," Spence said, "but Sunny's smart. She'll take her time. He already treats her like she's the only woman in the world."

Obviously, Spence hadn't noticed that he treated every female that way. "Ted and Sunny together." He chuckled. "Now that would really clinch the deal here."

Right then, she figured out the answer to the question everyone in town had been asking: Why had Spence changed his mind about Wynette?

Last spring, Spence had rejected the town in favor of San Antonio, but a little over a month ago, he'd reappeared and announced that Wynette was once again in the running. And now Meg knew it was because of Sunny. His daughter had first met Ted when he was still engaged to Lucy. But he wasn't engaged now, and what Sunny wanted, Spence would do his best to make sure Sunny got.

"Tell me about your new Cleaner You toilet," Meg said. "I'm dying to hear the details."

He eagerly launched into a description of a toilet that automatically washed the user's butt. That quickly led to his next favorite topic, her life in Hollywood. "All those famous people's houses . . . I'll bet you've seen some great bathrooms."

"I mainly grew up in Connecticut, and I spend a lot of time traveling."

That didn't stop him from asking if she knew his favorite stars, a list that included Cameron Diaz, Brad Pitt, George Clooney, and inexplicably, Tori Spelling.

The fireworks began as soon as it was dark. While the guests gathered on the back lawn, eleven-year-old Peter Traveler, Shelby and Warren's son, raced around the yard with his friends, and the sleepy younger children curled up on oversize beach towels next to their parents. One of Torie's daughters entwined her fingers in her mother's hair. Kenny and Emma's three children sprawled across their parents, the smallest tucking herself under her father's arm.

Meg, Spence, Ted, and Sunny sat on a blanket Shelby provided. Spence squeezed in too close, and Meg eased onto the grass. Ted braced his weight on his elbows and listened as Sunny enumerated the chemical compounds used to make specific colors of fireworks. He seemed fascinated, but Meg suspected his mind was someplace else. The guests cheered as the first pinwheels exploded in the sky. Spence dropped one hot, hairy paw over Meg's hand. The moist evening air made the stench of his cologne more pungent, and as a rocket shot into the air, the black stone in his pinkie ring winked at her like an evil eye.

The cologne . . . the heat . . . too much wine . . . "Excuse me," she whispered. She extricated herself and made her way through the blankets and beach towels to French doors that opened into a spacious family room. The cozy, English country decor featured soft-cushioned couches and easy chairs; end tables holding magazines and silver-framed family photographs; and bookcases displaying model airplanes, board games, and a complete set of Harry Potter.

The door opened behind her. Spence had followed her inside, and her stomach clenched. She was tired, out of sorts, and she couldn't take it any longer. "I'm in love with Ted Beaudine. Passionately in love with him."

"You've got a weird way of showing it."

Shit. Not Spence at all. She spun around to see Ted standing just inside the French doors, his tall, absolutely perfect body silhouetted against the night. A rocket exploded in the sky forming a golden starburst behind his head. It was so infuriatingly predictable she could have screamed. "Leave me alone."

"Passion sure does make you crabby." As he moved away from the door, the golden sparks tumbled to oblivion in an aerial waterfall. "Just checking to see if you're okay. You looked a little peaked."

"The stench of too much cologne, and that's bull. You want to get away from Sunny."

"I don't know why you'd say that. She's a real smart girl. Hot, too."

"And she'd be perfect for you, except you don't really like her, not that you'd admit to disliking anybody except me. Still, if you can manage to fall in love with her, you'll have that awful golf resort built before you know it. Spence told me himself that a match between you and Sunny would seal the deal. *That's* why he came back to Wynette." She shot him a dark look. "As I'm sure you've already figured out."

He didn't bother to deny it. "Wynette needs the resort, and I'm not apologizing for doing everything I can to make it happen. There's hardly a person in this town who won't benefit."

"You're going to have to marry her, then. What does one man's happiness mean against the well-being of the multitudes?"

"We barely know each other."

"Not to worry. Sunny's a woman who goes after what she wants."

He rubbed the bridge of his nose. "She's just having fun."

"*Au contraire.* You are the one and only Ted Beaudine, and the mere sight of you makes women—"

"Shut up." Harsh words, gently delivered. "Just shut up, will you?"

He looked as tired as she felt. She slumped down on the damask upholstered couch, propped her elbows on her knees, and rested her chin in her hands. "I hate this town."

"Maybe. But you also like the challenge it's giving you."

Her head shot up. "Challenge? I'm sleeping in a hot, unfurnished church and selling Bud Light to pampered golfers who can't be bothered to recycle their beer cans. Oh, yeah, I love the challenge all right."

His eyes seemed to see right through her. "That only makes it more interesting, doesn't it? You're finally getting a chance to test yourself."

"Finally?" She jumped up off the couch. "I've kayaked the Mekong

River and gone diving with great whites off Cape Town. Don't talk to me about tests."

"Those weren't tests. That's your idea of fun. But what's happening here in Wynette is different. You finally get to see what you're made of without Mom and Dad's money. Can you survive in a place where Spence Skipjack is the only person impressed by your last name and where, let's face it, nobody likes you?"

"Torie sort of likes me. And Haley Kittle." The way he was studying her made her uncomfortable, so she went over to the bookcase and pretended to inspect the titles.

He came up behind her. "It's interesting watching you. Can Meg Koranda survive on nothing but her wits? That's the real challenge for you, isn't it?"

He wasn't exactly right, but he wasn't entirely wrong, either. "What do you know? You're the all-American success story in reverse. Raised by rich parents and brought up with all the advantages. You should have ended up as spoiled as me, but you didn't."

"You're not spoiled, Meg. Stop saying that about yourself."

Once again he'd unbalanced her. She stared at a row of reference books. "What do you know? You've never screwed up in your life."

"You're wrong there. When I was a kid, I vandalized the Statue of Liberty."

"You and a Magic Marker. Big deal." She ran her thumb down the spine of a dictionary.

"Oh, it was worse than that. I climbed into the crown, broke a window, and tossed out a No Nukes banner."

That shocked her so much she finally turned to face him. "Lucy never told me about that."

"Didn't she?" He tilted his head so she couldn't quite see into his eyes. "I guess we never got around to talking about it."

"How could you not have talked about something so important?"

He shrugged. "Other things on our minds."

"The experience must have been at least a little traumatic."

His expression relaxed, and he smiled. "It was the worst moment of my childhood. And the best."

"How could it have been the best? Surely you got caught?"

"Oh, yes." He gazed at the English landscape hanging over the fireplace. "I didn't meet my father until I was nine—long story—and when we did meet, it didn't go well. He expected something else in a kid, and I expected a different kind of father. We were both pretty miserable. Until that day at the Statue of Liberty."

"What happened?"

He smiled again. "I learned I could count on him. That changed both our lives, and from then on, nothing was the same between us."

Maybe it was the wine. The fact that they were both tired from a long day and the strain of dealing with Spence and Sunny. All she knew was that they were staring into each other's eyes one moment, and the next, for no discernible reason, they both moved, and their bodies touched. She tilted her chin and he lowered his head, his eyelids dropped, and just like that, they were kissing.

She was so shocked that her arm flew up and banged him in the elbow, but her clumsiness didn't stop either of them. He cupped her face in his hands and tilted her head to exactly the right angle. She was too curious and too turned on to pull away.

He tasted good, like beer and bubble gum. His thumb slid into the tender place behind her earlobe while his other hand tunneled into her curls. No doubt about it. She was on the receiving end of one of the best kisses of her life. Not too hard. Not too soft. Slow and perfect. But of course it was perfect. He was Ted Beaudine, and he did everything impeccably.

She didn't remember putting her arms around his shoulders, but there they were, and as his silver tongue worked its magic against her own, she melted.

He eased away first. Her eyelids fluttered, and as she gazed up, she met a look of shock that must have matched her own. Something had happened. Something unexpected. And neither of them was happy about it. Slowly he released her.

She heard a noise. He straightened. Sanity returned. She hooked a piece of hair behind her ear and turned to see Sunny Skipjack standing inside the French doors, hand at her throat, her customary self-confidence crumpling. Meg had no idea whether the kiss had been the same impulsive act for Ted that it had been for her or whether he'd known Sunny was standing there all along and recklessly initiated the kiss to discourage her. Either way, he regretted it, something that was as clear as the trembling in her knees. He was tired, his defenses had been down for once, and he knew he'd just screwed up royally.

Sunny struggled for composure. "One of life's awkward moments," she said.

If Sunny bolted because of this, the people of Wynette would sure enough blame Meg, and she had enough problems without that. As she gazed up at Ted, she reassembled her features into a portrait of a damsel in distress. "I'm sorry, Ted. I know I can't keep throwing myself at you like this. I understand how uncomfortable it makes you. But you're just so . . . so . . . frickin' irresistible."

One dark eyebrow shot up.

She looked over at Sunny, girlfriend to girlfriend. "Too much wine. I swear it won't happen again." And then, because she was only human, "He's so vulnerable now. So sweet and helpless from the mess with Lucy. I took advantage."

"I'm not vulnerable or helpless," he said tightly.

She pressed her index finger to his lips. "An open wound." With the dignity of a brave woman suffering from unrequited love, she edged past Sunny and headed for the patio, where she reclaimed her purse and set off for what currently passed as her home.

SHE'D JUST WASHED HER FACE and slipped the HAPPY PRINTING COMPANY T-shirt over her head when she heard a car outside. A random Texas serial killer could have just shown up, but she was putting her money on Sunny Skipjack. She took her time hanging the Modigliani dress in the old choir robe closet, then let herself out the door by the altar into the main section of the church.

She was wrong about Sunny.

"You forgot your party favor," Ted said.

She didn't like the heady rush she felt at the sight of him standing at the rear of the sanctuary holding up a wooden paddleball stenciled with an American flag. "Shelby had a basket of patriotic yoyos, too, but I figured you'd like a paddle better. Or maybe that was just me projecting what I thought you needed." He slapped the paddle hard against his hand.

Although her HAPPY PRINTING COMPANY T-shirt hung over her hips, she wore only an ivory thong beneath. She needed more clothes, like chain mail and a chastity belt. He took a few swipes at the rubber ball with the paddle and sauntered forward, his eyes all over her. "Thanks for helping me out back there with Sunny, although I could have done without your commentary."

She eyed the paddle and then him. "You brought it on yourself. You shouldn't have kissed me."

His brow knit with phony indignation. "What are you talking about? You're the one who kissed me."

"I did not. You were all over me."

"In your dreams." He gave the paddleball an extra-hard slap. She cocked her head. "If you break a window with that thing, I'm reporting you to my landlord."

He caught the ball, gazed at what he could see of her bottom, and ran his thumb along the curve of the paddle. "The strangest idea just came into my head." The high ceiling fan ruffled his hair. Once again, he slapped the paddle against his palm. "I'd tell you about it, but it'd only make you mad."

Sex hung in the air between them as explosive as the evening's fireworks. Regardless of who had initiated their kiss, something had irrevocably shifted between them, and they both knew it.

So much for playing games. Although nothing was more repugnant to her than becoming another of Ted Beaudine's sexual conquests, the idea of making him one of her sexual conquests was worth pondering. "You can have any woman in this town. Probably in the whole state. Leave me alone."

"Why?"

"What do you mean, why? Because you've treated me like crap ever since I got here."

"Wrong. I was perfectly nice to you at the rehearsal dinner. I didn't start treating you like crap until after Lucy ran off."

"Which wasn't my fault. Admit it."

"I don't want to. I might have to blame myself, and who needs that?"

"You do. Although, to be fair, Lucy should have figured it out before things went so far."

He gave the paddleball a couple of whacks. "What else have you got on your grievance list?"

"You forced me to go work for Birdie Kittle."

He dropped the paddle on the brown chair, as if the temptation to use it was becoming too strong to resist. "It kept you out of jail, didn't it?"

"And you made sure I was paid less than the other maids."

He played dumb. "I don't remember that."

She nursed all the injustices. "That day at the inn, when I was cleaning . . . You stood in the doorway and watched me nearly kill myself trying to turn that mattress."

He grinned. "I have to admit, that was entertaining."

"Then, after lugging your bag of clubs for eighteen holes, you gave me a one-dollar tip."

She shouldn't have brought that up because he still held a grudge. "Three holes you cost me. And don't think I haven't noticed that all my new head covers are missing."

"You were my best friend's fiancé! And if that's not good enough, don't forget that I basically hate you."

He hit her full force with those golden brown eyes. "You basically like me, too. Not your fault. It just happened."

"I'm going to make it un-happen."

His voice turned to smoke. "Now why would you want to do that when we're both more than ready to take the next step? Which I highly recommend we do naked."

She swallowed. "I'm sure you'd like that, but maybe I'm not ready." Coyness wasn't her strong suit, and he looked disappointed in her for making the attempt. She threw up her hands. "Okay, so I'll admit I'm curious. Big deal. We both know what that leads to. Dead cat."

He smiled. "Or one hell of a lot of fun."

She hated that she was seriously thinking about going ahead with this. "I'm not seriously thinking about going ahead with this," she said, "but if I were, I'd have a ton of conditions."

"Such as?"

"This would only be about sex—no cute pet names, no nighttime confidences. No"—she wrinkled her nose at the idea—"friendship."

"We already have a kind of friendship."

"Only in your twisted mind because you can't stand the idea that you're not friends with everybody on the planet."

"I don't see what's wrong with that."

"It's impossible, that's what's wrong with it. If this went any further, you could never tell anybody about us. I mean it. Wynette is the gossip capital of the world, and I have enough trouble on my plate. We'd have to sneak around. In public, you'd need to keep on pretending to hate me."

His eyes narrowed. "I can handle that easy."

"And don't even think of using me to discourage Sunny Skipjack."

"Subject to discussion. That woman scares the hell out of me."

"She doesn't scare you at all. You just don't want to deal with her."

"Is that all?"

"No. I'd need to talk to Lucy first."

That caught him by surprise. "Why would you have to do that?"

"A question that once again proves how little you know me."

He reached in his pocket, pulled out his cell, and tossed it to her. "Go for it."

She tossed it right back. "I'll use my own."

He pocketed his phone and waited.

"Not now," she said, starting to feel more frazzled than she wanted to be.

"Now," he said. "You just told me it's a precondition."

She should kick him out, but she wanted him too much, and she was predestined to make bad choices when it came to men, which was why her female friendships had always been so important. She shot him a dirty look, the closest she could get to a face-saving gesture, and stomped toward the kitchen, where she banged the door behind her. As she grabbed her cell, she told herself she'd take it as a sign if Lucy didn't answer.

But Lucy answered. "Meg? What's up?"

She sank down on the linoleum and pressed her spine to the refrigerator door. "Hey, Luce. I hope I didn't wake you up." She unstuck a Cheerio she'd dropped that morning, or possibly last week, and crumbled it between her fingers. "So how's it going?"

"It's one in the morning. How do you think it's going?"

"Really? It's only midnight here, but since I have *no idea* where you are, it's a little tough to allow for time differences."

Meg regretted her testiness as Lucy sighed. "It won't be much longer. I'll . . . tell you as soon as I can. Right now everything's a little . . . confusing. Is something wrong? You sound worried."

"Something's wrong, all right." There was no easy way to say this. "What would you think about—" She pulled her knees tighter against her chest and took a deep breath. "What would you think about me hooking up with Ted?"

There was a long silence. "Hooking up? As in—?"

"Yes."

"With Ted?"

"Your former fiancé."

"I know who he is. You and Ted are a . . . couple?"

"No!" Meg dropped her knees to the floor. "No, not a couple. Never. This is just about sex. And forget it. I'm not exactly thinking clearly right now. I should never have called. God, what was I thinking? This is a total betrayal of our friendship. I shouldn't have—"

"No! No, I'm glad you called." Lucy actually sounded excited. "Oh, Meg, this is perfect. Every woman should have Ted Beaudine make love to her."

"I don't know about that, but—" She pulled her knees back up. "Really? You wouldn't mind?"

"Are you kidding?" Lucy sounded almost giddy. "Do you know how guilty I still feel? If he sleeps with you . . . You're my best friend. He'd be sleeping with my best friend! It'll be like getting absolution from the pope!"

"You don't have to sound so broken up about it."

The door opened. Meg quickly lowered her knees as Ted ambled in. "Tell Lucy hello from me," he said.

"I'm not your messenger boy," she retorted.

"Is he there right now?" Lucy asked.

"That would be a yes," Meg replied.

"Tell him hello from me, then." Lucy's voice grew small again, full of guilt. "And that I'm sorry."

Meg cupped her hand over the phone and gazed up at him. "She said she's having the time of her life, screwing every man she meets, and dumping you was the best move she ever made."

"I heard that," Lucy said. "And he'll know you're lying. He knows things like that."

Ted rested the heel of his hand against a top cabinet and slanted her his superior look. "Liar."

She glowered at him. "Go away. You are totally creeping me out."

Lucy sucked in her breath. "Did you just tell Ted Beaudine that he was creeping you out?"

"I might have."

Lucy let out a long exhalation. "Wow . . ." She sounded a little dazed. "I sure didn't see this coming."

Meg frowned. "See what coming? What are you talking about?"

"Nothing. Love you. And enjoy!" She hung up.

Meg snapped her phone closed. "I think we can safely assume Lucy's recovered from her guilt."

"Does that mean she gave us her blessing?"

"Me. She gave me her blessing."

He adopted a faraway look. "I sure do miss that woman. Smart. Funny. Sweet. She never gave me a moment's trouble."

"Gosh, I'm sorry about that. I knew it was boring between you two, but not that bad."

He smiled and stretched out his hand. She let him pull her to her feet, but he didn't stop there. In one smooth motion, he drew her against him and began kissing the breath right out of her. Because of their height, their bodies were a surprisingly comfortable fit, but that was the only comfortable thing about this lusty, bone-shattering kiss.

He smelled so good, tasted so good, felt so good. The heat of his skin, the feel of sturdy muscle and hard tendon. It had been so long.

He didn't grab her ass or shove his hand under her shirt where he would quickly have discovered lots of bare skin bisected only by that fragile ivory thong. Instead, he concentrated on her mouth, her face, her hair—stroking and exploring, sliding his fingers through her curls, finding her earlobes with his thumbs. It was as if he'd memorized a diagram of all the nonobvious erogenous zones on her body. It was heady and thrilling and oh so arousing.

Their mouths parted. He pressed his forehead to hers and spoke softly. "I'd like to go to my place, but I'm not risking having you change your mind on the way, so it'll have to be here." A nibble at her bottom lip. "Doubt it'll be the first time two people have got it on in that choir loft, although I thought my days of getting sweaty on a futon had ended when I graduated from college."

She tried to get her breath back as he caught her wrist and drew her out into the church. "Stop." Her heels skidded on the old pine floor. "We're not taking another step toward that futon until we have The Conversation."

He wasn't dumb. He groaned, but he stopped walking. "I'm disease free. There's been nobody since Lucy, and since that was four fricking months ago, you'll have to understand if I'm a little impatient."

"Nobody since Lucy? Really?"

"What part of four fricking months don't you get?" He regarded her stubbornly, as if he expected a fight. "And I don't go anywhere without a condom. You can make whatever you want out of that. It's just the way it is."

"You being Ted Beaudine and all."

"Like I said."

"Four months, huh? It hasn't been nearly that long for me." A lie. Her disastrous affair with Daniel, the Aussie river-rafting guide, had ended eight months ago. She'd never indulged in one-night stands, something she attributed to the conversations her mother had initiated about sex. Unfortunately, those conversations hadn't kept her from making some bad choices. More than one of her friends had said Meg deliberately chose men she knew would never commit because she wasn't ready to be a grown-up herself.

"I also am disease free," she said loftily, "and I'm on the pill. Don't let that stop you, however, from using one of those condoms you undoubtedly purchase by the gross. Since this is Texas, land of the barely concealed weapon, if I got pregnant, I would locate one of those weapons and blow your brains out. Fair warning."

"Good. We're clear." He caught her wrist and dragged her up the winding choir loft steps, not that he had to do much dragging.

"I also don't do one-night stands," she said when they reached the top. "So consider this the beginning of a short-term sexual commitment."

"Even better." He whipped off his T-shirt.

"And you can't let me get fired from the club."

He stopped. "Hold on. I want to get you fired."

"I know," she said, "but you want uncomplicated sex more."

"Good point." He dropped the T-shirt.

Before she knew it, they were on the lumpy futon and he was kissing her again. His hands curled around the bare cheeks of her bottom, and a thumb slid into the top of the silky floss that rode in her crack. "I pretty much enjoy it all when it comes to sex." His erection pressed hard against her leg. "You be sure to let me know if I do anything that scares you."

The blood supply that normally fed her brain had surged to other parts of her body, so she had no idea whether he was putting her on or not. "You worry about yourself" was the best she could do.

He played with the floss for a long, heated moment, then withdrew his thumb to drag it over her dragon tattoo. Although she loved the fantasy of having a man slowly undress her, she'd never known one of them who did it really well, and she wasn't giving Ted a chance to be the first. Sitting up on the narrow space beside him, she leaned back on her heels and pulled her T-shirt over her head.

In the age of silicone-enhanced breasts, hers weren't particularly memorable, but Ted was too much of a gentleman to criticize. He paid attention, but he didn't make any clumsy grabs. Instead, he curled his fingers around her rib cage, pulled himself up using only his spectacular abs, and bestowed a slow trail of kisses across her midriff.

Her skin pebbled. It was time to get serious. She was naked except for her thong, but he still wore his khaki shorts along with whatever was or wasn't underneath. She tugged the fastener to find out.

"Not yet," he whispered, pulling her down next to him. "Let's get you warmed up first."

Warmed up? She was ready to ignite!

He rolled to his side and offered her body his complete attention. His gaze lingered on the hollow at the base of her throat. The curve of her breast. The pucker of her nipple. The patch of ivory lace below her belly. But he didn't touch any of it. Any of her.

She arched her back, inviting him to get to it before she went up in flames. He dipped his head toward her breast. She closed her eyes in anticipation only to feel his teeth nip at her shoulder. Had the man never studied basic female anatomy?

It went on like that for a while. He investigated the sensitive spot at the inside of her elbow, the pulse point at her wrist, and the bottom curve of her breast. But only the bottom curve. By the time he touched the soft skin of her inner thigh, she was quivering with desire and fed up with his torture. But when she rolled over to take control, he shifted his weight, deepened his kisses, and somehow she was once again at his mercy. How could a man who'd gone four months without sex be so restrained? It was as if he weren't human. As if he'd used his genius inventor skills to create some kind of sexual avatar.

With the world's largest erection.

The exquisite torture went on, his caresses never quite reaching where she so desperately needed them to be. She tried not to moan, but the sounds slipped out. This was his revenge. He was going to foreplay her to death.

She didn't realize she'd reached for herself until he caught her hand. "I'm afraid I can't allow that."

"Allow it?" With lust-fueled strength, she twisted out from under him, threw one leg across his hips, and yanked at the snap on his shorts. "Put up or shut up."

He trapped her wrists. "These stay on until I take them off."

"Why? Are you afraid I'll laugh?"

His thick hair was rumpled from where she must have dug her

fingers into it, his bottom lip a little swollen from where she might possibly have bitten it, his expression vaguely regretful. "I didn't want to have to do this yet, but you're leaving me no choice." He flipped her beneath him, pinioning her with his body, fastened his mouth on her nipple, and delivered the perfect suction, just this side of pain. At the same time, he slipped a finger under the thin strip of lace between her legs and then inside her. She groaned, pulled her heels high on the bed, and shattered.

As she lay helpless in the aftermath, his lips brushed her earlobe. "I thought you'd have a little more self-control. But I guess you did your best." She was dimly aware of a tug at her lace chastity belt, then the slide of his body down over hers. He caught her legs and parted them wide. His beard stubble brushed the inside of her thighs. And then his mouth covered her.

A second cataclysmic explosion claimed her, but even then he didn't enter her. Instead, he tortured, comforted, tortured again. By the time her third orgasm hit, she'd become his sexual rag doll.

He was finally naked, and when he entered her, he did it slowly, giving her time to accept him, finding the perfect angle, nothing clumsy, no groping, no accidental finger scratch or elbow jab. He delivered a steady angled stroke followed by a hard thrust, flawlessly orchestrated, designed to deliver maximum pleasure. She'd never experienced anything like it. It was as if her pleasure was all that counted. Even as he came, he supported his weight so she didn't have to bear all of it.

She slept. They woke, made love again, and then once more. Sometime during the night, he drew the sheet over her, brushed her lips with a kiss, and left.

She didn't fall back to sleep right away. Instead, she thought about what Lucy had said. *Every woman should have Ted Beaudine make love to her.*

Meg couldn't argue with that. She'd never been loved so thoroughly, so unselfishly. It was as if he'd memorized all the sex manuals ever written—something, she realized, he was perfectly capable of having done. No wonder he was a legend. He knew exactly how to drive a woman to her maximum sexual pleasure.

So why was she so disappointed?

chapter twelve

THE CLUB WAS CLOSED the next day because of the holiday, so Meg did her laundry, then headed out to the cemetery to attack weeds with a couple of rusty tools she'd found near what was left of the storage shed. As she cleared some of the oldest headstones, she tried not to obsess too much about Ted, and when her cell rang, she didn't even take his call, although she couldn't resist listening to his message. An invitation to dinner Friday night at the Roustabout. Since Sunny and Spence would undoubtedly be part of their dining party, she didn't return the call.

She should have known it wouldn't be that easy to discourage him. Around three, he pulled up in his powder blue truck. Considering the way the town's females primped for him, she was happy with her dirt-streaked arms, bare legs, and the tight-fitting Longhorns T-shirt she'd rescued from the trash bin in the ladies' locker room, then modified by chopping off its sleeves and neckband. All in all, she looked just the way she wanted to.

As he stepped out of the cab, a couple of indigo buntings perched in the box elders burst into joyous song. She shook her head in disbelief. He wore a baseball cap and another in his seemingly endless wardrobe of broken-in shorts—these were tan chinos—along with an equally broken-in green T-shirt sporting a faded Hawaiian print. How did he manage to make whatever haphazard piece of crap he'd tossed on that morning look like high fashion?

The memory of last night intruded, all those embarrassing moans and humiliating demands. To compensate, she came out swinging. "If you're not planning to take off your clothes, you're dead to me."

"You California women are too damned aggressive." He gestured toward the cemetery. "I send a maintenance crew out here once a month to clean up. You don't have to do that."

"I like being outside."

"For a spoiled Hollywood brat, you have some unusual ways of entertaining yourself."

"It beats hauling your clubs around." She pulled off her baseball cap and swiped at her sweaty forehead with the back of a grimy arm. Her messy curls fell in her eyes and stuck to the back of her neck. She needed a haircut, but she didn't want to part with the money. "I'm not going to the Roustabout with you on Friday. Too many Skipjacks." She slammed her cap back on. "Besides, the less time we spend together in public, the better."

"I never said they'd be there."

"You didn't say they wouldn't, either, and I've had more than enough of them both." She was hot, cranky, and determined to be disagreeable. "Be honest, Ted. This whole thing with the golf resort . . . Do you really want to let the Skipjacks ruin another natural area just so more idiots can knock around a stupid white ball? You already have the country club. Isn't that enough? I know about the benefits to the local economy, but don't you think somebody, like maybe the mayor, should think about the long-term impact?"

"You're getting to be a real pain in the ass."

"As opposed to being an ass-kisser?"

She'd genuinely angered him, and he stalked back to his truck. But instead of tearing off in a huff, he jerked open the passenger door. "Get in."

"I'm not exactly dressed for an outing."

"The only person you'll see is me, which is a good thing, because you look like hell and I'm guessing you smell worse."

She was glad he'd noticed. "Is your truck air-conditioned?"

"Find out for yourself."

She wasn't going to pass up a mystery outing so she could hang around here pulling weeds. Still, she took her time meandering toward the truck. As she climbed inside, she noticed a missing dashboard, some odd-looking controls, and a couple of circuit boards mounted in what had once been a glove compartment.

"Don't touch those wires," he said as he slid behind the wheel, "unless you want to get electrocuted."

Naturally, she touched them, which made him surly. "I might have been telling the truth," he said. "You didn't know for sure."

"I like living on the edge. It's a California thing. Besides, I've noticed that 'truth' is a flexible word around here." As he slammed the door, she poked a grimy fingernail toward a series of dials near the steering wheel. "What are those?"

"Controls for a solar-powered air-conditioning system that doesn't work like I want it to."

"Great," she grumbled. "That's just great." As he pulled away from the church, she inspected a small screen set between the seats. "What's this?"

"The prototype for a new kind of navigation system. It's not working right, either, so keep your mitts off it, too."

"Is there anything in this truck that does work?"

"I'm pretty happy with my latest hydrogen fuel cell."

"Solar-powered air-conditioning, navigation systems, hydrogen fuel cells . . . You really have earned your geek blue ribbon."

"You sure are jealous of productive people."

"Only because I'm mortal and therefore subject to normal human emotions. Never mind. You wouldn't understand what that means."

He smiled and turned out onto the highway.

He was right. The solar air-conditioning system didn't work very well, but it worked well enough to keep the truck's cab cooler than the blistering outside temperature. They drove along the river for a few miles without talking. A vineyard gave way to a field of lavender. She tried not to think about the way she'd let him turn her into a gooey mess of moaning need.

He took a sharp left onto a narrow road paved in crumbling asphalt. They bumped past some rocky scrub and rounded a limestone bluff before the landscape opened into an expansive, treeless mesa that rose unnaturally about ten stories higher than the surrounding area. He turned off the ignition and climbed out of the truck. She followed him. "What is this? It looks weird."

He hooked his thumbs in his back pockets. "You should have seen it five years ago before they capped it."

"What do you mean 'capped it'?"

He nodded toward a rusted sign she hadn't noticed. It hung crookedly between a set of weathered metal posts not far from some abandoned tires. INDIAN GRASS SOLID WASTE LANDFILL. She gazed out over the weeds and scrub. "This was the town dump?"

"Also known as that unspoiled natural area you're so worried about protecting from development. And it's not a dump. It's a landfill."

"Same thing."

"Not at all." He launched into a brief but impressive lecture about compacted clay liners, geotextile mats, leachate collection systems, and all the other features that distinguished old-fashioned dumps from modern landfills. It shouldn't have been interesting, and it probably wouldn't have been to most people, but this was the kind of thing she'd been studying when she'd dropped out of college her senior year. Or maybe she just wanted to watch the play of expressions on his face and the way his brown hair curled around the edge of his baseball cap.

He gestured toward the open space. "For decades, the county leased this land from the city. Then two years ago the landfill hit capacity and had to be closed permanently. That left us with lost revenue and a hundred and fifty acres of degraded land, plus another hundred acres of buffer. Degraded land, in case you haven't already figured it out, is land that's not good for much of anything."

"Except a golf course?"

"Or a ski resort, which isn't too practical in central Texas. If a golf course is done right it can offer a lot of natural advantages as a wildlife sanctuary. It'll also support native plants and improve air quality. It can even moderate temperature. Golf courses can be about more than idiots chasing balls."

She should have known someone as smart as Ted would have thought about all this, and she felt a little stupid for having been so self-righteous.

He pointed toward some pipes coming out of the ground. "Landfills give off methane, so that has to be monitored. But methane can be captured and used to generate electricity, which we plan to do."

She gazed up at him from beneath the bill of her baseball cap. "It all sounds a little too good."

"This is the golf course of the future. We can't afford to build any more Augusta Nationals, that's for damn sure. Courses like that are dinosaurs, with their overtreated fairways you can eat off of and manicured roughs sucking up water."

"Has Spence bought into any of this?"

"Let's just say that once I started outlining the publicity value of building a truly environmentally sensitive golf course—how important it would make him, and not just in the golfing world—he got very interested."

She had to admit it was a brilliant strategy. Being heralded as an environmental trailblazer would be fertilizer to Spence's huge ego. "But I've never heard Spence mention any of this."

"He was too busy looking at your breasts. Which are, by the way, definitely worth looking at."

"Yeah?" She leaned against the truck's fender, hips thrust slightly forward, shorts riding low on her hip bones, more than happy to buy a little time to think through what she'd just learned about Ted Beaudine.

"Yeah." He gave her his best crooked smile, which almost looked genuine.

"I'm all sweaty," she said.

"I don't care."

"Perfect." She wanted to shatter that cool confidence, rattle him like he rattled her, so she pulled off her cap, grabbed the ragged hem of her too-tight cropped T-shirt, and whipped it over her head. "I'm the answer to your hound-dog dreams, big boy. Sex without all the messy emotional crap you hate."

He took in the navy demi-bra that clung damply to her skin. "What man doesn't?"

"But you *really* hate it." She let her shirt drop to the ground. "You're an emotional-sidelines kind of guy. Not that I'm complaining about last night. Absolutely not." *Shut up,* she told herself. *Just shut up.*

One eyebrow arched ever so slightly. "Then why does it sound that way?"

"Does it? Sorry. You are who you are. Take off your pants."

"No."

She'd sidetracked him with her big mouth. And, really, what did she have to complain about? "I've never known a guy so anxious to keep his clothes on. What's with you, anyway?"

The man who was never defensive lashed out. "Do you have a problem with last night that I'm not aware of? You weren't *satisfied*?"

"How could I not have been satisfied? You should market what you know about the female body. I swear you took me on that rocket ride to the stars at least three times."

"Six."

He'd been counting. She wasn't surprised. But she *was* crazy. Why else would she insult the only lover she'd ever known who cared more about her pleasure than his own? She needed to see a therapist.

"Six?" She quickly reached behind her back and unfastened her bra. Holding her hands over the cups, she let the straps slip down her shoulders. "Then you'd better take it easy on me today."

Lust trumped his indignation. "Or maybe I just need to take a little more time with you."

"Oh, God, no." She groaned.

But she'd challenged his legendary lovemaking skills, and a look of grim determination had settled over his features. With one long stride, he covered the distance remaining between them. The next thing she knew, her bra was on the ground and her breasts were in his hands. There, on the perimeter of the landfill, with decades of garbage decomposing in compacted cells, with methane meters sniffing the air and toxic leachate trickling through underground pipes, Ted Beaudine pulled out all the stops.

Not even last night's slow torture could have prepared her for to-day's meticulously calculated torment. She should have known better than to have even hinted that she wasn't completely satisfied, because now he was determined to make her eat her words. He bit the dragon on her bottom as he leaned down to pull off her shorts and panties. He bent her and turned her. He stroked, caressed, and explored with his deft inventor's fingers. Once again, she was at his mercy. She'd need shackles and handcuffs if she ever intended to take over control from this man.

While the hot Texas sun beat down on them, his clothes disap-peared. Sweat slicked his back, and twin furrows creased his forehead as he ignored the urgent demands of his own body to earn an A-plus in inciting hers. She wanted to scream at him to let go and enjoy, but she was too busy screaming her other demands.

He threw open the door of the cab, lifted her limp body onto the seat, and propped her legs wide. Keeping his own feet on the ground, he toyed and tormented, using his fingers as sweet weapons of inva-sion. Naturally, one orgasm wasn't good enough for him, and when she shattered, he pulled her from the cab and pressed her front-first against the side of the truck. The heated metal acted like a sex toy against her already provoked nipples as he played with her from behind. Finally, he turned her and started all over again.

By the time he entered her, she'd lost count of her orgasms, al-though she was sure he hadn't. He held her against the side of the truck with seeming ease, her legs wrapped around his waist, her bottom in the palms of his hands. Supporting her weight couldn't have been comfortable for him, but he showed no signs of strain.

His strokes were deep and controlled, her comfort paramount, even as he arched his neck, turned his face to the sun, and found his own release.

WHAT MORE COULD ANY WOMAN want in a lover? All the way back home, she asked herself that question. He was spontaneous, generous, inventive. He had a great body, and he smelled fantastic. He was absolutely perfect. Except for that emotional hole inside him.

He'd been prepared to marry Lucy and spend the rest of his life with her, but her desertion didn't seem to have made even a ripple in his daily existence. Something to remember if she ever found herself entertaining the vaguest notion of a more permanent future together. The only thing Ted felt deeply was his sense of responsibility.

As he turned into the lane that led to the church, he started fiddling with one of the truck's mystery controls. She suspected he was waiting for his report card as a lover, and how could she give him anything but an A-plus? Her lingering disappointment was her problem, not his. Only a total bitch would dump on a guy who did everything—almost everything—right.

"You're a great lover, Ted. Really." She smiled, meaning every word.

He glanced over at her, his expression stony. "Why would you tell me that?"

"I don't want you to think I'm ungrateful."

She should have kept her mouth shut because golden storm signals flashed in his eyes. "I don't need your damned gratitude."

"I just meant . . . It was amazing." But she was only making things worse, and the way his knuckles tightened on the worn steering wheel proved that all those people who claimed nothing ever upset Ted Beaudine clearly didn't know what they were talking about.

"I was there, remember?" His words were metal shards.

"Absolutely," she said. "How could I forget?"

He slammed on his brakes. "What the hell is wrong with you?"

"I'm just tired. Forget I said anything."

"I damned sure will." He reached across her and shoved open the passenger door.

Since her attempt to be conciliatory had failed dismally, she reverted to her true personality. "I'm taking a shower, and you're not invited in. As a matter of fact, don't ever touch me again."

"Why would I want to?" he shot back. "Some women are too damned much trouble."

She sighed, more disgusted with herself than with him. "I know."

He pointed one long finger in the general direction of her head. "You'd better be ready at seven on Friday night because that's when I'm picking you up. And don't expect to see me before then because I have business in Santa Fe. And I'm not calling, either. I have more important things to do than argue with a crazy woman."

"Forget about Friday. I told you I didn't want to spend any more time with the Skipjacks . . . or with you." She hopped out of the truck, but her still wobbly legs gave her an awkward landing.

"You tell me a lot of bullshit," he retorted. "I've yet to pay attention to any of it." He slammed the door in her face, the ignition roared, and he was off in a cloud of stardust.

She recovered her balance and turned to the steps. They both knew she'd rather spend an evening with the Skipjacks than stare at the walls of her too-silent church. And despite what they'd each just said, they both also knew this affair was far from over.

THE NEXT TWO DAYS WERE busy ones at the club. Word of Spence's infatuation with her had spread since Shelby's party, and her tips picked up as the golfers realized she might influence the plumbing king. Even Kayla's father, Bruce, slipped her a dollar. She thanked them for their generosity and reminded them to recycle their bottles and cans. They told her she was welcome and reminded her that people were watching her every move.

On Thursday, the boxes she'd asked her parents' housekeeper to pack up arrived from L.A. She traveled too much to have an elaborate wardrobe, and she also tended to give things away, but she needed her shoes. Even more important, she needed the big plastic bin that contained the spoils of her travels—the beads, amulets, and coins, many of them antiquities, that she'd picked up all over the world.

Ted didn't call from Santa Fe, but she hadn't expected him to. Still, she missed seeing him, and her heart gave a crazy little hiccup when he and Kenny stopped at her cart on Friday afternoon midway through their round. Kenny told her Spence and Sunny had just gotten back from Indianapolis and they'd be at the Roustabout that night for dinner. She told Ted she'd drive herself, so he needn't pick her up. He didn't like that, but he also didn't want an argument in front of Kenny, so he sauntered over to the ball washer, jammed in his pristine Titleist Pro V1, and pumped the handle far more vigorously than he needed to.

As he teed off, the morning sunlight washed him in gold, but at least the birds stayed quiet. Did he ever lose control? She tried to imagine a dark turbulence roiling beneath his easy polish. Occasionally, she even thought she caught a glimpse of vulnerability when his lazy smile took a second too long to form or a flicker of weariness shadowed his eyes. But those impressions faded as quickly as they appeared, leaving his shiny surface intact.

MEG WAS THE LAST TO ARRIVE at the Roustabout. She'd chosen the black-and-white Miu Miu mini from the resale shop, along with an acid yellow tank and one of her favorite pair of shoes, elaborately beaded and embroidered pink canvas platform sandals. But as she made her way to the table, her resale skirt drew more attention than her fabulous shoes.

In addition to Ted and the Skipjacks, all the Travelers and their spouses had gathered around the big wooden table: Torie and Dexter, Emma and Kenny, Warren Traveler and Shelby. Sunny had positioned herself to Ted's right where she could better demand his undivided attention. As Meg approached, he took in her mini, then gave her a pointed look that she interpreted as a command to sit on his other side. She'd been more than clear about hiding their affair, and she wedged a chair between Torie and Shelby, directly across the table from Emma.

The easy affection between Torie, Emma, and Shelby made her miss her own friends. Where was Lucy now and how was she getting along? As for the others . . . She'd been dodging phone calls from Georgie, April, and Sasha for weeks, unwilling to let any of her accomplished friends know how perilous her situation was, but since they were used to the way she dropped out of sight, her lack of response didn't seem to have raised any alarms.

The wily Traveler family flattered the Skipjacks outrageously. Shelby asked detailed questions about Viceroy's new product line, Torie lavished Sunny with compliments about her shiny dark hair and classic wardrobe choices, Kenny pointed out the strengths of Spence's putting game. The atmosphere was congenial, almost relaxing, right up to the moment Meg made the mistake of addressing Kenny's wife as "Emma."

One by one, all the locals at the table fell silent. "What did I do?" she said as they turned to stare at her. "She told me to call her Emma."

Emma grabbed her wineglass and drained it.

"It's just not done," Shelby Traveler replied, her mouth pinching with disapproval.

Emma's husband shook his head. "Never. Not even by me. At least not as long as she's got her clothes on."

"Bad manners," Torie added with a swish of her long dark hair.

"Disrespectful," her father, Warren, agreed.

Ted kicked back in his chair and regarded her gravely. "I'd have thought by now you'd know better than to insult somebody you barely know."

Emma slowly lowered her head and banged her forehead against the table three times.

Kenny rubbed his wife's back and smiled. Amusement danced in Ted's eyes.

Meg had distinctly heard both Sunny and Spence refer to Kenny's wife as Emma, but she knew it would be useless to point that out. "Deepest apologies, *Lady* Emma," she drawled. "I hope I get a last meal before the beheading."

Torie sniffed. "No need to be sarcastic."

Emma gazed across the table at Meg. "They can't help themselves. Really."

Her husband planted a satisfied kiss on his wife's lips, then returned to a discussion of Spence's new Callaway irons. Ted tried to join in, but Sunny wanted his full attention, and she knew how to get it. "What's the tank-to-wheel efficiency of your new fuel cell?"

Meg had no idea what that even meant, but Ted was his normal accommodating self. "Thirty-eight, forty-two percent, depending on the load."

Sunny, all rapt attention, moved in closer.

Spence invited Meg to dance, and before she could refuse, two sets of female hands grasped her arms and pushed her to her feet. "She thought you'd never ask," Shelby said sweetly.

"I sure wish Dex was as light on his feet as you are, Spence," Torie cooed.

Across the table, Emma looked as worried as someone in a sunflower-splashed yellow top could look, and Meg swore she caught the shadow of a frown cross Ted's face.

Fortunately, the first song was up-tempo, and Spence made no attempt to engage her in conversation. Too soon, however, Kenny Chesney began to croon "All I Need to Know," and Spence drew her close. He was too old for the cologne he'd chosen, and she felt as though she'd been enveloped by an Abercrombie & Fitch store. "You're making me more than a little crazy, Miz Meg."

"I don't want to make anybody crazy," she said carefully. *Except Ted Beaudine.*

Out of the corner of her eye, she saw Birdie, Kayla, and Zoey settle at a table near the bar. Kayla looked sexy in a tight, one-shoulder white top that hugged her breasts without being slutty and a tropical print mini that set off her shapely legs. Birdie and Zoey were more casually dressed, and all three watched Meg closely.

Spence curled his hand around hers and drew it to his chest. "Shelby and Torie told me about you and Ted."

Her internal alarm rang. "What exactly did they say?"

"That you finally found your backbone and accepted the fact that Ted's not the man for you. I'm proud of you."

She lost a step as she silently cursed both women.

He squeezed her fingers, a gesture she assumed was meant to be comforting. "Sunny and I don't have any secrets. She told me about you throwing yourself at him at Shelby's party. I guess the way he rejected you finally woke you up to the truth, and I just want to say that I'm proud of you for facing it. You're going to feel a whole lot better about yourself, now that you've stopped chasing him. Shelby sure thinks so, and Torie said— Well, never mind what Torie said."

"Oh, no. Tell me. I'm sure it'll be good for my . . . personal growth."

"Well . . ." He rubbed her spine. "Torie said that when a woman obsesses over a man who's not interested in her, it kills her soul."

"Quite the philosopher."

"I was surprised myself. She seems a little flaky. She also told me you were planning to get my name tattooed on your ankle, which I don't believe." He hesitated. "It's not true, is it?"

When she shook her head, he looked disappointed. "Some of the people in this town are odd," he said. "Have you noticed that?"

They weren't odd at all. They were wily as foxes and twice as smart. She unlocked her rigid knees. "Now that you mention it."

Torie dragged her husband onto the dance floor and maneuvered as close to Spence and Meg as she could get, undoubtedly hoping to eavesdrop. Meg shot her a death ray and pulled away from Spence. "Excuse me. I need to use the restroom."

She'd barely gotten inside before Torie, Emma, and Shelby stormed in to confront her. Emma pointed toward the closest stall. "Go ahead. We'll wait for you."

"Don't bother." Meg whirled on Shelby and Torie. "Why did you tell Spence I wasn't in love with Ted anymore?"

"Because you never were." Shelby's brightly colored enameled bangles jingled at her wrist. "At least I don't think so. Although Ted being Ted . . ."

"And you being female . . ." Torie crossed her arms. "Still, it was obvious you made up the whole thing to avoid Spence, and we'd all have gone along with it if Sunny hadn't shown up."

The restroom door swung open, and Birdie came in, followed by Kayla and Zoey.

Meg threw up her hands. "Great. I'm going to get gang-raped."

"You shouldn't crack jokes about a serious issue like that," Zoey said. She wore white cropped pants, a navy T-shirt that read WYNETTE PUBLIC SCHOOLS HONOR ROLL, and earrings that looked like they'd been made from drinking straws.

"That's the way Hollywood people are," Birdie said. "They don't have the same moral compass as the rest of us." And then, to Shelby, "Did you tell her she has to leave Ted alone now that Sunny's fallen for him?"

"We're gettin' there," Shelby said.

Emma took command. It was remarkable how much authority a relatively small woman with baby-doll cheeks and a cheery cap of butterscotch curls could possess. "You mustn't think no one understands your situation. I was once an outsider in Wynette myself, so I—"

"You still are," Torie observed in a loud whisper.

Emma ignored her. "—so I'm not unsympathetic. I also know what it's like to have the attentions of a man to whom you're not attracted, although the Duke of Beddington was far more odious than Mr. Skipjack. Still, my unwelcome suitor didn't hold the economic fate of this town in his hands. But I also didn't try to use Ted to discourage him."

"You kind of did," Torie said. "But Ted was only twenty-two at the time, and Kenny saw through you."

Emma's wide mouth tightened at the corners, emphasizing her plump bottom lip. "Your presence has doubly complicated an already delicate situation, Meg. You obviously find Spence's attentions objectionable, and we understand that."

"I don't." Kayla adjusted the rimless Burberry sunglasses she'd pushed on top of her blond hair. "Do you have any idea how rich that man is? And he's got great hair."

"Unfortunately, your method of discouraging him involves Ted," Emma went on, "which might have been acceptable if Sunny hadn't appeared."

Birdie tugged on the hem of the silky tomato red top she wore with a cotton skirt. "Anybody with two eyes can see how crazy Spence is about his daughter. You might be able to get away with rejecting him, but you can't get away with throwing yourself at the man his baby girl is falling in love with."

Torie nodded. "What Sunny wants, Sunny gets."

"She's not going to get Ted," Meg said.

"Something Ted will make certain she doesn't figure out until the ink on the land deal is dry," Emma said briskly.

Meg had heard enough. "Here's a scary thought. What if your sainted mayor decides to toss you all to the wolves and fend for himself?"

Zoey pointed a principal's accusing finger toward her, a remarkably effective gesture for a woman who was only a year older than Meg herself. "This is a big joke to you, but it's not a joke to the kids at my school who are jammed into overcrowded classrooms. Or the teachers trying to make do with outdated textbooks and no aides."

"It sure isn't a joke to me." Kayla stole a surreptitious look at herself in the mirror. "I hate running a resale shop full of old-lady clothes, but right now there aren't more than a handful of women in this town who can afford to buy the kind of fashion I was destined to sell." Her eyes swept over Meg's resale skirt.

"I've been wanting to open a tearoom and bookstore next to the inn ever since I took over the place," Birdie said.

Shelby pushed her blond bob behind one ear, revealing small gold hoops. "I have a husband who barely sleeps at night for feeling guilty because his company can't provide enough jobs to keep the town afloat."

"Dex feels the same," Torie said. "A town this size can't survive on one industry."

Meg spun on Emma. "What about you? What reason do you have for expecting me to prostitute myself with Spencer Skipjack?"

"If this town dies," Emma said quietly, "Kenny and I have enough money to do just fine. Most of our friends don't."

Torie tapped the toe of a studded leather T-strap sandal on the floor. "Between Spence, Sunny, and Ted, you're making things too complicated, Meg. You need to leave Wynette. And unlike everybody else, I happen to like you a lot, so this isn't personal."

"I don't dislike you," Emma said.

"I do," Birdie said.

"I don't dislike you either," said Shelby. "You have a very nice laugh."

Kayla gestured toward the embellished skeleton-key necklace Meg had assembled a few hours earlier. "Zoey and I love your jewelry."

Birdie puffed up like an angry parakeet. "How can y'all say anything nice to her? Have you forgotten about Lucy? Thanks to Meg, Ted got his heart broken."

"He seems to have recovered," Emma said, "so I'm prepared to overlook that."

Shelby opened her purse, a pink and brown paisley Juicy clutch, and pulled out a folded piece of paper that Meg quickly realized was a check. "We know you're short on cash, so we have a little something to help you get a fresh start somewhere else."

For the first time since Meg had met her, Torie seemed embarrassed. "You can consider it a loan if it makes you uncomfortable."

"We'd appreciate it if you took it," Emma said kindly. "It'll be best for everybody."

Before Meg could tell them all to go to hell, the restroom door swung open and Sunny sauntered in. "Is there a party?"

Shelby quickly slipped the check back in her purse. "It didn't start out that way, but we got to talking."

"And now we need your opinion." Torie deliberately turned to the mirror and pretended to look for mascara smears. "Charlize Theron or Angelina Jolie? Which one would you go gay for?"

"I say Angelina Jolie." Kayla pulled out her lip gloss. "Seriously. Any woman who says she wouldn't is either a liar or in deep denial. That woman oozes sex."

"In your opinion." Zoey, who'd been so morally righteous earlier, began fussing with her hair. "I'd choose Kerry Washington. A strong black woman. Or Anne Hathaway. But only because she went to Vassar."

"You would not go gay for Anne Hathaway," Birdie protested. "Anne Hathaway's a great actress, but she's not your sexual type."

"Since I'm not gay, my sexual type isn't the point." Zoey grabbed Kayla's lip gloss. "I'm merely commenting that if I were gay, I'd want a partner with brains and talent, not just beauty."

Emma straightened her sunflower shirt. "I must admit that I find Keira Knightley oddly compelling."

Kayla retrieved her lip gloss. "You always go for the Brits."

"At least she got over her thing for Emma Thompson." Torie tugged a paper towel from the dispenser. "What about you, Meg?"

Meg was more than a little sick of being manipulated. "I prefer men. Specifically hunky Texas men. Do you have any ideas?"

All around her, she could hear mental wheels grinding as the crazy women of Wynette tried to figure out how to respond. She headed for the door and left them to ponder.

By the time she'd returned to the table, she'd reached three conclusions: Ted's problems with Sunny were his own to resolve. She would handle Spence on a day-by-day basis. And nobody was going to drive her out of this horrible town until she was good and ready to leave.

chapter thirteen

MEG SAW TED ON THE COURSE the next day, but he was playing with Spence and Sunny, and he steered clear of her drink cart. When she got home that evening, she found a delivery truck parked at her front steps waiting for her. Ten minutes later, she'd sent the truck, along with its load of furniture, on its way.

She stomped into the hot, airless church. People kept trying to give her things she didn't want. Last night Shelby had slipped the getaway check into her purse, leaving Meg to tear it up. And now this. Granted, she needed furniture, and when she'd spotted the portable air conditioners, she'd almost set aside her principles. Almost, but not quite.

She threw open the church windows, turned on the fans, and poured a glass of iced tea from the refrigerator. This was the second time in a week that somebody had tried to pay her to leave town. If she let herself think about it, she'd get depressed, and she didn't want to be depressed. She wanted to be angry. After a quick shower, she pulled on shorts, a tank, slipped into a pair of flip-flops, and set off.

Stone pillars marked the entrance to the Beaudine estate. She wound through a grove of hardwood trees and crossed an old stone bridge before the road branched into a series of meandering lanes. The main house was easy to identify—low and sprawling, built in the Texas hacienda style of limestone and stucco with arched windows and doors framed in dark wood. Behind a low wall, she glimpsed a spacious pool, pool house, courtyard, gardens, and two smaller buildings in the same hacienda style, probably guest cottages. This wasn't so much an estate, she realized, as a compound, and everywhere she looked, breathtaking views spread before her.

When the road circled back on itself, she chose another lane but found only a putting green and maintenance buildings. She tried again and came upon a small stone and brick ranch with Skeet Cooper's pickup visible inside the open garage door. Nothing like keeping your caddy close by.

The last lane wound uphill where it opened onto a rocky bluff. And there it stood, a modern structure of perfectly balanced cream stucco rectangles topped by a butterfly roof. Sweeping sheets of glass faced south, along with sharp overhangs to shade the interior. Even without the small, sleek wind turbines mounted on the roof, she would have known this was his house. Its beauty, inventiveness, and functionality spoke volumes about its owner.

The front door opened before she could ring the bell, and he stood before her barefoot in a black T-shirt and gray athletic shorts. "Did you enjoy your tour?"

Either someone had tipped him off or security cameras monitored the property. Knowing his love of gadgetry, she suspected the latter. "The mighty ruler of the Kingdom of Beaudine is indeed all-knowing."

"I do my best." He moved back to let her in.

The house was open and airy, decorated in pale shades of gray and white—a cool, calming retreat from the punishing summer heat and the equally punishing demands of being Ted Beaudine. The furniture sat low, each piece carefully chosen for both its comfort and quiet, unimposing beauty. The most startling feature was a glass-enclosed rectangular room suspended above the soaring living area.

The house was almost monastically spare. No sculptures stood in the corners; no paintings graced its walls. The art lay outside in the views of river bluffs, granite hills, and distant, shadowed valleys.

She'd grown up in grand houses—her family's rambling Connecticut farmhouse, their Bel Air home, the weekend house on Morro Bay—but this was something quite special. "Nice digs," she said.

As he crossed the bamboo floor, a foyer light that had come on when he'd admitted her automatically shut off. "If you've shown up for sex, I'm bored with you," he said.

"That would explain the large bed on the delivery truck, along with those comfy, man-size chairs."

"And the couch. Don't forget the couch. Not to hurt your feelings, but your place isn't too comfortable. And from the phone call I just got, I hear you want to keep it like that. Why did you send that truck away?"

"Did you really think I was going to take presents from you?"

"The furniture was for me, not you. I'll be damned if I spend another night on that futon."

"Good thing you're bored with me."

"I might change my mind. As a matter of fact—"

"It isn't your job to furnish my place," she said. "I'll do it when I get around to it. Although I have to admit you almost sucked me in with those air conditioners. Unfortunately, I've developed this totally asinine sense of personal pride."

"Your loss."

"You have enough people to take care of, Mr. Mayor. You don't have to take care of me, too."

She'd finally caught him off balance. He looked at her oddly. "That's not what I was doing."

"Oh, yes, you were." She did her best to contain the thread of tenderness unraveling inside her. "I came here to rip your head off, but this house seems to have sucked away most of my righteous indignation. Do you happen to have anything to eat?"

He tilted his head. "Back there."

The stunning stainless-steel kitchen wasn't large, but it was dauntingly efficient. A limousine-long central island began as a workspace, then seamlessly extended into a sleek table large enough for a dinner party, with four wire-back chairs pushed under it on each side. "I don't like dining rooms," he said. "I like to eat in the kitchen."

"I think you're onto something."

Forgetting her hunger, she wandered over to the room's most striking feature, another colossal sheet-glass wall, this one looking down upon the Pedernales Valley where the river ran like a blue-green ribbon over jagged limestone shelves. Beyond the valley, the setting sun outlined the purple hills in a tangerine blaze. "Extraordinary," she said. "You designed this house, didn't you?"

"It's an experiment in net zero energy."

"Meaning?"

"The house produces more energy than it consumes. Right now about forty percent. There are photovoltaic and solar panels in the roof, along with rainwater collection. I have a gray water system, geothermal heating and cooling machines, appliances with kill switches to keep them from drawing power in the off mode. Basically, I'm living off the grid."

Ted had made his fortune helping towns optimize electrical usage, so the house was a natural extension of his work, but it was still remarkable.

"We use too damned much power in this country." He pulled

open the refrigerator door. "I've got some leftover roast beef. Or there's stuff in the freezer."

She couldn't keep the wonder out of her voice. "Is there anything you can't do?"

He slammed the door and whipped around. "Apparently, I can't make love according to your specifications, whatever the hell they might be."

Once again, she'd inadvertently ventured into the killing zone. "I didn't mean to hurt your feelings."

"Yeah. Telling a guy he's a bust-out in the sack is guaranteed to make him feel great."

"You're not a bust-out. You're perfect. Even I know that."

"Then what the hell is your gripe?"

"Why do you care?" she said. "Did you ever think it might be my problem instead of yours?"

"You're damned right it's your problem. And I'm not perfect. I wish you'd quit saying that."

"True. You have an overdeveloped sense of responsibility, and you've gotten so good at hiding what you're really feeling that I doubt you even know what you feel anymore. Case in point. Your fiancée left you at the altar, and you barely seem to have noticed."

"Let me get this straight." He leveled his finger at her. "A woman who's never held a job, who has no direction, and whose own family seems to have given up on her—"

"They haven't given up on me. They're just—I don't know—taking a short break." She threw up her hands. "You're right. I'm jealous because you're everything I'm not."

Some of the wind went out of his sails. "You aren't jealous, and you know it."

"A little jealous. You don't show anyone what you feel. I show everything to everybody."

"Way too much."

She couldn't hold it back. "I just think you could be so much more."

He gaped at her. "You're driving a drink cart!"

"I know. And the sad thing is, I don't entirely hate it." With a snort of disgust, he reached for the refrigerator again. She gasped. Lunging forward, she grabbed his hands and stared at his palms. "Oh, my God. *Stigmata.*"

He snatched them away. "A marking-pen accident."

She clutched her heart. "Give me a second to get my breath back, and then show me the rest of the house."

He rubbed at the red smears on his palms and sounded sullen. "I should throw you out is what I should do."

"You don't have it in you."

He stalked from the kitchen, and she thought he might really do it, but when he reached the main living area, he turned away from the front door toward a floating staircase that led to the suspended, glass-walled room. She followed him up and entered his library.

It felt a little like walking into a well-appointed tree house. Walls of books surrounded a comfortable seating area. An open archway in the back wall led to a glass-enclosed walkway that connected this part of the house to a small, separate room constructed against the hillside. "Bomb shelter?" she asked. "Or safe zone to hide out from the ladies?"

"My office."

"Cool." She didn't wait for his permission but crossed the walkway. Twin panels of ceiling lights came on automatically as she went down two steps into a spare room with high windows; a massive computer workstation of tempered glass and black steel; several ergonomic chairs; and some sleek, built-in storage cabinets. The office was spare, almost sterile. All it revealed about its owner was his efficiency.

"No nudie calendars or I-Heart-Wynette coffee mugs?"

"I come here to work."

She retraced her steps and returned to the suspended library. "*The Chronicles of Narnia,*" she said, taking in a shelf of well-read children's classics. "I loved that series. And *Tales of a Fourth Grade Nothing*. I must have read it a dozen times."

"Peter and Fudge," he said, coming back into the room from behind her.

"I can't believe you held on to these."

"Hard to get rid of old friends."

Or any friends, for that matter. The whole world made up Ted's inner circle. Yet how close was he to any of them?

She surveyed his collection and found both literary and genre fiction, biographies, nonfiction on a head-spinning variety of topics, and technical volumes: texts on pollution and global warming; on plant biology, pesticide use, and public health; books about soil conservation and safe water; about creating natural habitats and preserving wetlands.

She felt ridiculous. "All my yammering about how golf courses are destroying the world. You've been on top of this from the beginning." She pulled a volume called *A New Ecology* from the shelf. "I remember this from my college reading list. Can I borrow it?"

"Go ahead." He sat on a low couch and crossed an ankle over his knee. "Lucy told me you dropped out your senior year, but she didn't tell me why."

"Too hard."

"Don't give me that."

She ran a hand over the book's cover. "I was restless. Stupid. I couldn't wait for my life to begin, and college felt like a waste of time." She didn't like the bitter edge to her words. "Your basic spoiled brat."

"Not exactly."

She didn't like the way he was looking at her. "Sure I was. Am."

"Hey. I was a rich kid, too, remember?"

"Right. You and Lucy. The same übersuccessful parents, the same advantages, and look how you two turned out."

"Only because we both found our passions early on," he said evenly.

"Yeah, well, I found mine, too. Bumming around the world having a good time."

He toyed with a pen he picked up from the floor. "A lot of young people do that while they're trying to figure things out. There isn't much of a road map for people like us, the ones who've grown up with high-achieving parents. Every kid wants to make his family proud, but when your parents are the best in the world at what they do, it's a little tough to pull off."

"You and Lucy did. So have my brothers. Even Clay. He's not making much money now, but he's amazingly talented, and he will."

He clicked the pen. "You can match every success story with one about a trust-fund baby living an aimless, club-hopping life between stints at rehab, something you seem to have avoided."

"True, but . . ." Her words, when she finally spoke them, sounded small and fragile. "I want to find my passion, too."

"Maybe you've been looking in the wrong place," he said quietly.

"You forget that I've been everywhere."

"Traveling around the world is a lot more fun than traveling around inside your own head, I guess." He discarded the pen and rose from the couch. "What makes you happy, Meg? That's the question you need to answer."

You make me happy. Looking at you. Listening to you. Watching the way your mind works. Kissing you. Touching you. Letting you touch me.

"Being outside," she retorted. "Wearing funky clothes. Collecting old beads and coins. Fighting with my brothers. Listening to birds. Smelling the air. Useful stuff like that."

Jesus wouldn't sneer, and neither did Ted. "Well, then. That's where your answer lies."

The conversation had gotten way too deep. She wanted to psychoanalyze him, not the other way around. She plopped on the couch he'd just vacated. "So how's that fabulous contest coming along?"

His expression darkened. "I don't know and I don't care."

"Last I heard, the bidding for your services had gone over seven thousand."

"Don't know. Don't care."

She'd successfully diverted the conversation away from her own defects, and she propped her feet on the footstool. "I saw yesterday's *USA Today* at the club. I can't believe how much national attention this thing has started to attract."

He grabbed a couple of books from a narrow table and shoved them back on the shelf.

"Great headline in their Life section." She sketched it out in the air. "'Jilted Jorik Fiancé for Sale to Highest Bidder.' They painted you as quite the philanthropist."

"Will you just shut up about it?" He actually snarled.

She smiled. "You and Sunny are going to have a great time in San Francisco. I highly recommend you take her to the de Young Museum." And then, before he could yell, "Can I see the rest of your house?"

Again that snarl. "Are you going to touch anything?"

She was only human, and as she rose, she let her eyes drift over him. "Definitely."

That one word blew the summer storm clouds from his eyes. He cocked his head. "Then how about I show you my bedroom first?"

"Okay."

He headed toward the door, then came to an abrupt stop and turned back to glare at her. "Are you going to critique?"

"I've just been in a mood, that's all. Ignore."

"I intend to," he said, with a healthy dose of malevolence.

His bedroom had a pair of soft, spare chairs for reading; lamps with curled metal shades; and high windows that admitted light but not the views the rest of the house afforded, which gave this room a deep sense of privacy. An ice gray duvet covered the platform bed—a duvet that hit the polished bamboo floor even faster than their clothes.

Right away she could tell he was determined to correct past mistakes, even though he had no idea what those mistakes were. She'd never been kissed so thoroughly, caressed so meticulously, stimulated so exquisitely. He seemed certain that all he needed to do was try a little harder. He even put up with her attempts to take over. But he was a man who served others, and his heart wasn't in it. All that mattered was her fulfillment, and he suspended his own satisfaction to deliver another pitch-perfect performance on her body. Carefully researched. Perfectly executed. Everything done by the book. Exactly as he'd made love to every other woman in his life.

But who was she to criticize when she brought so little added value to the process? This time she vowed to keep her opinions to herself, and when she could finally gather her thoughts, she rolled onto one elbow to face him.

He was still breathing hard, and who wouldn't be after what he'd gone through? She stroked his sweaty, deliciously un-manscaped chest and licked her lips. "Ohmigod, I saw stars!"

His eyebrows slammed together. "You're still not happy?"

His mind-reading tricks were getting out of hand. She manufactured a gasp. "Are you kidding? I'm delirious. The luckiest woman in the world."

He just stared at her.

She fell back into the pillows and moaned. "If I could only market you, I'd make a fortune. That's what I should do with my life. That should be my life's purpose, to—"

He threw himself out of bed. "Jesus, Meg! What the hell do you want?"

I want you to want me, not just to make me want you. But how could she say that without making herself look like another Beaudine groupie? "Now you're getting paranoid. And you still haven't fed me."

"I'm not going to either."

"Sure you are. Because that's what you do. You take care of people"

"Since when did that become a bad thing?"

"Never." She gave him a wobbly smile.

He stalked into the bathroom, and she lay back in the pillows. Ted not only cared about others, but he followed up on that caring with action. Instead of giving him a sense of entitlement, his agile, gifted brain had cursed him with the obligation to look after everyone and everything he cared about. He was almost certainly the best human being she'd ever met. And maybe the loneliest. It must be exhausting to carry such a heavy load. No wonder he hid so many of his feelings.

Or maybe she was rationalizing the emotional distance he kept from her. She didn't like knowing he treated her the same as he'd treated all his other conquests, although she couldn't imagine him being as rude to Lucy as he was with her.

She tossed back the sheet and climbed out of bed. Ted made everyone feel as though he shared a special relationship only with them. It was the biggest rabbit in his silk hat of tricks.

Spence and Sunny left Wynette with nothing settled. The town teetered between relief that they were gone and concern that they wouldn't come back, but Meg wasn't worried. As long as Sunny believed she had a shot at Ted, she'd be back.

Spence called Meg daily. He also sent a luxury tissue holder, a soap dish, and Viceroy Industries' finest towel bar. "I'll fly you out to L.A. this weekend," he said. "You can show me around, introduce me to your parents, some of their friends. We'll have a great time."

His ego was too big to comprehend rejection, and trying to navigate the increasingly thin line between keeping her distance and not pissing him off was becoming more difficult every day. "Gee, Spence, sounds great, but they're all out of town right now. Maybe next month."

Ted was traveling on business, too, and Meg didn't like how much she missed him. She made herself concentrate on regrouping emotionally and building up her bank account by taking advantage of her downtime on the drink cart while she waited for the golfers to play through. She found a jewelry supply store on the Internet that offered free shipping. With the tools and materials she bought, along with a couple of artifacts from the collection in her plastic bin, she worked between customers, assembling a necklace and a pair of earrings.

The day after she finished the pieces, she wore them, and the morning's first female foursome noticed. "I've never seen earrings like those," the group's sole Diet Pepsi drinker said.

"Thanks. I just finished them." Meg slipped them from her ears and held them up. "The beads are Tibetan Sherpa coral. Quite old. I love the way the colors have worn."

"What about that necklace?" another woman asked. "It's very unusual."

"It's a Chinese needle case," Meg said, "from the Chin people of Southeast Asia. Over a hundred years old."

"Imagine owning something like that. Are you selling your work?"

"Gosh, I hadn't really thought about it."

"I want those earrings," Diet Pepsi said.

"How much for the necklace?" another golfer asked.

Just like that, she was in business.

The women loved the idea of owning a beautiful piece of jewelry that doubled as a historical artifact, and by the following weekend, Meg had sold another three items. She was scrupulously honest about authenticity, and she attached a card to each design documenting its provenance. She noted which materials were genuine antiquities, which might be copies, and she adjusted her prices accordingly.

Kayla heard about what she was doing and ordered some pieces on consignment for her resale shop. Things were going almost too well.

After two long weeks away, Ted showed up at the church. He was barely inside the door before they were pulling at each other's clothes. Neither of them had the patience to negotiate the stairs to the hot choir loft. Instead, they fell on the couch she'd recently rescued from the Dumpster at the club. Ted cursed as he banged against the wicker arm, but it didn't take him long to forget his discomfort and focus all his brainpower on remedying the mysterious flaws in his lovemaking technique.

She gave in to him as she always did. They rolled from the couch to the hard floor. The fans stirred the air over their naked bodies as he went through all the steps in the sex instruction video he must play in his head. Lights flashed, a sweeping arc across the tin ceiling. She clung to him. Begged. Commanded. Gave in.

When they were done, he sounded both wrung out and a little peevish. "Was that good enough for you?"

"Dear God, yes!"

"Damn right. Five! And don't try to deny it."

"Stop counting my orgasms."

"I'm an engineer. I like statistics."

She smiled and nudged him. "Help me move my bed downstairs. It's too hot to sleep up there."

She shouldn't have introduced the subject because he jumped off the couch. "It's too hot everywhere in this place. And that's not a bed, it's a fricking futon, which would be fine if we were nineteen, but we're not."

She tuned out his very un-Ted-like rant to enjoy the unrestricted views of his body. "I finally have furniture, so quit complaining."

The ladies' locker room had recently been refurbished, and she'd been able to snag the castoffs. The worn wicker pieces and old lamps looked right at home in her church, but he didn't seem impressed. A fragment of memory distracted her from her visual survey, and she came up off the floor. "I saw lights."

"Glad to hear it."

"No. When we were going at each other . . ." *When you were going at me.* "I saw headlights. I think somebody drove up to the church."

"I didn't hear anything." But he pulled on his shorts and went outside to look. She followed him and saw only her car and his truck.

"If anybody was here," he said, "they had the good sense to leave."

The idea that someone might have seen them together made her uneasy. She was allowed to pretend to be in love with Ted. But she didn't want anybody to know it might be more than pretense.

SEX WITH A LEGENDARY LOVER wasn't as fulfilling as she'd like, but two days later, she sold her most expensive piece, a blue glass Roman cabochon she'd wrapped with fine silver, using a technique she'd learned from a silversmith in Nepal. Her life was going too well, and she was almost relieved when she left the club the next evening and discovered someone had keyed the Rustmobile.

The scratch was long and deep, running from front fender to trunk, but considering the car's overall dilapidated condition, hardly a catastrophe. Then other cars started honking at her for no reason. She couldn't figure it out until she spotted the crude bumper stickers plastered on the back.

I'm Not Free but I'm Cheap
Mean People Suck. I Swallow

Ted found her crouched down in the employees' parking lot, trying to peel off the disgusting stickers. She didn't mean to yell, but she couldn't hold it back. "Why would somebody do this?"

"Because they're creeps. Here. Let me."

His gentleness as he moved her aside nearly undid her. She grabbed for a tissue in her purse and blew her nose. "It's not my idea of a joke."

"Mine either," he replied.

She turned away as he began methodically peeling up the edges of the second sticker. "People in this town are mean," she said.

"Kids. That doesn't excuse it, though."

She crossed her arms over her chest and hugged herself. The sprinklers went on in the flower beds. She blew her nose a second time.

"Hey, are you crying?" he asked.

She wasn't exactly, but she was close. "I'm not a crier. Never have been. Never will be." She'd had so little to cry about until the past few months.

He must not have believed her because he rose and set his hands on her shoulders. "You've put up with Arlis Hoover, and you've put up with me. You can handle this."

"It's just so . . . nasty."

He brushed her hair with his lips. "It only says something about the kid who did it."

"Maybe it wasn't a kid. There are so many people here who don't like me."

"Fewer all the time," he said quietly. "You've stood up to everybody, and that's earned you some respect."

"I don't know why I even care."

His expression grew so tender she wanted to weep. "Because you're trying to build something for yourself," he said. "With no help from anybody."

"You help me."

"How?" He dropped his hand, once again frustrated with her. "You won't let me do anything. You won't even let me take you out to dinner."

"Setting aside the issue of Sunny Skipjack lusting after you, I don't need everybody in this town knowing a sinner like me is getting it on with their sainted mayor."

"You're being paranoid. The only reason I've put up with it is because I've been out of town the past couple of weeks."

"Nothing's going to change now that you're back. Our secret fling is staying that way."

He temporarily dropped the subject and invited her to a private dinner that night at his place. She accepted his offer, but as soon as she reached his house, he dragged her upstairs and began playing his precise, calculated sexual games. By the end, he'd satisfied every cell in her body without touching any part of her soul. Exactly as it should be, she told herself.

"You're a magician," she said. "You've spoiled me forever for other men."

He threw back the covers, dropped his legs hard over the side of the bed, and disappeared.

She found him in the kitchen a short while later. She'd pulled his abandoned black T-shirt over her panties, but left the rest of her clothes tangled in the duvet on his bedroom floor. His dark brown hair was rumpled from her fingers, he was still bare-chested and barefoot, wearing only a pair of shorts. His boxers, she happened to know, were tangled in the sheets.

He had a beer in his hand and a second waiting for her on the counter. "I'm not good in the kitchen," he said, looking gorgeous and sulky.

She tore her eyes away from his chest. "I don't believe you. You're good at everything." She blatantly stared at his crotch in a sad attempt to make up for her disappointment. "And I do mean everything."

He could read her mind, and he practically sneered. "If I'm not living up to your standards, I apologize."

"You're delusional, and I'm hungry."

He rested his hips against the sink, not done with being surly. "Choose what you want from the freezer, and maybe I'll defrost it."

He would never have talked to another woman so rudely, and her spirits rose. As she moved behind the center island, she thought about bringing up the contest, but since the national publicity had just boosted the bidding past nine thousand dollars, she couldn't be so mean.

A man's refrigerator told a lot about him. She opened the door and took in sparkling glass shelves holding organic milk, beer, cheese, sandwich meat, and some neatly labeled food storage containers. A peek in the freezer revealed more containers, pricey frozen organic dinners, and chocolate ice cream. She looked over at him. "This is a total chick refrigerator."

"Your refrigerator looks like this?"

"Well, no. But if I were a better woman it would."

The corner of his mouth kicked up. "You do understand, don't you, that I'm not actually the person who cleans and stocks it?"

"I know that Haley buys your groceries, and I want a personal assistant, too."

"She's not my personal assistant."

"Don't tell her that." She pulled out two labeled and dated containers, ham and sweet potatoes. Although she wasn't a great cook, she was a lot better than either of her parents, thanks to the housekeepers who'd put up with the Koranda kids raiding their kitchen.

She leaned over the bottom hydrator looking for salad greens. The front door opened, and she heard the click of heels across the bamboo floors. A prickle of uneasiness scuttled through her. She quickly straightened.

Francesca Day Beaudine sailed into the room and flung open her arms. "Teddy!"

chapter fourteen

TED'S MOTHER WORE BLACK SKINNY pants and a hot pink corset top that shouldn't have looked so good on a woman approaching her midfifties. Her shiny chestnut hair showed no signs of gray, so she was either lucky or she had a skillful colorist. Diamonds glittered at her earlobes, the base of her throat, and on her fingers, but nothing about her was overdone. Instead, she reflected the elegance of a self-made woman possessed of beauty, power, and personal style. A woman who still hadn't spotted Meg as she launched herself at her beloved son's bare chest.

"I've missed you!" She looked so petite in the arms of her tall offspring, it was hard to believe she could have given birth to him. "I rang, honestly, but your bell is out of order."

"It's disconnected. I'm working on an entrance lock that can read fingerprints." He returned her hug, then released her. "How did your interview with the hero cops go?"

"They were marvelous. All my interviews went well, except for that beastly actor person, whose name I shall never again speak." She threw up her hands. And that's when she spotted Meg.

She must have seen the Rustmobile parked outside, but the shock that widened her green cat's eyes suggested she'd assumed the car either belonged to a service person or the most lowborn of Ted's unorthodox group of friends. Meg's and Ted's disheveled appearances made it more than obvious exactly what they'd been up to, and every part of her bristled.

"Mom, you remember Meg, I'm sure."

If Francesca had been an animal, the fur would have stood up on the back of her neck. "Oh. Yes."

Her enmity would have been comical if Meg hadn't felt like throwing up. "Mrs. Beaudine."

Francesca turned away from Meg and focused on her beloved son. Meg was used to seeing anger in a parent's eyes, but she couldn't stand seeing Ted on the receiving end of it, and she cut in before Francesca could say anything. "I threw myself at him just like every other woman in the universe. He couldn't help it. I'm sure you've seen this at least a hundred times."

Francesca and Ted both stared at her, Francesca with overt hostility, Ted with disbelief.

Meg tried to tug the hem of his T-shirt lower over her bottom. "Sorry, Ted. It . . . uh . . . won't happen again. I'll—be going now." Except she needed the car keys stuffed in the pocket of her shorts, and the only way she could retrieve them was to return to his bedroom.

"You're not going anywhere, Meg," Ted said calmly. "Mom, Meg didn't throw herself at me. She can barely stand me. And this isn't any of your business."

Meg shot up her hand. "Really, Ted, you shouldn't talk to your mother that way."

"Don't even try to suck up to her," he said. "It won't do any good."

But she made one final attempt. "It's me," she told Francesca. "I'm a bad influence."

"Cut it out." He gestured toward the food containers on the counter. "We're getting ready to eat, Mom. Why don't you join us?"

That so wasn't going to happen.

"No, thank you." Her clipped British accent made the words even icier. She drew back on her strappy heels and gazed up at her son. "We'll talk about this later." She shot from the kitchen, her shoes beating a furious tattoo across the floor.

The front door shut, but the scent of her perfume, faintly overlaid with hemlock, lingered behind. Meg regarded him glumly. "The good news is, you're too old for her to ground you."

"Which won't stop her from trying." He smiled and lifted his beer bottle. "It sure is tough having an affair with the most unpopular woman in town."

"HE'S SLEEPING WITH HER!" FRANCESCA exclaimed. "Did you know this was going on? Did you know he was sleeping with her?"

Emma had just sat down to breakfast with Kenny and the children when the doorbell rang. Kenny had taken one look at Francesca's face, grabbed the muffin basket, snatched up the kids, and disappeared. Emma ushered Francesca onto the sunporch, hoping her favorite place in the house would soothe her friend, but a scented morning breeze and a lovely view of the pasture weren't nearly enough to calm her.

Francesca jumped up from the shiny black rattan chair she'd

just collapsed into. She hadn't bothered with makeup, not that she needed much of it, and she'd shoved her small feet into a pair of clogs Emma happened to know she only used for gardening. "This was her plan from the beginning." Francesca's small hands flew. "Precisely what I told Dallie. First get rid of Lucy, then move in on Teddy. But he's so wise about people. I never thought for an instant he'd fall for it. How can he be so blind?" She stepped over a battered copy of *Fancy Nancy and the Posh Puppy*. "He's still in shock or he'd see right through her. She's wicked, Emma. She'll do anything to get him. And Dallie is completely useless. He says Ted is a grown man and I should butt out, but would I butt out if my son had a serious illness? No I would not, and I won't butt out now." She snatched up *Fancy Nancy* and pointed the book at Emma. "You had to have known. Why didn't you call me?"

"I had no idea it had gone so far. Let me get you a muffin, Francesca. And would you like some tea?"

Francesca tossed the book on a chair. "Someone must have known."

"You haven't been here, so you can't comprehend how complicated things have gotten with the Skipjacks. Spence is obsessed with Meg, and Sunny wants Ted. We're fairly sure that's why Spence came back to Wynette after the wedding fell through."

Francesca dismissed the Skipjacks. "Torie told me about Sunny, and Ted can handle her." Hurt shadowed her eyes. "I can't understand why you or Torie didn't call me?"

"It's been confusing. Meg did tell certain people she was in love with Ted, that's true. But we assumed she was merely using him to get Spence to back off."

Francesca's green eyes widened with astonishment. "Why wouldn't you believe she was in love with him?"

"Because she didn't act like it," Emma explained patiently. "I've never seen any woman, other than Torie, give him such a hard time. Meg doesn't get starry-eyed around him or hang on to his every word. She openly disagrees with him."

"She's even smarter than I thought." Francesca plowed a hand through her already unkempt hair. "He's never had a woman give him trouble. It's the novelty that's attracting him." She sagged onto the couch. "I hope she isn't on drugs. It wouldn't surprise me. The drug culture is everywhere in Hollywood."

"I don't think she's on drugs, Francesca. And we did try to persuade her to leave. Sunny Skipjack doesn't want any competition for Ted, and Spence dotes on his daughter. It's getting too messy. We knew Meg didn't have any money, so we offered her a check. Not our finest hour, I assure you. Anyway, she refused."

"Of course she refused. Why take your paltry check when she has Ted and his money in her sights?"

"Meg might be a bit more complicated than that."

"I'm sure she is!" Francesca retorted hotly. "Her own family has disowned her, and you can't tell me that was done lightly."

Emma knew she had to proceed carefully. Francesca was an intelligent, rational woman, except when it came to her son and husband. She loved both men ferociously, and she'd fight off armies to protect them, even if neither wanted her protection. "I know it might be difficult, but if you got to know her . . ."

Francesca grabbed a *Star Wars* figure that had been jabbing her in the hip and tossed it aside. "If anyone—and that includes my husband—thinks I'm going to stand by and watch that woman bewitch my son . . ." She blinked. Her shoulders collapsed, and all the energy seemed to seep out of her. "Why did this have to happen now?" she said softly.

Emma went over to sit next to her on the couch. "You're still hoping Lucy will come back, aren't you?"

Francesca rubbed her eyes. From the shadows underneath, it was obvious she hadn't slept well. "Lucy didn't return to Washington after she ran off," she said.

"No?"

"I've talked to Nealy. We both think this is a positive sign. Being away from home, from her job and her friends, will give her the opportunity to come to a deeper understanding of herself and what she's given up. You saw her with Ted. They loved each other. *Love* each other. And he refuses to talk about her. That tells you something, doesn't it?"

"It's been two months," Emma said carefully. "That's an awfully long time."

Francesca was having none of it. "I want everything to stop." She was up off the couch again, pacing. "Just long enough to give Lucy a chance to change her mind. Can you imagine if she finally returns to Wynette only to discover Ted's having an affair with the woman she considers her best friend? It doesn't bear thinking about." She spun on Emma, lines of stubborn determination forming around her mouth. "And I'm not going to let it happen."

Emma tried again. "Ted is quite capable of looking after himself. You mustn't—you really mustn't do anything rash." She gave her friend a worried look, then headed for the kitchen to make tea. As she filled the kettle, she pondered one of Wynette's most frequently recounted legends. According to local lore, Francesca had once flung a pair of four-carat diamonds into a gravel quarry to prove a point about how far she'd go to protect her son.

Meg had better take care.

The day after Meg's encounter with Francesca Beaudine, she received a summons to report to the office. As she drove the drink cart past the pro shop, Ted and Sunny emerged. Sunny wore a short blue-and-yellow harlequin print golf skirt and a sleeveless polo with a diamond quatrefoil pendant nestled in the open neck. She looked well organized, confident, self-disciplined, and perfectly capable of bearing Ted a genius baby in the morning, then heading to the course for a quick nine holes.

Ted's pale blue polo coordinated with hers. They both wore high-tech golf shoes, although he wore a ball cap instead of the yellow clip visor she slipped into her dark hair. Meg couldn't help but think how completely at ease he seemed with this woman who was holding him for ransom in exchange for a golf resort and condo development.

Meg parked the cart and made her way through the club to the office of the assistant manager. Minutes later, she was leaning across his desk trying not to yell. "How can you fire me? Two weeks ago, you offered me a promotion to snack shop manager." A promotion she'd turned down because she didn't want to be stuck inside.

He tugged on his stupid pink necktie. "You've been running a private business from the drink cart."

"I told you about it from the beginning. I made a bracelet for your mother!"

"It's against club policy."

"It wasn't last week. What's happened since then?"

He wouldn't meet her eyes. "I'm sorry, Meg. My hands are tied. This has come down from the top."

Meg's thoughts raced. She wanted to ask him who was going to tell Spence she'd been fired? Or Ted? And what about the retirees who played every Tuesday morning and liked the way she kept coffee for them on the cart? Or the golfers who noticed that she never screwed up their drink orders?

But she didn't say any of that.

When she got to her car, she saw that someone had tried to rip off her windshield wipers. The seat covers burned the backs of her thighs as she slid behind the wheel. Thanks to her jewelry sales, she had enough money to get back to L.A., so why did she care about this shitty job?

Because she liked her shitty job, and she liked her church with its shitty, makeshift furnishings. And she liked this shitty town with its big problems and weird people. Ted was right because, most of all, she liked being forced to live on her own hard work and wits.

She drove home, took a shower, and pulled on jeans, a white boho top, and her pink canvas platform sandals. Fifteen minutes later, she passed through the stone pillars of the Beaudine compound, but she didn't head for Ted's house. Instead she pulled the Rustmobile into the circular drive in front of the sprawling limestone and stucco home where his parents lived.

Dallie answered the door. "Meg?"

"Is your wife home?"

"She's in her office." He didn't seem too surprised to see her, and he stepped back to let her in. "Easiest way to get there is to follow the hallway to the end, go out the door, and cross the courtyard. Big set of arches in the wing on the right."

"Thanks."

The house had roughly plastered walls, beamed ceilings, and cool, tile floors. A fountain splashed in the courtyard, and the faint scent of charcoal suggested someone had fired up the grill for dinner. An arched portico shaded Francesca's office. Through the door panes, Meg saw her sitting at her desk, reading glasses perched on her small nose as she perused the paper in front of her. Meg knocked. Francesca looked up. When she saw who'd come to call, she leaned back in her chair to think it over.

Despite the Oriental rugs on the tile floors, the carved wooden furniture, folk art, and framed photographs, this was a working office with two computers, a flat-screen TV, and bookcases piled with papers, folders, and binders. Francesca finally rose and crossed the floor in rainbow flip-flops. She'd pulled her hair away from her face with a pair of small silver heart barrettes that counterbalanced the more mature half-glasses. Her fitted T-shirt announced her loyalty to the Texas Aggies, and her denim shorts displayed still-trim legs. But the informal wear hadn't made her give up her diamonds. They sparkled at her earlobes, around a slender wrist, and on her fingers.

She opened the door. "Yes?"

"I understand why you did it," Meg said. "I'm asking you to undo it."

Francesca pulled off the half-glasses but didn't budge. Meg had briefly entertained the notion that Sunny had been responsible, but this was an emotional act, not a calculated one. "I have work to do," Francesca said.

"Thanks to you, I don't." She stared down the green icicles shooting from Francesca's eyes. "I like my job. Embarrassing to admit, since it's hardly a big-time career, but I'm good at it."

"Interesting, but as I said, I'm busy."

Meg refused to move. "Here's the thing. I want my job back. In exchange, I won't rat you out to your son."

Francesca displayed her first trace of wariness. After a short pause, she stepped aside just far enough to let Meg in. "You want to deal? All right, let's do that."

Family photos filled the office. One of the most prominent showed a younger Dallie Beaudine celebrating a tournament win by lifting Francesca off her feet. She hung above him, a lock of her hair tumbling over her cheek, a silver earring brushing her jaw, her feet bare, and one very feminine red sandal balanced on the top of his golf shoe. There were also photos of Francesca with Dallie's first wife, the actress Holly Grace Jaffe. But most of the pictures were of a young Ted. They showed a skinny, homely boy with oversize glasses, pants pulled up nearly to his armpits, and a solemn, studious expression as he posed with model rockets, science fair projects, and his father.

"Lucy loved those pictures." Francesca settled behind her desk.

"I'll bet." Meg decided on a little shock treatment. "I got her permission before I slept with your son. And her blessing. She's my best friend. I'd never have done something like that behind her back."

Francesca hadn't expected that. For a moment, her face seemed to collapse, and then her chin came up.

Meg plunged on. "I'll spare you any more details about your son's sex life except to say he's safe with me. I have no illusions about marriage, babies, or settling into Wynette forever."

Francesca scowled, not as relieved by that statement as she should have been. "Of course you don't. You're a live-for-the-moment person, aren't you?"

"In a way. I don't know. Not so much as I used to be."

"Ted's been through enough. He doesn't need you messing up his life right now."

"I've noticed a lot of people in this town have strong ideas about what they think Ted needs and doesn't need."

"I'm his mother. I'm fairly clear on the subject."

Here came the tricky part, not that it had been exactly smooth sailing so far. "I guess an outsider, someone without preconceived notions, sees a person a little differently from those who've known him for a long time." She picked up a photo of a very young Ted with the Statue of Liberty in the background. "Ted is brilliant," she went on. "Everybody knows that. And he's wily. A lot of people know that, too. He has an overdeveloped sense of responsibility. He can't help that. But here's what most people, especially the women who fall for him, don't seem to notice. Ted intellectualizes what most people process emotionally."

"I have no idea what you're talking about."

She set down the photo. "He doesn't get swept away in romantic relationships like other people do. He adds up the pros and cons in some kind of mental ledger and acts accordingly. That's what happened with Lucy. They fit together in his ledger."

Outrage propelled Francesca from her chair. "Are you saying that Ted didn't love Lucy? That he doesn't feel things deeply?"

"He feels a lot of things very deeply. Injustice. Loyalty. Responsibility. Your son is one of the smartest and most morally upright people I've ever met. But he's totally practical about emotional relationships." The more she spoke, the more depressed she got. "That's what women don't pick up on. They want to sweep him off his feet, but he's not sweepable. Lucy's decision traumatized you more than him."

Francesca shot around the side of the desk. "This is what you want to believe. You couldn't be more wrong."

"I'm not a threat, Mrs. Beaudine," she said more quietly. "I'm not going to break his heart or try to trick him into marriage. I'm not going to hang on to him. I'm a safe place to stash your son until a more appropriate woman comes along." That hurt a lot more than she wanted it to, but she somehow managed a carefree shrug. "I'm your dream girl. And I want my job back."

Francesca had herself under control again. "You can't really see a future in doing menial work at a small-town country club."

"I like it. Who knew, right?"

Francesca picked up a notepad from her desk. "I'll get you a job in L.A. New York. San Francisco. Wherever you want. A good job. What you do with it is up to you."

"Thanks, but I've gotten used to getting things for myself."

Francesca set down the notepad and twisted her wedding ring, finally looking uncomfortable. Several more seconds ticked by. "Why didn't you take your grievance against me straight to Ted?"

"I like to fight my own battles."

Francesca's brief moment of vulnerability vanished, and steel took over her spine. "He's been through enough. I don't want him hurt again."

"Trust me when I tell you that I'm not important enough for that ever to happen." Another painful pang. "I'm his rebound girl. I'm also the only woman, other than Torie, that he can be bad-tempered with. It's restful for him. As for me . . . He's a nice break from the losers I generally hook up with."

"You're certainly pragmatic."

"Like I said. I'm your dream girl." Somehow she managed a cocky smile, but as she left the office and headed back across the courtyard her bravado faded. She was sick of feeling unworthy.

WHEN SHE SHOWED UP FOR WORK the next day, no one seemed to remember that she'd been fired. Ted stopped by her drink cart. True to her word, she didn't mention what had happened or his mother's part in it.

The day turned blistering hot, and by the time she got home that evening, she was a sweaty, sodden mess. She couldn't wait to get to the swimming hole. She pulled her polo over her head as she walked past the battered old table that held her jewelry supplies. One of the ecology books she'd borrowed from Ted lay open on the worn couch. In the kitchen, a stack of dirty dishes waited for her in the sink. She kicked off her sneakers and opened the bathroom door.

All the blood drained from her head as she saw what was scrawled across the mirror in a vicious smear of crimson lipstick.

GO AWAY

chapter fifteen

H ER HANDS SHOOK AS SHE tried to scrub the words away, and queer little sounds escaped from her throat.

GO AWAY

Leaving lipstick messages on mirrors was the biggest cliché in the world, something that only a person with no imagination would do. She needed to get a grip. But knowing an intruder had sneaked into her house when she was gone and touched her things made her nauseated. She didn't stop shaking until she'd erased the awful words and searched the church for other signs of invasion. She found nothing.

As her panic faded, she tried to imagine who had done this, but there were so many potential candidates she couldn't sort through them all. The front door had been locked. The back door was locked now, but she hadn't checked it before she'd left. For all she knew, the intruder had gotten in that way, then locked it afterward. She pulled her damp polo back on, went outside, and walked around the church but found nothing unusual.

She finally took her shower, darting nervous glances at the open door as she washed. She hated being frightened. Hated it even more when Ted loomed without warning in the open doorway, and she screamed.

"Jesus!" he said. "What's wrong with you?"

"Don't sneak up on me like that!"

"I knocked."

"How was I supposed to hear?" She jerked off the faucet.

"When did you get so skittish?"

"You took me by surprise, that's all." She couldn't tell him. She knew that right away. His status as a certified superhero meant he'd refuse to let her live here alone any longer. She couldn't afford to live anywhere else, and she wasn't letting him pay rent on another place. Besides, she loved her church. Maybe not at this precise moment, but she would again, as soon as she got over being creeped out.

He pulled a towel from the new Viceroy towel rack, Edinburgh line, that she'd recently installed. But instead of giving it to her, he draped it over his shoulder.

She held out her hand, even though she had a pretty good idea what was coming. "Give me that."

"Come and get it."

She wasn't in the mood. Except, of course she was because this was Ted standing in front of her, steady and sexy and smarter than any man she'd known. What better way to shake off her remaining jumpiness than to lose herself in lovemaking that demanded so little of her?

She stepped out of the shower and pressed her wet body against him. "Give it your best shot, lover boy."

He grinned and did exactly as she asked. Better than she'd asked.

Each time he took more care and postponed his satisfaction longer. After it was over, she wrapped a sarong around herself with one of the silk pieces she'd worn to his rehearsal dinner, then retrieved beers for both of them from the twelve-pack he'd stashed in her refrigerator. He'd already pulled on his shorts, and he took a folded piece of paper from the pocket.

"I got this in the mail today." He sat on the couch, one arm draped along the back, and crossed his ankles on an abandoned wooden wine crate she'd turned into a coffee table.

She took the paper from him and glanced down at the letterhead. TEXAS DEPARTMENT OF HEALTH. He didn't usually share the more mundane aspects of his mayoral job, and she sat on the arm of a wicker chair with faded tropical print cushions to read. Within seconds, she'd shot up only to discover her knees were too rubbery to hold her weight. She sank back into the cushions and reread the pertinent paragraph.

> *Texas Law requires that any person who tests positive for a sexually transmitted disease including, but not limited to, chlamydia, gonorhea, HPV, and AIDS, must provide a list of recent sexual partners. This is to notify you that* Meg Koranda *has listed you as one of these partners. You are urged to visit your physician immediately. You are also urged to cease all sexual contact with the above named infected person.*

Meg gazed up at him, feeling sick. "Infected person?"

"*Gonorrhea* is misspelled," he pointed out. "And the letterhead is bogus."

She crumpled the paper in her fist. "Why didn't you show me this as soon as you got here?"

"I was afraid you wouldn't put out."

"Ted . . ."

He eyed her casually. "Do you have any idea who might be behind this?"

She thought of the message on her bathroom mirror. "Any one of the millions of women who lust after you."

He ignored that. "The letter was mailed from Austin, but that doesn't mean much."

Now was the moment to tell him his mother had tried to get her fired, but Meg couldn't imagine Francesca Beaudine doing anything as vile as sending this letter. Besides, Francesca would almost certainly have checked for spelling errors. And she doubted Sunny would have made the mistake in the first place, unless she'd done it deliberately to throw them off track. As for Kayla, Zoey, and the other women holding on to fantasies about Ted . . . Meg could hardly throw around accusations based on dirty looks. She threw the paper on the floor. "Why didn't Lucy have to put up with this crap?"

"We spent a lot of time in Washington. And, frankly, Lucy didn't rile people like you do."

Meg came up off the chair. "Nobody knows about us except your mother and whoever she might have told."

"Dad and Lady Emma, who would probably have told Kenny."

"Who, I'm sure, told Torie. And if big-mouth Torie knows—"

"If Torie knew, she'd have been on the phone to me right away."

"That leaves our mysterious visitor from three nights ago," she said. Ted's wandering eyes indicated her sarong was slipping, and she tightened it. "The idea that someone might have been watching us through the window . . ."

"Exactly." He set his beer bottle on the wine crate. "I'm starting to think those bumper stickers on your car might not have been the work of kids."

"Somebody tried to break off my windshield wipers."

He frowned, and she once again debated mentioning the scrawl on her mirror, but she didn't want to be locked out of her home, and that's exactly what would happen. "How many people have keys to the church?" she asked.

"Why?"

"I'm wondering if I should be nervous."

"I changed the locks when I took over the place," he said. "You have the key I kept outside. I have one. Lucy might still have one, and there's a spare at the house."

Which meant the intruder had probably come in through the unlocked back door. Leaving it unlocked was a mistake Meg would make sure she didn't repeat.

It was time to ask the big question, and she poked the crumpled ball of paper with her bare toes. "That letterhead looked authentic. And lots of government workers aren't great spellers." She licked her lips. "It could have been true." She finally met his eyes. "So why didn't you ask me about it right away?"

Incredibly, her question seemed to annoy him. "What do you mean? If there was a problem, you'd have told me a long time ago."

She felt as if he'd ripped the floorboards right out from under her. All that trust . . . in her integrity. Right then she knew the worst had happened. Her stomach fell to her knees. She'd fallen in love with him.

She wanted to rip her hair out. Of course she'd fallen in love with him. What woman hadn't? Falling in love with Ted was a female rite of passage in Wynette, and she'd just joined the sisterhood.

She was starting to hyperventilate, so she did what she always did when she felt cornered. "You have to go now."

His gaze wandered down the thin silk sarong. "If I do that, this won't be anything more than a booty call."

"Right. Exactly the way I want it. Your glorious body, with as little conversation as possible."

"I'm starting to feel like the chick in this relationship."

"Consider it a growth experience."

He smiled, rose from the couch, pulled her into his arms, and began kissing her senseless. Just as she started to fall into another Beaudine-induced sexual coma, he enacted his legendary self-control and pulled away. "Sorry, babe. If you want more of what I've got, you have to go out with me. Get dressed."

She pulled herself back to reality. "Two words I never again want to hear coming out of your mouth. What's wrong with you, anyway?"

"I want to go out to dinner," he said evenly. "The two of us. Like normal people. At a real restaurant."

"A really bad idea."

"Spence and Sunny have an international trade show coming up that'll keep them out of the country for a while, and while they're away, I'm going to catch up on my sadly neglected business." He tucked a curl behind her ear. "I'll be gone almost two weeks. Before I take off, I want a night out, and I'm sick of sneaking around."

"Tough," she retorted. "Stop being so selfish. Think about your precious town, then picture the expression on Sunny's face if she found out the two of us—"

His cool faded. "The town and Sunny are my business, not yours."

"With that kind of self-centered attitude, Mr. Mayor, you'll never get reelected."

"I didn't want to be elected the first time!"

She finally agreed to a Tex-Mex restaurant in Fredericksburg, but once they got there, she maneuvered him into a chair that faced the wall so she could keep a lookout. That aggravated him so much he ordered for both of them without consulting her.

"You never get mad," she said when their server left the table. "Except at me."

"That's not true," he said tightly. "Torie can get me going."

"Torie doesn't count. You were obviously her mother in a previous life."

He retaliated by hogging the chip basket.

"I'd never have taken you for a sulker," she said after a long, heavy silence. "Yet look at you."

He shoved a chip into the hottest bowl of salsa. "I hate sneaking around, and I'm not doing it any longer. This affair is coming out of the closet."

His mulish determination scared her. "Hold it right there. Spence is used to getting what he wants for Sunny and for himself. If you didn't believe that, you wouldn't have encouraged me to stay all palsy-walsy with him."

He snapped a chip in half. "That's going to stop, too. Right now."

"No, it's not. I'll handle Spence. You deal with Sunny. As for the two of us . . . I told you from the beginning how it was going to be."

"And I'm telling you . . ." He jabbed the broken chip in the general direction of her face. "I've never sneaked around in my life, and I'm not doing it now."

She couldn't believe he was saying this. "You can't jeopardize something so important for a few meaningless rolls in the hay. This is a temporary fling, Ted. Temporary. Any day now, I'll pull up stakes and head back to L.A. I'm surprised I haven't done it already."

If she'd hoped he'd insist their relationship wasn't meaningless, she'd set herself up for disappointment. He leaned across the table. "It doesn't have anything to do with what's temporary. It has to do with the kind of person I am."

"What about the kind of person I am? Somebody who's completely comfortable with sneaking around."

"You heard me."

She regarded him with dismay. This was the unwelcome consequence of having a lover with honor. Or at least what he saw as honor. What she saw was a looming choice between disaster and heartbreak.

BETWEEN TRYING NOT TO THINK about falling in love with Ted and thinking too much about a possible reappearance by her mysterious home invader, Meg didn't sleep well. She used her wakeful nights to make jewelry. The pieces were becoming more complicated, as her small group of customers showed a distinct preference for jewelry that used genuine relics instead of copies. She researched Internet dealers who specialized in the kind of ancient artifacts she wanted to use and plowed an alarming chunk of her nest egg into an order with a Boston-area anthropology professor who had a reputation for honesty and who provided a detailed provenance for everything she sold.

As Meg unpacked some Middle Eastern coins, Roman cabochons, and three small, precious mosaic face beads from around the second century, she found herself wondering if making jewelry was her business or a distraction from figuring out what she should really be doing with her life?

A week after Ted left town, Torie called and ordered Meg to show up for work an hour early the next morning. When Meg asked why, Torie acted as if Meg had just failed an IQ test. "Because Dex will be home then to watch the girls. Jeez."

As soon as Meg got to the club the next morning, Torie dragged her to the practice range. "You can't live in Wynette without picking up a golf club. It's a city ordinance." She handed over her five-iron. "Take a swing."

"I won't be here much longer, so there's no point." Meg ignored the pang that tweaked at her heart. "Besides, I'm not rich enough to be a golfer."

"Just swing the damn thing."

Meg did and missed the ball. She tried again and missed again, but after a few more swings, she somehow sent the ball in a perfect arc to the middle of the practice range. She let out a whoop.

"A lucky shot," Torie said, "but that's exactly how golf sucks you in." She took the club back, gave Meg a few pointers, then told her to keep working.

For the next half hour, Meg followed Torie's instructions, and since she'd inherited her parents' natural athleticism, she began connecting with the ball.

"You could be good if you practiced," Torie said. "Employees play free on Mondays. Take advantage of your day off. I have a spare set of clubs in the bag room you can borrow."

"Thanks for the offer, but I don't really want to."

"Oh, you want to, all right."

That was true. Watching so many other people play had piqued her interest. "Why are you doing this?" she asked as she carried Torie's bag back to the clubhouse.

"Because you're the only woman other than me who's ever told Ted the truth about his dancing."

"I don't understand."

"Sure you do. I also might have noticed that Ted went strangely quiet when I brought up your name in our phone conversation this week. I don't know if you two have a future—providing he doesn't have to marry Sunny—but I'm not taking any chances."

Whatever that meant. Still, Meg found herself adding Torie O'Connor to the list of all she'd miss when she finally left Wynette. She slipped the bag of clubs off her shoulder. "Regardless of Sunny, how could Ted and I have a future? He's the Lamb of God, and I'm the town bad girl."

"I know," Torie said brightly.

That evening, as Meg hosed off the day's dust from the drink cart, the catering manager approached and told her one of the members wanted to hire her to serve at a ladies' luncheon at her home the next day. The few townspeople who could afford it routinely hired staff to help at private parties, but no one had ever requested her, and she needed all the money she could get to make up for the materials she'd just bought. "Sure," she said.

"Pick up a white server's shirt in the catering office before you leave. Wear a black skirt with it."

The closest thing Meg had was her black-and-white Miu Miu mini from the resale shop. It would have to do.

The catering manager handed over a piece of paper with the directions. "Chef Duncan is cooking, and you'll be working with Haley Kittle. She'll show you the ropes. Be there at ten. And this is a big deal, so do a good job."

After she got back from the swimming hole that evening, Meg finally looked at the information the catering manager had given her. There was something familiar about the directions. Her gaze flew to the bottom of the page where the name of the person she'd be working for was typed out.

Francesca Beaudine

She crumpled the paper in her fist. What kind of game was Francesca playing? Did she really think Meg would take the job? Except Meg had already done exactly that.

She yanked on her HAPPY PRINTING COMPANY T-shirt and stomped around the kitchen for a while, cursing Francesca, cursing herself for not reading the information earlier when she could still have refused. But would she have? Probably not. Her stupid pride wouldn't let her.

The temptation to pick up her phone and call Ted was nearly unbearable. She made herself a sandwich instead and carried it out to the cemetery only to discover she'd lost her appetite. It was no coincidence this was happening while he was gone. Francesca had executed a stealth attack designed to put Meg in her place. It probably made little difference to her whether Meg accepted or not. She wanted to make a point. Meg was an outsider, a down-on-her-luck drifter forced to work for a meager hourly wage. An outsider who'd only be allowed in Francesca's house as one of the help.

Meg pitched the sandwich into the weeds. Screw that.

SHE REACHED THE BEAUDINE COMPOUND a little before ten the next morning. She'd chosen her sparkly pink platforms to wear with the white catering blouse and Miu Miu mini. They wouldn't be the most comfortable shoes to work in, but the best defense against Francesca was a strong offense, and they'd send the message that she had no intention of being invisible. Meg would hold her head high, smile until her cheeks ached, and do her job well enough to put a crimp in Francesca's satisfaction.

Haley pulled up in her red Ford Focus. She barely spoke as they walked into the house together, and she looked so pale Meg grew concerned. "Are you feeling okay?"

"I've got . . . really bad cramps."

"Can you get someone to work for you?"

"I tried, but nobody's around."

The Beaudine kitchen was both luxurious and homey with sunny saffron walls, a terra-cotta floor, and handcrafted cobalt blue tile work. An enormous wrought-iron chandelier bearing colorful glass cups hung in the center of the room, and open shelves displayed copper pots and hand-thrown pottery.

Chef Duncan was unpacking the food he'd prepped for the event. A short man in his early forties, he had a big nose and a graying shrub of wiry auburn hair protruding from beneath his toque. He frowned as Haley disappeared into the bathroom, then barked at Meg to get to work.

While she set up the glassware and began organizing the serving dishes, he detailed the menu: bite-size puffed pastry hors d'oeuvres filled with melted Brie and orange marmalade, minted fresh pea soup served in demitasse cups that still needed to be washed, a fennel-laced salad, warm pretzel rolls, and the main course, asparagus frittata and smoked salmon, which they'd plate in the kitchen. The pièce de résistance was dessert, individually potted chocolate soufflés the chef had been working all summer to perfect and which must, must, must be served as soon as they came out of the oven and placed gently, gently, gently in front of each guest.

Meg nodded at the instructions, then carried the chunky green water goblets into the dining room. Palm and lemon trees grew in Old World urns placed in the corners, and water trickled from a stone fountain set in a tiled wall. The room held two temporary tables in addition to a long wooden permanent table with a distressed surface. Instead of formal linens, Francesca had chosen hand-woven place mats. Each table had a copper tray centerpiece holding assorted clay herb pots of oregano, marjoram, sage, and thyme, along with earthenware pitchers brimming with golden yellow blooms. Through the expansive dining room windows, she could see part of the courtyard and a shady pergola where a book lay abandoned on a wooden bench. It was hard not to like a woman who'd created such a beautiful setting to entertain her friends, but Meg intended to give it her best effort.

Haley still hadn't emerged from the bathroom when Meg returned to the kitchen. She'd just begun washing the pottery demitasse cups when the *tap-tap-tap* of heels on the tile floor announced the approach of their hostess. "Thank you for helping me out today, Chef Duncan," Francesca said. "I hope you're finding everything you need."

Meg rinsed a cup, turned from the sink, and gave Francesca her brightest smile. "Hello, Mrs. Beaudine."

Unlike her son, Francesca had a lousy poker face, and the play of emotions that crossed her face was fairly easy to decode. First came surprise. (She hadn't expected Meg to accept the job.) Then came puzzlement. (Exactly why had Meg shown up?) Discomfort appeared next. (What would her guests think?) Then doubt. (Perhaps she should have thought this through more carefully.) Followed by distress. (This had been a terrible idea.) All of it ending in . . . resolution.

"Meg, may I speak with you in the dining room?"

"Of course."

She followed the tapping heels out of the kitchen. Francesca was so petite Meg could almost have tucked her under her chin, although she couldn't imagine doing anything like that. Francesca was stylishly dressed as always—an emerald top and a cool white cotton skirt she'd cinched with a peacock blue belt. She stopped by the stone fountain and twisted her wedding ring. "I'm afraid there's been a mistake. My own, of course. I won't need you after all. Naturally, I'll pay you for your time. I'm sure money is tight or you wouldn't have felt the need to . . . show up today."

"Not as tight as it used to be," Meg said cheerfully. "My jewelry business is doing a lot better than I dreamed."

"Yes, I'd heard." Francesca was clearly flustered and just as clearly determined to settle this. "I suppose I didn't think you'd accept the job."

"Sometimes I even surprise myself."

"This is my fault, of course. I tend to be impulsive. It's caused me more trouble than you can imagine."

Meg knew all about being impulsive.

Francesca straightened to her full, unimpressive height and spoke with stiff dignity. "Let me get my checkbook."

Incredibly tempting, but Meg couldn't do it. "You have twenty guests coming, and Haley's not feeling well. I can't leave Chef in the lurch."

"I'm sure we'll manage somehow." She fingered a diamond bracelet. "It's too awkward. I don't want to make my guests uncomfortable. Or you, of course."

"If your guests are who I think they're going to be, they'll love this. As for me . . . I've been in Wynette for two and a half months, so it takes a lot to make me uncomfortable."

"Really, Meg . . . It's one thing for you to work at the club, but this is something else entirely. I know that—"

"Excuse me. I need to finish washing the cups." Meg's sparkly pink platforms made their own satisfying *tap-tap-tap* as she headed back to the kitchen.

Haley had emerged from the bathroom, but as she stood at the counter, she didn't look any better, and Chef was getting harried. Meg snatched the bottle of peach nectar from her hands and, following Chef's instructions, poured a little down the inside of each flute. She added champagne, slipped in a sliver of fresh fruit, and turned the tray over to Haley, hoping for the best. As Haley carried it away, Meg took the platter of toasty pastry puffs Chef had pulled from the oven, picked up a stack of cocktail napkins, and followed.

Haley had staked out a place by the front door so she didn't have to walk around. The guests arrived promptly. They wore brightly colored linens and cottons, their outfits dressier than what their California counterparts would have donned for such an affair, but in Texas, underdressing was a mortal sin even in the younger set.

Meg recognized some of the women golfers from the club. Torie was talking to the only person in the room dressed entirely in black, a woman Meg had never seen. Torie's champagne flute stalled halfway to her lips as she saw Meg approaching with the serving tray. "What the hell are you doing here?"

Meg dipped a fake curtsy. "My name is Meg, and I'm your server today."

"Why?"

"Why not?"

"Because . . ." Torie waved her hand. "I'm not sure why not. All I know is, it doesn't seem right."

"Mrs. Beaudine needed some help, and I had a free day."

Torie frowned, then turned to the thin woman at her side, who had a fierce black bob and glasses with red plastic frames. Ignoring the breach of protocol, she introduced them. "Lisa, this is Meg. Lisa is Francesca's agent. And Meg is—"

"I highly recommend the puff pastries." Meg couldn't be certain Torie wasn't about to identify her as the daughter of the great Fleur Savagar Koranda, the superstar of talent agents, but she knew Torie well enough by now not to take that chance. "Make sure you save room for dessert. I won't spoil the surprise by telling you what it is, but you're not going to be disappointed."

"Meg?" Emma appeared, her small brow knit, a pair of earrings Meg had fashioned from colorful nineteenth-century carnelian beads bobbing at her ears. "Oh, dear . . ."

"Lady Emma." Meg held out the tray.

"Just Emma. Oh, never mind. I don't know why I even bother."

"I don't either," Torie said. "Lisa, I'm sure Francesca has told you all about our local member of the British royal family, but I don't think the two of you have met. This is my sister-in-law, Lady Emma Wells-Finch Traveler."

Emma sighed and extended her hand. Meg slipped away and, under Francesca's watchful, worried eyes, headed over to serve the local mafia.

Birdie, Kayla, Zoey, and Shelby Traveler clustered together by the windows. As Meg drew nearer, she heard Birdie say, "Haley was with that Kyle Bascom again last night. I swear to God, if she gets pregnant . . ."

Meg remembered Haley's pale face and prayed that hadn't already happened. Kayla saw Meg and poked Zoey so hard she splashed champagne on her hand. All the women inspected Meg's skirt. Shelby shot Kayla an inquisitive look. Meg held out the stack of napkins to Birdie.

Zoey fingered a necklace that looked as though it had been made of shellacked Froot Loops. "I'm surprised you still have to work parties, Meg. Kayla said your jewelry's selling great."

Kayla fluffed her hair. "Not that great. I marked the monkey necklace down twice, and I still couldn't move it."

"I told you I'd redo it." Meg had to agree the monkey necklace wasn't her best piece, but nearly everything else she'd given Kayla had sold quickly.

Birdie tugged on a spike of her woodpecker red hair and regarded Meg loftily. "If I was going to hire catering help, I'd specify who I wanted. Francesca's too casual about this kind of thing."

Zoey glanced around. "I hope Sunny's not back yet. Imagine if

Francesca invited her with Meg here. None of us need that kind of stress. At least I don't, not with school starting in a few weeks and me down to one kindergarten teacher."

Shelby Traveler turned to Kayla. "I love monkeys," she said. "I'll buy that necklace."

Torie slipped into the circle. "Since when do you love monkeys? Right before Petey turned ten, I heard you tell him they were filthy little beasts."

"Only because he'd just about talked Kenny into buying him one for his birthday."

Torie nodded. "Kenny'd do it, too. He loves Petey as much as he loves his own kids."

Kayla shook her hair. "That French girlfriend of Ted's, the model, I always thought she sort of looked like a monkey. Something about her teeth."

The Crazy Women of Wynette were off and running. Meg slipped away.

When she got to the kitchen, Haley had disappeared, and she found Chef fuming as he stepped over broken champagne flutes. "She's worthless today! I sent her home. Leave the fucking glass alone and start plating the salads."

Meg did her best to follow his rapid-fire orders. She raced around the kitchen, avoiding the broken glass and cursing her pink platforms, but when she returned to the living room with a fresh tray of drinks, she deliberately slowed her steps, as though she had all the time in the world. Maybe she didn't have any experience as a server, but nobody needed to see that.

Back in the kitchen, she unearthed three small pitchers for salad dressing as Chef dashed to the oven to check on the frittatas. "I want these served hot."

The next hour flew by as Meg tried to do the work of two people while Chef worried over the chocolate dessert soufflés. Torie and Emma both seemed determined to engage her in conversation every time she appeared in the dining room, as if Meg were another guest. Meg appreciated their good intentions but wished they'd let her concentrate on her job. Kayla forgot her animosity long enough to tell Meg she wanted another pre-Columbian stone necklace and earrings for a friend who owned a shop in Austin. Even Francesca's agent wanted to talk, not about Meg's parents—apparently no one had tipped her off—but about the frittata and whether she detected a touch of curry.

"You have an amazing palate," Meg said. "Chef used the barest hint. I can't believe you caught it."

Francesca must have realized Meg had no idea whether the frittata contained curry or not because she quickly diverted Lisa's attention.

As Meg served, she picked up snippets of conversation. The guests wanted to know when Ted was getting back and what he intended to do about various local problems ranging from someone's noisy rooster to the Skipjacks' return trip to Wynette. As Meg poured Birdie a fresh glass of iced tea, Torie chided Zoey about her Froot Loops necklace. "Just once, couldn't you wear normal jewelry?"

"Do you think I enjoy walking around with half a grocery store hanging off me?" Zoey whispered, snatching a roll from the basket and ripping it in half. "But Hunter Gray's mother is sitting at the next table, and I need her to organize this year's book fair."

Torie looked up at Meg. "If I was Zoey, I'd establish stronger boundaries between my work and my personal life."

"That's what you say now," Zoey retorted, "but remember how excited you got when I wore those macaroni earrings Sophie made for me?"

"That was different. My daughter's artistic."

"Sure she is." Zoey smirked. "And you set up the school phone tree for me that very same day."

Meg somehow managed to clear the dishes without dumping leftovers in anyone's lap. The female golfers asked if she had any Arizona iced tea. In the kitchen, Chef's face was slicked with sweat as he pulled the perfectly puffed individual chocolate soufflés from the oven. "Hurry! Get these on the table before they collapse. Gently! Remember what I told you."

Meg heaved the heavy tray into the dining room. Serving the soufflés was a two-person job, but she braced the edge against her hip and reached for the first pot.

"Ted!" Torie exclaimed. "Look who's here, everybody!"

Meg's heart leaped into her throat, her head jerked up, and she wobbled on her pink platforms as she saw Ted framed in the doorway. In the space of seconds, the soufflés began to shift . . . And all she could think about was the baby carriage.

Her dad had pointed out the phenomenon when she was a kid. If you were watching a movie and you saw a baby carriage, you knew a speeding car was heading its way. The same went for a florist's cart, a wedding cake, or a plate-glass window being maneuvered across a street.

Sit back in your seat, kiddo, and hold on because a car chase is coming your way.

It was just like that with the chocolate soufflés.

She barely had the tray supported. She was losing her balance. The soufflés had started to slide. A car chase was heading her way.

But life wasn't a movie, and she'd eat the broken glass off the kitchen floor before she'd let those white pots fall. Even as she teetered on her shoes, she shifted her weight, repositioned her hip, and focused every ounce of her willpower on regaining her balance.

The pots resettled. Francesca rose from her chair. "Teddy, darling, you're just in time for dessert. Come and join us."

Meg lifted her chin. The man she loved was staring at her. Those tiger eyes that grew so smoky when they made love were now clear and fiercely perceptive. His gaze shifted to the tray she was carrying. Back to her. Meg looked down. The soufflés began to deflate. One by one. *Pfft . . . Pfft . . . Pfft . . .*

chapter sixteen

"LADIES." TED'S GAZE FLICKED from Meg's white server's apron to his mother, who'd suddenly turned into a whirlwind of motion.

"Find a chair, darling. Squeeze in next to Shelby." Her small hand flew from hair to bracelets to napkin, a bird of paradise searching for a safe place to land. "Fortunately, my son is a man at home in the company of women."

Torie snorted. "You can say that again. He's dated half the room."

Ted inclined his head toward the assemblage. "And enjoyed every moment."

"Not every moment," Zoey said. "Remember when Bennie Hanks plugged up all the toilets right before the fifth-grade choral concert? We never did make it to dinner that night."

"But I got to see a dedicated young educator in action," Ted said gallantly, "and Bennie learned a valuable lesson."

A momentary yearning softened Zoey's features, an indulgence in the memory of what might have been. To her credit, she shook herself out of it. "Bennie's at space camp in Huntsville. Let's hope they do a better job of guarding their toilets."

Ted nodded, but he'd fixed his attention back on his mother. His eyes were steady, his mouth unsmiling. Francesca lunged for her water glass. Emma darted an anxious glance between them and quickly stepped into the breach. "Did you have a successful business trip, Ted?"

"I did." He slowly withdrew his gaze from his mother and focused on Meg. She pretended she didn't notice and served the first of the soufflés with a flourish, as if the dessert was intended to have a giant crater in its middle.

He came toward her, his jaw set in a stubborn line. "Let me help you, Meg."

Yellow caution lights flashed in her head. "No need." She swallowed. "Sir."

His eyes narrowed. She picked up the next pot. Francesca and Emma both knew she and Ted were lovers, and so did the mysterious nighttime Peeping Tom, who might also be her home invader. Was that person here right now, watching them? The possibility accounted for only part of her growing sense of foreboding.

Ted took the ramekin from her and began serving each guest with an easy smile and a perfectly chosen compliment. Meg seemed to be the only person who noticed the tension lurking at the corners of that smile.

Francesca made cheery conversation with her guests, acting as if her son always helped out the serving staff. Ted's eyes darkened when Shelby announced that the bidding to Win a Weekend with Ted Beaudine had hit eleven thousand dollars. "We've got bids coming in from everywhere thanks to all the publicity we've gotten."

Kayla didn't seem as happy about that as the others, which suggested Daddy had cut off her bidding money.

One of the golfers waved to catch his attention. "Ted, is it true a crew from *The Bachelor* is coming to Wynette to tape background footage?"

"Not true," Torie said. "He couldn't pass their stupidity test."

The tray was finally empty, and Meg tried to make her escape, but as she dashed for the kitchen, Ted followed.

Chef was all smiles when he saw who'd barged in. "Hey, Mr. Beaudine. Great to see you." He abandoned the coffee carafes he'd just filled. "I heard you were out of town."

"Just got back, Chef." Ted's effortless good humor vanished as he focused on Meg. "What are you doing serving at my mother's party?"

"I'm helping out," she said, "and you're in my way." She grabbed an extra dessert from the counter and shoved it at him. "Sit down and eat."

Chef tore around the center island. "You can't give him that. It's already fallen."

Fortunately, Chef didn't know about the twenty others that had met an identical fate. "Ted won't notice," she said. "He eats Marshmallow Fluff straight from the jar." She was the one who did that, but life in Wynette had taught her the value of prevarication.

Ted returned the dessert pot to the counter, his mouth grim. "My mother set you up, didn't she?"

"Set me up? Your mother?" She lunged for the coffee carafes, but she wasn't quick enough, and he snatched them out from under her. "Give those back," she said. "I don't need your help. What I need is for you to get out of my way so I can do my job."

"Meg!" Chef's already florid face developed a purple tinge. "I apologize, Mr. Beaudine. Meg hasn't served before, and she has a lot to learn about how to treat people."

"Tell me about it." Ted disappeared through the door with the coffee.

He was going to mess everything up. She didn't know how. She only knew he was going to do something awful, and she had to stop it. She grabbed the iced tea pitcher and charged after him.

He'd already started filling cups without asking what anybody wanted, but even the tea drinkers didn't protest. They were too busy fussing over him. Ted wouldn't look at his mother, and twin furrows had formed in Francesca's otherwise smooth forehead.

Meg headed for the opposite side of the dining room and began refilling iced tea glasses. The woman Zoey had identified as Hunter Gray's mother gestured toward Meg. "Torie, that looks just like your Miu Miu skirt. The one you wore when we all went to see Vampire Weekend in Austin."

Ted broke off his conversation with Francesca's agent. Torie flicked her lazy, rich girl's eyes over Meg's skirt. "They knock off everything these days. No offense to you, Meg. It's a fairly decent knockoff."

But this was no knockoff, and Meg suddenly understood the veiled looks she received whenever she wore any of the garments she'd picked up at Kayla's resale shop. All this time, she'd been wearing Torie O'Connor's castoffs, clothes so immediately identifiable that no one else in town would buy them. And everyone had been in on the joke, including Ted.

Birdie shot Meg a smug look as she handed over her iced tea glass. "The rest of us have too much pride to wear Torie's old clothes."

"Not to mention, we don't have the body for it," Zoey said.

Kayla fluffed her hair. "I keep telling Torie she'd make a lot more money if she sent her things to a consignment shop in Austin, but she says it's too much trouble. Until Meg came along, I could only sell her things to out-of-towners."

The comments would have stung, except for one thing. All of the women, even Birdie, kept their voices low enough so only Meg could hear their barbs. She didn't have time to ponder why they'd done that because Ted was setting down both coffee carafes and heading right toward her.

Although his easy smile was firmly fixed, his determined eyes told a more dangerous story. A car crash was heading toward her, and she couldn't think of a single way to avoid it.

He stopped in front of her, pulled the iced tea pitcher from her hand, and passed it over to Torie. Meg took a step back only to feel his fingers curling around the nape of her neck, anchoring her in place. "Why don't you go help Chef in the kitchen, sweetheart. I'll clear off these dishes."

Sweetheart?

The engine roared, the tires squealed, the brakes smoked, and the speeding car slammed into the baby carriage. Right there in front of the biggest gossips in Wynette, Texas, Ted Beaudine lowered his head, sealed his legendary lips over hers, and announced to the whole world that there'd be no more sneaking around. Meg Koranda was the new woman in his life.

A furious Kayla came out of her chair. Shelby groaned. Birdie knocked over her iced tea glass. Emma buried her face in her hands, and Zoey, who looked as befuddled as one of her second graders, cried, "I thought she was making it up to get rid of Spence."

"Ted and *Meg*?" Hunter Gray's mother exclaimed.

Francesca sagged back in her chair. "Teddy . . . What have you done?"

With the possible exception of her agent, everyone else in the room understood the import of what had just happened. Kayla watched her boutique slip away. Birdie saw her new tearoom and bookstore go up in smoke. Zoey mourned the school improvements that would never happen. Shelby and Torie envisioned more sleepless, guilt-ridden nights for their husbands. And Francesca saw her only son slipping into the grasp of a scheming, unworthy woman.

Meg wanted to cry from the sheer, exhilarating joy of knowing he'd do something so colossally stupid for her.

He brushed his knuckles down her cheek. "Go on now, sweetheart. Mom appreciates the way you stepped in to help her today, but I'll take over now."

"Yes, Meg," Francesca said quietly. "We can handle it from here."

Meg was more important to him than this town. Her heart surged with a giddy intoxication that made her dizzy, but the woman she'd become didn't let her enjoy the moment for long. She dug her nails into her palms and faced his mother's guests. "I'm . . . I'm . . . sorry you were forced to see that." She cleared her throat. "He's, uh, had a tough time lately. I'm trying to be kind, but . . ." She took a shaky, shallow breath. "He can't accept the fact that I'm . . . just not that into him."

Ted picked up what was left of Torie's soufflé, took a bite, and listened patiently as Meg tried her best to do the right thing and dig him out of the beautiful mess he'd created. "It's me, not you." She turned to him, urging him with her eyes to go along with her. "Everybody else thinks you're fabulous, so it has to be me, right? Nobody else seems to find you just a little bit . . . creepy."

He cocked an eyebrow.

Francesca swelled up in her chair. "Did you just call my son 'creepy'?"

Ted spooned up another bite of chocolate, interested in what else she'd come up with. He wasn't going to help at all. She wanted to kiss him, yell at him. Instead, she returned her attention to the women. "Be honest." Her voice gained strength with the rightness of what she was doing. "You all know what I mean. The way the birds start to sing when he walks outside. That's creepy, right? And those halos that keep popping up around his head?"

No one moved. No one said a word.

Her mouth had gone dry, but she plowed on. "What about the *stigmata*?"

"Stigmata?" Torie said. "That's a new one."

"Marking-pen accident." Ted devoured the last spoonful of chocolate and set the dish aside. "Meg, honey—and I'm only saying this because I care so much—you're acting kind of crazy. I sure do hope you're not pregnant."

A dish banged in the kitchen, taking her resolve with it. He was a master of cool. She was merely a wannabe and she'd never be able to beat him at his own game. This was his town, his problem to solve. She grabbed the iced tea pitcher and made a dash for the kitchen.

"I'll see you tonight," he called after her. "Same time. And wear that dress of Torie's. It looks a hell of a lot better on you than it ever did on her. Sorry, Torie, but you know it's true."

As Meg slipped through the door, she heard Shelby's wail. "But what about the contest? This is going to ruin everything!"

"Screw the contest," Torie said. "We've got bigger problems. Our mayor just gave Sunny Skipjack the finger and San Antone a new golf resort."

TED WISELY DIDN'T RETURN to the kitchen. As Meg helped Chef clean up, her mind was spinning in a dozen different directions. She heard the guests leaving, and before long Francesca came into the kitchen.

Her face was pale. She was barefoot, her party clothes exchanged for shorts and a T-shirt. She thanked Chef and paid him, then handed Meg her check.

It was twice what Meg had been promised.

"You did the work of two people," Francesca said.

Meg nodded and gave it back. "My contribution to the library fund." She held Francesca's gaze just long enough to display a little dignity, then returned to her work.

It was almost dinnertime before the last dishes were put away and she could leave, toting the generous sack of leftovers Chef had given her. She couldn't stop smiling all the way back to the church. Ted's truck was parked by the steps. As tired as she was, all she could think about was tearing his clothes off. She grabbed the leftovers and dashed inside only to come to a screeching halt.

The church had been ransacked. Overturned furniture, slashed pillows, strewn clothing . . . Orange juice and ketchup were smeared on the futon, and her jewelry supplies were scattered everywhere—her precious beads, the tools she'd just purchased, tangled lengths of wire.

Ted stood in the middle of the mess. "The sheriff's on his way."

THE SHERIFF FOUND NO SIGN of forcible entry. When the subject of keys came up, Ted said he'd already put in a call to have the locks changed. As the sheriff advanced the theory that a vagrant had done the job, Meg knew she had to come clean about the message smeared on her bathroom mirror.

Ted exploded. "You're just getting around to telling me? What the hell were you thinking? I wouldn't have let you stay here another day."

She just looked at him. He glared right back—no halo in sight.

The sheriff asked with a straight face if anybody held a grudge against her. She thought he was putting her on until she remembered he worked for the county and might not be tuned in to local gossip.

"Meg's had some run-ins with a few people," Ted said, "but I can't imagine any of them doing this."

The sheriff pulled out his notebook. "What people?"

She tried to pull herself together. "Basically anybody who likes Ted isn't too fond of me."

The sheriff shook his head. "That's an awful lot of people. Could you narrow it down?"

"There's not really much point in throwing out random names," she said.

"You're not accusing anybody. You're giving me a list of people who have a grudge against you. I need your cooperation, Miz Koranda."

She saw his point, but it didn't feel right.

"Miz Koranda?"

She tried to muster the energy to begin. "Well, there's . . ." She barely knew where to start. "Sunny Skipjack wants Ted for herself." She gazed at the destruction around her and took a deep breath. "Then there's Birdie Kittle, Zoey Daniels, Shelby Traveler, Kayla Garvin. Kayla's father, Bruce. Maybe Emma Traveler, although I thought she'd come around."

"Not a single one of them would tear the place up like this," Ted said.

"Somebody did," the sheriff replied, flipping to a fresh page in his notebook. "Go on, Miz Koranda."

"All of Ted's old girlfriends, especially after what happened at the luncheon today." That involved a brief explanation, which Ted thoughtfully provided, along with his commentary on the cowardice of people who wanted to sneak around instead of being up front about their relationships.

"Anybody else?" The sheriff turned another page in his notebook.

"Skeet Cooper saw me mash one of Ted's golf balls into the ground to keep Ted from winning his match against Spencer Skipjack. You should have seen the way he looked at me."

"You should have seen the way I looked at you," Ted said with disgust.

Meg picked at a hangnail.

"And?" The sheriff clicked his pen.

She pretended to look out the window. "Francesca Beaudine."

"Now wait a minute!" Ted exclaimed.

"The sheriff wanted a list," she retorted. "I'm giving him a list, not making accusations." She turned back to the sheriff. "I saw Mrs. Beaudine a little more than an hour ago at her house, so it would have been very hard for her to have done this."

"Hard, but not impossible," the sheriff said.

"My mother did not trash this place," Ted declared.

"I don't know about Ted's father," Meg said. "He's hard to read."

Now it was the sheriff who puffed up with outrage. "The great Dallas Beaudine isn't a vandal."

"Probably not. And I think we can safely eliminate Cornelia Jorik. It would be tough for a former president of the United States to sneak into Wynette without getting noticed."

"She could have sent her henchmen," Ted drawled.

"If you don't like my list, you come up with one," she shot back. "You know all the suspects a lot better than I do. Bottom line—somebody is sending me a clear message that they want me out of Wynette."

The sheriff looked at Ted. "How about it, Ted?"

Ted shoved his hand through his hair. "I can't believe any of these people would do anything so ugly. What about somebody you work with at the club?"

"Those are my only positive relationships."

The sheriff flipped his notebook closed. "Miz Koranda, you shouldn't stay here by yourself. Not until this thing is settled."

"Believe me, she's not going to stay," Ted said.

The sheriff promised to talk to the police chief. Ted walked him out to his squad car, and Meg's cell rang in her purse. When she glanced at the display, she saw it was her mother, the last person she should talk to right now and the person whose voice she most wanted to hear.

She moved through her trashed kitchen and out the back door. "Hi, Mom."

"Hi, honey. How's the job?"

"Great. Really great." She sank down on the step. The cement still carried the day's heat, and she felt its warmth through Torie O'Connor's castoff skirt.

"Your dad and I are so proud of you."

Her mother was still under the illusion that Meg was the activities coordinator at the club, something she'd have to correct very soon. "Honestly, it's not much of a job."

"Hey, I know better than anyone what it's like to work with giant egos, and you have to see a lot of that at a country club. Which brings me to the reason I called. I have some great news."

"Belinda died and left me all her money."

"You wish. No, your grandmother will live forever. She's one of the undead. The great news is . . . Your father and I are coming to visit you."

Oh, God . . . Meg jumped up from the step. A dozen ugly images flashed through her head. The ripped sofa cushions . . . The broken glass . . . The drink cart . . . The faces of everyone who held a grudge against her.

"We miss you, and we want to see you," her mother said. "We want to meet your new friends. We're so proud of the way you've turned things around for yourself."

"That's . . . that's great."

"We have some scheduling we need to work out, but we'll settle that soon. A low-key visit. Just a day or so. I miss you."

"I miss you, too, Mom." She'd have time to clean up the mess inside, but that was only the tip of the iceberg. What about her job? She assessed the probability of being promoted to activities coordinator before their visit and concluded she had a better chance of being invited to Birdie's house for a slumber party. She shuddered at the thought of introducing her parents to Ted. It didn't take much imagination to picture her mother falling to her knees and begging Ted not to wise up.

She picked the most straightforward of her troubles. "Mom, there's just one thing . . . My job. It's not that impressive."

"Meg, stop putting yourself down. I can't change the fact that you've grown up in a family of wacko overachievers. We're the strange ones. You're a normal, intelligent, beautiful woman who let herself get sidetracked by all the craziness around her. But that's behind you now. You've made a fresh start, and we couldn't be prouder. I have to run. I love you."

"Love you, too," Meg said weakly. And then, after her mother had hung up: "Mom, I'm a cart girl, not the activities coordinator. But my jewelry's selling great."

The back door opened, and Ted appeared. "I'll send somebody tomorrow to clean up."

"No," she said wearily. "I don't want anyone to see this."

He understood. "Then stay out here and relax. I'll deal with it."

All she wanted to do was curl up in a ball and think about everything that had happened, but she'd spent too many years letting other people clean up after her. "I'm fine. Let me change my clothes first."

"You shouldn't have to do this."

"Neither should you." That kind, beautiful face made her ache. A few weeks ago, she'd have asked herself what a man like Ted was doing with a woman like her, but something had started to happen inside her, a sense of accomplishment that had begun to make her feel just a little bit worthy.

He dragged the ruined futon outside, followed by the damaged couch and chairs she'd gotten from the club. He cracked a few jokes as he worked to lift her spirits. She swept up broken glass, examining it so she didn't accidentally throw away any of her precious beads. When she was satisfied, she went into the kitchen to clean up the mess there, but he'd already done it.

By the time they were finished, it was nearly dark, and they were both hungry. They carried the luncheon leftovers and two bottles of beer into the graveyard and spread everything out on one of the bath towels. They ate directly from the containers, their forks occasionally touching. She needed to talk about what had happened at his mother's house, but she waited until they were finished before she broached the subject. "You should never have done what you did at the luncheon."

He leaned against Horace Ernst's tombstone. "And what was that?"

"Don't play games. Kissing me." She worked to suppress the exhilaration that still wanted to bubble over inside her. "By now, it's all over town that we're a couple. Spence and Sunny won't be back for more than five minutes before they'll hear about it."

"You let me worry about Spence and Sunny."

"How could you do something so stupid?" *So wonderful.*

Ted extended his legs toward the Mueller plot. "I want you to move in with me for a while."

"Are you paying attention to anything I'm saying?"

"Everybody knows about us now. There's no reason not to move in."

After all he'd done for her, she couldn't fight with him any longer. She picked up a stick and peeled the bark with her thumbnail. "I appreciate the offer, but moving in with you would be like thumbing my nose at your mother."

"I'll take care of my mother," he said grimly. "I love her, but she doesn't run my life."

"Yeah, that's what we all say. You. Me. Lucy." She stabbed the stick into the dirt. "These are powerful women. They're sane, they're smart, they rule their worlds, and they love us ferociously. A potent combination that makes it tough to pretend they're normal mothers."

"You're not staying here alone. You don't even have a place to sleep."

She gazed through the trees toward the trash pile that now held her futon. Whoever had done this wasn't going to stop, not as long as Meg stayed in Wynette. "All right," she said. "But only for tonight."

She followed him back to his house in the Rustmobile. They'd barely gotten inside before he drew her to his chest and made a one-handed phone call. "Mom, somebody broke into the church and trashed the place, so Meg'll be staying with me for a couple of days. You scare her, I'm mad at you, and you're not welcome here right now, so leave us alone." He hung up.

"She doesn't scare me," Meg protested. "Not much, anyway."

He kissed her on the nose, turned her in the general direction of the stairs, and patted her bottom, lingering on the dragon. "As much as I hate saying this, you're dead on your feet. Go to bed. I'll be up later."

"Hot date?"

"Even better. I'm going to rig up a surveillance camera at the church." His voice developed a hard edge. "Something I'd have done right away if you'd told me about the first break-in."

She wasn't foolish enough to try to defend herself. Instead, she wrapped her arms around him and pulled him down on the bamboo floor. After everything that had happened today, this time would be different. This time he'd touch something other than her body.

She rolled on top of him, grabbed his head between her hands, and kissed him ferociously. He kissed her back with his customary competency. Aroused her with his intoxicating ingenuity. Left her sweaty and breathless and almost . . . but not quite . . . satisfied.

chapter seventeen

MEG WASN'T USED TO AIR-CONDITIONING, and with only a sheet covering her, she got chilly during the night. She curled against Ted, and when she opened her eyes, it was morning.

She rolled to her side to study him. He was as irresistible asleep as awake. He had the best kind of bed head, a little flat here, a little spiky there, and her fingers itched to sort it out. She studied the distinct tan line across his bicep. No respectable Southern California glamour boy would be caught dead with a tan line like that, but Ted wouldn't spare it a thought. She pressed her lips to it.

He rolled to his back, dragging part of the sheet with him, and stirring up the musky scent of their sleeping bodies. She was instantly aroused, but she needed to be at the club soon, and she forced herself out of bed. By now, everyone would know all about what had happened at the luncheon yesterday, and it wouldn't occur to any of them to blame Ted for that kiss. A day full of problems stretched in front of her.

She was stocking the cart for the Tuesday morning women golfers when Torie emerged from the locker room. With her ponytail swinging, she marched toward Meg and, in typical Torie fashion, got down to business. "Obviously, you can't stay at the church after what happened, and you sure can't stay at Ted's, so we all decided the best thing is for you to move into Shelby's guest suite. I lived there between my first two unfortunate marriages. It's private and comfortable, plus it has its own kitchen, something you wouldn't have if you stayed with Emma or me." She set off for the pro shop, ponytail bouncing, and then called over her shoulder, "Shelby's expecting you by six. She gets upset when people are late."

"Hold on!" Meg stalked after her. "I'm not moving into your childhood home."

Torie planted her hand on her hip, looking as serious as Meg had ever seen her. "You can *not* stay at Ted's."

Meg already knew that, but she hated being ordered around. "Contrary to popular belief, none of you get a vote. And I'm going back to the church."

Torie snorted. "Do you really think he'll let you do that after what happened?"

"Ted doesn't *let* me do anything." She stomped back to the cart. "Thank Shelby for her generosity, but I've made my plans."

Torie came after her. "Meg, you can't move in with Ted. You really can't."

Meg pretended not to hear and drove off.

She wasn't up to working on her jewelry while she waited for customers, so she pulled out a copy of *American Earth* she'd borrowed from Ted, but not even the words of the country's most astute environmentalists could hold her attention. She set the book aside as the first foursome of women appeared.

"Meg, we heard about the break-in."

"You must have been terrified."

"Who do you think did it?"

"I'll bet they wanted to get to your jewelry."

She scooped ice into paper cups, poured drinks, and answered their questions as briefly as she could. Yes, it was scary. No, she didn't have any idea who'd done it. Yes, she intended to be a lot more careful in the future.

When the next foursome appeared, she heard more of the same, but it still didn't sink in right away. Only after they were all out on the fairway did it occur to her that not one of those eight women had mentioned Ted's kiss at the luncheon or his declaration that he and Meg were a couple.

She didn't understand it. The women in this town loved nothing more than to pry into other people's business, especially Ted's, so politeness wasn't holding them back. What was going on?

She didn't put the pieces together until the next foursome began pulling their carts up to the tee. And then she understood.

None of the women she'd spoken to had been at the luncheon, and they didn't know. The twenty guests who'd witnessed what had happened had formed a conspiracy of silence.

She sank back into the cart and tried to imagine the telephone lines buzzing last night. She could hear each of Francesca's guests swearing on her Bible, or the latest issue of *InStyle* magazine, not to breathe a word to anyone. Twenty gossipy Wynette women had taken a vow of silence. It couldn't last, not under normal circumstances. But where Ted was concerned, it just might.

She served the next group, and sure enough, they only talked about the break-in, with no mention of Ted. But that changed half an hour later when the final group, a twosome, pulled up. As soon as she saw the women getting out of the cart, she knew this conversation would be different. Both of them had been at the luncheon. Both of them had seen what had transpired. And they were both coming toward her with decidedly unfriendly grimaces on their faces.

The shorter of the two, a leathery brunette everybody called Cookie, got right to the point. "We all know you're the one behind that break-in at the church, and we know why."

Meg should have seen this coming, but she hadn't.

The taller woman yanked on her golf glove. "You wanted to move in with him, and he didn't want you to, so you decided to make it impossible for him to refuse. You trashed your own place before you went to work that morning at Francesca's."

"You can't really believe that," Meg said.

Cookie yanked a club from her bag without getting her customary drink. "You didn't really think you could pull this off, did you?"

After they left, Meg stomped around the tee for a while, then slumped down on the wooden bench by the tee marker. It wasn't even eleven o'clock, and ripples of heat already hung in the air. She should leave. She had no prospects here. No real friends. No job worth doing. But she was staying anyway. She was staying because the man she'd fallen so stupidly in love with had jeopardized the future of this town he cared so much about to let the world know how important she was to him.

She hugged the knowledge to her heart.

HER CELL BEGAN TO RING not long after. The first call came from Ted. "I hear the local female mafia is trying to get you out of my house," he said. "Don't pay attention to them. You're staying with me, and I hope you're planning to make something good for dinner." A long pause. "I'll take care of dessert."

Her next call came from Spence, so she didn't answer, but he left a message saying he'd be back in two days, and he'd be sending a limo to pick her up for dinner. After that Haley called asking Meg to meet her at the snack shop on her two o'clock break. When Meg got there, she found an unwelcome surprise in the form of Birdie Kittle sitting across from her daughter at one of the green metal bistro tables.

Birdie was dressed for work in an aubergine knit suit. She'd draped the jacket over the back of the chair, revealing a white camisole and plump, lightly freckled arms. Haley hadn't bothered with makeup, which would have improved her appearance if she hadn't been so pale and tense. She jumped up from the table like a jack-in-the-box. "Mom has something to tell you."

Meg didn't want to hear anything Birdie Kittle had to say, but she took the empty chair between them. "How are you feeling?" she asked Haley. "Better than yesterday, I hope."

"Okay." Haley sat back down and started picking at the chocolate chip cookie lying on a square of waxed paper in front of her. Meg recalled the conversation she'd overheard at the luncheon.

"Haley was with that Kyle Bascom again last night," Birdie had said. *"I swear to God, if she gets pregnant . . ."*

Last week, Meg had seen Haley in the parking lot with a gangly kid about her own age, but when she'd mentioned it, Haley had been evasive.

She broke off a piece of the cookie. Meg had tried selling those same cookies from the cart, but the chips kept melting. "Go ahead, Mom," Haley said. "Ask her."

Birdie's mouth pinched, and her gold bracelet clinked against the edge of the table. "I heard about the break-in at the church."

"Yes, it seems everybody has."

Birdie ripped off the straw wrapper and poked it into her soft drink. "I talked to Shelby a couple of hours ago. It was nice of her to invite you to stay at her house. She didn't have to, you know."

Meg kept her response neutral. "I realize that."

Birdie pushed the straw through the ice. "Since it doesn't seem as though you're willing to stay there, Haley thought . . ."

"Mom!" Haley shot her a murderous look.

"Well, pardon meee. *I* thought you might be more comfortable at the inn. It's closer to the club than Shelby's, so you wouldn't have to drive as far to work, and I'm not booked up right now." Birdie jabbed at the bottom of the paper cup hard enough to poke a hole through it. "You can stay in the Jasmine Room, my compliments. There's a kitchenette that you might remember from all the times you cleaned it."

"Mom!" Color flooded Haley's pale face. There was a frantic air about her that worried Meg. "Mom wants you to stay. It's not just me."

Meg highly doubted that, but it meant a lot that Haley valued their friendship enough to stand up to her mother. She took a piece of the cookie Haley wasn't eating. "I appreciate the offer, but I already have plans."

"What plans?" Haley said.

"I'm moving back into the church."

"Ted will never let you do that," Birdie said.

"He's had the locks changed, and I want to be back in my own place." She didn't mention the surveillance camera he intended to finish installing today. The fewer people who knew about that, the better.

"Yes, well, we can't always get what we want," Birdie said, channeling her inner Mick Jagger. "Are you ever planning to think about somebody other than yourself?"

"Mom! It's good she's going back. Why do you have to be so negative?"

"I'm sorry, Haley, but you refuse to acknowledge what a mess Meg has made of everything. Yesterday, at Francesca's . . . You weren't there, so you can't possibly—"

"I'm not deaf. I heard you on the phone with Shelby."

Apparently the code of silence had a few holes.

Birdie nearly upset her drink as she got up from her chair. "We're all doing our best to clean up your messes, Meg Koranda, but we can't do it by ourselves. We could use a little cooperation." She grabbed her jacket and strode away, her red hair blazing in the sun.

Haley crumbled her cookie inside the wax-paper square. "I think you should go back to the church."

"You seem to be the only one." As Haley stared off into the distance, Meg regarded her with concern. "Obviously, I'm not doing a great job dealing with my own problems, but I know something's bothering you. If you want to talk, I'll listen."

"I don't have anything to talk about. I need to get back to work." Haley grabbed her mother's abandoned soda cup along with the macerated cookie and returned to the snack shop.

Meg headed back to the clubhouse to pick up the drink cart. She'd left it near the drinking fountain, and just as she got there, a very familiar, very unwelcome figure came striding around the corner of the clubhouse. Her designer sundress and Louboutin stilettos suggested she hadn't shown up for a round of golf. Instead, she beat a determined path toward Meg, her stilettos tap-tap-tapping along the asphalt, then going silent as she stepped into the grass.

Meg resisted the urge to hold up her fingers in the sign of the cross, but as Francesca came to a stop in front of her, she couldn't repress a groan. "Please don't say what I think you're going to say."

"Yes, well, I'm not precisely on top of the world about this, either." A quick flick of her hand pushed the Cavalli sunglasses to the top of her head revealing those luminous green eyes, the lids dusted with bronze, and silky dark mascara embracing her already thick lashes. What little makeup Meg had begun the day with, she'd sweated off hours ago, and while Francesca smelled of Quelques Fleurs, Meg smelled of spilled beer.

She looked down at Ted's diminutive mother. "Could you at least hand me a gun first so I can kill myself?"

"Don't be foolish," Francesca retorted. "If I had a gun, I'd have already used it on you." She swatted at a fly that had the audacity to buzz too close to her exquisite face. "Our guest cottage is detached from the house. You'll have it all to yourself."

"Do I get to call you Mom, too?"

"Good God, no." Something happened to the corner of her mouth. A grimace? A smirk? Impossible to tell. "Call me Francesca like everyone else."

"Peachy." Meg slipped her fingers into her pocket. "Out of curiosity, is anybody in this town even remotely capable of minding her own business?"

"No. And that's why I insisted from the beginning that Dallie and I keep a place in Manhattan. Did you know Ted was nine years old the first time he came to Wynette? Can you imagine how many of the local peculiarities he'd have picked up if he'd lived here from birth?" She sniffed. "It doesn't bear thinking about."

"I appreciate the offer, just as I appreciated Shelby's offer and Birdie Kittle's, but would you please inform your coven that I'm going back to the church."

"Ted will never allow that."

"Ted doesn't get a vote," Meg snapped.

Francesca gave a small coo of satisfaction. "Proving you don't know my son nearly as well as you think you do. The guest cottage is unlocked, and the refrigerator is stocked. Don't even think about defying me." And off she went.

Across the grass.

Down the cart path.

Tap . . . tap . . . Tap . . . tap . . . Tap . . . tap . . .

MEG REVIEWED HER MISERABLE DAY as she pulled out of the employees' parking lot that evening and headed down the service drive toward the highway. She had no intention of moving into Francesca Beaudine's guesthouse, or Shelby Traveler's, or the Wynette Country Inn. But she also wasn't staying with Ted. As angry as she might be with the meddling women of this town, she wouldn't thumb her nose at them, either. No matter how awful they were, how intrusive and judgmental, they were doing what they believed was right. Unlike so many other Americans, the inhabitants of Wynette, Texas, didn't understand the concept of citizen apathy. They also had reality on their side. She couldn't live with Ted as long as the Skipjacks were around.

Out of nowhere, something came flying toward her car. She gasped and hit the brakes, but she was too late. A rock slammed into her windshield. She caught a flicker of movement in the trees, slammed the car into park, and jumped out. She slid on some loose gravel but regained her balance and raced toward the grove of trees that lined the service drive.

Stickers grabbed at her shorts and scratched her legs as she plunged into the undergrowth. She saw another flicker of motion, but she couldn't even tell whether it came from a person. She only knew that someone had once again attacked her, and she was sick of being a victim.

She plunged deeper into the woods, but she wasn't sure which way to go. She stopped to listen but heard nothing except the rasp of her own breathing. Eventually, she gave up. Whoever had thrown that rock had gotten away.

She was still shaking when she returned to her car. A spiderweb of shattered glass spread from the center of the windshield, but by craning her neck she could almost see well enough to drive.

By the time she reached the church, her anger had steadied her. She badly wanted to see Ted's truck parked outside, but he wasn't there. She tried to use her key to get in, but the lock had been changed, just as she expected. She stomped back down the steps and looked under the stone frog, knowing even as she picked it up that he wouldn't have left a new key for her. She stomped around some more until she located a security camera mounted in the pecan tree that had once sheltered the faithful as they'd come from worship.

She shook her fist at it. "Theodore Beaudine, if you don't get over here right away and let me in, I'm going to break a window!" She plopped down on the bottom step to wait, then hopped up again and cut across the cemetery to the creek.

The swimming hole waited for her. She stripped down to bra and panties and dove in. The water, cool and welcoming, closed over her head. She swam to the rocky bottom, kicked off, and came to the surface. She dove again, willing the water to wash away her terrible day. When she'd finally cooled down, she stuffed her wet feet into her sneakers, grabbed her dirty work clothes, and headed back toward the church in her sodden underwear. But as she stepped out of the trees, she came to a dead stop.

The great Dallas Beaudine sat on a black granite tombstone, his faithful caddy, Skeet Cooper, standing at his side.

Cursing under her breath, she ducked back into the trees and pulled on her shorts and sweaty polo. Facing down Ted's father was a whole different ball game from dealing with the women. She dragged her fingers through her wet hair, told herself to show no fear, and sauntered into the cemetery. "Checking out your future resting site?"

"Not quite yet," Dallie said. He rested comfortably on the grave marker, his long, jean-clad legs stretched out before him, dappled light playing in the silver threads of his dark blond hair. Even at fifty-nine, he was a beautiful man, which made Skeet's leathery ugliness all the more pronounced.

Her feet sloshed in her sneakers as she moved closer. "You could do worse than this place."

"I s'pose." Dallie crossed his ankles. "The surveyors showed up a day early, and Ted's out at the landfill with them. This resort deal might go through after all. We told him we'd help you move your things to his house."

"I've decided to stay here."

Dallie nodded, as if he were thinking it over. "Doesn't seem too safe."

"He's set up at least one security camera."

Dallie nodded again. "Truth is, Skeet and I already moved your things."

"You had no right to do that!"

"Matter of opinion." Dallie turned his face into the breeze, as if he were checking wind direction before he made his next golf shot. "You're staying with Skeet."

"With *Skeet*?"

"He doesn't talk much. Figured you'd rather move in there than have to deal with my wife. I might as well tell you I don't like it when she gets upset, and you sure do upset her."

"She gets upset about the damnedest things." Skeet shifted his toothpick from one side of his mouth to the other. "Not much you can do to talk her out of it either, Francie being Francie."

"With all due respect . . ." Meg sounded like a lawyer, but Dallie's calm assurance rattled her in a way the women didn't. "I don't want to live with Skeet."

"Don't see why not." Skeet shifted his toothpick. "You'll have your own TV, and I won't bother you none. I like to keep the place neat, though."

Dallie rose from the tombstone. "You can follow us over, or Skeet'll drive your car and you can ride with me."

His steady gaze testified that the decision had been made, and nothing she said would change it. She weighed her options. Returning to the church clearly wasn't an option right now. She wasn't moving in with Ted. If he didn't understand why, she did. That left Shelby and Warren Traveler's house, the inn, Francesca's guesthouse, or staying with Skeet Cooper.

With his grizzled, sun-cured face and Willie Nelson ponytail falling between his shoulder blades, Skeet looked more like a derelict than a man who'd picked up a couple of million dollars caddying for a golf legend. She pulled her shredded pride together and regarded him loftily. "I don't let my roommates borrow my clothes, but I do enjoy a little spa party on Friday nights. Manis and pedis. You do mine. I'll do yours. That kind of thing."

Skeet shifted his toothpick and gazed at Dallie. "Looks like we got ourselves another live one."

"Seems that way." Dallie pulled his car keys from his pocket. "Still too soon to tell, though."

She had no idea what they were talking about. They set off ahead of her, and she heard Skeet chuckle. "Remember that night we almost let Francie drown in the swimming pool?"

"Sure was tempting," Francie's loving husband replied.

"Good thing we didn't."

"The Lord works in mysterious ways."

Skeet flicked his toothpick into the scrub. "He sure seems to be workin' overtime these days."

SHE'D SEEN SKEET'S SMALL, STONE, ranch-style house when she'd first explored the Beaudine compound. Double-hung windows flanked a front door painted a nondescript tan. An American flag, the only decorative feature, hung listlessly from a pole near the front walk.

"We tried not to mess up your things too much when we moved them," Dallie said as he held the front door open for her.

"Thoughtful." She stepped into an immaculately neat living area, which was painted a lighter version of tan than the front door and dominated by a pair of high-end, exceptionally ugly, brown recliners pointed directly at a large, wall-mounted flat-screen television. Dead center above it hung a multicolored sombrero. The room's only true aesthetic touch came from a beautiful earth-toned rug similar to the ones in Francesca's office, a rug Meg suspected Skeet hadn't chosen himself.

He picked up the remote and turned on the Golf Channel. The wide opening opposite the front door revealed part of a hallway and a functional kitchen with wooden cabinets, white countertops, and a set of ceramic canisters shaped like English cottages. A smaller flat-screen television hung above a round wooden dinette table with four padded swivel chairs.

She followed Dallie down the hallway. "Skeet's bedroom's at the end," he said. "He snores like crazy, so you might want to buy yourself some earplugs."

"It gets better and better, doesn't it?"

"Temporary. Until things settle down."

She wanted to ask him exactly when he expected that might be but thought better of it. He led her into a sparsely furnished bedroom with mass-produced Early American—style furniture: a double bed covered in a quilted, geometrical-print bedspread; a dresser; an upholstered chair; and another flat-screen television. The room was painted the same tan as the rest of the house, and her suitcase, along with some packing boxes, sat on a bare tiled floor. Through the open closet door, she saw her wardrobe hanging from a wooden rod and her shoes neatly lined up beneath.

"Francie's offered more than once to decorate the place for him," Dallie said, "but Skeet likes to keep things simple. You have your own bathroom."

"Hooray."

"Skeet's office is in the bedroom next door. As far as I can tell, he doesn't use it for a damn thing, so you can set up your jewelry making in there. He won't notice, not unless you lose the remote control he keeps on top of the file cabinet."

The front door slammed, and even the Golf Channel couldn't drown out the sound of angry footsteps followed by the demanding bellow of Wynette's favorite son. "Where is she?"

Dallie gazed toward the hallway. "I told Francie we should have stayed in New York."

chapter eighteen

SKEET TURNED UP THE VOLUME in response to Ted's intrusion. Meg pulled herself together and poked her head out into the living room. "Surprise."

Ted's ball cap shaded his eyes, but his rigid jaw indicated stormy weather. "What are you doing here?"

She made a grand gesture toward the recliner. "I've taken a new lover. Sorry you had to find out like this."

"*Golf Central*'s on," Skeet grumbled, "and I can't hear a damn thing."

Dallie came out of the hallway behind her. "That's because you're going deaf. I been telling you for months to buy some damned hearing aids. Hey there, son. How did things go at the landfill?"

Ted's hands stayed aggressively planted on his hips. "What's she doing here? She's supposed to be staying with me."

Dallie turned his attention back to her, his blue eyes as clear as a Hill Country sky. "I told you he wouldn't be happy about this, Meg.

Next time you need to listen to me." He shook his head sadly. "I tried my damnedest to talk her out of it, son, but Meg sure does have a mind of her own."

She had a couple of choices. She picked the one that didn't involve punching someone. "It's better this way."

"Better for whom?" Ted retorted. "It sure as hell isn't better for me. And it's not better for you, either."

"As a matter of fact, it is. You have no idea—"

"Best you two have this discussion in private." Dallie looked embarrassed, which he wasn't. "Your mom and I are eating at the club tonight. Normally, I'd invite you both to join us, but there seems to be a lot of tension."

"You're damned right there's tension," Ted said. "She's got some wacko out there gunning for her, and I want her where I can keep an eye on her."

"Doubt she'll come to much harm here." Dallie headed for the front door. "Except for her eardrums."

The door closed behind him. Ted's censorious gaze, along with her damp clothes and clammy underwear, gave her goose bumps. She stomped down the hallway to her bedroom and knelt before her suitcase. "I've had a hard day," she said as he stalked into the room behind her. "You can go away now, too."

"I can't believe you let them get to you!" he exclaimed. "I thought you had more backbone."

She wasn't surprised that he'd seen through his father's charade. She pulled a bag, neatly packed with her toiletries, from the suitcase. "I'm hungry, and I need a shower."

His pacing stopped. The mattress sighed as he sat on the edge. Seconds ticked by before he spoke so softly she could barely hear. "Sometimes I want to leave this town so bad I can taste it."

A rush of tenderness filled her. She set aside the bag and went to him. As the sounds of a Viagra commercial echoed from the living room, she smiled and pulled off his ball cap. "You are this town," she whispered. And then she kissed him.

Two days later, as she sat in the shade by the fifth tee reading about large-scale composting, one of the junior caddies buzzed toward her in a cart. "You're wanted in the pro shop," he said. "I'll take over here."

She drove his cart back to the clubhouse with a sense of foreboding that turned out to be justifiable. No sooner had she stepped into the pro shop than a pair of large, sweaty hands settled over her eyes. "Guess who?"

She suppressed a groan, then pulled herself together. "The manly drawl suggests Matt Damon, but something tells me . . . Leonardo DiCaprio, right?"

A hearty laugh, the hands dropped, and Spencer Skipjack turned her to face him. He wore his Panama hat, an aqua sports shirt, and dark pants. A big grin stretched his big mouth over his big square white veneers. "I have definitely missed you, Miz Meg. You're one of a kind."

Plus, she had ultrafamous parents, and she was more than twenty years his junior, an irresistible combination to an egomaniac. "Hey, Spence. Thanks for the presents."

"That soap dish is from our new line. Retails for a hundred and eighty-five dollars. Did you get my message?"

She played dumb. "Message?"

"About tonight. What with all my traveling, I've been neglecting you, but that's going to change starting right now." He made a vague gesture toward the front offices. "I sprung you from work for the rest of the day. We're flying to Dallas." He grabbed her arm. "First, a little shopping trip for you at Neiman's, then drinks at the Adolphus and dinner at the Mansion. My plane's waiting for us."

He'd dragged her halfway to the door, and this time he wasn't going to let her put him off as she'd done before. The most appealing of her options involved telling him to go to hell, but the land surveyors were still in town, the resort deal was practically signed, and she wouldn't be the ultimate spoiler. "You're the most thoughtful man."

"Neiman's was Sunny's idea."

"She's amazing."

"She's spending the day with Ted. The two of them have a lot of catching up to do."

Sunny might not have heard about the luncheon kiss, but she would almost certainly have heard about Ted's legendary lovemaking skills, and Meg suspected she'd be doing everything she could to find out for herself if the stories were true. Meg also knew Ted wouldn't touch her. Having that much faith in a man unsettled her. Hadn't she trusted men before? But none of those men were Ted.

Ted . . . who'd claimed her in front of the town and damned the consequences. A stupid, boneheaded thing to do that meant everything to her.

She tugged her bottom lip between her teeth. "We know each other well enough that I can be honest, right?"

The sight of his narrowing eyes wasn't encouraging, so she dumped her dignity and tried a pout. "What I'd really like is a golf lesson."

"A golf lesson?"

"You have such a beautiful swing. It reminds me of Kenny's, but I can't exactly ask him for a lesson, and I want to learn from the best. Please, Spence. You're such a great player. It'd mean a lot more to me than another trip to Dallas, where I've been at least a thousand times."

More like once, but he didn't know that, and twenty minutes later, they were on the practice range.

Unlike Torie, Spence was a miserable teacher, more interested in having her admire his swing than helping her develop her own, but Meg acted as though he was the king of all golf instructors. As he droned on, she found herself wondering if he was as committed to building an environmentally conscious resort as Ted believed. When they finally sat on the bench to take a break, she decided to go on a fishing expedition. "You're so good at this. I swear, Spence, your love for the game shows through in everything you do."

"I've been playing since I was a kid."

"That's why you have so much respect for the sport. Look at you. Anybody with money can build a golf course, but how many men have the vision to build a course that'll set the benchmark for future generations?"

"I believe in doing what's right."

That was encouraging. She amped it up a little. "I know you'll say all the environmental awards you're sure to win aren't what's most important, but you deserve every bit of the recognition that's coming to you."

She thought she'd gone too far, but she'd once again underestimated his bottomless ego. "Somebody has to set the new standard," he said, echoing words she'd heard from Ted.

She pressed a little harder. "Don't forget to hire a photographer to take photos of the landfill the way it is now. I'm not a journalist, but I'm guessing the various award committees are going to want really good before and after pictures."

"Now don't be putting the cart ahead of the horse, Miz Meg. I haven't signed anything yet."

She hadn't really expected him to reveal his final decision to her, but she'd hoped. A hawk soared overhead, and Spence started making noises about a romantic dinner at one of the local vineyards. If she had to eat with him, she wanted to do it someplace where she'd have lots of company, so she insisted that only the Roustabout's barbecue could satisfy her appetite.

Sure enough, they'd barely been seated before reinforcements began to arrive. Dallie sauntered in first, followed by Shelby Traveler, who hadn't even taken time to put on her mascara. Kayla's father, Bruce, still wearing his workout shorts, rushed in next, darting dirty looks at Meg while he ordered. They had no intention of leaving her alone with Spence, and by nine o'clock, their group occupied three tables, with Ted and Sunny noticeably missing.

Meg had taken a shower in the locker room before they'd left the club and changed into her spare outfit: an unimpressive funnel-neck gray top, swirly skirt, and sandals, but dressing down didn't discourage Spence, who couldn't keep his hands to himself. He took advantage of any excuse to press against her. He ran his finger over her wrist, readjusted the paper napkin in her lap, and brushed her breast with his arm as he reached for a bottle of Tabasco. Lady Emma did her best to distract him, but Spence had all the power, and he intended to use it to get what he wanted. Which was how she ended up standing in the parking lot under the red and blue neon ROUSTABOUT sign with her phone pressed to her ear.

"Dad, I have one of your biggest fans here," she said when her father picked up. "I know you've heard of Spencer Skipjack, the founder of Viceroy Industries. They make the most luxurious plumbing products. He's basically a genius."

Spence grinned, and his chest inflated in the neon flicker like one of Chef's pre—car crash soufflés.

She'd pulled her father away from his ancient Smith Corona

typewriter or from her mother. Either way, he wasn't happy. "What's this about, Meg?"

"Can you believe it?" she replied. "As busy as he is, he gave me a golf lesson today."

His annoyance shifted to concern. "Are you in some kind of trouble?"

"Absolutely not. Golf is the most amazing game. But then, you know that."

"You'd better have a good reason for this."

"I do. Here he is."

She shoved the phone at Spence and hoped for the best.

Spence immediately adopted an embarrassing intimacy with her father, peppering a movie critique with plumbing advice, offering the use of his private jet, and telling Jake Koranda where he should eat in L.A. Apparently her father didn't say anything to offend him because Spence was beaming when he finally handed her phone back.

Her father, however, wasn't nearly as happy. "That guy's an idiot."

"I knew you'd be impressed. Love you." Meg flipped her phone shut and gave Spence a thumbs-up. "My father doesn't usually take to people so quickly."

One look at Spence's beaming expression told her the conversation had only intensified his fixation on her. He curled his hands around her arms and began to pull her to him just as the Roustabout's door flew open and Torie, who'd finally realized they were missing, came flying out to the rescue. "Hurry up, you two. Kenny just ordered three of every dessert on the menu."

Spence didn't take his predatory eyes off Meg. "Meg and I have other plans."

"The molten lava cake?" Meg cried.

"And the spicy peach cobbler!" Torie exclaimed.

They managed to get Spence back inside, but Meg was sick of being held hostage. Fortunately, she'd insisted on driving herself, and after four bites of lava cake, she got up from the table. "It's been a long day, and I have to work tomorrow."

Dallie was immediately on his feet. "I'll walk you to your car."

Kenny shoved a beer at Spence, stopping him before he could follow. "I sure could use some business advice, Spence, and I can't think of a better man to turn to."

She made her escape.

Yesterday when she'd come out of work, she'd discovered that the Rustmobile's broken windshield had been replaced with a new one. Ted denied having done it, but she knew he was responsible. So far, nothing else of hers had been vandalized, but it wasn't over. Whoever hated her wouldn't give up, not as long as she stayed in Wynette.

When she got to the house, she found Skeet asleep in the recliner. She tiptoed past him into her bedroom. As she kicked off her sandals, the window slid open and Ted's lanky body squeezed through. Little eddies of pleasure swirled inside her. She cocked her head. "I'm sure glad we're not sneaking around anymore."

"I didn't want to talk to Skeet, and not even you can make me mad tonight."

"Sunny finally put out?"

"Even better." He grinned. "The announcement's coming tomorrow. Spence picked Wynette."

She smiled. "Congratulations, Mr. Mayor." She started to hug him, then pulled back. "You do know you're making a deal with the devil."

"Spence's ego is his weakness. As long as we control that, we control the man."

"Ruthless, but true," she said. "I still can't believe all those women kept their mouths shut."

"About what?"

"Your temporary lapse of sanity at your mother's luncheon. Twenty women! Twenty-one if we count Mummy."

But he had something more pressing on his mind. "I have a P.R. firm standing by. The minute the ink's dry on the land contract, a press release is going out crowning Spence the leader of golf's green movement. I'm going to make sure he's in too deep right from the beginning to ever pull out."

"I love it when you talk dirty."

Even as she teased him, an uneasiness came over her, a feeling that she was missing something, but she forgot about it as she began pulling at his clothes. He cooperated beautifully, and they were soon naked on her bed, the breeze from the open window falling across their skin.

This time she wasn't going to let him take over. "Close your eyes," she whispered. "Tight."

He did as she asked, and she nuzzled her way to a small, taut nipple. She dawdled there for a while, then slipped her hand between his thighs. She kissed him, cupped him, stroked.

His eyelids inched open, lids heavy. He reached for her, but she slid on top of him before he could take over. Slowly, she began guiding him into her body—a body not completely ready for such a formidable invasion. But the reluctant stretch and ache excited her.

Now his eyes were fully open. She began to pull herself down hard upon him only to feel his hands gripping her thighs, holding her back. His brow furrowed. She didn't want to see concern there. She wanted ravishment.

But he was too much the gentleman.

He arched his back and settled his mouth over her breast. The movement raised his thighs and lifted her off him. "Not so fast," he whispered against her moist nipple.

Yes, *fast*! she wanted to cry out. Fast and awkward and crazy and passionate.

But he'd felt her tightness, and he was having none of it. He wouldn't let her endure even a moment's discomfort in pursuit of his own satisfaction. As he teased her nipple, he reached between their bodies and began to perform his magic tricks, arousing her until she was mindless. Another A-plus performance.

She recovered first and rolled out from under him. His eyes were closed, and she tried to find reassurance in the rapid rise and fall of his chest, his sweat-slicked skin. But despite his rumpled hair and the slight puffiness she'd inflicted on his bottom lip, she couldn't make herself believe she'd really touched him, not in any lasting way. Only the memory of that reckless public kiss told her she wasn't being a fool.

THE TOWN ERUPTED WITH THE NEWS that Spence had chosen Wynette. For the next three days, people hugged each other on the street, the Roustabout poured free beers, and the barbershop blasted out old Queen anthems from an ancient boom box. Ted couldn't go anywhere without men pounding him on the back and women hurling themselves at him, not that they didn't do that anyway. The good news even eclipsed Kayla's announcement that the contest bidding had reached twelve thousand dollars.

Meg barely saw him. He was either on the phone with Spence's lawyers, who were due to fly in any day to finalize the contracts, or he was involved in Operation Avoid Sunny. She missed him dreadfully, right along with their less-than-satisfactory sex life.

She was doing her own avoidance dance with Spence. Fortunately, the local citizens had joined the effort to keep him away from her. Still, the uneasiness she'd been carrying around for days wouldn't go away.

On Sunday after work she made a detour to the swimming hole to cool off. She'd developed a deep affection for both the creek and the Pedernales River that fed it. Although she'd seen photos of the way a sudden rainstorm could transform the river into a raging corridor of destruction, the water had always been gentle with her.

Cypress and ash grew near the creek's bank, and she sometimes caught sight of a whitetail deer or an armadillo. Once a coyote came out from behind some buttonbush and looked as startled to see her as she was to see it. But today the cool waters failed to work their magic. She couldn't get past the disquieting notion that she was missing something important. It dangled in front of her, a piece of fruit she couldn't quite reach.

A cloud rolled in, and a scrub jay scolded her from the branch of a nearby hackberry tree. She shook the water from her hair and dove under again. When she came up, she wasn't alone.

Spence loomed above her on the riverbank, the clothes she'd abandoned hanging from his big hands. "You shouldn't go swimming by yourself, Miz Meg. It's not safe."

Her toes dug into the mud, and water lapped at her shoulders. He must have followed her here, but she'd been too preoccupied to notice. A stupid mistake that someone with so many enemies should never have made. The sight of him holding her clothes made her stomach knot. "No offense, Spence, but I'm not in the mood for company."

"Maybe I'm tired of waiting for you to be ready." Still holding her clothes, he sat on a big rock by the river's edge next to the towel she'd left there and studied her. He was dressed for business in navy pants and a long-sleeved blue oxford dress shirt he'd begun to sweat through. "It seems every time I start to have a serious conversation with you, you manage to slip away."

She was naked except for a sodden pair of panties, and as much as she might like to think of Spence as a buffoon, he wasn't. A cloud skittered over the sun. She clenched her fists under the water. "I'm a happy-go-lucky person. I don't like serious conversations."

"Comes a time when everybody has to get serious."

The way he slid her bra through his fingers gave her chills, and she didn't like being frightened. "Go away, Spence. You weren't invited."

"Either you come out or I'm coming in."

"I'm staying where I am. I don't like this, and I want you to leave."

"That water looks damned inviting." He set her clothes next to him on the rock. "Did I ever tell you I swam competitively in college?" He began taking off his shoes. "I even thought about training for the Olympics, but I had too much else going on."

She sank deeper into the water. "If you're seriously interested in me, Spence, you're going about this the wrong way."

He pulled off his socks. "I should have been up front with you earlier, but Sunny says I can be too blunt. My mind works faster than most people's. She says I don't always give people enough time to get to know me."

"She's right. You should listen to your daughter."

"Cut the bull, Meg. You've had plenty of time." His fingers worked at the buttons of his blue oxford dress shirt. "You think all I want is a roll in the hay. I want more than that, but you won't stay still long enough to hear me out."

"I apologize. I'll meet you in town for dinner, and you can say whatever you want to."

"We need privacy for this discussion, and we won't have that in town." He unfastened his cuffs. "The two of us have a future together. Maybe not marriage, but a future. Being together. I knew that the first time I met you."

"We don't have a future. Be real. You're only attracted to me because of my father. You don't even know me. You just think you do."

"That's where you're wrong." He took off his shirt revealing a gruesomely hairy chest. "I've been around longer than you have, and I understand human nature a lot better." He stood. "Look at you. Driving a fucking drink cart at a third-rate public course that calls itself a country club. Some women do just fine on their own, but you're not one of them. You need someone picking up the check."

"You're wrong."

"Am I?" He came toward the riverbank. "Your parents brought you up soft. It was a mistake I didn't make with Sunny. She worked at the plant from the time she was fourteen, so she learned early on where a dollar came from. But that's not the way it was with you. You had all the advantages and none of the responsibility."

There was enough truth in his words to sting.

He stopped at the riverbank. A raven called out. The water rushed around her. She shivered from the chill and from her vulnerability.

His hands dropped to his belt buckle. She sucked in her breath as he pulled it open. "Stop right there," she said.

"I'm hot and that water looks real good."

"I mean it, Spence. I don't want you here."

"You just think you don't." He pulled off his pants, tossed them aside, and stood in front of her. His hairy belly hung over white boxers, pasty legs protruding beneath.

"Spence, I don't like this."

"You brought it on yourself, Miz Meg. If you'd gone to Dallas with me like I wanted yesterday, we could have had this discussion on my plane." He dove in. The splash hit her in the eyes. She blinked, and within seconds, he'd surfaced beside her, his hair plastered to his head, rivulets of water running through his blue-black beard. "What's the real problem, Meg? You think I won't take care of you?"

"I don't want you to take care of me." She didn't know if he intended to rape her or if he merely wanted to make her submit to his authority. She only knew she had to get away, but as she backed toward the riverbank, his arm shot out and he grabbed her wrist. "Come here."

"Let me go."

His thumbs dug into her upper arms. He was strong, and he lifted her off the rocky bottom, exposing her breasts. She saw his lips coming toward her, those big square teeth aiming for her mouth.

"Meg!"

A figure shot out of the trees. Slim, dark-haired, dressed in hip-hugging shorts and a retro Haight-Ashbury T-shirt.

"Haley!" Meg cried.

Spence jumped back as if he'd been hit. Haley came closer, then stopped. She hugged herself, crossing her arms over her chest and clutching her elbows, unsure what to do next.

Meg didn't know why she'd shown up, but she'd never been so glad to see anyone. Spence's heavy, drawn eyebrows jutted ominously over his small eyes. Meg made herself look at him. "Spence was just leaving, weren't you, Spence?"

The fury in his expression told her that their love affair was over. By puncturing his ego, she'd moved to the top of his enemies list.

He pulled himself out of the water. His white briefs clung to his buttocks, and she looked away. Haley stood frozen in the shade, and he didn't spare her a glance as he jerked on his pants and shoved his feet into his shoes without his socks. "You think you got the best of me, but you haven't." His voice was almost a growl as he snatched up his shirt. "Nothing happened here, and don't either of you try to say otherwise."

He disappeared up the path.

Meg's teeth were chattering, and her knees had locked so she couldn't move.

Haley finally found her tongue. "I've—I've got to go."

"Not yet. Help me out. I'm a little shaky."

Haley came toward the bank. "You shouldn't swim here by yourself."

"Believe me, I won't be doing it again. It was stupid." A sharp stone bit into the ball of her foot, and she winced. "Here, give me your hand."

With Haley's help, she made it up onto the riverbank. She was dripping and naked except for her panties, and her teeth wouldn't stop chattering. She grabbed the towel she'd brought with her and sank down onto the sun-heated rock. "I don't know what I'd have done if you hadn't shown up."

Haley looked toward the path. "Are you going to call the police?"

"Do you really think anybody wants to take Spence on right now?"

Haley rubbed her elbow. "What about Ted? Are you going to tell him?"

Meg imagined the consequences of doing just that and didn't like what she saw. But she also wasn't keeping this to herself. She rubbed her hair with the towel, then balled it up. "I'll call in sick at work for the next few days and make sure Spence can't find me. But as soon as that bastard's down payment is in the bank, I'm telling Ted exactly what happened. A few other people, too. They need to know how ruthless Spence can be." She clutched the towel. "For now, keep it to yourself, okay?"

"I wonder what Spence would have done if I hadn't shown up?"

"I don't want to think about it." Meg grabbed her T-shirt from the ground and pulled it on, but she couldn't make herself touch the bra he'd held. "I don't know what stroke of luck brought you here today, but I sure am glad. What did you want?"

Haley twitched, as if the question startled her. "I was— I don't know." Color flooded her face beneath her makeup. "I was driving, and I thought you might want to . . . go get burgers or something."

Meg's hands stalled on the hem of her T-shirt. "Everybody knows I'm staying at Skeet's. How did you find me here?"

"What difference does it make?" She spun around and headed for the path.

"Wait!"

But Haley didn't wait, and her reaction was so extreme, so out of proportion to their conversation, that Meg was taken aback. Then everything clicked into place.

Her chest constricted. She shoved her feet into her flip-flops and ran after her. She took the shortcut through the cemetery instead of following the path. Her flip-flops slapped her heels, and weeds grabbed her still-damp legs. She reached the front of the church just as Haley ran around from the back, and she blocked her path. "Stop right there! I want to talk to you."

"Get out of my way!"

Haley tried to get past her, but Meg wouldn't let her. "You knew I was here because you followed me. Just like Spence did."

"You don't know what you're talking about. Let me go!"

Meg tightened her grip. "It was you."

"Stop it!"

Haley tried to free her arm, but Meg held fast as water dripped icy fingers down the back of her neck. "All this time. You're the one who broke into the church. You're the one who sent that letter and threw the rock at my car. All along. It was you."

Haley's chest heaved. "I don't— I don't know what you're talking about."

Meg's damp T-shirt clung to her skin, and goose bumps broke out on her arms. She felt sick. "I thought we were friends."

Her words cut something loose inside Haley. She jerked her arm away, and her sneer distorted her mouth. "Friends! Yeah, you were a friend, all right."

The wind picked up. An animal scuttled in the brush. Meg finally understood. "This is because of Ted . . ."

Haley's face crumpled with fury. "You told me you weren't in love with him. You told me you were just saying that to get rid of Spence. And I believed you. I was so stupid. I believed you until that night I saw you together."

The night Meg and Ted had made love at the church and Meg had seen those headlights. Her stomach twisted. "You spied on us."

"I didn't spy!" Haley cried. "It wasn't like that! I was driving around, and I saw Ted's truck go by. He'd been out of town, and I wanted to talk to him."

"So you followed him here."

She shook her head, the movement jerky. "I didn't know where he was going. I just wanted to talk to him."

"And you accomplished that by spying on us through the window."

Tears of rage spilled over her lids. "You lied to me! You told me it was all fake!"

"I didn't lie. That's the way it started out. But things changed, and I sure as hell wasn't going to make a big announcement about it." Meg regarded her with disgust. "I can't believe you did those things to me. Do you have any idea how it felt?"

Haley swiped at her nose with the back of her hand. "I didn't hurt you. I only wanted you to *go away.*"

"What about Kyle? That's what I don't understand. I thought you were crazy about him. I've seen you together."

"I told him to leave me alone, but he kept showing up at work." Dirty mascara tears smeared her cheeks. "Last year, when I liked him, he wouldn't even talk to me. Then, when I stopped liking him, all of a sudden he wanted to go out."

The pieces came together. "You didn't change your mind about going to U.T. because of Kyle. All along, it was because of Ted. Because he and Lucy weren't getting married."

"So what?" Her nose was red, her skin blotchy.

"Did you do this kind of thing to her? Harass her like you've harassed me?"

"Lucy was different."

"She was going to marry him! But you left her alone and went after me. Why? I don't get that."

"I didn't love him then," she said fiercely. "Not the way I do now. Everything changed after she ran out on him. Before then—I had a crush on him like everybody else, but it was a kid thing. After she left, it was like I could see all the pain in his heart, and I wanted to make it go away. Like I understood him when nobody else did."

One more woman who thought she understood Ted Beaudine.

Haley's eyes were fierce. "I knew then that I'd never love anybody like I love him. And if you love somebody that much, they have to feel it back, don't they? I had to make him see me for who I am. It was working, too. I only needed more time. And then you went after him."

Haley was long overdue for a reality check, and Meg was angry enough to deliver it. "It was only working in your fantasies. Ted was never going to fall in love with you. You're too young, and he's too difficult."

"He's not difficult! How can you say that about him?"

"Because it's true." Meg stepped away from her in disgust. "You're a baby. Eighteen going on twelve. Real love makes you a better person. It doesn't turn you into a sneak and a vandal. Do you really think Ted could love someone who's been hurting another person the way you have?"

Her words hit home, and Haley's face crumpled. "I didn't want to hurt you. I just wanted you to leave."

"Obviously. What were you planning to do to me today?"

"Nothing."

"Don't lie to me!"

"I don't know!" she cried. "I— When I saw you swimming, I guess I was going to take your clothes. Maybe burn them."

"Real mature." Meg paused and rubbed her wrist where Spence had grabbed her. "Instead, you came out of hiding to protect me."

"I wanted you to go away, not get raped!"

Meg didn't think Spence would have raped her, but she tended to be an optimist.

The sound of tires on gravel interrupted their drama. They turned together and saw a powder blue pickup racing down the lane.

chapter nineteen

M EG HAD FORGOTTEN THE SECURITY camera, and Haley didn't know about it. Her head shot up in panic. "You're going to tell him what I've done, aren't you?"

"No. You're going to tell him." Haley had been spiteful and destructive, but she'd also protected Meg from Spence today, and Meg owed her something for that. She grabbed her by the shoulders. "Listen to me, Haley. Right now you have a chance to change the course of your life. To stop being a sneaky, destructive, love-struck child and start being a woman with a little character." Haley winced as Meg dug her fingers into her arms, but Meg didn't let go. "If you don't stand up right now and face the consequences of what you've done, you're going to be living your life in the shadows—always ashamed, always knowing you're a mean little rat who betrayed a friend."

Haley's face crumpled. "I can't do it."

"You can do whatever you set your mind to. Life doesn't give you many moments like this, and you know what I think? I think that how you act in the next few minutes will dictate the person you're going to be from now on."

"No, I—"

Ted jumped out of his truck and rushed toward Meg. "The security people called. They said Spence showed up. I got here as fast as I could."

"Spence is gone," Meg said. "He left when he saw Haley."

With one sweep of his eyes, he took in Meg's bare legs and the damp T-shirt that didn't quite cover her wet panties. "What happened? He gave you trouble, didn't he?"

"Let's just say he wasn't pleasant. But I haven't blown your big deal, if that's what you want to know." Of course it was what he wanted to know. "At least I don't think I have," she added.

Was the relief she saw on his face a reflection of his concern for her or for the town? She wanted more than anything to tell him what had happened, but that would put him in an impossible situation. No matter how hard it would be, she was going to bide her time, just for a few days.

He finally noticed Haley's red eyes and blotchy face. "What happened to you?"

Haley looked at Meg, waiting for Meg to bust her, but Meg stared right back. Haley dipped her head. "I—got a bee sting."

"A bee sting?" Ted said.

Haley gazed at Meg again, daring her to say something. Or maybe begging her to do what Haley couldn't manage for herself. Seconds ticked by, and when Meg didn't say anything, Haley began to pull at her bottom lip. "I've got to go," she finally mumbled in a small, coward's voice.

Ted knew something more than a bee sting had transpired. He looked at Meg for an explanation, but Meg kept her focus on Haley.

Haley dug into the pocket of her microscopic shorts for her car keys. She'd parked her Focus facing the lane, presumably to make a fast getaway after she'd burned Meg's clothes. She pulled her keys out and studied them for a moment, still waiting for Meg to expose her. When that didn't happen, she began taking short, tentative steps toward her car.

"Welcome to the rest of your life," Meg called out.

Ted regarded her curiously. Haley faltered, then stopped. When she finally turned around, her eyes were bleak, pleading.

Meg shook her head.

Haley's throat muscles worked. Meg held her breath.

Haley turned back toward her car. Took another step. Stopped and faced him. "It was me," she said in a rush. "I'm the one who did those things to Meg."

Ted stared at her. "What are you talking about?"

"I'm—I'm the one who vandalized the church."

Ted Beaudine wasn't often at a loss for words, but this was one of those moments. Haley twisted the keys in her hands. "I sent that letter. I put the bumper stickers on her car and tried to break off the wipers and threw the rock at her windshield."

He shook his head, trying to take it all in. Then he rounded on Meg. "You told me a rock fell off a truck."

"I didn't want you to worry," Meg said. *Or take it upon yourself to replace my Rustmobile with a Humvee, something you're perfectly capable of doing.*

He spun back to confront Haley. "Why? Why would you do all that?"

"To—to make her leave. I'm . . . sorry."

For a genius, he was slow on the uptake. "What did she ever do to you?"

Once again, Haley faltered. This would be the hardest part for her, and she looked at Meg for help. But Meg wasn't giving it. Haley's fist curled around her keys. "I was jealous of her."

"Jealous of *what*?"

Meg wished he didn't sound so incredulous.

Haley's voice dropped to a whisper. "Because of you."

"Me?" More incredulity.

"Because I fell in love with you," Haley said, each word wrapped in misery.

"That's the stupidest thing I ever heard." Ted's disgust was so palpable that Meg almost felt sorry for Haley. "How could tormenting Meg show your so-called *love*?" The word was a snarl that sent Haley's fantasy world crashing around her.

She pressed her hands to her stomach. "I'm sorry." She started to cry. "I . . . never meant for it to go so far. I'm—so sorry."

"Sorry doesn't cut it," he shot back. And then he delivered the final proof of exactly how unrequited her feelings for him were. "Get in your car. We're going to the police station. And you'd better call your mother on the way because you're going to need all the support you can get."

Tears rolled down Haley's cheeks, and small, choked sobs caught in her throat, but she kept her head up. She'd accepted her fate, and she didn't argue with him.

"Hold on." Meg blew air into her cheeks, and then released it. "I have to vote no on the police."

Haley stared at her. Ted waved her off. "I'm not arguing with you about this."

"Since I'm the victim, I get the final say."

"Like hell you do," he said. "She terrorized you, and now she's going to pay."

"For whatever it cost you to put in my new windshield, that's for sure."

He was so furious that his skin had gone pale beneath his tan. "For more than that. She's broken at least a dozen laws. Trespassing, harassment, vandalism—"

"How many laws did you break," Meg said, "when you vandalized the Statue of Liberty?"

"I was *nine*."

"And a genius," she pointed out, while Haley watched them, not sure what was going on or how it would affect her. "That means you were at least nineteen in IQ years. That's a year older than she is."

"Meg, think about what she did to you."

"I don't have to. Haley's the one who needs to think, and I could be wrong about this, but I have a feeling she's going to be doing a lot of that. Please, Ted. Everybody deserves a second chance."

Haley's future rested with Ted, but she was looking at Meg with an expression that combined shame and wonder.

Ted glared down at Haley. "You don't deserve this."

Haley wiped her cheeks with her fingers and gazed at Meg. "Thank you," she whispered. "I won't ever forget this. And I promise. Somehow I'll make it up to you."

"Don't worry about making it up to me," Meg said. "Make it up to yourself."

Haley took that in. Finally, she nodded—a small, hesitant motion—and then she nodded more decisively.

As Haley walked to her car, Meg remembered the nagging feeling that she'd let something important slip past her. This must be it. Somewhere in her subconscious, she must have suspected Haley, although she wasn't sure how she could have.

Haley drove away. Ted kicked the gravel with his heel. "You're too soft, do you know that? Too damned soft."

"I'm a spoiled celebrity child, remember? Being soft is all I know."

"This is no time for joking around."

"Hey, if you can think of a bigger joke than Ted Beaudine hooking up with a mere mortal like Meg—"

"Stop it!"

The day's tension was getting to her, but she didn't want him to see how vulnerable she felt. "I don't like it when you're crabby," she said. "It defies the laws of nature. If you can turn into a grouch, who knows what's next? The entire universe might blow up."

He ignored that. Instead, he hooked one of her wet curls behind her ear. "What did Spence want? Other than your rapt attention and an introduction to your celebrity friends?"

"That . . . basically covers it." She turned her cheek into his palm.

"There's something you're not telling me."

She turned her voice into a sexy purr. "Babe, there's lots I'm not telling you."

He smiled and touched his thumb to her bottom lip. "You can't go running off by yourself. Everybody is trying to make sure you're never alone with him, but you have to do your part, too."

"I know. And believe me, it won't happen again. Although I can't tell you how much it bothers me that I'm the one who has to go into hiding just because some horny zillionaire—"

"I know. It's not right." He pressed his lips to her forehead. "Just stay out of his way for a couple more days, and then you can tell him to go to hell. As a matter of fact, I'll do it for you. You can't imagine how sick I am of having that clown run my life."

The feeling returned without warning. The sensation of something lying in wait for her. Something that had nothing to do with Haley Kittle.

The sky had grown darker, and the wind pressed her T-shirt to her body. "Don't you . . . Don't you think it's odd that Spence hasn't heard about us? Or that Sunny hasn't heard? So many people know, but . . . not them. Sunny doesn't know, does she?"

He glanced up at the clouds. "Doesn't seem to."

She couldn't get enough air into her lungs. "Twenty women saw you kiss me at that luncheon. Some of them must have told their husbands, a friend. Birdie told Haley."

"It figures."

The racing clouds threw his face into shadow, and the fruit she'd been trying so hard to touch came closer. She sucked in more air. "All those people know we're a couple. But not Spence and Sunny."

"This is Wynette. Everybody pulls together."

The fruit hung so close she could catch its scent, no longer pleasant, but fetid and cloying. "Such loyal people."

"They don't make them any better."

And just like that, she had the poisoned fruit in her hand. "You knew all along that nobody would say anything to Spence or Sunny."

A distant roll of thunder . . . He craned his neck toward the video camera in the tree, as if he wanted to make sure it hadn't moved. "I don't understand what you're getting at."

"Oh, you understand, all right." She spoke the rest on a single, painful breath. "When you kissed me . . . When you told all those women we were a couple . . . You knew they'd keep it a secret."

He shrugged. "People'll do what they're going to do."

The fruit split open in her hands, revealing its wormy, rotten flesh. "All your talk about openness and honesty, about how much you hated sneaking around. I bought it."

"I do hate sneaking around."

The clouds rushed overhead, the thunder rumbled, and a wave of fury caught her in its grip. "I was so *touched* when you kissed me in front of everyone. So giddy that you were willing to make that kind of sacrifice. For me! But you . . . *you* weren't risking a thing."

"Wait a minute." His eyes flamed with righteous indignation. "You lit into me that night. You said what I did was stupid."

"That's what my head said. But my *heart* . . . My stupid heart . . ." Her voice broke. "It was singing."

He winced. "Meg . . ."

The play of emotions on the face of this man who would never willingly hurt anyone was painfully easy to decipher. His dismay. His concern. His pity. She hated it—hated him. She wanted to hurt him as he'd hurt her, and she knew exactly how to punish him. With her honesty.

"I've fallen in love with you," she said. "Just like the others."

He couldn't hide his dismay. "Meg . . ."

"But I don't mean any more to you than the rest of them. Any more to you than Lucy did."

"Hold it right there."

"I'm such an idiot. That kiss meant so much to me. I let it mean so much." She gave a harsh laugh that was mainly a sob, no longer certain which of them she was most angry with. "And the way you wanted me to stay at your house . . . Everybody was so worried about that, but if it had happened, they'd have killed themselves covering for you. You knew that."

"You're making a big deal out of nothing." But he wouldn't meet her eyes.

She took in his strong, clean profile. "Just the sight of you made me feel like dancing," she whispered. "I've never loved a man like I love you. Never imagined the kind of feelings I have for you."

His mouth twisted and his eyes darkened with pain. "Meg, I care. Don't think I don't care. You're— You're wonderful. You make me . . ."

He paused, searching for a word, and she sneered at him through her tears. "Do I make your heart sing? Do I make you feel like dancing?"

"You're upset. You—"

"My love is hot!" The words burst from her. "It's a burning thing. It boils and churns and runs deep and strong. But all your emotions are cool and spare. You stand on the sidelines where you don't have to sweat too much. That's why you wanted to marry Lucy. It was neat. It was logical. Well, I'm not neat. I'm messy and wild and disruptive, and you have broken my heart."

With a clap of thunder, the rain began to fall. His face twisted. "Don't say that. You're upset."

He tried to reach out to her, but she jerked away. "Get out of here. Leave me alone."

"Not like this."

"Exactly like this. Because you only want what's best for people. And right now what's best for me is to be alone."

The rain was falling more heavily now. She could see his internal scales working away. Weighing the pros and cons. Wanting to do the right thing. Always do the right thing. That's how he was made. And by letting him see how much he'd hurt her, she couldn't have hurt him more.

A crack of lightning split the air. He pulled her up the steps and beneath the overhang above the church doors. She jerked away. "Leave! Can't you at least do that?"

"Please, Meg. We'll sort this out. We just need a little time." He tried to touch her face, but when she flinched, he let his arm drop to his side. "You're upset. And I understand. Later tonight, we'll—"

"No. Not tonight." *Not tomorrow. Not ever.*

"Listen to me. Please . . . I have meetings all day tomorrow with

Spence and his people, but tomorrow night, we'll . . . We'll have dinner at my house where there won't be any interruptions. Just the two of us. We'll both have had time to think about all this, and we can talk it through."

"Right. Time to think. That's going to fix everything."

"Be fair, Meg. This has come out of nowhere. Promise me," he said roughly. "Unless you promise to meet me tomorrow night, I'm not going anywhere."

"All right," she said woodenly. "I promise."

"Meg . . ."

Once again he tried to touch her, and once again she resisted. "Just go. Please. We'll talk about it tomorrow."

He studied her for so long she didn't think he'd leave. But eventually he did, and she stood at the top of the church stairs, watching him drive away in the rain.

When he was out of sight, she did what she hadn't been able to do before. She walked around the side of the church and broke a window. A single pane she could reach through to unfasten the latch. Then she shoved the window open and climbed into her dusty, empty sanctuary.

He expected her to meet him tomorrow night for a calm, logical discussion about her unrequited love. She'd promised him.

As a clap of thunder shook the building, she thought how easily that kind of promise could be broken.

IN THE CHOIR LOFT, SHE found a pair of jeans Dallie and Skeet had overlooked when they'd packed up her things. There was still food in the kitchen, but she had no appetite. Instead, she paced the old pine floor and thought of everything that had brought her to this moment.

Ted couldn't change who he was. Had she really believed he could love her? How could she have thought, even for a moment, that she was different from the rest?

Because he'd shown her parts of himself he'd never shown anyone else, and that had made her feel different. But it had all been an illusion, and now she had to leave because staying here was impossible.

The thought of never seeing him again nearly made her crumple, so she focused on the practicalities. The old, irresponsible Meg would have jumped in her car that night and run off. But her new, improved version had obligations. Tomorrow was her day off, so no one would be expecting her at work, and she had time to do what she needed to.

She waited until she was sure Skeet would be asleep before she returned to his house. As his snores rumbled down the hallway, she sat at the desk in his office where she'd been working on her jewelry and picked up a yellow pad. She made notes for whoever would take over the drink cart, explaining how best to stock it, listing the preferences of the regulars, adding a few lines about recycling cups and cans. Maybe her job wasn't brain surgery, but she'd more than doubled the revenue from the drink cart, and she was proud of that. At the end, she wrote, *A job is what you make it.* But she felt foolish and crossed it out.

As she finished a bracelet she'd promised Torie, she tried not to think about him, but that was impossible, and by dawn, when she slipped the bracelet into a padded envelope, she was bleary-eyed and exhausted, sadder than she could ever remember.

Skeet was eating his Cap'n Crunch at the kitchen table, the sports page propped in front of him, when she came out. "Good news," she said, forcing a smile. "My stalker has been identified and neutralized. Don't ask me for details."

Skeet looked up from his cereal. "Ted know about this?"

She struggled against the wave of pain that threatened to drown her whenever she thought of never seeing him again. "Yes. And I'm moving back into the church." She didn't like lying to Skeet, but she needed an excuse to pack up her things without arousing his suspicions.

"Don't see why you need to hurry off," he grumbled.

As he returned to his Cap'n Crunch, she realized she'd miss the old curmudgeon, right along with a lot of other people in this crazy town.

Lack of sleep and too much pain had worn her out, and she'd barely started packing before she gave in and lay down. Despite her bleak dreams, she didn't awaken till early afternoon. She finished packing quickly but still didn't get to the bank until nearly three o'clock. She withdrew all but twenty dollars from her meager account. If she closed the account, every teller in the place would start quizzing her, and five minutes after she walked out the door, Ted would know she was leaving. She couldn't bear another confrontation.

The town's only mailbox sat by the front steps of the small post office. She mailed her drink-cart notes and her letter of resignation to Barry, the assistant manager. As she dropped in the envelope with Torie's bracelet, a car pulled into the no-parking zone. The driver's window slid down, and Sunny Skipjack poked out her head. "I've been looking for you. I forgot the club was closed today. Let's grab a drink so we can talk."

Sunny was all sleek efficiency with her shiny dark hair and platinum jewelry. Meg had never felt more breakable. "Not a good time, I'm afraid," she said. "I have a million things to do." *Like get in my car and turn my back on the man I love so much.*

"Cancel them. This is important."

"Is it about your father?"

Sunny looked at her blankly. "What about my father?"

"Nothing."

A few people on the sidewalk stopped to watch, none of them trying to be discreet about it. Sunny, the busy executive, tapped impatient fingers on the steering wheel. "Are you sure you can't spare a few minutes from your busy schedule to discuss a possible business venture?"

"Business venture?"

"I've seen your jewelry. I want to talk. Get in."

Meg's plan for the future was foggy at best. She weighed the risk of postponing her departure for an hour against the benefit of hearing what Sunny had to say. Sunny might be a pain in the ass, but she was also a smart businesswoman. Meg set aside her reluctance to enter an enclosed space with another Skipjack and got in the car.

"Did you hear there was an article in the *Wall Street Journal*, of all places, about Ted's contest?" Sunny said as she pulled out into the street. "Part of a series on creative approaches to charitable fundraising."

"No, I hadn't heard that."

She drove with one hand on the wheel. "Every time one of those stories comes out, the bidding goes up. All this national attention is getting pricey, but I haven't splurged on anything for a long time." Sunny's cell rang. She slipped it under the sickle of shiny dark hair that swung over her ear. "Hi, Dad."

Meg stiffened.

"Yes, I read the memo, and I spoke to Wolfburg," Sunny said. "I'll call Terry this evening."

They talked for another few minutes about lawyers and the land deal. Meg's thoughts drifted back to Ted, only to be brought up short as Sunny said, "I'll have to check on that later. Meg and I are hanging out right now." She looked over at Meg and rolled her eyes. "No, you're not invited to join us. Talk to you later." She listened for a moment, frowned, then disconnected. "He sounded pissed. What's up with you two?"

Meg welcomed the flood of anger. "Your father isn't good at taking no for an answer."

"That's why he's successful. He's smart and focused. I don't understand why you're giving him such a hard time. Or maybe I do."

Meg didn't want to have this conversation, and she regretted getting in the car. "You wanted to talk about my jewelry," she said as they turned out onto the highway.

"You're underselling. Your pieces are distinctive, and they have snob appeal. You need to reposition yourself for the high-end market. Go to New York. Use your contacts to meet the right buyers. And stop wasting your merchandise on the locals. You can't build a serious design reputation in East Jesus, Texas."

"Good advice," Meg replied as they passed the Roustabout. "I thought we were going for a drink."

"Short detour to the landfill."

"I've already seen it, and I really don't want to go back."

"I need to take some pictures. We won't stay long. Besides, we can talk in private there."

"I'm not sure we need a private conversation."

"Sure we do." Sunny turned into the lane that led to the landfill. It had received a fresh coat of gravel since Meg was last here, the time she and Ted had made love against the side of the truck. Another wave of pain punched her in the chest.

Sunny pulled up next to the rusted sign, grabbed a camera from her purse, and got out, every gesture, every movement, purposeful. Meg had never met anyone so self-confident.

She wasn't going to cower in the car, and she stepped out, too.

Sunny put the camera to her eye and focused on the landfill. "This is the future of Wynette." The shutter clicked. "At first, I was opposed to building here, but after I got to know the town and the people better, I changed my mind."

After you got to know Ted Beaudine, Meg thought.

She took more shots, shifting her angle. "It's really a unique place. The bedrock of America and all that. Generally, Dad's not crazy about small towns, but everybody's been so great to him here, and he loves being able to play with guys like Dallie and Ted and Kenny." She lowered the camera. "As for me . . . It's no secret I'm interested in Ted."

"You and the rest of the female universe."

Sunny smiled. "But, unlike the rest, I'm also an engineer. I can meet him as an intellectual equal, and how many other women can say that?"

Not me, Meg thought.

She walked behind the landfill sign and pointed her camera toward the methane pipes. "I understand the technology that interests him." The shutter clicked. "I appreciate his passion for ecology on both a scientific and a practical level. He has an amazing mind, and not many people can walk in lockstep with that kind of intellect."

Still another woman who thought she knew what he needed. Meg couldn't resist. "And Ted returns your feelings?"

"We're getting there." She lowered the camera again. "At least I hope so. I'm a realist. Maybe it won't happen the way I want, but I'm like my father. I don't back down from a challenge. I believe Ted and I have a future, and I intend to do everything I can to make it happen." She gazed directly into Meg's eyes. "Cards on the table. I want you to leave Wynette."

"Do you now?" She saw no reason to tell Sunny she'd have been on her way if Sunny hadn't stopped her. "And why is that?"

"It's not personal. I think you're good for my father. He's been depressed lately. Getting older and all that. You've taken his mind off it. The problem for me is, you're holding Ted back. He'd never admit he's leaning on you, but it's obvious."

"You think Ted's leaning on me?"

"I see it in the way he looks at you, the way he talks about you. I know you and Lucy Jorik were best friends. You're a reminder of her, and as long as you're around, it's going to be very hard for him to move forward."

So smart, and yet so dumb.

"I'm also a big believer in women watching out for women," Sunny said. "Being around him so much isn't good for you. I've heard from more people than I can count that you're over him, but we both know that's not quite true. Face it, Meg. Ted's never going to go for you. The two of you have nothing in common."

Except famous parents, a privileged upbringing, a passion for ecology, and a high tolerance for the absurd, something Sunny would never understand.

"Ted is comfortable with you because you remind him of Lucy," Sunny went on. "But that's all it will ever be. Staying here is holding you back, and it's making my relationship with him more complicated."

"You certainly are blunt."

She shrugged. "I believe in being honest."

But what Sunny called honesty was nothing more than a callous disregard for any feelings or opinions that weren't her own.

"Subtleties have never worked for me," she said, proudly flying the flag of her self-importance. "If you're willing to disappear, I'm willing to help you get started with your jewelry business."

"Blood money?"

"Why not? You aren't a bad investment. By incorporating genuine relics in your pieces, you've stumbled on a nice little niche market that could be very profitable."

"Except I'm not sure I want to be in the jewelry business."

Sunny couldn't comprehend anyone turning her back on a viable business, and she barely concealed a sneer. "What else are you going to do?"

She was about to tell Sunny she'd handle her future her own way when she heard tires spinning on gravel. They both turned as an unfamiliar car braked to a stop behind them. The sun was in her eyes, so she couldn't see who was driving, but the interruption didn't surprise her. The good citizens of Wynette wouldn't leave her alone with a Skipjack for long.

But as the car door opened, her stomach sank. The person getting out of the dark sedan was Spence. She turned to Sunny. "Take me back to town."

But Sunny's eyes were on her father as he approached them, his Panama hat shadowing the upper half of his face. "Dad, what are you doing here?"

"You told me you were taking pictures today."

Meg had no reserves left to deal with this. "I want to go back to town now."

"Leave us alone," Spence said to his daughter. "I have a few things I need to say to Meg in private."

"No! Don't leave."

Meg's alarm confused Sunny, whose welcoming smile for her father faded. "What's going on?"

Spence angled his head toward his daughter's car. "I'll meet you back in town. Go on."

"Stay where you are, Sunny," Meg said. "I don't want to be alone with him."

Sunny looked at her as if she were maggot-infested. "What's wrong with you?"

"Meg's a coward," he said. "That's what's wrong with her."

Meg wouldn't be his helpless victim yet again. "Sunny, your father assaulted me yesterday."

chapter twenty

"Assaulted?" Spence gave a rough bark of laughter. "That's a good one. Show me a mark anywhere on you, and I'll give you a million dollars."

Sunny's customary composure had vanished, and she regarded Meg with revulsion. "How could you say something so vile?"

More cars were bumping down the gravel lane, not just one, but a whole stream, everyone sensing trouble. "Shit," Spence exclaimed. "A man can't take a crap in this town without everybody showing up to watch."

Kayla jumped out from the passenger side of a red Kia being driven by one of the waitresses at the Roustabout. "What are y'all doin' out here," she chirped, rushing toward them as if she'd just stumbled on a roadside picnic.

Before anyone could reply, Torie, Dexter, and Kenny disgorged from a silver Range Rover. Torie's Hawaiian print sarong clashed with her plaid bikini top. She had wet hair and no makeup. Her husband wore a dark blue business suit, and Kenny raised a hand decorated with a Spider-Man Band-Aid. "Afternoon, Spence. Sunny. Nice weather after yesterday. Not that we didn't need the rain."

Zoey leaped from a navy blue Camry. "I was on my way to a science curriculum meeting," she said to no one in particular.

More cars fell in behind hers. The whole town seemed to sense a catastrophe in the making, and they were all determined to prevent it.

Dexter O'Connor gestured toward the landfill. "You're a lucky man, Spence. So many possibilities."

Instead of looking at him, Spence kept his angry gaze on Meg, and the relief she'd felt at the appearance of all these people began to fade. She tried to tell herself she was wrong. Surely he'd let this go. Surely he wouldn't press this in front of so many people. But she'd known from the beginning that he couldn't tolerate having anyone get the best of him.

"The contracts aren't signed yet," he said ominously.

A collective expression of panic fell over the faces of the onlookers. "Dad . . ." Sunny put her hand on her father's arm.

Torie took charge. Tightening the knot on her sarong, she marched toward Spence. "Me and Dex are planning to throw a couple of steaks on the grill tonight. Why don't you and Sunny join us, that is if you don't mind kids, or maybe we'll ship them over to Dad's house? Sunny, have you ever seen emus close up? Dex and me have a whole flock of them. Basically, I married him so I could pay my feed bill. He isn't as crazy about them as I am, but they're the sweetest creatures you ever met." Torie went on to deliver a breathless and very lengthy monologue describing the care and feeding of emus and their benefit to humankind. She was stalling for time, and since everybody kept glancing down the lane, Meg didn't have any trouble figuring out why. They were waiting for a knight in a powder blue pickup to appear and save the town from disaster.

More vehicles streamed into the lane. Torie was running out of emu material, and she cast an imploring eye at the others. Her brother reacted first, slipping one arm across Spence's shoulders and gestured toward the landfill with the other. "I've been giving a lot of thought to the routing."

But Spence turned away from him and studied the growing crowd. His gaze returned to Meg, and the way his eyes narrowed told her it was payback time. "Turns out, that might be a little premature, Kenny. I have a reputation to consider, and Meg here was just telling my daughter something pretty shocking."

Dread kicked her in the stomach. He wanted revenge, and he knew exactly how to get it. If she stood her ground, she'd hurt so many people, but the thought of backing down made her ill. How could doing the right thing feel so wrong? She dug her fingers into her palms. "Forget it."

But Spence wanted his pound of flesh for every wound she'd inflicted on his ego, and he pressed. "Oh, I can't do that," he said. "Some things are too serious to forget. Meg says I— What was that word you used?"

"Let it go," she said, even as she knew he wouldn't.

He snapped his fingers. "I remember. You said I *assaulted* you. Do I have that right, Meg?"

A murmur went up from the crowd. Kayla's glossed lips grew slack. Zoey pressed her hand to her throat. More cells snapped open, and Meg fought down her nausea. "No, Spence, you don't have it right," she said woodenly.

"But that's what I heard you say. What my daughter heard you say." He jutted out his chin. "I remember going swimming with you yesterday, but I sure don't remember any assault."

Her jaw didn't want to move. "You're right," she murmured. "I got it wrong."

He shook his head. "How could you get something so serious wrong?"

He was going to hammer her into the ground. The only way she could win was by letting him win, and she struggled to hold herself together. "Easy. I was upset."

"Hey there, everybody."

The crowd turned in unison as their savior ambled forward. He'd arrived unnoticed because he'd been driving the dark gray Benz they all tended to forget he owned. He looked tired. "What's going on here?" he said. "A party I forgot about?"

"I'm afraid not." Even as Spence frowned, she could see he was reveling in the power he held over all of them. "I sure am glad you showed up, Ted. It seems we have an unanticipated problem."

"Oh? And what's that?"

Spence rubbed his jaw where the day's stubble cast a blue-black shadow. "It's going to be hard for me to do business in a town where a person can go around throwing out false accusations and getting away with it."

He wasn't going to cancel the deal. Meg didn't believe it. Not with Sunny giving him those pleading glances. Not with an entire town lined up to fawn over him. He was playing a cat-and-mouse game, flexing his muscle by humiliating her and letting them all see who was in charge.

"I'm sorry to hear that, Spence," Ted said. "I guess misunderstandings can happen anywhere. The good thing about Wynette is that we try to fix our troubles before they get too big to cause problems. Let me see if I can't help straighten this out."

"I don't know, Ted." Spence gazed toward the empty landfill. "Something like this is going to be hard to get past. Everybody's counting on me to sign those contracts tomorrow, but I can't imagine that happening with this false accusation hanging over me."

Tense murmurs rippled through the crowd. Sunny didn't see through her father's game, and her face was a picture of dismay as she envisioned her future with Ted slipping away. "Dad, we need to talk about this privately."

Mr. Cool pulled off his ball cap and scratched his head. Did anyone but her see his weariness? "You have to do what you think is right, that's for sure, Spence. But I'm betting I can help fix this if you'll just tell me what the problem is."

Meg couldn't stand it any longer. "I'm the problem," she declared. "I insulted Spence, and now he wants to punish the town for it. But you don't have to do that, Spence, because I'm leaving Wynette. I'd be gone by now if Sunny hadn't stopped me."

Ted shoved his hat back on his head, and even as he glared at her, his voice was calm. "Meg, why don't you let me handle this?"

But Spence was out for blood. "You think you can just drive away with no harm done after making such a serious accusation in front of my daughter? That doesn't work for me."

"Now hold on here," Ted said. "How about we start at the beginning?"

"Yes, Meg," Spence sneered. "Why don't we do that?"

She couldn't look at Ted, so she focused on Spence. "I've admitted that I lied. You were a perfect gentleman. There was no assault. I . . . made the whole thing up."

Ted spun on her. "Spence assaulted you?"

"That's what she told my daughter." Spence's words dripped with contempt. "She's a liar."

"You assaulted her?" Ted's eyes blazed. "You son of a bitch." With

no more warning than that, Mr. Cool launched himself at the town's last great hope.

A gasp of stunned disbelief went up from the crowd. The plumbing king sprawled to the ground, his Panama hat rolling away in the dirt. Meg was so shocked she couldn't move. Sunny let out a strangled scream, and everyone stood in frozen horror as their unflappable mayor—their very own Prince of Peace—grabbed Spencer Skipjack by the collar of his dress shirt and dragged him back to his feet.

"Who the hell do you think you are?" Ted shouted in his face, his own features twisting in dark fury.

Spence lashed out with his foot, catching Ted in the leg and sending them both tumbling back into the dirt.

It was all a bad dream.

A bad dream that turned into a full-fledged nightmare as two familiar figures emerged from the crowd.

She was imagining them. It couldn't be. She blinked, but the awful vision wouldn't go away.

Her parents. Fleur and Jake Koranda. Staring at her with appalled faces.

They couldn't be here. Not without telling her they were coming. Not here at the landfill witnessing the greatest personal disaster of her life.

She blinked again, but they were still standing there, with Francesca and Dallie Beaudine right behind them. Her mother, gloriously beautiful. Her father—tall, craggy, and ready to spring.

The brawlers were on their feet, then back on the ground. Spence had Ted by a good fifty pounds, but Ted was stronger, more agile, and fueled by an anger that had transformed him into a man she didn't recognize.

Torie clutched her sarong. Kenny released a blistering obscenity.

Kayla started to cry. And Francesca tried to run to the aid of her precious baby boy only to have her husband snatch her back.

No one, however, thought to restrain Sunny, who wouldn't let any man, not even the one she fancied herself in love with, attack her beloved father. "Daddy!" With a cry, she threw herself on Ted's back.

It was more than Meg could stand. *"Get off him!"*

She ran to intercede, slipped in the gravel, and fell on Sunny, trapping Ted beneath them both. Spence took advantage of Ted's temporary captivity and sprang to his feet. Meg watched with alarm as he drew his leg back to kick Ted in the head. With her own shriek of rage, she twisted to her side and slammed into him, knocking him off balance. As he fell, she grabbed Sunny by the back of her designer blouse. Ted would never hit a woman, but Meg possessed no such scruples.

Torie and Shelby Traveler eventually pulled Meg off a sobbing Sunny, but the town's peace-loving mayor was out for blood, and it took three men to restrain him. He wasn't the only one being held back. Meg's mother, Skeet, Francesca, and the fire chief all had to work together to contain her father.

A vein throbbed in the side of Ted's neck as he struggled to free himself so he could finish what he'd started. "You even *think* about going near her again, and you'll regret it."

"You're crazy!" Spence shouted. "You're all crazy!"

Ted's lips thinned with contempt. "Get out of here."

Spence snatched his hat from the ground. Oily hanks of black hair hung over his forehead. One of his eyes was beginning to swell shut, and his nose was bleeding. "This town always needed me more than I ever needed it." He slapped his hat against his leg. "While you're watching this place rot, Beaudine, think about what you gave up." He slammed his hat on his head and gazed at Meg, his expression venomous. "Think about how much that nobody cost you."

"Daddy . . ." Sunny's dirty blouse was torn, she had a scraped arm and a scratch over her cheek, but he was too wrapped up in his own rage to give her the comfort she craved.

"You could have had it all," he said, blood trickling from his nostril. "And you gave it up for a lying bitch."

Only her mother throwing herself at her father kept him from leaping on Spence, while the men holding Ted back nearly lost their struggle to contain him. Dallie sauntered forward, his eyes steel blue chips. "I advise you to get out of here while you can, Spence, because all it'll take from me is a nod, and those ol' boys keeping Ted from finishing the job he started out to do are going to let him go."

Spence took in the sea of hostile faces and began backing toward the cars. "Come on, Sunny," he said with a bravado that didn't ring true. "Let's get out of this shithole."

"You're the loser, asshole!" Torie called out. "I could hit a five-iron better than you when I was in junior high. And, Sunny, you're a stuck-up bitch."

Father and daughter, sensing they could have an angry mob on their heels, rushed to their cars and threw themselves inside. As they drove away, one set of eyes after another landed on Meg. She felt their anger, saw their despair. None of this would ever have happened if she'd left town when they'd wanted her to.

Somehow she managed to keep her head up, even as she blinked back tears. Her exquisite mother, all six feet of her, began coming toward her, moving with the authority that had once carried her down the world's greatest runways. The crowd's attention had been so focused on the unfolding calamity that no one had noticed the strangers in their midst, but the Glitter Baby's stripy blond hair, dramatic marking-pen eyebrows, and wide mouth made her instantly recognizable to everyone over thirty, and a buzz went up. Then Meg's father moved to her mother's side, and the buzz stopped as the onlookers tried to absorb the astonishing fact that the legendary Jake Koranda had stepped off the silver screen to walk among them.

Meg took them in with an unhappy combination of love and despair. How could someone as ordinary as herself be the offspring of these two magnificent creatures?

But her parents never got close to her because Ted had lost it. "Everybody get the hell out of here!" he exclaimed. "Everybody!" For some inexplicable reason, he included her parents in his proclamation. "You, too."

Meg wanted nothing more than to leave and never come back, but she had no car, and she couldn't bear the idea of riding back with her parents before she'd had a chance to pull herself together. Torie seemed to be her best option, and she cast a beseeching look in her direction only to have Ted's arm shoot out. "You stay right where you are."

Each word had a jagged edge and icy point. He wanted a final showdown, and after all this, he deserved it.

Her father took Ted's measure, then turned to her. "Do you have a car here?"

When she shook her head, he pulled out his keys and tossed them at her. "We'll hitch a ride back to town and wait for you at the inn."

One person after another began moving away. No one wanted to defy Ted, not even his mother. Francesca and Dallie led Meg's parents to their Cadillac. As the cars began to leave, Ted walked toward the rusted sign, where he gazed out over the vast stretch of tainted land now stripped of all its future promise. His shoulders slumped. She'd done this to him. Not intentionally, but she'd done it all the same by staying in Wynette when every sign pointed to the absolute necessity of her leaving. Then she'd compounded her stupidity by falling so absurdly in love with the man least likely to love her back. Her self-indulgence had led to this moment where everything had fallen apart.

The sun hung low in the sky, etching his profile in fire. The last car disappeared, but it was as if she'd ceased to exist, and he didn't move. When she couldn't stand it any longer, she forced herself to go to him. "I am so sorry," she whispered.

She lifted her hand to wipe the blood from the corner of his mouth, but he caught her wrist before she could touch him. "Was that *hot* enough for you?"

"What?"

"You think I don't feel things." His voice was hoarse with emotion. "That I'm some kind of robot."

"Oh, Ted . . . That's not what I meant."

"Because you're a drama queen, you're the only one who's allowed to have feelings, is that right?"

This wasn't the conversation they needed to have. "Ted, I never meant for you to get caught up in this thing with Spence."

"What was I supposed to do? Let him get away with assaulting you?"

"He didn't exactly do that. I don't honestly know what would have happened if Haley hadn't shown up. He—"

"I sweat!" he exclaimed, which made no sense at all. "You said I never sweat."

What was he talking about? She tried again. "I was alone at the swimming hole when he showed up. I asked him to leave, and he wouldn't. It got nasty."

"And the son of a bitch paid for it." He grabbed her arm. "Two months ago I was getting ready to marry another woman. Why can't you cut me some slack? Just because you jumped off the deep end doesn't mean I have to jump right in, too."

She was used to reading his mind, but not this time. "What exactly do you mean by 'jump off the deep end'?"

His mouth twisted in scorn. "Fall in love."

The words were so contemptuously uttered, they should have left blisters on his lips. She pulled away and took a step back. "I'd hardly call falling in love 'jumping off the deep end.'"

"Then exactly what would you call it? I was ready to spend the rest of my life with Lucy. The rest of my life! Why can't you get that?"

"I get it. I just don't understand why we're talking about this now, after what just happened."

"Of course you don't." His face had gone pale. "You don't understand anything about reasonable behavior. You think you know me so well, but you don't know anything about me."

One more woman who thought she understood Ted Beaudine . . .

Before she could get them back on track, he resumed his attack. "You brag about how you're all emotion. Well, a big frigging round of applause. I'm not like that. I want things to make sense, and if that's a sin in your eyes, then tough."

It was as if he'd suddenly started spouting a foreign language. She understood his words, but not the context. Why weren't they talking about the part she'd played in the disaster with Spence?

He swiped a trickle of blood from the corner of his mouth with the back of his hand. "You say you love me. What does that even mean? I loved Lucy, and look how meaningless that turned out to be."

"You loved Lucy?" She didn't believe it. Didn't want to believe it.

"Five minutes after I met her, I knew she was the one. She's smart. She's easy to be with. She cares about helping people, and she understands what it's like to live in a fishbowl. My friends loved her. My parents loved her. We wanted the same things out of life. And I've never been more wrong about anything." His voice faltered. "You expect me to forget all that? You expect me to snap my fingers and make all that go away?"

"That's not fair. You acted as if she didn't matter. You didn't seem to care."

"Of course I cared! Just because I don't go around broadcasting every emotion doesn't mean I don't feel them. You said I broke your heart. Well, she broke mine."

A pulse ticked in his throat. She felt as if he'd slapped her. How could she not have known this? She'd been convinced he hadn't loved Lucy, but the opposite was true. "I wish I'd realized," she heard herself say. "I didn't understand."

He made a harsh, dismissive gesture. "And then you came along. With all your mess and all your demands."

"I never made a single demand!" she exclaimed. "You're the one who made demands, right from the beginning. Telling me what I could and couldn't do. Where I could work. Where I could live."

"Who are you kidding?" he said roughly. "Everything about you is a demand. Those big eyes—blue one minute, green the next. The way you laugh. Your body. Even that dragon tattooed on your butt. You demand everything of me. And then you criticize what you get."

"I never—"

"The hell you didn't." He moved so quickly she thought he was going to hit her. Instead, he jerked her against him and shoved his hands under her short cotton skirt, pushing it to her waist, grabbing her bottom. "You think this isn't a demand?"

"I—hope so," she said in a voice so small she barely recognized it.

But he was already dragging her to the side of the gravel lane. He didn't even allow her the courtesy of the backseat of his car. Instead, he pulled her down into a patch of sandy soil.

With only the blazing sun above them, he tangled his hands in her panties, tossed them away, and splayed her legs on each side of his hips. As he reared back on his heels, the sun fell hot on the vulnerable inner skin of her thighs. He never took his eyes off the moist softness he'd exposed even as his hands went to his zipper. He was out of control, this man of logic and reason. Stripped of his gentleman's veneer.

The shadow of his body blocked the sun. He opened his jeans. She could have yelled at him to stop—could have pushed him off—could have smacked him in the head and told him to snap out of it. He would have. She knew that. But she didn't. He'd gone wild, and she wanted to race into the unknown with him.

He reached under her and angled her hips so she had to take all of him. No drawn-out foreplay, no painstaking torment and exquisite teasing. Only his own need.

Something sharp scraped her leg . . . A rock dug into her spine . . . With a dark moan, he drove into her. As his weight pressed her into the ground, he shoved up her top and bared her breasts. His beard scraped her tender skin. An awful tenderness filled her as he used her body. Without courtesy, without restraint or civility. He was a fallen angel, consumed by darkness, and he took no care with her at all.

She shut her eyes against the blinding sun as he pumped inside her. Gradually, the wildness that had claimed him claimed her as well, but it happened too late. With a hoarse cry, he bared his teeth. And then he flooded her.

The harsh sound of his breathing rasped in her ears. His weight pushed the air from her lungs. Finally, he fell off her with a moan. And then everything was still.

This was what she'd wanted since the first time they'd made love. To break through his control. But the cost to him had been too great, and as he came back to himself, she saw exactly what she knew she'd see. A good man stricken by remorse.

"Don't say it!" She slapped her hand over his bruised mouth. Slapped his jaw. "Don't say it!"

"Jesus . . ." He scrambled to his feet. "I can't . . . I'm sorry. I'm so fucking sorry. Jesus, Meg . . ."

As he pulled his clothes together, she jumped up next to him, shoved her skirt down. His face was twisted, agonized. She couldn't bear to hear his tormented apology for being human instead of a demi-god. She had to do something quickly, so she poked him hard in the chest. "Now that's what I've been talking about all along."

But he'd gone pale, and her attempt at deflection fell flat. "I can't— I can't believe I did that to you."

She wouldn't give up so easily. "Could you do it again? Maybe a little slower this time, but not much."

It was as if he didn't hear her. "I'll never forgive myself."

She hid behind bravado. "You're boring me, Theodore, and I have things to do." First she'd try to give him back his self-respect. Then she had to face her parents. After that? She needed to turn her back on this town forever.

She grabbed her panties and adopted a cockiness she was far from feeling. "I realize I have managed to royally screw up the future of Wynette, so stop messing around here and do what you do best. Start cleaning up other people's messes. Find Spence before he gets away. Tell him you lost your mind. Say that everybody in town knows I'm unreliable, but you still let yourself get sucked in. Then apologize for fighting with him."

"I don't give a damn about Spence," he said flatly.

His words struck terror in her heart. "You will. You really, really will. Please. Do what I say."

"Is that asshole all you can think about? After what just happened . . ."

"Yes. And it's all I want you to think about. Here's the thing . . . I need an undying declaration of love from you, and you're never going to be able to give me that."

Frustration, regret, impatience—she saw them all in his eyes. "It's too fast, Meg. It's too damned—"

"You've been more than clear." She cut him off before he could say any more. "And no big guilt trip after I go. To be honest, I fall in and out of love fairly quickly. It won't take me long to get over you." She was talking too fast. "There was this guy named Buzz. I went through a good six weeks feeling sorry for myself, but, honestly, you're no Buzz."

"What do you mean, after you go?"

She swallowed. "Strangest thing, but Wynette's lost its appeal. I'm taking off as soon as I talk to my parents. And aren't you glad you don't have to be around to witness that conversation?"

"I don't want you to leave. Not yet."

"Why not?" She studied him, looking for some sign she might have missed. "What am I supposed to stay around for?"

He made an odd gesture of helplessness. "I—I don't know. Just stay."

The fact that he wouldn't meet her eyes told her everything. "Can't do it, pal. I—just can't."

It was strange to see Ted Beaudine look so vulnerable. She pressed her lips to the undamaged corner of his mouth and hurried to the car that her ever-thoughtful parents had left for her. As she drove away, she allowed herself one last glance in the rearview mirror.

He stood in the middle of the road, watching her leave. Behind him, the vast wasteland of the landfill extended as far as the eye could see.

chapter twenty-one

MEG CLEANED UP IN THE BATHROOM at the Chevron station on the highway, wiping away the worst of the dirt and covering up her tear streaks. She dug into the suitcase she'd wedged into the small restroom for her boho top, a clean pair of jeans to hid the scratches on her legs, and a gauzy green scarf to conceal the beard burn on her neck. Since the first time they'd made love, she'd wanted him to be so overcome by passion that he'd lose his legendary control. It had finally happened, but not in the way she'd dreamed.

She let herself in through the service entrance at the inn. Birdie would never permit guests as famous as her parents to stay anywhere but the recently renamed Presidential Suite, and she climbed the back stairs to the top floor. Each step was an exercise in willpower. From the very beginning, she'd gotten it all wrong with Ted. She hadn't believed he'd loved Lucy, but he'd loved her then, and he still loved her now. Meg was nothing more than his rebound girl, his temporary walk on the wild side.

She couldn't let herself give in to the pain, not when she was about to face such an excruciating reunion with her parents. She couldn't think about Ted, or her uncertain future, or the wreckage she'd be leaving behind when she drove away from Wynette.

Her mother answered the door of the suite. She still wore the tailored platinum tunic top and slim-legged pants she'd had on at the landfill. Ironically, her fashion model mother cared little about clothes, but she dutifully dressed in the exquisite outfits her brother Michel made for her.

In the background, Meg's father stopped pacing. She gave them both an unsteady smile. "You could have told me you were coming."

"We wanted to surprise you," her father said dryly.

Her mother took her by the elbows, gave her a long, hard look, then pulled her close. As Meg sank into that familiar embrace, she forgot for a moment that she was a full-grown woman. If only her parents were clueless and demanding, her life would be a lot less guilt-ridden, and she wouldn't have to expend so much energy pretending she didn't care about their good opinion.

She felt her mother's hand in her hair. "Are you all right, sweetheart?"

She swallowed her tears. "I've been better, but considering that train wreck you witnessed, I can't complain."

Her father took over the embrace, squeezing her tight, then giving her a light smack on the rear, just as he'd done since she was a little girl.

"Tell us everything," her mother said when he finally let her go. "How did you get tangled up with that awful man?"

"Dad's fault," Meg managed. "Spencer Skipjack is a celebrity worshiper, and I was the closest he could get to the mighty Jake."

"You have no idea how much I want to rip that bastard apart," the mighty Jake said.

That was a scary thought, considering her father was a Vietnam vet, and what he hadn't learned in the Mekong Delta, he'd picked up making movies involving every form of weaponry from samurai swords to AK-47s.

Her mother made a vague gesture toward her state-of-the-art phone. "I've already started digging. I haven't uncovered anything yet, but I will. A snake like that always leaves a slimy trail."

Their anger didn't surprise her, but where was their disappointment at having witnessed their oldest child once again at the center of a mess?

Her father returned to pacing the carpet. "He's not going to get away with this."

"It's only a matter of time before his sins catch up with him," her mother said.

They didn't understand the implications of what they'd witnessed. They didn't have a clue how important the golf resort was to the town or the part Meg had played in destroying that promise. All they'd seen was a slimeball insulting their beloved daughter, and a gallant younger man avenging her honor. Meg had been given a gift from heaven. Not even Dallie and Francesca seemed to have enlightened them on the drive back to the inn. If she got her parents out of town quickly enough, they'd never hear about the part she'd played in all of this.

And then she remembered the words she'd spoken to Haley . . . *how you act in the next few minutes will dictate the person you're going to be from now on.*

Her circumstances were different from Haley's, but the underlying truth remained the same. What kind of person did she want to be?

An odd sense of—not peace, because there'd be no peace for her, not for a very long time. More a sense of *rightness* came over her. The experiences of the past three months had torn away the fabrications she'd shrouded herself in. She'd been so convinced she could never live up to the accomplishments of the rest of her family that she hadn't made a fair attempt at anything except nurturing her role as the family gadabout. If she'd ever risked building something for herself, she would also have risked failing in their eyes. By not risking anything, she couldn't set herself up for failure. That's what she'd believed, so that, in the end, she'd been left with nothing.

It was time she claimed the woman she wanted to be—a person willing to walk her own path in her own way without worrying how others judged her success or her failure, including those she loved. She needed to create her own vision of what she wanted her life to be and follow it to the end. She couldn't do that by hiding.

"Here's the thing . . ." she said. "What happened today . . . It's a little more complicated than it might seem."

"It seems pretty straightforward to me," her father said. "The guy's a pompous jerk."

"True. Unfortunately, that's not all he is . . ."

She told them everything, starting with the day she'd arrived. Halfway through her story, her father attacked the minibar, and a few minutes later, her mother joined him, but Meg kept going. She told them everything except how deeply she'd fallen in love with Ted. That was her story alone to sort out.

When she got to the end, she was standing by the window, her back to City Hall, while her parents sat side by side on the low couch. She made herself keep her chin up. "So you see, it's because of me that Ted lost his temper for the only time in his adult life and got in that fight. It's because of me that the town is going to lose millions of dollars of revenue and all those jobs."

Her parents exchanged long looks, full of meaning to each other but incomprehensible to her. They'd always communicated like this.

Maybe that's why neither she nor her brothers were married. They wanted what their parents had and weren't willing to settle for less.

Ironically, that's what she'd started to believe she had with Ted. They'd gotten really good at reading each other's minds. Too bad she hadn't picked up on what she'd most needed to know about him. How much he loved Lucy.

Her father rose from the couch. "Let me get this straight . . . You kept Lucy from potentially destroying her life by marrying the wrong man. You supported yourself in a town full of nutty people hell-bent on making you the scapegoat for all their troubles. You weren't really the activities coordinator at that country club, but you worked hard at the job you did have. And you also managed to start your own small business on the side. Do I have that right?"

Her mother lifted one magnificent eyebrow. "You've forgotten to mention how long she was able to hold off that perverted blowhard."

"Yet she's the one who's apologizing?" Her father turned it into a question, and the Glitter Baby's famous gold-flecked eyes bored into her daughter's.

"For what, Meg?" she said. "Exactly what are you apologizing for?"

Their question left her speechless. Hadn't they been listening?

The model and the movie star waited patiently for her response. A lock of blond hair curled along her mother's cheek. Her father rubbed his hip, as if he were checking for one of the pearl-handled Colt revolvers he'd worn in his Bird Dog Caliber films. Meg started to respond. She even opened her mouth. But nothing came out because she couldn't think of a good answer.

Her mother tossed her hair. "Obviously, these Texans have brainwashed you."

They were right. The person she needed to apologize to was herself for not being wise enough to protect her heart.

"You can't stay here," her father said. "This isn't a good place for you."

In some ways, it had been a very good place, but she merely nodded. "My car's already packed. I'm sorry to run out on you after you came all this way, but you're right. I have to leave, and I'm going now."

Her mother switched to her no-nonsense voice. "We want you to come home. Take some time to regroup."

Her father slipped his arm around Meg's shoulders. "We've missed you, baby."

This was what she'd wanted since they'd kicked her out. A little security, a place to hole up while she sorted everything out. Her heart filled with love for them. "You're the best. Both of you. But I have to do this on my own."

They argued with her, but Meg held firm, and after an emotional farewell, she headed back down the rear stairs to her car. She had one more thing to do before she drove away.

THE CARS IN THE ROUSTABOUT parking lot overflowed onto the highway. Meg parked on the shoulder behind a Honda Civic. As she walked along the road, she didn't bother searching for Ted's Benz or his truck. She knew he wouldn't be here, just as she knew everyone else would have gathered inside to hash over the afternoon's catastrophe.

She took a deep breath and shoved the door open. The smell of fried food, beer, and barbeque rolled over her as she looked around. The big room was jammed. People stood along the walls, between tables, and in the hallway that led to the restrooms. Torie, Dex, and all the Travelers squeezed around a four-top. Kayla, her father, Zoey, and Birdie sat nearby. Meg didn't see either Dallie or Francesca, although Skeet and some of the senior caddies leaned against the wall next to the video games, sipping beer.

It took a while before anyone in the crowd noticed her, and then it started to happen. Small pockets of silence that grew bigger as the seconds ticked by. They spread to the bar first, then encompassed the rest of the room until the only sounds were the clink of glassware and the voice of Carrie Underwood coming from the jukebox.

It would have been so much easier to slink away, but these past few months had taught her she wasn't the loser she'd believed herself to be. She was smart, she knew how to work hard, and she finally had a plan, however shaky, for her future. So even though she'd started to feel dizzy, and the food smells were making her nauseated, she forced herself to walk over to Pete Laraman, who always gave her a five-dollar tip for the frozen Milky Ways she carried just for him. "May I borrow your chair?"

He relinquished his seat and even gave her a hand up, a gesture she suspected was motivated by curiosity, not courtesy. Someone pulled the plug on the jukebox, and Carrie broke off midsong. Standing on the chair might not have been her best idea because of her rubbery knees, but if she was going to do this, she had to do it right, and that meant everyone in the place needed to be able to see her.

She spoke into the silence. "I know you all hate me right now, and there's nothing I can do about that."

"You can get the hell out of here," one of the bar rats shouted.

Torie shot to her feet. "Shut up, Leroy. Let her have her say."

The brunette Meg recognized from Francesca's luncheon as Hunter Gray's mother piped up next. "Meg's said enough, and now we're all screwed."

The woman next to her came out of her chair. "Our kids are screwed, too. We can kiss those school improvements good-bye."

"The hell with the schools," another of the bar rats declared. "What about all those jobs we're not going to have thanks to her?"

"Thanks to Ted," his crony added. "We trusted him, and look what happened."

The dark murmur Ted's name elicited told Meg she was right to do this. Lady Emma tried to spring up to defend their mayor only to have Kenny pull her back into her chair. Meg surveyed the crowd. "That's why I'm here," she said. "To talk about Ted."

"There's nothing you can say about him that we don't already know," the first bar rat declared with a sneer.

"Is that right?" Meg countered. "Well, how about this? Ted Beaudine isn't perfect."

"We sure know that now," his friend shouted, looking around him for confirmation and not having any trouble finding it.

"You should have known it all along," she countered, "but you've always held him to a higher standard than you've held yourselves. He's so good at everything that you lost sight of the fact that he's human like the rest of us, and he can't always work miracles."

"None of this would have happened if it wasn't for you!" someone exclaimed from the back.

"That's exactly right," Meg said. "You stupid rednecks! Don't you get it? From the minute Lucy walked out on him, Ted didn't have a chance." She let that sink in for a moment. "I saw my opportunity and I moved in on him. Right from the beginning, I had him in the palm of my hand." She tried to duplicate the bar rat's sneer. "None of you think a woman can control Ted, but I cut my teeth on movie stars and rockers, so believe me, he was easy. Then, when the game got old, I dumped him. He's not used to that, and he got a little crazy. So blame me all you want. But don't you dare fix the blame on him because he doesn't deserve your crap." She felt her swagger slipping. "He's one of yours. The best you have. And if you don't all let him know that, you deserve what you get."

Her legs had started to shake so badly she could barely jump down from the chair. She didn't look around, didn't seek out Torie and the rest of the Travelers to say the only good-byes that meant anything to her. Instead, she made a blind dash for the door.

Her last sight of the town she'd both loved and hated was a distant glimpse of the Pedernales River and the sign in her rearview mirror.

YOU ARE LEAVING
WYNETTE, TEXAS
Theodore Beaudine, Mayor

She let herself cry, racking sobs that shook her body and tears that blurred her vision. She gave into her grief because her heart was broken and because, once this trip was over, she was never going to cry again.

chapter twenty-two

A DARK CLOUD HAD SETTLED over Wynette. A tropical storm blew in from the Gulf, flooding the river and taking out the bridge on Comanche Road. The flu season started too early, and everybody's kids got sick. A kitchen fire closed the Roustabout for three weeks, and the town's only two garbage trucks broke down on the same day. While they were still reeling from all that, Kenny Traveler duck-hooked his drive on the eighteen hole at Whistling Straits and missed the cut in the PGA Championship. Worst of all, Ted Beaudine had resigned as mayor. Right when they needed him the most, he resigned. One week he was in Denver; Albuquerque, the next. Chasing all over the country trying to help cities get off the grid instead of staying in Wynette where he belonged.

Nobody was happy. Before Haley Kittle set off for her freshman year at U.T., she sent out a mass e-mail with a detailed account of what she'd seen the day she'd come on Spencer Skipjack threatening Meg

Koranda at the swimming hole behind the old Lutheran church. Once everybody knew the truth about what had taken place, they couldn't in good conscience blame Ted for punching Spence. Sure, they wished it hadn't happened, but Ted could hardly turn his back on the insults Spence was throwing out. One person after another tried to explain that to him on the few occasions he returned to town only to have him nod politely and hop on a plane the next day.

The Roustabout finally reopened, but even when Ted was around, he didn't show up. Instead, a couple of people saw him hanging out at Cracker John's, a shabby bar near the county line.

"He's divorced us," Kayla moaned to Zoey. "He's divorced the whole town."

"It's our own damned fault," Torie said. "We expected too much from him."

Word had spread from various well-placed sources that Spence and Sunny had gone back to Indianapolis, where Sunny had buried herself in work and where Spence got shingles. Much to everyone's shock, Spence had broken off negotiations with San Antonio. Word was, after being courted so vigorously by the people of Wynette, he'd lost interest in being a small fish in a big pond, and he'd given up his plans to build a golf resort anywhere.

With all the upheaval, people had almost forgotten about the Win a Weekend with Ted Beaudine contest until the library rebuilding committee reminded everybody the bidding closed at midnight on September 30. That night, the committee gathered in Kayla's first-floor home office to commemorate the occasion, as well as to show Kayla their appreciation for the way she'd continued to run the online contest even after her father cut off her bidding.

"We couldn't have done this without you," Zoey said, from the Hepplewhite settee opposite Kayla's desk. "If we ever get the library reopened, we're putting up a plaque in your honor."

Kayla had recently redecorated the office with Liberty print fabric walls and neoclassic furniture, but Torie elected to sit on the floor. "Zoey wanted to hang the plaque in the children's section," she said, "but we voted to put it by the fashion shelves. We figured that's where you'll be spending most of your time."

The others shot her a dirty look for reminding Kayla she'd be reading about fashion instead of setting trends at the boutique she'd always dreamed of owning. Torie hadn't meant to be tactless, so she got up to refill Kayla's mojito and admire the way her skin looked since her chemical peel.

"One minute to midnight," Shelby chirped with false enthusiasm.

The real suspense had ended a month earlier when Sunny Skipjack had stopped bidding. For the past two weeks, the top bidder, at fourteen thousand five hundred dollars, was a TV reality star only the teenagers had ever heard of. The committee made Lady Emma break the news to Ted that it looked as though he'd be spending a weekend in San Francisco with a former stripper who'd specialized in turning over tarot cards with her butt cheeks. Ted had merely nodded and said she must have excellent muscle control, but Lady Emma said his eyes were empty, and she'd never seen him look so sad.

"Let's count it down, just like New Year's Eve," Zoey said brightly.

And so they did. Watching the computer screen. Counting backward. At exactly midnight, Kayla hit the refresh button, and they all started to call out the name of the winner, only to fall silent as they saw that it wasn't the butt-talented stripper at all, but . . .

"Meg Koranda?" A collective gasp went up, and then they all started talking at once.

"Meg won the contest?"

"Hit the button again, Kayla. That can't be right."

"Meg? How could it be Meg?"

But it was Meg, all right, and they couldn't have been more shocked.

They talked for an hour, trying to figure it out. Every one of them missed her. Shelby had always admired the way Meg could anticipate what each of the women golfers might want to drink on any particular day. Kayla missed the profit Meg's jewelry had brought in, along with Meg's quirky fashion sense and the fact that nobody else would touch Torie's castoffs. Zoey missed Meg's sense of humor as well as the gossip she generated. Torie and Lady Emma simply missed her.

Despite the trouble she'd caused, they all agreed Meg had fit perfectly into the town. It was Birdie Kittle, however, who'd turned into Meg's most outspoken advocate. "She could have had Haley arrested the way Ted wanted, but she stood up for her. Nobody else would have done that."

Haley had told her mother and Birdie's friends everything. "I'm going to keep seeing a counselor at school," she'd said. "I want to learn how to respect myself better so nothing like that ever happens again."

Haley was so honest about what she'd done and so ashamed of her actions that none of them had been able to stay angry with her for long.

Shelby, who'd switched from mojitos to Diet Pepsi, slipped out of her new pewter flats. "It took guts to face down everybody at the Roustabout the way Meg did. Even if nobody believed a word she said."

Torie snorted. "If we hadn't all been so depressed, we'd have fallen off our chairs laughing when she talked about how she controlled Ted, then dumped him, like she was some big man-eater."

"Meg has honor, and she has heart," Birdie said. "That's a rare combination. She was also the hardest-working maid I ever had."

"And the worst paid," Torie pointed out.

Birdie immediately got defensive. "You know I'm trying to make up for that. I sent a check in care of her parents, but I haven't heard a word."

Lady Emma looked worried. "None of us have. She should at least have kept her phone number so we could call her. I don't like the way she's disappeared."

Kayla gestured toward the computer screen. "She picked a heck of a way to resurface. This is a desperation move on her part. A last attempt to get Ted back."

Shelby tugged on the waistband of her too-tight jeans. "She must have borrowed the money from her parents."

Torie wasn't buying it. "Meg's too proud to do that. And she's not the kind of woman who'll chase after a man who won't commit."

"I don't believe Meg placed that bid," Zoey said. "I think her parents did it."

They pondered the idea. "You might be right," Birdie finally said. "What parents wouldn't want their daughter to end up with Ted?"

But Lady Emma's quick brain had taken a different path. "You're all wrong," she said firmly. "Meg didn't place that bid, and neither did her parents." She exchanged a long look with Torie.

"What?" Kayla said. "Tell us."

Torie set aside her third mojito. "Ted placed the bid in Meg's name. He wants her back, and this is how he's going to get her."

THEY ALL WANTED TO SEE his reaction, so the committee members spent the next half hour arguing about who would inform Ted that Meg had won the contest. Would he pretend shock or come clean about his ruse? Eventually Lady Emma pulled rank on them and announced that she would do it herself.

Ted returned to Wynette on a Sunday, and Lady Emma showed up at his house early Monday morning. She wasn't altogether surprised when he didn't answer the door, but it wasn't in her nature to be put off, so she parked her SUV, pulled a lavishly illustrated biography of Beatrix Potter from her tote, and prepared to wait him out.

Less than half an hour later, the garage door opened. He took in the way she'd blocked both his truck and his Benz, then approached her car. He was wearing a business suit and aviator sunglasses, and carrying a laptop in a black leather case. He leaned down to address her through the open window. "Move."

She snapped her book closed. "I'm here on official business. Something I would have told you if you'd answered the door."

"I'm not the mayor any longer. I have no official business."

"You're the mayor in absentia. We've all decided. And it's not that kind of business."

He straightened. "Are you going to move your car or am I going to do it for you?"

"Kenny would not approve of you manhandling me."

"Kenny would cheer me on." He pulled off his sunglasses. His eyes looked tired. "What do you want, Emma?"

The fact that he didn't address her as "Lady Emma" alarmed her as much as his pallor, but she concealed how worried she was. "The contest is over," she said, "and we have a winner."

"I'm thrilled," he drawled.

"It's Meg."

"Meg?"

She nodded and waited for his reaction. Would she see satisfaction? Shock? Was her theory right?

He slipped on his sunglasses and told her she had thirty seconds to move her damn car.

FRANCESCA'S VAST, WALK-IN CLOSET WAS one of Dallie's favorite places, maybe because it reflected so many of his wife's contradictions. The closet was both luxurious and homey, chaotic and well organized. It smelled of sweet spice. It testified to overindulgence and rock solid practicality. What the closet didn't show was her grit, her generosity, or her loyalty to the people she loved.

"It's never going to work, Francie," he said as he stood in the doorway watching her pull a particularly fetching lace bra from one of the closet's built-in drawers.

"Rubbish. Of course it will." She shoved the bra back in the drawer as if it had personally offended her. That was all right with him because it left her standing in front of him in nothing but a pair of low-cut purplish lace panties. Whoever said a woman in her fifties couldn't be sexy hadn't seen Francesca Serritella Day Beaudine naked. Which he had. Many times. Including not half an hour ago when they'd been tangled up in their unmade bed.

She pulled out another bra that looked pretty much the same as the last one. "I had to do something, Dallie. He's wasting away."

"He's not wasting away. He's reassessing. Even when he was a kid, he liked taking his time to think things over."

"Rubbish." Another bra met with her displeasure. "He's had over a month. That's long enough."

The first time he'd seen Francie, she'd been stompin' down the side of a Texas highway, dressed like a southern belle, mad as hell, and determined to hitch a ride with him and Skeet. It had turned out to be the luckiest day of his life. Still, he didn't like letting her get too far ahead of him, and he pretended to inspect a nick on the doorjamb. "What did Lady Emma have to say about your little plan?"

Francie's sudden fascination with a bright red bra that didn't come close to matching her panties told him she hadn't mentioned her plan to Lady Emma. She slipped on the bra. "Did I tell you Emma is trying to talk Kenny into renting an RV and driving around the country with the children for a few months? Homeschooling them while they're on the road."

"I don't believe you did," he replied. "Just like I don't believe you told her you were going to set up an e-mail account in Meg's name and make the winning bid in that stupid-ass contest. You knew she'd try to talk you out of it."

She pulled a dress the same color as her eyes from a hanger. "Emma can be overly cautious."

"Bull. Lady Emma is the only rational person in this town, and I'm including you, me, and our son."

"I resent that. I have a great deal of common sense."

"When it comes to business."

She turned her back to him so he could pull up her zipper. "All right, then . . . *You* have a great deal of common sense."

He brushed the hair away from the nape of her neck and kissed the soft skin beneath. "Not when it comes to my wife. That got wiped out the day I picked you up on that highway."

She turned and gazed up at him, her lips parting, her eyes going all dewy. He could drown in those eyes. And, damn it, she knew that. "Stop trying to distract me."

"Please, Dallie . . . I need your support. You know how I feel about Meg."

"No, I don't." He zipped the dress. "Three months ago you hated her. In case you've forgotten, you tried to drive her out of town, and when that didn't work, you did your best to humiliate her by making her wait on all your friends."

"Not my finest hour." She wrinkled her nose, then grew thoughtful. "She was magnificent, Dallie. You should have seen her. She didn't bend an inch. Meg is . . . She's rather splendid."

"Yeah, well, you thought Lucy was rah-ther splendid, too, and look how that turned out."

"Lucy is wonderful. But not for Ted. They're too much alike. I'm surprised we didn't see that as clearly as Meg did. Right from the beginning, she's fit in here in ways Lucy could never quite manage."

"Because Lucy's too levelheaded. And we both know that 'fitting in' isn't exactly a compliment when you're talking about Wynette."

"But when we're talking about our son, it's essential."

Maybe she was right. Maybe Ted was in love with Meg. Dallie had thought so, but then he'd changed his mind when Ted had let her go as easily as he'd let Lucy go. Francie seemed sure, but she wanted grandbabies so much that she wasn't objective. "You should have just given the library committee the money right from the beginning," he said.

"You and I talked about that."

"I know." Experience had taught them that a few families, no matter how well off, couldn't support a town. They'd learned to pick their causes, and this year, the expansion of the free clinic had won out over the library repairs.

"It's only money," said the woman who'd once lived on a jar of peanut butter and slept on the couch of a five-hundred-watt radio station in the middle of nowhere. "I don't really need a new winter wardrobe. What I need is to have our son back."

"He hasn't gone anywhere."

"Don't pretend not to understand. More than losing the golf resort is bothering Ted."

"We don't know that for sure, since he won't talk to any of us about it. Even Lady Emma can't get him to open up. And forget about Torie. He's been dodging her for weeks."

"He's a private person."

"Exactly. And when he discovers what you've done, you're on your own, because I'm going to be conveniently out of town."

"I'm willing to take that risk," she said.

It wasn't the first risk she'd taken for their son, and since it was easier to kiss her than argue, he gave up.

Francesca had an immediate problem. The committee had used the e-mail address Francesca had established in Meg's name to notify her she'd won, which left Francesca with the job of locating her to deliver the news. But since Meg seemed to have disappeared, Francesca was forced to contact the Korandas.

She'd interviewed Jake twice in the past fifteen years, something of a record, given his obsession with privacy. His reticence made him a difficult interview subject, but off camera, he had a quick sense of humor and was easy to talk to. She didn't know his wife as well, but Fleur Koranda had a reputation for being tough, smart, and completely ethical. Unfortunately, the Korandas' brief, awkward visit to Wynette hadn't given either Francesca or Dallie a chance to deepen their acquaintance.

Fleur was cordial, but guarded, when Francesca phoned her office. Francesca patched together a cobbled version of something approximating the truth, leaving out only a few inconvenient details, such as her part in all this. She spoke of her admiration for Meg and her conviction that Meg and Ted cared deeply about each other.

"I'm absolutely certain, Fleur, that spending a weekend together in San Francisco will give them the chance they need to reconnect and repair their relationship."

Fleur was no fool, and she zeroed in on the obvious. "Meg doesn't have nearly enough money to have placed that bid."

"Which makes this situation all the more tantalizing, doesn't it?"

A short pause followed. Finally, Fleur said, "You think Ted is responsible?"

Francesca wouldn't lie, but neither did she intend to confess what she'd done. "There's been a lot of speculation in town about that. You can't imagine the theories I've heard." She hurried on. "I won't pressure you for Meg's telephone number . . ." She paused, hoping Fleur would volunteer to hand it over. When she didn't, she pressed on. "Let's do this. I'll make sure the itinerary for the weekend is sent directly to you, along with Meg's round-trip plane ticket from L.A. to San Francisco. The committee had planned on using a private jet to fly them both from Wynette, but given the circumstances, this seems like a better solution. Do you agree?"

She held her breath, but instead of answering, Fleur said, "Tell me about your son."

Francesca leaned back in her chair and gazed at the snapshot of Teddy she'd taken when he was nine. Head too big for his small, skinny body. Pants belted too high on his waist. The too-serious expression on his face at odds with his worn T-shirt, which announced BORN TO RAISE HELL.

She picked up the photo. "The day Meg left Wynette, she went to our local hangout and told everyone that Ted's not perfect." Her eyes filled with tears she didn't try to blink away. "I disagree."

FLEUR SAT AT HER DESK replaying her conversation with Francesca Beaudine, but it was hard to think clearly when her only daughter was in so much pain. Not that Meg would admit anything was wrong. The time she'd spent in Texas had both toughened and matured her, leaving her with an unfamiliar reserve Fleur still hadn't adjusted to. But even though Meg had made it clear that the subject of Ted Beaudine was off-limits, Fleur knew Meg had fallen in love with him and that she'd been deeply hurt. Every maternal instinct she possessed urged her to protect Meg from more pain.

She considered the gaping holes in the story she'd just heard. Francesca's glamorous exterior concealed a razor-sharp mind, and she'd revealed only as much as she wanted to. Fleur had no reason to trust her, especially when it was clear that her son was her priority. The same son who'd put the new sadness in Meg's eyes. But Meg wasn't a child, and Fleur had no right to make a decision like this for her.

She reached for the phone and called her daughter.

THE CHAIR TED HAD COMMANDEERED in the lobby of San Francisco's Four Seasons Hotel gave him a clear view of the entrance without making him immediately visible to whoever walked in. Each time the doors swung open, something twisted in the pit of his stomach. He couldn't believe he'd been thrown off stride so badly. He liked taking life easy, with everybody having a good time and appreciating one another's company. But nothing had been easy since the night of his wedding rehearsal when he'd met Meg Koranda.

She'd been wrapped in a few twists of silky fabric that left one shoulder bare and hugged the curve of her hip. Her hair was a belligerent tangle around her head, and silver coins swung like nunchucks from her ears. The way she'd challenged him had been annoying, but he hadn't taken her nearly as seriously as he should have. From that very first meeting, as he'd watched her eyes change from clear blue to the green of a tornado sky, he should have taken everything about her seriously.

When Lady E. had told him Meg was the winning bidder in the stupid-ass contest, he'd experienced a surge of elation followed almost immediately by a crashing return to reality. Neither Meg's pride nor her bank account would have allowed her to place that bid, and it didn't take him long to figure out who'd done it. Parents had always liked him, and the Korandas were no different. Even though he and Meg's father hadn't done more than exchange a few glances, they'd communicated perfectly.

The doorman helped an elderly guest into the lobby. Ted made himself ease back into the chair. Meg's plane had landed well over an hour ago, so she should be walking in any minute. He still didn't know exactly what he'd say to her, but he'd be damned if he let her see even a hint of the anger that still simmered inside him. Anger was a counterproductive emotion, and he needed a cool head to deal with Meg. His cool to her hot. His orderly to her messy.

But he didn't feel either cool or orderly, and the longer he waited, the more anxious he got. He could barely sort out all the crap she'd thrown in his face. First she'd dumped on him about what had happened at the luncheon. So what if he'd known the women wouldn't say anything? He'd still made a public declaration, hadn't he? Then she'd announced she'd fallen in love with him, but when he'd tried to tell her how much he cared, she'd discounted it, right along with refusing to attach any importance to the fact that he'd stood at the altar three months earlier, ready to marry another woman. Instead, she wanted some kind of everlasting promise, and wasn't that just like her—jumping into something without putting the situation in any kind of context?

His head shot up as the lobby doors once again swung open, this time admitting an older man and a much younger woman. Even though the lobby was cool, Ted's shirt was damp. So much for her accusation that he stood on the sidelines where he didn't have to sweat too much.

He checked his watch again, then pulled out his phone to see if she'd sent him a text, just as he'd done so many times since she'd disappeared, but none of the messages were from her. He shoved the phone back in his pocket as the other memory crowded in. The one he didn't want to deal with. What he'd done to her that day at the landfill . . .

He couldn't believe he'd lost control like that. She'd tried to brush it off, but he'd never forgive himself.

He tried to think about something else, only to end up stewing over the mess in Wynette. The town refused to accept his resignation, so his desk at City Hall sat empty, but he'd be damned if he was jumping back into that disaster. The truth was, he'd let everybody down, and no matter how understanding they all tried to be, there wasn't a person in town who didn't know he'd failed them.

The lobby doors opened and closed. In the course of one summer, his comfortable life had been destroyed.

"I'm messy and wild and disruptive, and you have broken my heart."

The unbearable hurt in those green-blue eyes had cut right through him. But what about his heart? His hurt? How did she think he felt when the person he'd grown to count on the most left him in the lurch right when he needed her?

"My stupid heart . . . ," she'd said. *"It was singing."*

He waited in the lobby all afternoon, but Meg never appeared.

THAT NIGHT, HE WANDERED THROUGH Chinatown and got drunk in a Mission District bar. The next day he pulled up the collar of his jacket and walked the city in the rain. He rode a cable car, drifted through the tea garden in Golden Gate Park, poked into a couple of souvenir shops on Fisherman's Wharf. He tried to eat a bowl of clam chowder at the Cliff House to warm up but set it aside after a few bites.

"Just the sight of you made me feel like dancing."

He woke up too early the next morning, hungover and miserable. A cold, thick fog had settled in, but he hit the empty streets anyway and climbed to the top of Telegraph Hill.

Coit Tower wasn't open yet, so he walked the grounds, gazing out across the city and the bay as the fog began to lift. He wished he could talk this whole mess over with Lucy, but he could hardly call her up after all this time and tell her that her best friend was an immature, demanding, overly emotional, unreasonable nutcase, and what the hell was he supposed to do about that?

He missed Lucy. Everything had been so easy with her.

He missed her . . . but he didn't want to wring her neck like he wanted to wring Meg's. He didn't want to make love with her until her eyes turned to smoke. He didn't yearn for the sound of her voice, the joy of her laughter.

He didn't ache for Lucy. Dream about her. Long for her.

He didn't love her.

With a rustle of leaves and a chilly gust, the wind carried the fog out to sea.

chapter twenty-three

A FEW HOURS LATER, TED WAS headed south on I-5 in a rented Chevy Trailblazer. He drove too fast and stopped just once to grab a mug of bitter coffee. He prayed Meg had gone to L.A. with her parents when she'd left Wynette instead of heading off to Jaipur or Ulan Bator or some other place where he couldn't get to her and tell her how much he loved her. The wind that had carried away the San Francisco fog had also swept away the last of his confusion. He'd been left with a blinding clarity that cut through all the turmoil of old fiancées and aborted weddings, a clarity that let him see how skillfully he'd used logic to hide his fear of having his easy life disturbed by chaotic emotions.

He, of all people, should have known love wasn't orderly or rational. Hadn't his own parents' passionate, illogical love affair overcome deception, separation, and pigheadedness to last more than three decades? That kind of soul-deep love was what he felt for Meg—the complicated, disruptive, overpowering love he'd refused to admit was missing in his relationship with Lucy. He and Lucy had fit together so perfectly in his mind. His mind . . . but not his heart. It should never have taken him so long to figure that out.

He ground his teeth in frustration when he hit L.A. traffic. Meg was a creature of passion and impulse, and he hadn't seen her in over a month. What if time and distance had convinced her she deserved something better than a boneheaded Texan who didn't know his own mind?

He couldn't think like that. He couldn't let himself contemplate what he'd do if she'd gotten fed up with the whole idea of ever having fallen in love with him. If only she hadn't cut off her phone. And what about her history of hopping on planes and flying off to the farthest reaches of the planet? He wanted her to stay put, but Meg wasn't like that.

It was early evening by the time he reached the Korandas' Brentwood estate. He wondered if they knew Meg hadn't shown up in San Francisco. Although he couldn't be certain they were the ones who'd put up the winning bid, who else would have done it? The irony didn't escape him. What the parents of daughters most liked about him was his stability, but he'd never felt less stable in his life.

He identified himself over the intercom. As the gates swung open, he remembered he hadn't shaved for two days. He should have stopped at a hotel first to clean up. His clothes were wrinkled, his eyes bloodshot, and he had a bad case of flop sweat, but he wasn't going to turn back now.

He parked his car at the side of the English Tudor that was the Korandas' primary California home. Best-case scenario, Meg would be here. Worst-case scenario . . . He wouldn't think about worst-case scenarios. The Korandas were his allies, not his enemies. If she weren't here, they'd help him find her.

But the cool hostility Fleur Koranda exhibited when she opened the front door did nothing to bolster his shaken confidence. "Yes?"

That was all. No smile. No handshake. Definitely no hug. Regardless of age, women tended to go all melty-eyed when they saw him. It had happened so many times he barely noticed, but it wasn't happening now, and the novelty unbalanced him. "I need to see Meg," he blurted out, and then, stupidly, "I— We haven't been formally introduced. I'm Ted Beaudine."

"Ah, yes. Mr. Irresistible."

She didn't say it like it was a compliment.

"Is Meg here?" he asked.

Fleur Koranda looked at him exactly the way his mother had looked at Meg. Fleur was a beautiful six-foot Amazon with the same boldly slashed eyebrows Meg had, but not Meg's coloring or more delicate features. "The last time I saw you," Fleur said, "you were scrambling in the dirt, trying to knock a man's head off."

If Meg had the guts to stand up to his mother, he could face hers down. "Yes, ma'am. And I'd do it again. Now I'd appreciate it if you'd tell me where I can find her."

"Why?"

If you gave mothers like this an inch, they'd mow you down. "That's between her and me."

"Not exactly." The deep voice came from Meg's father, who'd appeared at his wife's shoulder. "Let him in, Fleur."

Ted nodded, stepped into a grand entrance hall, and followed them to a comfortable family room already occupied by two tall younger men with Meg's chestnut brown hair. One sat on the fireplace hearth, ankle crossed over his knee, strumming a guitar. The other tapped away at a Mac. These could only be Meg's twin brothers. The one with the laptop, Rolex, and Italian loafers had to be Dylan, the financial whiz, while Clay, the guitar-playing New York actor, had

shaggier hair, ripped jeans, and bare feet. Both of them were exceptionally good-looking guys and dead ringers for an old movie idol,
although he couldn't immediately recall which one. Neither resembled
Meg, who took after her father. And neither appeared to be any more
welcoming than the senior Korandas. Either they knew Meg hadn't
shown up in San Francisco and blamed him, or he'd gotten it dead
wrong from the start, and they weren't the ones who'd entered the
contest for her. Either way, he needed them.

Jake made perfunctory introductions. Both brothers uncoiled from
their respective seats, not to shake his hand, he quickly discovered, but
to meet him at eye level. "So this is the great Ted Beaudine," Clay said
with a drawl almost identical to the one his father used on-screen.

Dylan looked as though he'd sniffed out a hostile takeover. "No
accounting for my sister's taste."

So much for hopes of cooperation. Although Ted didn't have any practice dealing with animosity, he damned sure wasn't going to back away
from it, and he cut his gaze between the brothers. "I'm looking for Meg."

"I take it she didn't show up for your party in San Francisco,"
Dylan said. "That must have been quite a blow to your ego."

"My ego doesn't have anything to do with it," Ted countered. "I
need to talk to her."

Clay fingered the neck of his guitar. "Yeah, but here's the thing,
Beaudine . . . If our sister wanted to talk to you, she'd have done it by
now."

The atmosphere in the room crackled with an ill will he recognized as the same kind of antagonism Meg had confronted every day
she was in Wynette. "That's not necessarily true," he said.

Mother Bear's beautiful, blond fur bristled. "You had your chance,
Ted, and from what I understand, you blew it."

"Big-time," Papa Bear said. "But if you give us a message, we'll be
sure to pass it on."

Ted was damned if he'd spill his guts to any of them. "With all due respect, Mr. Koranda, what I have to say to Meg is between the two of us."

Jake shrugged. "Good luck, then."

Clay set down his guitar and stepped away from his brother. Some of his hostility seemed to have faded, and he regarded Ted with what seemed like sympathy. "No one else is going to tell you, so I will. She's left the country. Meg is traveling again."

Ted's stomach twisted. This was exactly what he'd feared. "No problem," he heard himself say. "I'm more than happy to get on a plane."

Dylan didn't share his brother's sympathetic attitude. "For a guy who's supposed to be some kind of genius, you're a little slow on the uptake. We're not telling you a damned thing."

"We're a family," Papa Bear said. "You may not understand what that means, but all of us do."

Ted understood exactly what it meant. It meant these tall, good-looking Korandas had circled their wagons against him just as his friends had done against Meg. Lack of sleep, frustration, and a self-disgust that was tinged with panic made him lash out. "I'm a little confused. Aren't you the same *family* who cut her off four months ago?"

He had them. He could see the guilt in their eyes. Until this exact moment, he'd never suspected he had a spiteful nature, but a person learned something new about himself every day. "I'll bet Meg never told you everything she went through."

"We talked to Meg all the time." Her mother's stiff lips barely moved.

"Is that right? Then you know all about how she was living." He didn't give a damn that he was about to do something grossly unfair.

"I'm sure you know she was forced to scrub toilets to buy food? And she must have told you she had to sleep in her car? Did she mention that she barely avoided going to jail on vagrancy charges?" He wasn't telling them who'd nearly sent her there. "She ended up living in an abandoned building with no furniture. And do you have any idea how hot a Hill Country summer is? To cool off, she swam in a snake-infested creek." He could see the guilt dripping from their pores, and he bore in. "She had no friends and a town full of enemies, so you'll forgive me if I'm not impressed with your notions of how to protect her."

Her parents had gone ashen-faced, her brothers wouldn't look at him, and he told himself to back off even as the words kept coming. "If you don't want to tell me where she is, then the hell with all of you. I'll find her myself."

He stormed out of the house, fueled by rage, an emotion so new to him he barely recognized it. By the time he reached his car, however, he regretted what he'd done. This was the family of the woman he loved, and even she believed they'd done the right thing by cutting her off. He'd accomplished nothing except venting his anger on the wrong people. How the hell was he supposed to find her now?

He spent the next few days fighting a grinding despair. An Internet search failed to yield any clues about Meg's whereabouts, and the people most likely to have information refused to talk to him. She could be anywhere, and with the whole world to search, he had no idea where to start.

Once it was obvious the Korandas hadn't been the high bidders in the contest, the identity of his matchmaker should have been immediately clear, but he still didn't figure it out right away. When he finally put the pieces together, he stormed to his parents' house and ran his mother to ground in her office.

"You made her life hell!" he exclaimed, barely able to contain himself.

She tried to wave him away with a flick of her fingers. "A dreadful exaggeration."

It felt good to have a target for his anger. "You made her life hell, and then suddenly, without warning, you turn into her champion?"

She regarded him with injured dignity, her favorite trick when she was backed into a corner. "Surely you've read Joseph Campbell. In any mythic journey, the heroine has to pass a series of difficult trials before she's worthy enough to win the hand of the beautiful prince."

His father snorted from across the room.

Ted stalked out of the house, afraid of this new anger that kept erupting. He wanted to hop on a plane, to bury himself in work, to slip out of the skin that had once fit him so comfortably. Instead he drove to the church and sat next to Meg's swimming hole. He imagined her disgust if she could see him like this—see what was happening to the town. With the mayor's office sitting empty, bills weren't getting paid and disputes were going unsettled. No one could even authorize the final repairs on the library that his mother's check had made possible. He'd failed the town. He'd failed Meg. He'd failed himself.

She would hate the way he'd fallen apart, and even in his imagination, he didn't like disappointing her more than he already had. He drove into town, parked his truck, and forced himself through the door of City Hall.

As soon as he stepped inside, everybody started toward him. He held up his hand, glared at each one of them, and sealed himself in his office.

He stayed there all day, refusing to answer either the ringing phone or the repeated knocks on his locked door as he shuffled through papers, studied the city budget, and contemplated the sabotaged golf resort. For weeks the seed of an idea had been trying to break through his subconscious only to wither in the bitter soil of his guilt, anger, and misery. Now, instead of gnawing over the ugly scene at the landfill, he applied the cool, hard logic that was his stock-in-trade.

One day passed, then another. Homemade baked goods began to pile up outside his office. Torie yelled through the door, trying to bully him into going to the Roustabout. Lady E. left the complete works of David McCullough on the passenger seat of his truck—he had no idea why. He ignored them all, and after three days, he had a plan. One that would make his life infinitely more complicated, but a plan nonetheless. He emerged from his seclusion and began making phone calls.

Another three days passed. He found a good lawyer and made more phone calls. Unfortunately, none of that solved the bigger problem or finding Meg. Despair gnawed at him. Where the hell had she gone?

Since her parents continued to dodge his calls, he made both Lady E. and Torie give it a try. But the Korandas wouldn't crack. He imagined her sick with dysentery in the jungles of Cambodia or freezing to death on her way up K2. His nerves were raw. He couldn't sleep. Could barely eat. He lost track of the agenda during the first meeting he called.

Kenny showed up at his house one evening with a pizza. "I'm seriously starting to worry about you. It's time you get a grip."

"Look who's talking," Ted retorted. "You went nuts when Lady E. ran out on you."

Kenny pleaded memory loss.

That night Ted once again found himself lying sleepless in his bed. How ironic that Meg used to call him Mr. Cool. As he stared at the ceiling, he imagined her gored by a bull or bitten by a king cobra, but when he began picturing her getting gang-raped by a band of guerrilla soldiers, he couldn't take it any longer. He threw himself out of bed, jumped in his truck, and drove to the landfill.

The night was cool and still. He left on his high beams and stood between the funnels of light as he stared out at the empty, polluted land. Kenny was right. He had to pull himself together. But how could he do that? He was no closer to finding her than when he'd begun, and his life had fallen apart.

Maybe it was the desolation, or the stillness, or the dark, empty land so full of untapped promise. For whatever reason, he felt himself standing straighter. And he finally saw what he'd missed—the glaring fact he'd overlooked in all his attempts to find her.

Meg needed money to leave the country. From the beginning, he'd assumed her parents had given it to her to make up for everything she'd gone through. That was what logic told him. His logic. But he wasn't the one calling the shots, and he'd never once gotten out of his own head to slip into hers.

He envisioned her face in all its moods. Her laughter and anger, her sweetness and sass. He knew her as well as he knew himself, and as he opened his mind to hers, the essential fact he should have picked up on from the beginning became blindingly clear.

Meg wouldn't take a penny from her parents. Not for shelter. Not for travel. Not for anything. Clay Koranda had lied to him.

chapter twenty-four

M EG HEARD THE CAR CREEPING along behind her. Although it was barely ten o'clock at night, the chilly October rain had emptied the streets of Manhattan's Lower East Side. She walked faster past the wet, black garbage bags that sagged at the curb. Rain dripped through the fire escapes above her head, and trash floated in the flooded gutters. Some of the former redbrick tenement buildings on Clay's block had been spruced up, but most hadn't, and the neighborhood was dodgy at best. Still, she hadn't thought twice about clearing her head with a trip to her favorite cheap deli for a hamburger. But she hadn't counted on the rain driving everyone inside on her way back.

The building that housed Clay's cramped fifth-floor walkup was almost two blocks away. She'd subleased his dingy apartment while he was in L.A. shooting a meaty role in an indie film that might be the break he'd been waiting for. The place was small and depressing, with only two minuscule windows admitting trickles of thready light, but it was cheap, and once she'd gotten rid of Clay's greasy old couch, along with the detritus left behind by various girlfriends, she had room to make her jewelry.

The car stayed with her. A quick glance over her shoulder showed a black stretch limo, not anything to get nervous about, but it had been a long week. A long six weeks. Her brain was fuzzy from exhaustion, and her fingers so sore from laboring over her jewelry collection that only willpower kept her going. But her hard work was paying off.

She didn't try to convince herself she was happy, but she knew she'd made the best decisions she could about her future. Sunny Skipjack had been on target when she'd said Meg should reposition herself for the high-end market. The boutique managers she'd shown her sample pieces to liked the juxtaposition of modern design and ancient relics, and the orders had come in more quickly than she'd dreamed possible. If her life's goal was to be a jewelry designer, she would have been ecstatic, but that wasn't her goal. Not now. Finally, she knew what she wanted to do.

The car was still right behind her, its headlights yellow smears on the wet asphalt. Rain had soaked through her canvas sneakers, and she pulled the purple trench she'd found at a secondhand store more tightly around her. Security grilles barred the windows of the sari shop, the Korean discount home-goods store, even the dumpling place—all closed for the night.

She walked faster still, but the steady hum of the engine didn't fade. It wasn't her imagination. The car was definitely following her, and she had a block to go.

A police car sped by on the cross street, siren blaring, red light pulsing in the rain. Her breath came more quickly as the limousine pulled up next to her, its dark windows menacing in the night. She started to run, but the car stayed with her. Out of the corners of her eyes, she saw one of the back windows slide down.

"Want a lift?"

The last face she'd ever have expected to see peered out at her. She stumbled on the uneven pavement, so dizzy she nearly fell. After everything she'd done to cover her tracks, here he was, framed in that open window, his features shadowed.

For weeks, she'd labored deep into the night, focusing only on her work, not letting herself think, refusing to sleep until she was too exhausted to go on. She was ragged and empty, in no condition to talk to anyone, let alone him. "No thanks," she managed. "I'm almost home."

"You look a little wet." A shaft of light from a streetlamp cut across one molded cheekbone.

He couldn't do this to her. She wouldn't let him. Not after all that had happened. She started to walk again, but the limo stayed even with her.

"You really shouldn't be out here by yourself," he said.

She understood him well enough to know exactly what lay behind his sudden appearance. A guilty conscience. He hated hurting people, and he needed to reassure himself that she wasn't permanently damaged. "Don't worry about it," she said.

"Would you mind getting in the car?"

"No need. I'm almost home." She told herself not to say any more, but curiosity got the best of her. "How did you find me?"

"Believe me, it wasn't easy."

She kept her eyes straight ahead and didn't slacken her pace. "One of my brothers," she said. "You got to them."

She should have known they'd cave. Last week, Dylan had taken a detour from Boston to tell her Ted's calls were driving them all nuts and she needed to talk to him. Clay sent her a stream of text messages. *Dude sounds desperate,* his last one said. *Who knows what he might do?*

Worst-case scenario? she'd replied. *He'll miss a 4-foot putt.*

Ted waited until a taxi passed before he replied. "Your brothers gave me nothing but trouble. Clay even told me you'd left the country. I forgot he was an actor."

"I told you he was good."

"It took me a while, but I finally realized you wouldn't accept money from your parents anymore. And I couldn't see you leaving the country with what you took out of your checking account."

"How do you know what I took out of my checking account?"

Even in the dusky light, she could see him raise his eyebrow. She moved on with a snort of disgust.

"I knew you'd ordered some of your jewelry materials on the Internet," he said. "I made a list of possible suppliers and got Kayla to call them."

She stepped around a broken whiskey bottle. "I'm sure she was more than willing to help you out."

"She told everyone that she owned a boutique in Phoenix and she was trying to find the designer of some jewelry she'd spotted in Texas. She described a few of your pieces—said she wanted to carry them in her store. Yesterday she got your address."

"And here you are. A wasted trip."

He had the nerve to sound angry. "Do you think we could have this conversation inside the limo?"

"No." He could deal with his guilt all by himself. Guilt didn't add up to love, an emotion she was done with forever.

"I really need you to get in the car." He grunted out the words.

"I really need you to go to hell."

"I just got back, and trust me, it's not all it's cracked up to be."

"Sorry about that."

"Damn it." The door swung open, and he jumped out while the limo was still moving. Before she could react, he was dragging her to the car.

"Stop it! What are you doing?"

The limo had finally braked. He pushed her inside, climbed in after her, and slammed the door. The locks clicked. "Consider yourself officially kidnapped."

The car began to move again, its driver hidden behind the closed partition. She grabbed the door handle, but it didn't budge. "Let me out! I don't believe you're doing this. What's wrong with you? Are you crazy?"

"Pretty much."

She'd delayed looking at him for as long as she could. Any longer, and he'd see weakness. Slowly she turned her head.

He was as dazzling as ever with those tiger eyes and bladed cheekbones, that straight nose and movie-star jaw. He wore a charcoal gray business suit with a white shirt and navy tie. She hadn't seen him so formally dressed since his wedding day, and she struggled against a dark tide of emotion. "I mean it," she said. "Let me out right now."

"Not until we've talked."

"I don't want to talk to you. I don't want to talk to anybody."

"What do you mean? You love to talk."

"Not anymore." The interior of the stretch had long seats running up the sides and tiny blue lights edging the roof. An enormous bouquet of red roses lay on the seat in front of a built-in bar. She dug into her coat pocket for her cell. "I'm calling the police and telling them I've been kidnapped."

"I'd rather you didn't."

"This is Manhattan. You're not God here. They'll send you to Rikers for sure."

"Doubtful, but no sense taking chances." He snatched the phone away and shoved it in the pocket of his suit coat.

She was an actor's daughter, and she produced a bored shrug. "Fine. Talk. And hurry up about it. My fiancé's waiting for me at the apartment." She pressed her hip against the door, as far away from him as she could get. "I told you it wouldn't take me long to forget you."

He blinked, then reached for his bouquet of guilt roses and set them in her lap. "I thought you might like these."

"You thought wrong." She flung them back at him.

As THE BOUQUET HIT HIM in the head, Ted accepted the fact that this reunion wasn't going any better than he deserved. Kidnapping Meg had been one more miscalculation on his part. Not that he'd planned to kidnap her. He'd intended to show up at her door with the roses and a heartfelt declaration of everlasting love, then sweep her off into the limo. But as the car turned onto her street, he'd spotted her, and all his common sense had vanished.

Even from the rear, with her body enveloped in a long purple trench coat, her shoulders hunched against the rain, he'd recognized her. Other women had the same long-legged gait, the same determined swing of the arms, but none of them made him feel as if his chest had imploded.

The dim blue lights in the limo's interior picked up the same shadows beneath her eyes that he knew had taken up residence under his own. Instead of the rustic beads and ancient coins he was used to seeing dangling from her ears, she wore no jewelry, and the tiny, empty holes in her lobes gave her a vulnerability that tore at him. Her jeans poked out beneath the hem of her wet purple trench coat, and her canvas sneakers were soaked. Her hair was longer than it was when he'd last seen her, spangled with raindrops, and bright red. He wanted her back the way she'd been. He wanted to kiss away the new hollows below her cheekbones and put the warmth back in her eyes. He wanted to make her smile. Laugh. Make her love him again as deeply as he loved her.

As she stared straight ahead at the partition that separated them from his mother's longtime Manhattan driver, he refused to consider the possibility that he was too late. She had to be lying about the fiancé. Except how could any man resist falling in love with her? He needed to be sure. "Tell me about this fiancé of yours."

"No way. I don't want you to feel any worse about yourself than you already do."

She was lying. At least he prayed she was. "So you think you know how I feel?"

"Definitely. You feel guilty."

"True."

"Frankly, I don't have the energy right now to reassure you. As you can see, I'm doing just fine. Now get on with your life and leave me alone."

She didn't look as though she was doing just fine. She looked exhausted. Worse, there was an aloofness—a gravity—about her so at odds with the funny, irreverent woman he knew that he couldn't make the pieces fit. "I've missed you," he said.

"Glad to hear it," she replied, in a voice as remote as those mountains he'd feared she might be climbing. "Could you please take me back to my apartment?"

"Later."

"Ted, I mean it. We have nothing more to talk about."

"Maybe you don't, but I do." Her determination to get away scared him. He'd witnessed firsthand how stubborn she could be, and he hated having that resolve turned against him. He needed a way to break through her ice. "I thought we . . . might take a boat ride."

"A boat ride? I don't think so."

"I knew it was a stupid idea, but the rebuilding committee insisted that was the way to go with you. Forget I mentioned it."

Her head shot up. "You talked this over with the *rebuilding committee*?"

That flash of temper gave him hope. "I might have mentioned it. In passing. I needed the female perspective, and they convinced me that all women appreciate the grand romantic gesture. Even you."

Sure enough, sparks flared in her eyes. "I cannot believe you talked over our personal business with those women."

Our business, she'd said. Not just his. He pressed harder. "Torie's really pissed with you."

"I don't care."

"Lady E., too, but she's more polite about it. You hurt all their feelings when you changed your phone number. You really shouldn't have done that."

"Send them my apologies," she said with a sneer.

"The boat was Birdie's idea. She's kind of become your champion because of Haley. And you were right about not bringing in the police. Haley's grown up a lot lately, and I'm not one of those men who can't admit it when he's wrong."

His hopes rose higher as she clenched her fists against her wet coat. "How many other people did you talk to about our private business?"

"A few." He stalled for time, frantically trying to figure out how to play this. "Kenny was worthless. Skeet's still mad at me. Who knew he'd take to you the way he did? And Buddy Ray Baker said I should buy you a Harley."

"I don't even know Buddy Ray Baker!"

"Sure you do. He works nights at the Food and Fuel. He sends his best."

Indignation had put some of the color back in those beautiful cheeks. "Is there anyone you didn't talk to?" she said.

He reached for the napkin next to the champagne bucket, where, in a premature burst of optimism, he had a bottle chilling. "Let me dry you off."

She grabbed the napkin from him and threw it down. He settled back in the seat and tried to sound as if he had it all under control. "San Francisco wasn't much fun without you."

"Sorry you had to waste your money like that, but I'm sure the rebuilding committee was grateful for your generous contribution."

Admitting he wasn't the one who'd made that expensive final bid hardly seemed like the best way to convince her of his love. "I sat in the hotel lobby all afternoon waiting for you," he said.

"Guilt is your thing. It doesn't work with me."

"It wasn't guilt." The limo pulled to the curb, and the driver, following Ted's earlier instructions, stopped on State Street across from the National Museum of the American Indian. It was still raining, and he should have chosen another destination, but he'd never have gotten her inside his parents' Greenwich Village co-op, and he couldn't imagine spilling his guts in a restaurant or bar. He sure as hell wasn't saying any more in this limo with his mother's driver eavesdropping on the other side of the partition. *The hell with it.* Rain or not, this was the place.

She peered out the window. "Why are we stopping here?"

"So we can take a walk in the park." He hit the locks, grabbed the umbrella from the floor, and pushed the door open.

"I don't want to take a walk. I'm wet, my feet are cold, and I want to go home."

"Soon." He caught her arm and somehow managed to get both her and the umbrella out onto the street.

"It's raining!" she exclaimed.

"Not too much now. Besides, you're already wet, that red hair should keep you plenty warm, and I have a big umbrella." He popped it, dragged her around the back of the limo and up onto the sidewalk. "Lots of boat docks here." He nudged her toward the entrance to Battery Park.

"I told you I wasn't going on a boat ride."

"Fine. No boat ride." Not that he'd planned one anyway. That would have taken a degree of organized thought he wasn't capable of pulling together. "I'm just saying there are docks here. And a great view of the Statue of Liberty."

She completely missed the significance of that.

"Damn it, Ted." She whirled on him, and the quirky humor that had once marched in lockstep with his own was nowhere to be seen. He hated seeing her this way, with all her laughter dimmed, and he knew he had only himself to blame.

"All right, let's get this over with." She scowled at a bike rider. "Say what you have to say, and then I'm going home. On the subway."

Like hell she was. "Deal." He steered her into Battery Park and down the closest path leading to the promenade.

Two people sharing one umbrella should have been romantic, but not when one of those people refused to get close to the other. By the time they hit the open promenade, rain had soaked his suit coat, and his shoes were nearly as wet as hers.

The vendors' carts had disappeared for the day, and only a few hearty souls hurried along the wet pavement. The wind had picked up, and the cold drizzle blowing in off the water hit him in the face. In the distance, the Statue of Liberty stood guard over the harbor. She was lit up for the night, and he could just make out the tiny lights shining through the windows in her crown. On a long-ago summer day, he'd broken one of those windows, unfurled a NO NUKES banner, and finally found his father. Now, with the statue standing there to give him courage, he prayed he would find his future.

He summoned up his courage. "I love you, Meg."

"Whatever. Can I go now?"

He tilted his head toward the statue. "The most important event of my childhood happened over there."

"Yeah, I remember. Your youthful act of vandalism."

"Right." He swallowed. "And it seems fitting that the most important event of my manhood should happen there, too."

"Wouldn't that have been when you lost your virginity? What were you? Twelve?"

"Listen to me, Meg. I love you."

She couldn't have been less interested. "You should get therapy. Seriously. Your sense of responsibility has gotten way out of control." She patted his arm. "It's over, Ted. Throw away all that guilt. I've moved on and, frankly, you're starting to seem a little pathetic."

He wouldn't let her get to him. "The truth is, I wanted to have this conversation out there on Liberty Island. Unfortunately, I was banned for life, so that's not possible. Being banned didn't seem like such a big deal when I was nine, but it sure as hell feels like one now."

"Do you think you could wind this up? I have some paperwork I need to get done tonight."

"What kind of paperwork?"

"My admission papers. I'm starting classes at NYU in January."

His gut churned. This was definitely not something he wanted to hear. "You're going back to school?"

She nodded. "I finally figured out what I want to do with my life."

"I thought you were designing jewelry?"

"That's paying the bills. Most of them, anyway. But it's not what satisfies me."

He wanted to be what satisfied her.

She finally started to talk without being prodded. Unfortunately, it wasn't about the two of them. "I'll be able to finish my bachelor's degree in environmental science by summer and go right into a master's program."

"That's . . . great." *Not great at all.* "Then what?"

"Maybe work for the National Park Service or something like the Nature Conservancy. I might be able to manage a land protection program. There are a lot of options. Waste management, for example. Most people don't see that as a glamorous field, but the landfill fascinated me from the beginning. My dream job is— " Just like that, she broke off. "I'm getting cold. Let's go back."

"What about your dream job?" He prayed she'd say something along the line of being his wife and the mother of his children, but that didn't seem too realistic.

She spoke briskly, stranger to stranger. "Turning environmental wastelands into recreational areas is what I'd really like to do, and you can consider yourself responsible. Now this has been loads of fun, but I'm out of here. And this time, don't try to stop me."

She turned her back and began to walk away, a grim, humorless, red-haired woman who was tough as nails and no longer wanted him in her life.

He panicked. "Meg! I love you! I want to marry you!"

"That's weird," she said without stopping. "Only six weeks ago, you were telling me all about how Lucy broke your heart."

"I was wrong. Lucy broke my brain."

That finally stopped her. "Your brain?" She looked back at him.

"That's right," he said more quietly. "When Lucy ran out on me, she broke my brain. But when you left . . ." To his dismay, his voice cracked. "When you left, you broke my heart."

He finally had her full attention, not that she looked at all dreamy-eyed or even close to being ready to throw herself into his arms, but at least she was listening.

He collapsed the umbrella, took a step forward, then stopped himself. "Lucy and I fit together so perfectly in my head. We had everything in common, and what she did made no sense. I had the whole town lining up feeling sorry for me, and I was damned if I was going to let anybody know how miserable I was. I—I couldn't get my bearings. And there you were in the middle of it, this beautiful thorn in my side, making me feel like myself again. Except . . ." He hunched his shoulders, and a trickle of rainwater ran down his collar. "Sometimes logic can be an enemy. If I was so wrong about Lucy, how could I trust the way I felt about you?"

She stood there, not saying a word, just listening.

"I wish I could say I realized how much I loved you as soon as you left town, but I was too busy being mad at you for bailing on me. I don't have a lot of practice being mad, so it took me a while to understand that the person I was really mad at was myself. I was so pigheaded and stupid. And afraid. Everything has always come so easy for me, but nothing about you was easy. The things you made me feel. The way you forced me to look at myself." He could barely breathe. "I love you, Meg. I want to marry you. I want to sleep with you every night, make love with you, have kids. I want to fight together and work together and—just be together. Now are you going to keep standing there, staring at me, or could you put me out of my misery and say you still love me, at least a little?"

She stared at him. Eyes steady. Unsmiling. "I'll think about it and let you know."

She walked away and left him standing alone in the rain.

He dropped the umbrella, stumbled over to the wet railing, and curled his fingers around the cold metal. His eyes stung. He'd never felt so empty or so alone. As he stared out into the harbor, he wondered what he could have said that would have convinced her. Nothing. He was too late. Meg had no patience for procrastinators. She'd cut her losses and moved on.

"Okay, I've thought it over," she said from behind him. "What are you offering?"

He spun around, his heart in his throat, rain splashing his face. "Uh . . . My love?"

"Got that part. What else?"

She looked fierce and strong and absolutely enchanting. Wet spiky lashes framed her eyes, which didn't seem either blue or green now, but a rain-soft gray. Her cheeks were flushed, her hair a flame, her mouth a promise waiting to be claimed. His heart raced. "What do you want?"

"The church."

"Are you planning to live there again?"

"Maybe."

"Then, no, you can't have it."

She appeared to think it over. He waited, the sound of his blood rushing in his ears.

"How about the rest of your worldly possessions?" she said.

"Yours."

"I don't want them."

"I know." Something bloomed inside his chest, something warm and full of hope.

She squinted up at him, rain dripping from the tip of her nose. "I only have to see your mother once a year. At Halloween."

"You might want to rethink that. She's the one who secretly put up the cash so you won the contest."

He'd finally thrown her off balance. "Your mother?" she said. "Not you?"

He had to lock his elbows to keep from embracing her. "I was still in my mad phase. She thinks you're— I'm going to quote her. She thinks you're 'magnificent.'"

"Interesting. Okay, how about this for a deal breaker?"

"There won't be any deal breakers."

"That's what you think." For the first time she looked unsure. "Are you . . . willing to live someplace other than Wynette?"

He should have seen this coming, but he hadn't. Of course she wouldn't want to move back to Wynette after everything that had happened to her there. But what about his family, his friends, his roots, which stretched so deep into that rocky soil he'd become part of it?

He gazed into the face of this woman who'd claimed his soul. "All right," he said. "I'll give up Wynette. We can move anywhere you want."

She frowned. "What are you talking about? I didn't mean forever. Jeez, are you crazy? Wynette's home. But I'm serious about getting my degree, so we're going to need a place in Austin, assuming I get into U.T."

"Oh, God, you'll get in." His voice cracked again. "I'll build you a palace. Wherever you want."

She finally looked as dewy-eyed as he felt. "You'd really give up Wynette for me?"

"I'd give up my life for you."

"Okay, you're seriously starting to freak me out." But she didn't say it like she was freaked out. She said it like she was really happy.

He looked deep into her eyes, wanting her to know exactly how serious he was. "Nothing is more important to me than you."

"I love you, Teddy Beaudine." She finally spoke the words he'd been waiting to hear. And then, with a happy whoop, she threw herself at his chest, plastering her wet, cold body against his; burying her wet, cold face in his neck; touching her wet, warm lips to his ear. "We'll work out our lovemaking problems later," she whispered.

Oh, no. She wasn't getting ahead of him that easily. "By damn, we'll work them out now."

"You're on."

This time she was the one dragging him. They raced back to the limo. He gave the driver a quick set of directions, then kissed Meg breathless as they rode the few short blocks to the Battery Park Ritz. They dashed into the lobby with no luggage and rainwater dripping from their clothes. Soon they were locked behind the door of a warm, dry room that looked out over the dark, rainy harbor.

"Will you marry me, Meg Koranda?" he said as he pulled her into the bathroom.

"Definitely. But I'm keeping my last name just to piss off your mother."

"Excellent. Now take off your clothes."

She did, and he did, hopping on one foot, holding on to each other, getting tangled in shirtsleeves and wet denim legs. He turned on the water in the roomy shower stall. She jumped in ahead of him, leaned against the marble tiles, and opened her legs. "Let me see if you can use your powers for evil instead of good."

He laughed and joined her. He picked her up in his arms, kissing her, loving her, wanting her as he'd never wanted anyone. After what had happened that ugly day at the landfill, he promised himself he'd never again lose control with her, but the sight of her, the feel of her against him, made him forget everything he knew about the right way to make love to a woman. This wasn't any woman. This was Meg. His funny, beautiful, irresistible love. And, oh God, he nearly drowned her.

His brain finally cleared. He was still inside her, and she was looking up at him from the floor of the shower, a grin like spangled sunshine spread over her mouth. "Go ahead and apologize," she said. "I know you want to."

It would take him a hundred years to understand this woman.

She pushed him over, reached up to slam off the water with the flat of her hand, and gave him a look that was full of sin. "Now it's my turn."

He didn't have the strength to resist.

When they finally made it out of the shower, they bundled themselves in robes, dried each other's hair, and rushed toward the bed. Just before they got there, he went to the window to close the drapes.

The rain had stopped, and in the distance the Lady of the Harbor gazed back at him. He could feel her smiling.

M EG REFUSED TO MARRY TED until she got her degree. "Boy ge-
niuses deserve to marry college graduates," she told him.

"This boy genius deserves to marry the woman he loves right now
instead of waiting till she gets a diploma." But despite his grumbling,
he understood how important this was to her, even if he wouldn't
admit it.

Life in Wynette was dull without Meg, and everybody wanted her
back, but despite numerous phone calls and occasional drop-in visits
from various residents to her tiny apartment in Austin, she wouldn't
set foot inside the city limits until her wedding. "I'd be tempting fate
if I came back before I had to," she told the members of the library's
rebuilding committee when they showed up at her door with a Rub-
bermaid pitcher of Birdie's mojitos and a half-empty bag of tortilla
chips. "You know I'll get into trouble with somebody as soon as I hit
town."

Kayla, who cut calories by eating only the broken chips, dug through the bag. "I have no idea what you're talking about. People went out of their way, right from the very beginning, to make you feel welcome."

Lady Emma sighed.

Shelby poked Zoey. "It's because Meg's a Yankee. Yankees don't appreciate southern hospitality."

"That's for sure." Torie licked the salt off her fingers. "Plus, they steal our men when we're not paying attention."

Meg rolled her eyes, drained her mojito, then kicked them all out so she could finish her paper on eutrophication. After that, she dashed off to supervise the undergraduate art major she'd hired to help fill the orders that continued to come in from New York. Over the outraged protests of Ted, his parents, her parents, her brothers, the library committee, and the rest of Wynette, she was still paying her own expenses, although she'd relaxed her principles long enough to accept Ted's engagement present of a shiny red Prius.

"You gave me a car," she said to him, "and all I have for you is this lousy money clip."

But Ted loved his money clip, which she'd fashioned from a rare Greek medallion of Gaia, the goddess of the earth.

Ted wasn't able to spend nearly as much time in Austin as they'd originally planned, and even though they talked several times a day, they desperately missed being together. But he needed to stay close to Wynette. The group of carefully selected investors he'd been assembling to build the golf resort had finally come together. The members included his father, Kenny, Skeet, Dex O'Connor, a couple of well-known touring pros, and a few Texas businessmen, none of them involved in plumbing. Amazingly, Spence Skipjack had resurfaced all full of bluster about putting the "misunderstanding" behind them.

Ted told him there was no misunderstanding, and he should stick to making toilets.

Ted had maintained controlling interest in the resort so he could build it exactly as he envisioned. He was jubilant about the project but overworked, and with construction scheduled to begin soon after their wedding, it would only get worse. Although he frequently talked about how much he needed someone who shared both his vision and his trust working at his side, it wasn't until Kenny drove to Austin and cornered Meg for a private conversation that she realized the person Ted wanted working with him was herself.

"He knows how much going back to school for your master's degree means to you," Kenny said. "That's why he won't ask you."

It didn't take Meg more than five seconds to decide her master's degree could wait. Working with the man she loved on a project like this was her dream job.

Ted was jubilant when she asked if she could work with him. They talked for hours about their future and the legacy they intended to build together. Instead of poisoned land, they'd create places where all families, not just wealthy ones, could gather to have a picnic or throw a ball—places where kids would be able to catch fireflies, listen to birds sing, and fish in clean, unpolluted water.

She ended up scheduling her wedding for exactly one year, minus one day, from the date Ted was to have walked Lucy down the aisle, a decision Francesca hotly protested. She was still complaining about it when Meg—diploma finally in her possession—returned to Wynette three days before the ceremony.

While Ted raced into town to unveil a new display at the reopened library, Meg plopped onto a counter stool in her future mother-in-law's kitchen for breakfast. Francesca passed a toasted bagel across the counter. "It's not as if you didn't have plenty of dates to choose from," she said. "Honestly, Meg, if I didn't know better, I'd swear you were trying to jinx the whole thing."

"Just the opposite." Meg slathered blackberry jam over her bagel. "I like the symbolism of bright new lives arising from the tragic ashes of the past."

"You're as odd as Teddy," Francesca said in exasperation. "I can't believe it took me so long to realize how perfect the two of you are for each other."

Meg grinned.

Dallie looked up from his coffee mug. "People round here like that she's a little odd, Francie. It makes her fit in better."

"She's more'n a little odd," Skeet said from behind his newspaper. "Hugged me yesterday for no reason at all. 'Bout gave me a heart attack."

Dallie nodded. "She's strange that way."

"Sitting right here," Meg reminded them.

But Skeet and Dallie had moved on to discuss which of them was better suited to give her golf lessons, disregarding the fact that Meg had already chosen Torie.

Francesca once again tried to get Meg to spill the details about her wedding gown, but Meg refused to talk. "You'll see it when everybody else does."

"I don't understand why you let Kayla see it, but not me."

"Because she's my fashion consultant, and you're merely my nagging future mother-in-law."

Francesca didn't bother to argue the second point, only the first. "I know as much about fashion as Kayla Garvin."

"More, I'm sure. But you're still not seeing it until I walk down the aisle." She gave Francesca a sticky kiss on the cheek, then ran off to the inn to meet her family. Not long after that, Lucy arrived.

"Are you sure you want me there?" Lucy had said over the phone when Meg had asked her to be part of the wedding party.

"I couldn't get married without you."

They had so much to talk about, and they drove to the church where they could catch up without anyone eavesdropping. Ted eventually found them lounging at the side of the swimming hole. The initial awkwardness between the former lovers had vanished long ago, and they chatted like the good friends they were always meant to be.

The rehearsal dinner was at the country club, just as it had been the first time around. "I feel like I've stepped through a time warp," Lucy whispered to Meg not long after they arrived.

"Except this time you can relax and enjoy yourself," Meg told her. "It'll be entertaining, I promise you."

And entertaining it was, as the locals cornered Jake and Fleur to sing Meg's praises. "Your daughter was the best executive employee I ever had at the inn," Birdie told them with all kinds of earnestness. "She practically ran the place. I hardly had to do anything."

"She's quite bright," her mother replied with a straight face.

Zoey tugged on an exquisite set of Egyptian earrings. "You have no idea how much she's improved my wardrobe." She slipped her hand into her pocket where Meg happened to know she'd stowed a glittery bottle-cap necklace she could slip on when Hunter Gray's mother appeared.

"The country club hasn't been the same since she left," Shelby gushed. "You would not believe how difficult it is for some people to distinguish between regular Arizona iced tea and diet."

It was Kayla's turn, but Birdie had to poke her in the ribs to drag her attention away from the gorgeous Koranda brothers. Kayla blinked and dutifully did her part to burnish Meg's reputation. "I swear I gained six pounds after she left, I was so depressed. Her jewelry was practically keeping my shop afloat. Plus, she's the only woman other than Torie and me with an appreciation for cutting-edge fashion."

"Y'all are too dear," Meg drawled. And then, loudly, to her parents, "They take their electroshock therapy together. That way, they get a group discount."

"There is no gratitude in that girl," Shelby sniffed to Lady Emma.

Torie grabbed a crab puff. "We could always put her in charge of the city playground committee. That'll teach her to disrespect us."

Meg groaned, Lady Emma smiled, and Lucy was befuddled. "What's happened?" she said when she caught Meg alone. "You totally fit in here. And that's not a compliment."

"I know," Meg replied. "It sort of sneaked up on me."

But Lucy was mildly miffed. "They were never anything but polite to me, so clearly, I wasn't good enough for them. Me, the daughter of the president of the United States. You, on the other hand—Miss Screwup—you, they love."

Meg smiled and lifted her glass toward the Crazy Women of Wynette. "We understand each other."

Fleur drew Lucy away, Ted joined Meg, and together, they watched Kayla and Zoey move in on Meg's brothers. Ted took a sip from his wineglass. "Shelby told your parents she's pretty sure you're pregnant."

"Not yet."

"I figured you'd probably tell me first." He gazed toward the women. "Or maybe not. You're absolutely sure you want to live here?"

Meg smiled. "I couldn't live anywhere else."

He slipped his fingers through hers. "One more night, and then that stupid sexual moratorium of yours is over. How I ever let you talk me into it, I'll never understand."

"I don't know that you can exactly call four days a moratorium."

"It sure as hell feels like one."

Meg laughed and kissed him.

By the next afternoon, however, she was a bundle of nerves, and neither Lucy, nor her five other bridal attendants, could calm her down. Georgie and April, along with their famous husbands, had flown in from L.A., while Sasha had arrived from Chicago. It hadn't felt right to get married without Torie and Lady Emma, and they all looked stunning in simply cut, sleeveless, dove gray silk dresses, each with a slightly different set of rhinestone buttons running down the back.

"Kayla's putting 'em all up on eBay for us when this shindig is over," Torie announced to Meg as they gathered before the ceremony in the church's antechamber. "She says we'll make a fortune."

"Which we'll give to charity," Lady Emma stated firmly.

Fleur got predictably teary-eyed when she saw Meg in her gown. So did Torie and Lady Emma, although for a different reason. "You're sure about this?" Torie whispered to Meg as the bridal party moved into the narthex for the processional.

"Some things are meant to be." Meg clutched her bouquet tighter as Lucy arranged the short train. The gown, with its structured corset top, fragile cap sleeves, and slim, delicately embellished silhouette, plunged to a deep V in the back. She wore it with her mother's finger-tip wedding veil and tiara of Austrian crystals.

The trumpets sounded, a signal for Ted to enter at the front of the church, along with Kenny, his best man. Although Meg couldn't see her bridegroom, she suspected a convenient shaft of sunlight would choose that moment to spill through the stained-glass windows and put another one of those ridiculous halos around him.

She was getting queasier by the minute.

Lady Emma had lined up the bridesmaids. With a gathering sense of panic, Meg watched April step off first, followed by Torie and then Sasha. Meg's hands were clammy, her heart beating too fast. Georgie disappeared. Only Lady Emma and Lucy were left.

Lucy whispered, "You look beautiful. Thanks for being my friend."

Meg tried to smile. Really she did. But Lady Emma was heading down the aisle, and only Lucy was left, and Meg was cold all over.

Lucy moved.

Meg's hand shot out, and she grabbed her by the arm. "Wait!"

Lucy looked over her shoulder.

"Get him," Meg said on a wheeze of panic.

Lucy gaped at her. "You are kidding me, right?"

"No." Meg gulped for air. "I have to see him. Right now."

"Meg, you can't do this."

"I know. It's horrible. But . . . Just get him, please?"

"I knew coming here was a bad idea," Lucy muttered. Then she took a deep breath, fixed her old White House smile on her face, and headed down the aisle.

She kept that smile firmly in place right up to the moment she stopped in front of Ted.

He studied her. She studied him.

"Uh-oh," said Kenny.

She licked her lips. "Uhm . . . Sorry, Ted. *Again.* Sorry again. But . . . Meg wants to see you."

"I strongly advise you not to go," Kenny whispered.

Ted turned to the Reverend Harris Smithwell. "Excuse me for a minute."

The crowd broke out in an uproar as he strode up the aisle, not looking to the right or the left, but straight ahead toward the woman waiting for him just beyond the sanctuary.

At first, he merely took in the sight of that beloved face framed in a froth of white. Her cheeks were pale, her knuckles white around her wedding bouquet. He stopped in front of her. "Hard day?" he asked.

She set her forehead against his jaw, poking him in the eye with the tiara that held her veil in place. "Do you know how much I love you?" she said.

"Almost as much as I love you," he replied, kissing her gently on the nose so he didn't mess up her makeup. "You look beautiful, by the way. Although . . . I swear I've seen that gown before."

"It's Torie's."

"Torie's?"

"One of her castoffs. It's kind of expected, right?"

He smiled. "I sure hope it was from her wedding to Dex and not her earlier failures."

"Uh-huh." She nodded and sniffed. "Are you—are you completely sure about this? I'm a very messy person."

His eyes drank her in. "There's such a thing as being too neat, sweetheart."

"Except . . . Let's face it. I'm smart, but I'm not as smart as you. I mean . . . hardly anybody is, but still . . . It's possible we'll have dumb kids. Not really dumb, but . . . Relatively speaking."

"I understand, sweetheart. Getting married for the first time can be nerve-racking for anybody, even a courageous person like yourself. Fortunately, I have experience with weddings, so I can help you." This time he risked messing up her makeup to give her a tender kiss on her lips. "The sooner we get through this, the sooner I can strip you naked, lose my self-control, and humiliate myself again."

"That's true." The color finally began to return to her cheeks. "I'm being stupid. But I'm under a lot of stress. And when I'm stressed, I sometimes forget that I'm good enough for you. Too good for you. You're still kind of screwed up, you know, with the people-pleasing thing."

"You'll protect me from myself." *And everyone else,* he thought.

"It's going to be a full-time job."

"Are you up for it?"

She finally smiled. "I am."

He stole another kiss. "You know how much I love you, right?"

"I do."

"Good. Hold on to that thought." He scooped her into his arms, and before she could tell him it was unnecessary—that she'd pulled herself back together and he needed to put her down *right this minute.* Before she could say any of that, he'd started down the aisle.

"This one," he announced to everybody, "is not getting away."

author's note

EVERY BOOK I WRITE STANDS on its own, which doesn't prevent the characters in one book from wandering into another. Lots of old friends wandered into this book—Francesca and Dallie Beaudine from *Fancy Pants;* Nealy Case and Mat Jorik from *First Lady;* Fleur and Jake Koranda from *Glitter Baby;* Kenny Traveler and Emma (oops . . . *Lady* Emma) from *Lady Be Good,* which also includes Torie and Dex's unorthodox love affair. You can catch an earlier glimpse of Meg in *What I Did for Love* and meet a younger version of Ted in both *Fancy Pants* and *Lady Be Good.* And, yes, Lucy Jorik deserves her happy ending. As I write this, I'm hard at work on her story.

I have so many people to thank for their encouragement, including my irresistible dear friend and editor Carrie Feron, my longtime agent, Steven Axelrod, and my wonderful cheerleaders at Harper-Collins, William Morrow, and Avon Books. Yes, I know exactly how lucky I am to have all of you in my corner.

Author's Note

I don't know what I'd do without my able assistant Sharon Mitchell, who makes my world run so much smoother. Huge thanks to my peerless golf adviser, Bill Phillips. Also to Claire Smith and Jessie Niermeyer for sharing their "Tales from a Drink Cart."

A standing ovation to my writing buddies: Jennifer Greene, Kristin Hannah, Jayne Ann Krentz, Cathie Linz, Suzette Van, and Margaret Watson, with a special round of applause for Lindsay Longford.

Hugs to the new friends I've made on Facebook and to all the incredible, extraordinary Seppies on my message board!

SUSAN ELIZABETH PHILLIPS

www.susanelizabethphillips.com